FIVE SECONDS OF
DEAD AIR

The Misadventures of Max Mason

Volume One

CHARLES SISK

ISBN: 978-1-54394-823-3 (print)
ISBN: 978-1-54394-824-0 (ebook)

Acknowledgments

Well, a lot of emotions (mostly good) went into writing about Max; but the people who encouraged, believed, and had faith that I could do it are the ones that made me a writer...who knew (other than my mother) !!!

Thanking people for their strength, love, encouragement, and belief starts with my beautiful & precious wife Kristina. You have taught me that I could do ANYTHING I put my mind to...I just needed to do it. I love you so much for your personality, your laughter, your honor, your trust & forgiveness, and yes...your occasional cold feet in bed. You have made writing Karen Tyler a joy and an honor...I love you forever & always, and I dedicate this book to you.

Raymond Earl, you have been my best friend, my conscience, my tech guru, and someone I have leaned on in both good times & bad for nearly 35 years. You were the second person to read the original manuscript for this book and I'll always remember the first words you said to me about it "Who the *%#@*k are you, this is REALLY good" yours & Kristina's approval was all I needed to push forward with Max...thank you so much.

Parke & Denise, I thank you BOTH for your support, encouragement, and editing expertise. Parke, you helped me become a writer with your advice & journalistic skills and I thank you for that.

Jason, Stephanie, Brenna, Rachel, Catherine, Ashley, and Sara you have ALL been the real "action heroes" of my life and I love you all so very much...thank you for letting your "old man" write about his incredible children.

Dave, Rachel, & Nathan your encouragement, support, and your ice cream (a lot of ice cream) helped get me to this place of having Max introduced into the literary world...thank you so much.

Patrice, Julie, Nashwan, Naila, Jean-Marie, Rashad, and Sonny; all of you blessed me with reading the book and giving me positive feedback from the female, young male, and older male perspectives on Max & his friends and I thank you <u>ALL</u> for that.

Lee & Daryl, you both gave me the courage, and the strength to bring Max & his adventures out into the public, and I thank you for that.

I know you were reading over my shoulder the entire time I was writing this book Donna Jean, probably concerned I was killing to many people off...but trust me, they were <u>ALL</u> bad. Thank you for keeping watch over everyone.

And finally, thanks to Max. His personality, his courage, and his wit (some call it sarcasm) has brought his character to life beyond my wildest dreams. I can't wait to write the next adventure for him

Thank you everyone.

Charles Sisk

CHAPTER 1

THE SUN WAS STARTING TO GO DOWN ON THIS
particularly warm July Saturday evening in the nation's capital as
the Presidential limousine slowly drove down the alley to the back
entrance loading dock of the Washington Majestic Hotel and came
to a stop. Secret Service agent Maxwell "Max" Mason stepped out of
the black Cadillac limo, stood at the door and looked around.

Max was rather tall - about 6'2" - dark hair, in his late 30s, a very
well-built and handsome man, dressed in a conservative black suit
and tie which was agency policy for public appearances. He touched
his ear piece communicator and raised his hand to his mouth, quietly speaking into the wrist transmitter he was wearing.

"Squirrel and Chipmunk have arrived," he said with a slight
grin. He knew those were the agency code names for President
Daryl Matthews' twin 11-year-old sons Scott and Steven, but he still
couldn't help snickering whenever he would call them that.

It was agency procedure that the boys arrive ahead of their parents, which they did when the Presidential family attended a func-
tion together. The President and First Lady were always about five
minutes behind them in separate protective limos.

They were all attending the Children's Global Hunger Charity
Gala, a worldwide charity that helped raise money to stop child

hunger around the world hosted by the Washington Majestic Hotel in downtown Washington, DC, just a few blocks from the White House. The Majestic Hotel was the historic favorite, dating back to its opening before World War II, for parties, galas, and Presidential inaugurations. Even President Matthews had his two inaugural balls there.

The hotel was posh, with oak wood floors, white marble pillars, crystal chandeliers, and vaulted ceilings with skylights. Max had done a walk-through a few hours before and was impressed with the style and staff of the Majestic. The lobby was decorated beautifully with flowers and other floral arrangements to welcome their guests year-round.

Both boys were dressed in fitted black suits with ties, and when they stood side-by-side no one could tell which was which, not even Max. They were identical twins, with the only distinction being that his charge Scott wore a Rocky squirrel pin on his jacket lapel that Max had given him some time ago. Scott Matthews loved that pin and wore it on every coat or shirt he wore in public. This was Max's way of figuring out which one was Scott when he and brother Steven Mathews dressed alike in public, which they did a lot.

Max walked up to the door of the back entrance of the hotel looked around and declared it was free of any threats. "All clear," he spoke into his wrist transmitter.

A second agent - also tall, early 30s and wearing the same suit as Max - got out of the limo, looked around, then looked back inside the limo to tell the boys they could come out. Agent Jason Carpenter was the "new guy" on the protective detail. He had only been with the agency eight months when he was given the responsibility of keeping Steven Matthews, code name "Chipmunk" safe. He looked at Max standing at the rear entry door and with a nod acknowledged he was bringing the boys out of the car.

Max looked at him, then glanced around the perimeter one more time and said, "We're good." Agent Carpenter nodded to Max in acknowledgment and stuck his head back inside the limo to address the two young boys.

The twins got out of the limo one at a time and walked toward Max with Jason closely behind them. Max knocked on the door and it was opened immediately by another agent already stationed inside. Max, Agent Carpenter and the two boys went inside quickly and the door closed behind them. They walked down a cleared hallway and observed several other agents positioned at each end of a banquet room in the hotel reserved for the First Family to wait to be announced by the charity's president and Master of Ceremonies Lila Baird.

Looking around the room, Max saw that the lavished hotel had put out an impressive catered buffet that had been cleared through the agency.

After looking it over, he told Agent Carpenter to keep an eye on the boys. "Don't let them eat too much," he said.

The boys did what any most 11-year-olds might, going right for the desserts. Max grinned then looked at Carpenter sternly to remind him what he said.

The front of the Washington Majestic Hotel for the Charity Gala that evening was like a movie premiere, with paparazzi, red carpet interviews and limousines arriving with dignitaries and celebrities. Hundreds of spectators strained their necks trying to see who was there, while Secret Service agents patrolled the area keeping watchful eyes on the crowd. The front of the hotel was brightly lit with marquee lights blinking, "Welcome, Children's Global Hunger Charity."

The Federal Protection Police had blocked off three city blocks in every direction and only allowed those vehicles with special stickers to approach the lobby entrance. Security was tight for this event especially since the First Family was attending.

Chatter was coming over Max's receiver from the agents in front of the hotel acknowledging who was coming out of the limos to attend the gala. Everyone from Congressmen, Senators, Corporate CEOs, the Prime Minister of England, several A-list movie stars, and a few professional sports stars were making their way to the hotel lobby. Max grinned and thought to himself he could be at home right

3

now watching baseball and eating wings with his two kids instead of all this.

Max's agency cell phone started buzzing in his pocket. He always put it on vibrate when he was working. He touched the ON button and spoke into the phone. "Agent Mason here," he said.

A familiar voice came over Max's phone. "Agent Mason, this is Agent Tyler with the President and First Lady's motorcade."

Max smiled when he heard who it was. Agent Karen Tyler was a special friend to Max in the agency. She was beautiful, with long blonde hair, tall even without heels, funny, smart, young - in her early 30s – and, yes, *very* lethal! Max loved her smile and enthusiasm for the job. She was very dedicated.

Max and Tyler had been colleagues at the agency for almost four years and were good friends, but nothing more. Max helped her in martial arts and shooting when they had down time to train at work. She was a *very* good student who picked up quickly on what he taught her.

Max stood in the room watching the twin boys enjoy their desserts, thought to himself for a moment, then spoke into the phone with a grin on his face. "Agent Tyler, after all we've meant to each other, we're still not on a first-name basis?" He chuckled knowing he could tease her without offending her. There was a long pause, then Max's face went flush. "We're on speaker, aren't we Agent Tyler?"

"Yes sir, we *are* -- with the President and First Lady," she replied, with a sly smile toward the First Lady.

Another familiar voice came through his ear piece and Max grimaced as he heard a slight giggle. "Hello, Max." It was First Lady Heather Matthews.

"Say hello, sweetheart," she said to her husband, President Daryl Matthews.

President Matthews looked up from the file he was reading. "Hello, Maxwell."

Max seemed to stand up a little straighter when he heard the President's voice. "Good evening, Mr. President, Mrs. Matthews."

"We're going to be delayed about 10 to 15 minutes to the hotel sir," Agent Tyler said, looking at both the President and First Lady sitting across from her in the limo.

"Off speaker please, Agent Tyler," Max requested.

The First Lady smiled at Tyler and nodded in agreement. Tyler spoke into the phone, now positioned against her ear. "Off speaker, sir."

Max seemed a bit concerned, some would say paranoid, when he asked, "Is there a problem, Agent Tyler?"

Tyler quickly responded to her superior, ready to explain. "No sir, there's no problem. Chariot 1 hit a serious pothole on Pennsylvania Avenue and damaged the front tire. We have since transferred to Chariot 3 and have continued on our way, but we have lost some time sir," Tyler informed Max.

Max felt a bit relieved but reminded her, "Keep your eyes open Tyler."

"Yes sir," Tyler replied, relieved that Max wasn't too upset at the delay.

First Lady Heather Matthews gestured to Agent Tyler to give her the phone. Tyler told Max, "Sir, the First Lady would like to speak with you." Mrs. Matthews knew there was a special bond between Max and her two boys and trusted him to take care of them in every situation.

"Max, there's no sense in the boys just hanging out in that stuffy banquet room," the First Lady told Max. Max smiled knowing her twin boys were indulging in a few desserts and didn't have issues staying there.

Mrs. Matthews continued, "Let the boys go sit in their seats in the ballroom and we'll be there in a couple of minutes."

"Yes ma'am, copy that," Max replied.

The First Lady handed the phone back to Agent Tyler who spoke again to Max. "We are en route and arriving shortly sir."

"Roger that, Agent Tyler, and we need to have a brief chat you and I," he said with a smile.

Tyler grinned and acknowledged, "Yes sir."

She hung up and placed the phone back in her suit coat pocket. "So what's going on between you and Max?" Heather Matthews asked grinning.

Tyler was a bit stunned by the First Lady's question and quickly responded. "Nothing ma'am," as she blushed ever so slightly. "We're just colleagues."

"Leave Agent Tyler alone, honey. We don't need to be meddling in things that don't concern us," President Matthews said, looking up from his file again at his wife.

"Shhhhh, Daryl. Karen and I are having girl talk," she said to her husband, smiling at Tyler.

"Heather!" her husband said firmly.

"It's okay, Mr. President," Tyler responded. "Agent Mason has been mentoring me the past year in martial arts and on the firing range sir. Nothing inappropriate," Tyler said shyly.

Mrs. Matthews wouldn't leave it at just that, and with a grin asked Tyler, "Is that okay with you, sweetie?" Tyler blushed a bit redder to the First Lady's question.

"It's okay right now, ma'am. Agent Mason has a lot on his plate outside the agency. I'm sure a relationship other than professional is the furthest from his mind, ma'am," the young agent said.

Mrs. Matthews continued to grin at Tyler. "Max Mason is a very handsome man, don't you think, sweetie?"

"*Really* Heather!" her husband said, rolling his eyes at her.

"Okay, okay. I won't pry anymore," she said giggling and stealing a sly look at Tyler.

Tyler turned to look out the car window with a very big smile on her face, thinking about what she and the First Lady talked about, something that she thought she never would --Max Mason!

Max had just turned his agency phone off and returned his earpiece back in his ear when he heard "Code 3, situation at entry point Alpha." Max knew that a Code 3 was a minimum security issue, usually an argument or disorderly conduct with a guest. "Entry point Alpha" was the front of the hotel at the lobby entrance. Max put his transmitter to his lips and asked, "What's the issue there Agent?"

The agent responded, "We have an invited female guest here, sir, with a medical ID card stating she has a pacemaker and can't go through the X-ray detector."

Max spoke again into his transmitter. "Does the medical card check out with the medical database?"

The agent, a female, scanned the card to the Medical Alert Identification database that holds all doctor-issued medical IDs for security purposes. The woman's ID came across the video screen as "ACCESS GRANTED".

"Yes sir, it seems to be legitimate," the agent replied as he handed the guest her ID card back.

"Then have one of the female agents there wand her and send her to her table," said Max. He knew that they were using top-of-the-line metal detector wands for this gala and needed to move this situation along to get everyone, especially the boys, to their tables before the President and First Lady arrived.

The woman's ID identified her as Brenda Danforth from New York City, an attractive African American woman, 42 years of age.

The medical ID she gave showed the X-ray of a pacemaker implant which coincided with the vertical chest scar everyone could see with the low-cut, red flowing evening dress she wore.

Max and the Secret Service knew that heart and orthopedic surgeons give these medical ID's to their patients so they legally don't have to walk through the X-ray metal detectors, mostly at airport security checkpoints. The handheld wands are less powerful and typically don't cause issues with pacemakers because they use a lower frequency, but they are still effective for security matters.

The female agent gestured to Ms. Danforth to come with her to the other side of the X-ray detector. Once there the agent requested, "Ma'am, please hold your arms out until I tell you to put them down." Danforth obliged and the agent proceeded to glide the electronic wand over the woman's body, only picking up beeps from over the scar on her chest.

"Ma'am, you're clear to go to your seat," said the agent.

Ms. Danforth smiled back at her. "Thank you." She looked at the watch on her wrist and started walking to the ballroom.

A handsome male Secret Service agent approached her and asked, "Ma'am, has your escort already been seated?"

Ms. Danforth gave him a wry smile. "No, I'm here alone to support the New York City chapter of the Children's Global Hunger charity." She politely handed him her invitation.

He looked it over and handed it back to her. "Have a good evening ma'am." She smiled again at the agent and continued walking to the ballroom.

Max informed Agent Carpenter what the First Lady said about seating the boys in the ballroom. They both went over to the twins and Max told them what their mother wanted them to do. Steven and Scott Matthews just shrugged their shoulders. "Okay," they said in unison.

First, they both wiped their hands off with napkins Carpenter handed to them, threw them in the wastebasket and headed for the door with the two agents. The four of them walked down the hallway together reaching the curtain-covered entrance to the ballroom.

Max brushed aside part of the curtain to get a look at the ballroom and could see it was brightly lit with multi-colored balloons on strings rising above every table.

Max could see between the curtains that each table in the room was nicely set with white linen, crystal glasses and fine silverware. He thought to himself while grinning, "this is a "fat cat, high roller, rich-folk-type party."

Waiters and waitresses dressed in white tuxedos moved around the large room with trays of champagne and hors d'oeuvres as guests shook hands with one another and the ladies were admiring one another's gowns. Max also observed that most of the room and seats were filled already since the invitation said 8pm and it was 7:50pm according to Max's watch.

The President and First Lady were scheduled to arrive at 7:45pm, but as Max and Agent Carpenter knew they were running late and wouldn't be there until 8pm because of the limousine issue. Max surveyed the room one last time and noticed the woman in red with the chest scar heading to her table near the front where the First Family was to be seated.

Max felt a tug on his jacket and looked back to see Scott Matthews. "Max, I have to use the restroom before we sit down," he said.

Max figured all the milk and desserts Steven and Scott enjoyed without their parents would catch up with them eventually, and it appeared it had already.

Max smiled at Scott Matthews and said, "Okay Squirrel."

Max glanced down the hallway and saw the men's restroom sign at the far end near one of the positioned agents. He looked at Agent Carpenter and said with a grin, "Squirrel needs the restroom. What about Chipmunk?"

Steven Matthews heard what Max said and spoke up. "I'm okay right now Max."

Agent Carpenter looked at Max, tilted his head slightly to the side, raised his eyebrows and said, "This could be a long night."

Max grinned back. "Don't I know it."

"I'm going to go ahead and take Chipmunk to his seat," Carpenter said.

Max nodded and started down the hallway with Scott Matthews. When he got to the door the other agent approached and acknowledged Agent Mason. The agent went into the restroom and returned seconds later declaring, "All clear sir, there's no one inside."

Max looked at Scott and smiled. "Let's make it quick Squirrel, your mom and dad are almost here." Max glanced at his watch again to see it was now 7:55pm and knew he had to get Scott to his seat before the President and First Lady made their entrance to the charity gala.

Scott Matthews came out of the restroom and Max instinctively asked him, "Did you wash your hands?"

Scott looked at him with a condescending scowl on his face. "Of course I did. I'm not a baby."

Max smiled and liked the fact that the young man took up for himself. "No sir, you're not. I'll make sure I remember that."

9

Scott gave Max a big smile. "Thanks Max."

Max put his hand on his shoulder and directed the President's son back down the hallway.

Just before they got to the curtained ballroom entrance, Max heard a loud voice of someone speaking into a microphone. He could make out that it was a woman's voice, thinking it was charity hostess Lila Baird making an announcement.

"We are all here for a great cause," Max heard still walking down the long hallway with Scott. "As am I," the voice echoed in the ballroom. Max had an eerie feeling, like hairs standing up on the back of his neck listening to the woman speak.

Max softly pulled Scott back behind him as they were almost to the curtained entrance of the ballroom feeling something was wrong.

The woman's voice had something sinister about it as she said, "The dragon breathes again."

Max had just moved the curtain a bit to see the woman wearing the red dress with the scar holding the microphone, standing in front of the First Family's reserved table where Agent Carpenter and Steven Matthews were sitting.

He watched as she smiled at everyone, looked at the clock on the wall that now said 8pm, and then there was a powerful explosion that blew her into small bloody pieces.

The force of the blast knocked Max back into Scott Matthews who was behind him. Max was stunned and disoriented for a moment, his ears ringing, but he quickly got to his knees and pulled out his service weapon, keeping Scott behind him.

"Scott, are you hurt? Scott, are you okay?" he shouted glancing over his shoulder to see the boy slowly rising up.

"What happened Max?" Scott asked a bit dazed and confused.

Smoke had started bellowing into the hallway and Max could hear people screaming and shouting in the ballroom.

"AGENTS DOWN! SECURE THE PERIMETER!" Max screamed into his wrist transmitter.

The fire sprinkler and alarm system in the ballroom and adjoining hallways engaged, soaking everyone, including Max and Scott

Matthews while both waited for agency backup to secure the President's son.

Five Secret Service agents with guns drawn emerged from the back hallway coming towards Max and Scott, all soaking wet. "Are you okay sir? Have you been injured?" one of the agents asked Max.

"I'm okay, I'm okay. Get Squirrel out of here!" Max yelled helping to pick the young boy up off the water-soaked carpeted floor.

"Don't leave me Max," Scott begged. The President's son was scared and Max could see it, but he knew he had to check on his brother Steven and Agent Carpenter's status inside the ballroom.

"Squirrel, I need you to help these guys get out of here. They're scared too and I know you can help them," Max said, trying to be reassuring to his young ward.

"Okay Max," he said. The five agents helped Scott up and surrounded him, with their guns drawn, slowly moving back down the hallway from where they had just come.

Max yelled to one of the agents as he was leaving with Scott. "Get someone to turn the damn sprinkler system off if the fire is contained." The agent turned and nodded to Max.

The President and First Lady's limousine had just pulled up to the front of the Washington Majestic Hotel when Agent Tyler got the "Code Red" repeatedly shouted in her earpiece. "Code Red" signified that the agency's positions or agents had been violently compromised. Go! Go! We've been attacked!" she screamed to the agent driver who put the limo back in drive and floored the accelerator.

As they were leaving, Tyler observed through the limo window that guests were running out the hotel exits through billows of smoke. She could also hear the sound of fire trucks and rescue vehicles coming in their direction.

The First Lady could also see the smoke and people seemingly running for their lives and started yelling, "Where are we going? What's happening Karen? Where are my boys?"

President Matthews tried to console his scared wife. "Heather, you need to stay calm. I'm sure they're fine with Agents Mason and Carpenter."

That didn't sit well with Heather Matthews and she shot back at her husband, "Don't tell me to stay calm, Daryl! My babies are missing after a terrorist attack and I don't know if they're safe," as she started crying on the President's shoulder.

President Matthews looked at Agent Tyler. "Get me an update now, Tyler, please!" he requested anxiously.

Tyler spoke into her transmitter. "Anyone got eyes on Squirrel and Chipmunk? Over."

An agent's voice came over her receiver. "Squirrel has been recovered and transported safely to Olympus. Over." Tyler knew Olympus was the code name for the White House.

"What about Chipmunk?" Tyler asked. "Over."

"No information yet on Chipmunk ma'am," the agent replied. "Over."

Tyler started to get nervous as she was not getting the information she wanted. "Where are Agents Mason and Carpenter? Over."

"Agent Mason went to secure the ballroom against any secondary attack ma'am. Over," the agent responded.

Max, with his gun drawn, slowly and cautiously pulled back the curtain leading into the ballroom. What he saw devastated and angered him. People running for the exit doors, fire, smoke, the screams and moans from wounded guests lying on the floor barely moving, as well as bodies that lay motionless from the explosion. Blood stains were everywhere -- on the floor, the walls and on the damaged tables and chairs.

Max looked around making sure there weren't any more possible threats and saw most of the fires dying out. His gun pointed wherever his eyes went. He fixated on the area Agent Carpenter and young Steven Matthews would have been when the bomb went off and slowly made his way in that direction. He then spoke into his transmitter. "Anyone copy? Wounded civilians in need of medical attention immediately!"

All he got was static in his earpiece. He thought to himself the impact of the explosion must have damaged his communications link, so he pulled the earpiece out and put it in his pocket.

Max slowly moved towards the front of the ballroom, evaluating and consoling those along the way who were wounded. "Help is on its way," he said, trying to assure them, continuously looking around for another possible attack.

Max could see tables and chairs stained with blood scattered on the ballroom floor near the front where the main explosion took place and where the entire First Family would have been seated if not for the damaged limousine that delayed their arrival.

Max finally made his way to some overturned tables near the front of the podium and saw a body underneath them. He slowly lifted them off, tossing them aside, and found Agent Jason Carpenter face down on the floor. Max closed his eyes and let out a heavy sigh at the sight of his fellow Secret Service agent.

Max pulled a pair of latex gloves from his coat pocket and put them on, so as not to contaminate the crime scene evidence. Max slowly turned Carpenter's body over, only to find Steven Matthews under him. Both were dead.

Steven Matthews' cold, dead eyes stared back at Max making him uneasy, angry and emotional to the point of tears slowly dripping down his face. Max kneeled down, placed his gun on the floor and slowly closed Steven's opened eyelids. He patted the young boy's chest, then stood up again. "Goodbye Chipmunk. Your brother and I will miss you. You were a good boy," he said with a heavy disheartened sigh.

Several FBI agents and uniformed Federal Protection Police with guns drawn came into the ballroom to find Max still kneeling over both Agent Carpenter and Steven Matthews. Max knew they were coming and heard them scream, "Show us your hands NOW!"

Max responded loudly, raising his hands in the air as he stood up. "Agent Maxwell Mason! I'm with the Secret Service!"

Two agents grabbed Max harshly while another kept his gun pointed at him, searched him and found his SA-XD handgun on the floor by his feet and his agency ID in his coat pocket. They confirmed his ID and apologized to him for the rough treatment. "Sorry Agent Mason."

"It's okay," Max replied. He knew that everyone's emotions were running high because of the grim circumstances and that they were just doing their jobs.

One of the FBI agents handed Max his gun and ID and informed him, "The President is trying to get in touch with you sir." Max knew telling the President his son was killed in the attack wasn't a conversation he wanted to have with either him or the First Lady, but he knew he had to.

He borrowed the agent's secure phone and called Agent Karen Tyler, knowing she was still with the President and First Lady. "Agent Tyler, this is Agent Mason. I need to speak with the President?" he asked when Tyler answered.

"Are you and the boys okay?" she asked solemnly.

Max paused and repeated his request. "Please, Karen, let me speak with the President," he stated solemnly.

Agent Tyler handed the phone to President Matthews. "It's Agent Mason for you, Mr. President," she said with conflicting thoughts.

Before he even had a chance to say anything to Max, Heather Matthews asked her husband, "Are our boys safe Daryl?"

"Max, it's Daryl Matthews. What's going on with my sons?"

Max felt a lump in his throat as he heard the President speak to him but knew what he had to say. "Mr. President, I'm sorry to have to inform you and the First Lady that your son Steven was killed in the blast this evening. I'm so, so sorry sir."

Daryl Matthews face showed his grief as he looked at his wife Heather who screamed, "Noooo!" as she fell into her husband's arms crying uncontrollably.

The President handed Tyler the phone so he could console his wife, wrapping his arms tightly around her, tears rolling down his face.

Tears inched down Tyler's face as well, and she wiped them away quickly so the President and First Lady couldn't see them. She felt terrible for what they were going through. She put the phone to her ear and asked Max, "What happened there sir?"

Max proceeded to explain what had happened with the lady in the red dress exploding, Scott Matthews being safe, but then finding Agent Carpenter and Steven Matthews' bodies in the rubble.

"Are you okay Max?" asked Tyler, her heart breaking knowing he had had to inform the President of his loss.

"I don't think I'll ever be okay with this," Max replied, and hung up the phone.

Max waited until everyone was given medical attention and transported to the hospital. He had given assistance where he could and took statements from those willing. He looked around with the FBI forensic teams hoping to find anything that could lead to who might be responsible for this horrific crime. Max almost lost his composure when the coroner came in to collect the bodies of Agent Carpenter and Steven Matthews. He knew he was only doing his job, but Max stopped him before he zipped the body bags up over their heads so he could say "goodbye" one last time to both.

FBI investigator John Evans approached Max. "I'm going to need your statement Agent Mason."

Max knew this was protocol but asked Special Agent Evans if they could possibly do it in the morning. "I would appreciate if you would keep me in the loop on this case," Max asked.

Evans thought for a moment, realized Agent Mason had been through a lot that evening and agreed to his request. "First thing in the morning, Agent Mason, my office," he countered. "We should have some of the forensic evidence in the morning." Max nodded and started heading towards the front of the ballroom.

The President and First Lady's limousine arrived back at the White House. Several agents with guns drawn came out of the front door and surrounded the car. Agent Tyler got out with her gun drawn as well, looking around for possible threats.

Then she looked back inside the car. "All clear, Mr. President. You both can come out now."

Mrs. Matthews was distraught and sobbing as the President helped his wife walk up the steps to the front door.

As they entered the foyer, Scott Matthews came running down the hallway to his parents. Heather Matthews dropped to her knees and hugged her baby boy tightly, continuing to cry. Scott had not yet heard what had happened to his brother so he was confused why his mom and dad were acting so unusual towards him.

"Dad, why is Mom crying so much," he asked, which made her cry even more. "Where are Steven and Max?" Scott asked.

Daryl Matthews hugged his worried son and kissed him on the top of his head. "I love you son. We have to talk about Steven."

Scott started to understand what was happening and tears began flowing from his eyes. "Did the explosion kill Steven?" he asked, with his young face flushed with fear. He watched as his mother continued to cry and he knew that's what had happened. He sat down on the floor and started to weep for his twin brother, feeling overwhelming guilt. "It's all my fault! It's all my fault!" he screamed.

The First Lady heard her son and gathered herself together. "No, no, it's not your fault Scott. Don't ever think that," she told him looking into his heartbroken eyes.

"If I didn't have to go to the bathroom he would still be alive," Scott cried to his mother.

His mother continued to console him. "Bad, evil people did this to your brother, not you sweetheart" she said, her voice starting to get an angry tone as she gave her husband a stern, maternal look.

"What about the other people? What about Max and Agent Carpenter?" a calmer Scott Matthews asked.

His father looked at him with authority. "You don't need to worry about any of that right now son."

The young boy was insistent to his father. "Please Dad, what happened to Max and Agent Carpenter?"

"Max is okay son. We don't know anything about Agent Carpenter yet."

Secret Service Director Dwayne Marshall approached the grieving First Family. "Please forgive me for intruding Mr. President. I'm very sorry for your loss. We have a preliminary report about the bombing tonight," he said softly.

President Matthews responded, "I want EVERYONE in my office in ten minutes."

"Yes Ssir," Marshall acknowledged, and he started walking back down the hallway.

Daryl Matthews returned his attention to his upset son Scott, assuring him, "We will find out who did this to our family, I promise son, and they will be brought to justice." The President turned to Agent Tyler who had been standing over in the corner the entire time. "Please take Heather and Scott upstairs Karen."

"Yes, Mr. President." she replied.

"Let's get you both upstairs ma'am," Tyler said as she helped the First Lady to her feet as she was still holding onto her son.

Heather Matthews started walking towards the stairs with Scott in hand, then suddenly turned toward her husband. "Find out who killed my son, Daryl, and make them pay! I *mean* it!" she said angrily.

President Matthews gave his grieving wife a determined look, nodding in agreement as she started climbing the stairs to the family quarters.

CHAPTER 2

AGENT MAX MASON WAS CLEARED BY WHITE
House security at the main gate and headed to the Secret Service
entrance, parked his car in the designated lot and started walking toward the White House. He walked through the service door,
showed his ID to the guard and was immediately met by Secret
Service Director Dwayne Marshall. "In my office *now* Mason!"
Marshall bellowed.

Marshall was an understanding, but stern, supervisor and was
already under extreme pressure answering to this case. Max and
the director got along famously, even having had beers many times
together away from the job.

Max knew this was going to be a "high profile" terrorism situation that the media was going to eat up and he did not envy his boss's
position right now.

"Yes sir," Max replied, looking down the hallway past Marshall.

Marshall and Max walked into the director's office, past his secretary's desk and into his private office. "Shut the door Mason," he
said sternly.

Before Max could latch the door completely closed Marshall lit
into him. "What the fuck happened Max?" he asked. "I've got the
President of the United States' 11-year-old son on a slab down at the

coroner's office, not to mention a dead agent, and no answers to one fucking thing," Marshall said.

Max understood his anger thinking about seeing Steven's lifeless eyes staring up at him in the ballroom. Max informed his boss that the suicide bomber was an African American woman. "The bomb was inside her disguised as a pacemaker," he said.

"How the hell is that even possible?" Marshall asked.

"I don't know sir, but it was powerful enough to practically take out half the room," Max explained.

"How did she get past the X-ray detectors in the lobby?" asked Marshall.

Max remembered the conversation he had had on the radio with the agent at the lobby entrance. "She had a medical ID card from her heart surgeon that the database cleared sir," he told his superior. "She was also hand-wanded by a female agent as she came in since her ID indicated she couldn't go through the full body scanners sir."

As Max continued watching Marshall's contorted face at his explanation he remembered the low-cut, bright red dress she wore that prominently showed her surgical scar just before she exploded. She made it a point that everyone could see it and now he understood why she did.

"So she's in the system?" Marshall asked.

Max remembered the agent scanning the medical card to get a match in the medical database. "Yes sir, she is."

"I understand now why Agent Carpenter and Steven Matthews were killed considering the proximity the First Family table was to the podium and the bomber, but where were *you* and Scott Matthews, Max? Why weren't the two of you killed as well?" Marshall asked.

Max thought about his boss's question and sternly responded, "Am I being accused of something here sir?"

"Not at all, Agent Mason. I just want to know why you and your charge were not at the table the same time Agent Carpenter and Steven Matthews were."

Max didn't like the tone of the question asked by his boss.

"Scott had to use the restroom before he sat down and Steven didn't sir, but Agent Carpenter wanted to get Steven in his seat before his parents got there and went ahead of us," Max explained. "Scott and I were coming down the hallway when the bomb went off...*sir,*" he forcibly exclaimed.

"So I have a dead President's son because he didn't have to take a piss and the other *did*? Is that what you're saying Agent Mason?"

Max paused for a moment of thought. "Yes sir, that's correct."

Marshall wasn't happy with the answer, raising his voice, "Agent Mason, do you expect me to tell the President of the United States who just lost his son to terrorists that his other son was only saved because he had to go to the bathroom?"

Max understood what his boss was trying to get across about his explanation. "It's the truth sir, and that's what my report will say." As he stood before his director, Max felt satisfied with his report on the tragedy at the gala.

Director Marshall looked straight into Agent Mason's eyes.

"Go home Max. Get some sleep, eat something...the world's gonna know your name tomorrow," he implied. "Be back in my office at 0900 tomorrow morning."

"Yes sir," said Max, and he turned and walked out of Marshall's office.

Agent Tyler had heard from another agent that Max Mason was in the White House and waited for him outside of Director Marshall's office in the hallway. "How bad was it sir?" she asked as he walked out and saw her standing there.

"Pretty bad," Max replied with a chuckle knowing Tyler was referring to the discussion with Dwayne Marshall.

Tyler knew how close he was to both Agent Carpenter and Steven Matthews and offered her condolences. "I'm so sorry about Jason and Steven."

Max looked at Tyler and smiled. "Thanks."

Tyler smiled back. "Where are you headed now sir?" she asked.

"I'm going home and have a drink Tyler," he responded with a grin.

"Would you like for me to bring you some food sir?" Tyler asked, knowing Max would not make any for himself when he got home.

"No thanks. I just need to be alone right now. Rain check?" he asked grabbing her hand and squeezing it gently.

"I would like that sir," replied Tyler. They smiled at one another and Max walked back down the hallway and out the service door where he had come in.

The President was waiting in his Oval Office when Director Marshall was announced. As Marshall walked in he saw CIA Director Aaron Oliver and FBI Director Michael James sitting on the couch eagerly awaiting Marshall's preliminary report.

"Mr. President, I have spoken with lead agent Maxwell Mason concerning this evening's tragedy," Marshall began.

"Agent Mason believes a female suicide bomber carried out this attack and that she carried the bomb inside her body concealed as a heart pacemaker sir."

Marshall knew how that sounded and both Director Oliver and James spoke up.

"Are your agents stoned, Marshall?" Oliver queried with a chuckle.

"How the hell is that even possible, Dwayne?" James asked.

Director Marshall knew he was on the hot seat for this but wasn't going to let anyone other than the President disrespect his agency or his agents. "Max Mason is a highly decorated agent, a former Navy SEAL and devoted father. His insights are always DEAD ON," Marshall replied.

"Dead seems to be a resounding issue with Mason," Oliver piped in with a smirk on his face.

"Mr. President, Agent Mason is not on trial here. We should be concentrating on who did this and why sir," Marshall argued.

"I agree that Agent Mason is not on trial here gentlemen, but he has answers to a good many questions, and I want those answers, and my *family* wants those answers," President Matthews replied.

"Where are we with forensics, Michael?" the President asked looking at FBI Director James.

"We are going over everything we took out of the ballroom, Mr. President. We should know something by morning."

"Has anyone taken credit for this bombing yet Aaron?" the President asked directing the question to CIA Director Oliver.

"No sir. All the chatter is about it happening, not who did it," Oliver explained.

"So right now we have absolutely *nothing* on who killed my son? Is that what you're all trying to tell me?"the President yelled.

Daryl Matthews angrily stood up and swiped his arm across his desk, throwing everything on the floor. Amy Reynolds, the President's secretary, and a Secret Service agent with his gun drawn clamored into the room. "Are you okay sir?" she asked.

"I'm fine Amy, thank you," he said frustrated. "Somebody get me information on the son of a bitch that did this. NOW!" he screamed.

"I want everyone connected to this case in my office by 10am, and we better know more than we know now. Do I make myself clear gentlemen?" the President said with anger in his voice.

All three directors nodded with shock on their faces. "Yes, Mr. President," they said in unison, and exited quickly.

Max Mason pulled into his driveway in Arlington, Virginia, about 20 minutes east of his office in Washington, DC, and walked into the single family home he lived in with his two teenage children. He noticed as he unlocked the front door that the bushes in front of the house could use some water, and maybe a little trim. Max went in and closed the door behind him. He walked through the family room into the kitchen and saw a note on the refrigerator door -- "Dinner in the fridge Daddy" -- which made him smile. His daughter was always taking care of him, even at 16 years old.

Max opened the fridge, saw his plate of food, decided he wasn't hungry and closed the door. He opened the cabinet above the fridge, pulled out a half empty bottle of Jamaican dark rum, grabbed a glass from the next cabinet and poured some into the glass. He slowly sipped some rum, put the glass down and then proceeded to wash his face in the kitchen sink. He downed the rest of the glass, put the bottle back in the cabinet, left the glass in the sink and slowly started up the stairs to his bedroom.

When he got to his door he heard the squeaking of a door opening. "Are you okay Daddy?" Max turned to see his daughter standing in her bedroom doorway half asleep.

Max walked over to her and gave her a big hug. "I am now. Go back to sleep princess," he said, kissing her on the forehead.

"Love you daddy," she said as she closed her door.

"Love you too princess," he replied, tears coming down his face. Max closed his door, rubbed his eyes, and lay down on his bed thinking tomorrow was going to be a *very* long day.

Max got back up and plugged his phone in to charge and noticed a text from Karen Tyler. "Hang in there Max," it said with a smiley face. A good feeling came over Max as he laid back down and closed his eyes.

After only four hours sleep, Max was back up, showered, got dressed and went down to the kitchen. His two kids were in high school and had already left so they were basically self-sufficient now. But he knew his daughter would always make coffee and leave it for him. He poured a cup and started sipping it, turned on the TV news and found - to no real surprise - every channel he turned to talking about the gala tragedy.

Max remembered what Marshall had said the previous night, that everyone was going to know his name. Yet after seeing four or five reports on different channels his name hadn't come up. He finished his coffee and put his cup in the dishwasher. He fixed his holstered SA-XD 9mm handgun on his hip, put his dress jacket on, straightened his tie and grabbed his keys.

Max Mason arrived at the White House entrance around 8:45am showed his Secret Service ID, was confirmed by the guard and let through the gate. He noticed that security was a little tighter than usual but understood under these particular circumstances. He again parked his car in the designated lot for Secret Service agents and went inside.

He met Director Marshall coming out of his office. "Good morning sir," Max said.

"Good morning Max," Marshall replied looking like he'd been there all night.

Max felt a little better when the director called him "Max" and not Agent Mason.

"Go have a seat I'll be right in," Marshall told Max.

"Yes sir" he replied.

Max sat down in the chair in front of the director's desk feeling like he was back in the school principal's office. Director Marshall came in with a cup of coffee, shut the door behind him and placed it on his desk.

"I read your report this morning Max." Marshall informed him.

Max had stayed up late to finish it to make sure it was in his email first thing this morning. "Your theory is plausible. *Unusual*, but still plausible," Marshall told him. "We found out from CIA informants last night that a new explosive is on the open market," he added with worry in his voice.

Max sat up in his chair a little straighter. "How powerful is the explosive sir?"

"Powerful enough that you can take out a whole city block with about the size of a walnut of this shit," Marshall explained.

"What about the pacemaker theory sir," Max asked. "Could someone have survived such a surgical procedure with an explosive inside them?" Max wanted to know.

"Agent Tyler is investigating the doctor who did this Brenda Danforth's heart surgery. She should know something soon," Marshall said.

"Does this explosive have a name like C-4 or plastique sir?" Max asked.

Marshall picked up a piece of paper from his desk and looked at it. "X-127. That's all it says here," Marshall read out loud. "Now for the bad news Max. The President wants a meeting with all those involved last night, especially you. It's scheduled for this morning.

"Max, you're a good agent and I will do what I can for you with the President, but understand he's an angry man and a grieving father right now," Marshall added.

Max looked at his boss, smiled, and said, "Thank you sir. I appreciate that."

Marshall's secretary stood at the door of his office and informed the two of them, "The President is assembling everyone in the Oval Office in 10 minutes gentlemen."

"Thank you Mary" Marshall responded. She smiled, left the doorway and returned to her desk. Marshall got up from his chair and looked at Max. "Are you ready for this?"

Max stood up. "Yes sir, I am." He knew what he had done last night was by the book and didn't have any concerns about how he had handled things.

Max and Director Marshall slowly walked towards the Oval Office, meeting Agent Karen Tyler on the way. "Good morning sirs," Tyler said.

Max smiled at Tyler and thought she looked quite good in her short skirt and blazer but decided not to say anything other than, "Good morning, Agent Tyler."

The hallway was bustling with agents, assistants and agency directors ready to meet President Matthews to discuss the terrorist bombing tragedy that had taken his son's life just hours before. The door of the Oval Office opened and his Chief of Staff stepped out and announced, "The President will see you all now."

Everyone filed into the Oval Office as all three directors sat on the sofa in front of the President's desk with their assistants standing behind them holding files and reports. Max and Tyler stood behind Director Marshall waiting for the President to arrive.

Another door opened and President Matthews, with two protective duty agents, walked in prompting everyone to stand at attention. President Matthews looked at everyone with sadness in his face. "Good morning everyone" he said solemnly.

"Good morning Mr. President," they all quickly responded.

President Matthews sat down at his desk, which allowed the directors to sit down.

"Where are we with this bombing?" the President asked. "Director Oliver, you start," the President commanded.

"We only have a bit of information, Mr. President," The CIA Director said. "Seems a terrorist cell called the "Dragon's Breath" early this morning claimed responsibility for the bombing. We don't have any information on them at the moment sir. They seem to be a new faction out of Southeast Asia," continued Oliver. " Mr. President, we have all our overseas contacts looking into getting more information on this cell as we speak sir."

Max thought to himself about what the woman in the red dress had said at the podium just before she blew herself up. "The dragon breathes again," she had declared, obviously making a direct context to the "Dragon's Breath" terrorist organization. But Max couldn't shake the feeling he had heard that name sometime in the past.

Oliver continued explaining to the President about the new experimental explosive that was used in the bombing -- X-127.

"Where did this explosive come from?" asked President Matthews.

"We have reliable intelligence, Mr. President, that it was smuggled out of North Korea," Oliver replied.

"How the hell did it get in the United States Aaron?"

"We don't know, Mr. President," Oliver replied feeling incompetent about his answer.

"Now, somebody tell me about this woman who killed my son last night," President Matthews demanded.

FBI Director James stood and received a file from his assistant behind him. "Her name was Brenda Danforth, Mr. President" James replied.

"She was from New York City, the Upper East Side, and according to her financials was very well off from family money, with no living relatives," James continued. "She was a major contributor to the Children's Hunger Charity the past two years which warranted her invitation to the gala last night," he explained.

"Her medical file showed she had open heart surgery two months ago here in a nearby Washington, DC, hospital to put in a pacemaker," James read.

"The surgeon, Dr. Oscar Williams, successfully transplanted the pacemaker and oversaw her recovery in a private medical facility in Arlington, Virginia" he explained.

"We have agents looking for Dr. Williams as we speak, Mr. President," James said concluding his report.

"Why haven't you found him yet?" the President asked the FBI chief a bit angrily.

Agent Tyler raised her hand apprehensively behind Director Marshall before speaking. "Mr. President, I had local law enforcement visit Dr. Williams' home early this morning and found both he and his wife had been murdered sir."

"According to the coroner's report, Mr. President, they had been dead for at least a week," Tyler continued.

"How did they die, Agent Tyler?" the President asked.

"Gunshot wounds to the back of their heads, execution style, Mr. President. It looks like they were shot on their knees."

"Okay. That doesn't sound suspicious at all," the President said sarcastically. "Anyone have any answers, theories, even fucking guesses on this bombing?" President Matthews loudly asked his directors.

"Agent Tyler, good work. I want you to adjust your schedule and continue looking into this case."

"Yes, Mr. President. Thank you sir," Tyler replied.

"Mr. President," FBI Director James said loudly. "Domestic investigations are the FBI's job, not the Secret Service," he proclaimed. "The Secret Service isn't allowed to investigate criminal acts of terrorism, Mr. President. They are nothing more than a protective agency. I must object, sir."

Director Marshall stood up. "That's enough slandering my agency Michael. One of my own agents was killed last night in the line of duty. That gives *my* agency the right to investigate," Marshall declared.

Director James looked at Dwayne Marshall. "With your agency's incompetence, we're lucky *only two* people were killed last night."

"ENOUGH!" the President screamed. "Agent Tyler, I want you to continue investigating this bombing," President Matthews said to her. Tyler nodded to the President.

"Director James, may I remind you one of those *only two* people killed last night was *my* 11-year-old son," President Matthews said standing behind his desk and looking down at James.

"I'm deeply sorry, Mr. President" James said embarrassed.

"Next time you open your mouth, try to think before you look like an asshole in front of everyone in the room," the President said.

"Yes, Mr. President. Again, my apology" James replied, feeling a bit foolish.

"Do we have any information on this Danforth woman?" President Matthews asked again. The room went silent with everyone looking at one another. "Any theories, or ideas about this bombing? Come on people, my wife is on sedatives and I can't grieve for my son until this fucking crisis is over! Give me something! The media is all over this already!"

Max spoke up. "Mr. President there was something that she said and did right before she blew herself up. She said 'the dragon breathes again.' Right after that she looked at the clock that said 8pm, smiled at everyone and exploded."

"That was in everyone's report Agent Mason. What's your point?" asked the President.

"Mr. President, what if the bomb was set to go off at exactly 8pm and she had to alter her plan because you and the First Lady weren't there yet sir," Max explained. "I believe she already knew she was exploding at 8pm, saw Agent Carpenter and your son at the table and figured they were the only high profile targets available before she died."

"So you're saying killing my son was her second choice, Agent Mason?'

"Yes sir, that's exactly what I'm saying, with my apology, Mr. President."

President Matthews turned and looked out the window, then back to Max thinking about what he had said, knowing he and his wife had not arrived at the gala on time because of the limo trouble. "No apology needed. Your theory has merit Max."

"Thank you sir," Max acknowledged.

"Anyone else want to add to Agent Mason's theory?" President Matthews asked. No one spoke up as they all looked around at each other. "Then get out of here and find me some answers," he said unpleasantly. "All except you, Agent Mason. A word, please," he said.

Everyone slowly walked out of the room looking back at President Matthews standing behind his desk. Max stood there with his hands behind his back in his accustomed "at ease" stance the Navy taught him many years ago. Agent Tyler walked by Max and smiled at him. He smiled back as she left through the door.

"I need to know how and why my son died Max," the President asked.

Max wasn't sure of the question. "Sir??" inquired.

"I know he was killed by a terrorist suicide bomber, but what I *don't* know is why Steven wasn't with you and his brother Scott?"

Max could see the sadness and fear in the President's eyes and thinking how he himself would feel if he lost one of his two children so horrifically. No parent should outlive their children, he thought. "Scott asked to use the restroom before he sat down sir," Max started to explain.

"I asked Steven if he needed to as well, and he said no." As Max continued he could see more sadness coming over President Matthews' face. "Agent Carpenter wanted to get him in his seat before you arrived and I escorted Scott to the restroom sir. When Scott was through, I escorted him back down the hallway. Just as I pulled the curtain back, the bomb went off, Mr. President. There was nothing I could do sir."

"You should have made him go Max," came the voice of the First Lady from behind. Heather Matthews had slipped into the room and slowly walked up to Max, looked him in the eyes and slapped him across the face with her right open hand. "My son is dead because of you," Mrs. Matthews said distraught with emotional pain and anger.

"HEATHER!" Daryl Matthews yelled from behind his desk. "You need to go back to our quarters NOW!"

"You're the President of the United States, Daryl. Have you taken even a minute to grieve for our son?" she asked, tears pouring down her face.

"That's not fair Heather. Of course I have. And we're trying to get the people responsible for it."

"Why, when we have the one person here who could have saved him but didn't!" she exclaimed.

"Agent Mason, you're dismissed," the President directed.

"Yes, Mr. President," Max replied, turning to leave the room.

"I don't want you to ever go near my *only* son again Max. Do you understand that?" the First Lady said in a furious tone.

"Yes ma'am. I'm *so* sorry for your loss," he acknowledged to the grieving Heather Mathews as he left the room.

Daryl Matthews pushed the button on his desk phone as his wife stood in front of him crying,

"Yes, Mr. President?" inquired secretary Amy Reynolds.

"Have Agent Tyler come into my office please."

"Yes, Mr. President," she replied and hung up the phone.

Agent Tyler arrived a few moments later and was escorted in by the President's secretary. "Agent Tyler, Mr. President," Reynolds announced.

"Thank you, Amy" President Matthews acknowledged. "Agent Tyler I need you to escort my wife back to our quarters please."

"Yes, Mr. President," Tyler replied, realizing she had come in during a very awkward and personal moment with the President and First Lady.

"I don't want that man *near* our son, Daryl. Do you understand that?"

"We will discuss this later Heather…alone. Please go upstairs with Karen sweetheart," he said lovingly to his wife. Heather Matthews turned towards the door and nodded to Karen Tyler and the two left the office together.

The President pushed the intercom button again and before his secretary could speak he said, "Have Director Marshall come to my office."

"Yes, Mr. President," she replied.

The Secret Service chief arrived a few minutes later and was ushered in. "Thank you Amy," said the President.

"I'm afraid we have a problem, Dwayne" the President said as Amy closed the door behind Director Marshall. "Heather refuses to let Max take care of Scott anymore. She blames him for Steven's death. As the President, I understand the situation he was put into, and as a father I thank him for saving my son Scott's life. But as a husband I have to take my wife's feelings into account and need to you to reassign Max away from Scott."

Marshall was perplexed by what the President was saying. "So you want me to reassign the best agent you have in your employ, that has saved countless lives over his tenure here, including your son's, with no thought or hesitation because your wife told you to, Mr. President?" Marshall knew that would get him a reprimand from the President but he was not happy he was disciplining one of his top agents.

"God damn it, Dwayne, this could put my wife's mental health into a *very* dark place that she may never get out of if I don't do this," President Matthews said frustrated. "I don't want to do this. Max has been with me for seven years. He's more than just a damn good agent to me. He's a friend. But I have to do what's best for my family first," he said turning away from Marshall. "I can't have him in DC, Dwayne. Heather would eventually run into him here."

"Get him to Los Angeles or Miami," the President commanded. "I'm sure his family would enjoy either of those two cities. I promise to give him the highest recommendation at whichever office he chooses and a pay raise for the inconvenience."

Director Marshall straightened his tie, looked at the President. "For the record, Mr. President, I think this is bullshit and you should be ashamed of yourself...SIR."

Marshall turned and walked out the door before the President could say anything else, walking slowly back towards his office where he knew Max was waiting for him.

Max stood up from his chair outside the door as his boss walked into his office. Marshall looked at Max. "Let's talk."

Max followed the director into his office and closed the door behind him. Marshall gave him a serious look. "Take a seat Max."

Max didn't like the way that sounded and stood at ease in front of Marshall's desk. "I'd rather stand, sir, if you don't mind."

"Max, the President believes it would be beneficial if you were to not be on Scott's protection detail anymore," Marshall informed his agent.

"Am I being fired sir?" Max asked confused.

"No, Max. He wants me to reassign you to either the Los Angeles or Miami office," Marshall explained. "He says either one you choose for your family he will personally call and set up the transfer for you."

Max was feeling all kinds of emotions after hearing this news -- anger, sadness, regret and anxiety. "How much time do I have to think about this sir?" Max asked.

"I need a choice after the memorial services tomorrow for both Steven and Agent Carpenter," Marshall insisted.

"And Max, I wouldn't advise trying to go to Steven Matthews' memorial service. The First Lady has had you barred from it."

"I would like to at least say goodbye to Scott if the President will allow it sir," Max requested.

"I will ask him Max, but don't get your hopes up. Take the rest of the day off, go home and talk to your kids, sleep on your decision and let me know tomorrow after Carpenter's service," Marshall said with sadness and guilt in his voice.

"Yes sir," Max replied, feeling a bit nauseous at his predicament.

He then drove home thinking about what Marshall had said to him, and walked through the door to find his daughter sitting on the couch in the family room reading a book. "Why are you home so early Daddy?" she asked.

"Wanted to spend some time with you and your brother princess," Max said with a smile.

She gave her father "The Look" she always did when he was trying to be upbeat, or trying to pull something over on them at home so they didn't worry. "What's going on Daddy?" she asked trying to get him to open up to her.

"Everything is fine princess," Max said smiling at her.

"I'm almost 17, not 6 Daddy. I know when you're trying to protect us from something."

"That's a father's job sweetheart. Let's not dwell on anything right now. How about getting your brother and training a bit with your old man?"

"*Really?*" she responded enthusiastically.

"We haven't trained in a while sweetie. I know your brother and you have missed it," Max said remembering how much they loved training with him since they were little.

"I know. I'll go get him and we'll meet you in the training room," she said with a big smile on her face. "Can we shoot today?"

"I don't see why not princess." Max felt some joy knowing how they both liked to shoot in the firing range he had built in the basement level of the house. She ran upstairs to get her brother while Max thought about what their future would be like after tomorrow.

Agent Tyler sat at her desk looking at reports that were coming in from the FBI concerning the bombing when her phone rang. "Agent Tyler," she acknowledged.

"Agent Tyler I need to see you in my office." Director Marshall was on the other end.

"Yes sir," Tyler replied. Tyler walked down the hallway and into her boss's office to find him sitting behind his desk.

"Close the door Karen." She closed the door behind her and stood in front of Marshall's desk. "Any new information on the bombing or murders?" he asked.

"Ballistics came back negative from the bullets taken from the doctor and his wife from any firearm we have in our database sir."

"Sounds like a professional hit to me," Marshall said.

"We are going over the medical files for Brenda Danforth's pace-maker. It seems to be larger than the normal pacemaker that medical manufacturers use for transplants, which leads me to believe it was specially made for her by Dr. Williams," Tyler explained. "That's about it at the moment sir. This organization seems to be ghosts. They clean up their mess before they disappear. We've got no leads beyond Danforth and Dr. Williams. The two of them have no financial transactions or political affiliations connecting them to each other outside of the heart surgery sir."

"Thank you Agent Tyler. Please stay on top of this," Marshall requested. "Now...I need to reassign you to Scott Matthews's protection detail starting immediately," Marshall hesitantly told her.

"What about Agent Mason sir?" Tyler asked.

"Agent Mason has been reassigned to another office effective the day after tomorrow." he answered.

"This isn't Agent Mason's fault sir," Tyler said protecting her colleague.

"I know, Karen, but it's out of my hands. It's what the President and First Lady want, especially the First Lady," Marshall said, still trying to understand it himself. "You will be the lead agent on Scott Matthews's protection detail effective tomorrow morning at 0800," he ordered.

"Yes sir. May I be dismissed sir?"

"Dismissed," Marshall replied, not feeling good at all about what he had to do to his friend Max Mason or Karen Tyler.

Tyler walked back to her desk and immediately called Max on his cell phone, but after a few rings got his voicemail instead.

"This is Max, please leave a message," said the recording.

"Max, I just heard what happened...please call me!" Tyler pleaded into the phone. "I need to know you're alright."

After Max awoke the next day, he showered, shaved, got dressed and headed to the kitchen where he knew his daughter had made coffee for him. When he walked in he was surprised to see his son and daughter sitting at the kitchen island waiting for him. He knew they had missed the bus for school. "Aren't both of you going to be late for school?"

His daughter spoke up first. "This is an intervention Daddy." Max giggled and smiled at her statement but realized they were both serious.

"What's going on Pop?" his son asked.

Max always told them the truth and didn't hesitate this time either.

"I've been removed from Scott Matthews' protection detail and the President wants me to take another assignment in another city," he informed his children.

"Why are we being chased out of town for something you had *no* control over daddy?" his daughter asked.

Max hadn't thought of it that way. His guilt told him to leave town for not being able to save the lives of Steven Matthews or Jason Carpenter.

"We have lived here since Mom died, Pop. Why should we leave because the President says we should? Don't we have a right to stay here if we want?" his son asked.

"We would have to tighten our belts for a bit if we stay," Max said to them, thinking they were both right.

"We love you Daddy. Whatever *you* want to do, we will go along with. You know that," she said. His son nodded in agreement with his younger sister.

Max walked up to each of them, kissed them on the forehead. "I love you both so much."

"We know," they both said together smiling at one another.

Max drove them to school and then headed to the White House. He called a financial advisor he knew about what his options were. He pulled up to the security gate, offered up his ID to the guard on duty with a smile and drove to the agent lot and parked. He was informed by an agent as he came in that Agent Carpenter's memorial service would be at 10am in the White House chapel.

Max walked down the hallway to the director's office said "Good morning" to Mary and asked to see the director.

"He will see you Max," she said as she returned from the chief's office.

Max walked into Director Marshall's office and stood in front of his desk. "Good morning sir."

"Good morning Max. I hope you made a decision on where you wanted to go. I think your kids would love Miami."

Max changed the subject for the moment. "Were you able to talk to the President about saying good-bye to Scott sir?"

"Yes I did. He said he would allow you five minutes with Scott before Agent Carpenter's memorial service," Marshall informed him.

"Thank you sir, I will give you my decision after Carpenter's service" Max informed Marshall.

"Why can't you tell me now Max?" Marshall asked anxiously.

"It would ruin the surprise sir," Max said with a condescending smile on his face.

"Do I need to worry about you Agent Mason?" Dwayne Marshall asked concerned.

"No sir. Not at all. Everything is fine," Max replied with a grin.

Max followed Director Marshall to the Oval Office so he could say his goodbye to Scott Matthews. Marshall stood in front of Amy Reynolds' desk and asked if the President was ready for Agent Mason. She picked up the phone.

"Mr. President, Director Marshall and Agent Mason are here to see you sir."

She hung up the phone and informed them, "The President will see you both now."

Max followed Marshall into the President's office and saw Scott Matthews sitting on the couch while his father sat behind his desk.

"MAX!!!" Scott shouted as he saw him come in the room.

Max smiled at the young boy. "Hey Squirrel, look at you!" Scott was still wearing his Rocky Squirrel pin on the lapel of his black suit he was wearing for his brother's and Agent Carpenter's memorial services. Max looked over at the President who nodded to him in acknowledgment.

Scott got up and ran to his friend hugging him at the waist. "When are you coming back Max?" he asked looking up at him.

Max glanced over at the President who just stared at Max with sorrow for his son. "Do you remember Agent Tyler?" Max asked.

"Yeah. She's pretty," Scott Matthews said smiling.

"Yes, she is," Max responded with a glint in his eyes. "Well, she is going to be taking over my duties with you starting today."

"What's wrong Max?" the young boy asked not understanding what he was saying.

"I feel after what happened to your brother and Agent Carpenter, I need to spend some quality time with *my* two kids. I've missed them."

"You're not moving away, are you Max?" Scott asked.

Max looked at the President and with a stern look said, "No, Scott. I'm *not* moving away. My family's home is here." Max could see the puzzled, yet stern, look the President gave him, thinking they had an understanding about him leaving town.

"That's awesome Max!" Scott said with excitement.

President Matthews stood up from behind his desk and addressed his son. "It's time for you to go upstairs and get ready for the service Scott."

"Okay Dad. I'll talk to you later Max," as he hugged the agent again then walked out of his father's office.

"Have Director Marshall join us Amy," the President said over his intercom. The FBI chief had waited outside for Max until his reunion with Scott Matthews was over.

Marshall walked into the President's office to find Max and the President standing staring at each other with Max in his usual respectful "at ease" stance.

"What the hell Dwayne! I thought we had an understanding about all this!" the President said in anger.

Director Marshall had a deer-in-the-headlights look, not understanding what the President meant. "I'm sorry, Mr. President, I'm not following what you're asking."

"Agent Mason just told my son he *wasn't* moving away. What is that suppose to mean?"

Director Marshall looked at Max who gave him a half grin and asked, "What are you pulling Mason?"

"Nothing, sir. I've been reminded that what you have you don't necessarily need, but what you need you may already have and should treasure it while you have it," Max said smiling.

"What the fuck is that supposed to mean?" the director yelled. "Is that another one of your fucking Zen statements Mason?"

"It means, sir, that I am taking early retirement from the agency as of tomorrow. I signed the papers with H/R before I came in sir," Max informed both his boss and the President.

Max looked at the President with a stern look on his face and firmly stated, "With all due respect, sir, *no one* chases my family out of town, not even *you*, Mr. President.

"I'm sorry you and your wife lost your son in such a horrific way, but my conscience is clear. I did *my job* by protecting Scott for you; How you and your wife view my actions on that night is between you two, Mr. President. It has been an honor serving you all these years."

The now former-agent Mason then extended his hand to the President who took it hesitantly.

"I'm sorry for all this Max," President Matthews said with remorse. "Good luck to you and your family."

"Thank you, Mr. President."

Max then looked at Director Marshall. "I will turn over my badge and ID to you after Carpenter's service sir."

Marshall nodded to Max with a scowl on his face. Max smiled thinking Marshall was actually trying to intimidate him. Max thought to himself, "Guess I might be off his Christmas card list now."

Max then addressed both of them. "I hope to see you both at Jason Carpenter's memorial service." He turned and walked out of the Oval Office with a satisfying grin on his face.

Marshall followed Max out. Are you sure about this Mason?"

"Yes, sir, I am." he replied with a grin.

"That was pretty ballsy talking to the President that way," Marshall said, not happy with his agent.

"I'm retired, sir. I'm just a taxpayer now. He now works for me . .
. and for that matter, so do *YOU*," Max said with a smirk.

Marshall sort of understood what Max was doing but knew the
President would come down on *him* knowing Mason was *not* leaving
town. "Anytime you want to come back into the government, I'm
sure we can find something that fits you," Marshall said.

"I appreciate that, sir, but right now I have two people I answer to
and I'm looking forward to them bossing me around," Max said with
a chuckle referring to his two teens at home.

Max shook the director's hand. "It's been fun, sir," he said with
a smile.

"Yes it has, Max, yes it has," Marshall replied with a grin. He knew
he and the President were losing the best agent the Secret Service
ever had, but he understood Max's decision.

Agent Tyler met Max and Marshall before they went into the
director's office. "I believe you two have some things to discuss,"
Marshall said with a grin as he walked into his office. "I'll see you
both at the service."

"Is it true Max are you quitting the service?" she asked with sadness on her face.

Max smiled at Tyler. "Not quitting, retiring."

"What's the difference? You won't be here anymore," she replied,
obviously upset at his decision.

"It's time I played Dad for a while," Max said laughing, looking
forward to spending most of his time with his kids.

"My son and daughter have a couple of years before they go off
to college or the military and I'd like to give them my full attention
for once" he explained.

"They've been *very* understanding and patient all these years
with a Navy SEAL and Secret Service dad," he laughed. "It's *their* time
now," Max said smiling.

"But what about us and my training, Max? Are you just going to
throw that away?" Karen asked.

"You know I haven't had to train you in a while now," Max
responded with a grin.

"You are an exceptional woman, Karen Tyler. Your service career and new assignment is going to keep you busy for a *very* long time. We live our lives through our dedication to the job, to protecting those who are responsible for making our country safe. Max said.

"I've always been proud of you Karen. I wish you nothing but the best in your life," Max continued, taking her face in his hands and giving her an extended kiss on her cheek. Karen closed her eyes, tears rolling down her face and reached up to hold his hands. Moments later, he turned and walked away towards the chapel.

Tyler then heard Marshall's secretary behind her. "Agent Tyler, the director needs to see you ma'am." Tyler wiped the tears from her eyes and turned to go into his office, glancing back at Max walking down the hallway. She thought, sadly, it might be the last time she would see Max Mason.

CHAPTER 3

THE FIRST THING STACY MICHAELS SAW AS SHE was helped out of the limousine was how huge the banner was that hung across the front of the Global Broadcast Network building. Her blue eyes got really big and excited seeing the multi-colored sign with big, black bold lettering that read "Global Broadcasting Network Welcomes Children's Global Hunger TV/Radio Telethon". The banner ran the entire length of the five-story building and covered down over the 4th and 5th stories. She couldn't help but smile when she saw it. She thought it was beautifully endorsed.

Stacy looked at the empty GBN parking lot, the steel partitions around the building's block and thought how secure it was outside the GBN building. She noticed how nicely the shrubs and trees were landscaped along the front of the building.

Standing on the sidewalk, she adjusted her skirt down a bit, then watched as her boss Jonathan Mayer stepped out of the limo. Two black-suited men approached them from the front of the building, one carrying a clipboard. "We're with the Secret Service," the young agent with the clipboard said to Stacy and Mayer. "We need to confirm your invitation."

Mayer smiled at Stacy and looked at the agent. "I'm Jonathan Mayer, and this is my assistant Stacy Michaels from Mayer Financial."

The agent looked down the page of his clipboard and looked at them both. "We need to see some ID before we can allow you to enter Mr. Mayer, Ms. Michaels." Both Michaels and Mayer handed the agent their driver's licenses. He looked them both over and handed them back. "Please enjoy the telethon," the agent said allowing them to proceed to the front entrance.

Mayer looked at his assistant, smiled, buttoned his jacket and asked "What's the first thing on my agenda Stacy?"

"You have a group meet and greet with Congressman David Young, GBN Director of Broadcasting Brian Jurgens, and GBN Security Chief Charles Lee in ten minutes sir."

Stacy Michaels was working as an assistant for one of the richest and financially smartest men in the world. She had been with him for over a year and this was her first official business trip with him. They flew in a private jet from their Virginia Beach headquarters, were picked up by a limousine and had lunch at the five-star Washington Majestic Hotel where they were staying -- firsts for Stacy, who was enjoying all of it.

Jonathan Mayer was a financial genius when it came to stock trading, banking, financial planning and investment management. He had built Mayer Financial Corp. into one of the largest financial banking institutions in the world. Mayer had been contracted by the Children's Global Hunger Charity President Nelson Roberts to oversee the financial donations generated worldwide by the GBN TV/Radio telethon. His security knowledge on bank accounts was second to none.

Mayer had a PHD in financial banking and took over Mayer Financial when his father passed away under what some believed suspicious circumstances 15 years ago. He was tall, late 40s, handsome and an ex-CIA computer analyst. He was a good boss to Stacy and had treated her with respect since she began working for him.

Stacy looked at her watch and saw it was almost time for her boss's meeting and put her glasses back up on her nose. She was young and smart, having just turned 21, graduating early from college with an international affairs degree. She had long blonde hair, beautiful blue eyes, and with her four-inch heals she was almost six feet tall, with a model's figure.

"Your meeting with the Congressman is in five minutes sir," she reminded him. Mayer looked around the entrance of the building and its surroundings, smiled, straightened his tie and proceeded to walk through the front door with Stacy close behind.

GBN Security Chief Charles Lee, a tall Asian American was waiting at the security desk when Mayer and Stacy announced themselves to one of the guards.

The guard handed them both visitor passes and asked them to go through the metal detectors. Lee walked up and introduced himself and ushered them past the metal detectors, waving off the security guards.

Stacy noticed that many people coming in also did not have to go through the metal detectors. They only had to show their ID badges to the guard. She thought that was a bit strange considering the security aspects related to the event. She knew that several high profile children and teens would be present to participate in the telethon that evening, including the teenage daughter of President of the Unites States Keith Bradshaw, Stephanie Bradshaw.

"Welcome to GBN, Mr. Mayer," Lee said shaking his hand.

"Thank you. This is my assistant Stacy Michaels," Mayer said.

"Hi," Stacy replied, shaking Lee's hand.

"Nice to meet you both. The Congressman and director are waiting for you in the conference room," Lee said as they walked down the hallway of the large building that had its walls decorated with the colored flags of different countries.

"How many countries do you broadcast to Mr. Lee?" Stacy asked curiously.

"We broadcast to 45 different countries simultaneously on TV and radio 24 hours a day, 365 days a year."

"Even on Christmas Day?" Stacy asked.

"Yes, even on Christmas Day," Lee said with a laugh.

"How is your computer security?" Mayer asked Lee.

"We have federal cyber encryption analysts on staff to protect our servers." Lee ensured Mayer.

"Very nice," Mayer replied with a smile. "I'd like to see them if I could. The servers, I mean," he explained.

"I believe the director can arrange that for you," Lee said.

The three of them arrived at the conference room, passing the armed security guard standing by the glass door entrance. The guard opened the door and everyone followed Lee in. Stacy smiled at the guard and said "Thank you" to him as she entered. The guard gave her a smile back, closing the door quickly behind them.

As the three of them entered the large conference room they could see brightly-colored banners around the room representing various countries of the world. Stacy thought the room was beautifully decorated.

There was a small group of men gathered in the middle of the room, and as Stacy, Mayer, and Lee approached they smiled at the three of them.

"Mr. Mayer, nice to finally meet you. I'm Congressman David Young of Virginia," the well-dressed politician said extending his hand out to Mayer. He'd recognized him from his photo in the Business Journal magazine.

"Very nice to meet you, Congressman. This is my assistant Stacy Michaels," Mayer replied taking the Congressman's firm hand shake.

"How do you do, Congressman," Stacy said shaking his hand as well.

"Let me introduce some major players in the making of today's event," Rep. Young said with a smile. "This is Brian Jurgens, Director of Broadcasting here at GBN."

Brian Jurgens was in his early 40s, about six feet tall, with short brown hair, and well-built. Stacy thought he looked a little young to be in charge of a Federal agency even if it was just a TV and Radio station's day to day operations. She also thought "He must have pictures on someone high up." He was dressed in a dark blue suit and tie, looking like an advertising model, Stacy thought with a grin.

"He is the one in charge of ALL the broadcasting on TV and radio, as well as the internet streaming," the Congressman said to them. "Mr. Jurgens and his Associate Director Marcus Grant worked hard to help set all this up for the charity."

Jonathan Mayer stepped forward and extended his hand to Jurgens who shook it and said, "It's nice to meet you, Mr. Mayer. This is Marcus Grant."

Stacy felt a little uneasy around Grant. She noticed he had been eyeing her and smiling the entire time since she'd walked in. She could tell when someone was trying to hit on her.

Marcus Grant was African American, had an athletic build, was sharply dressed, and probably early to mid 30s, she thought. "Nice to meet you both," Grant said shaking Mayer's hand, then moving to Stacy's.

"Nice to meet you," Stacy replied to Grant, forcing a smile to him.

"You should come work for *us*," Grant said looking Stacy up and down with a big grin.

"No thank you. I love my job at the beach," Stacy said, shooting him down quickly.

"I'll talk you into it before you leave," Grant said with a bigger grin on his face.

"I seriously doubt it," Stacy replied with a stern look on her face.

"We would like to give you both a private tour of our broadcasting facility and let you know what GBN is all about before the telethon begins this evening," Brian Jurgens said looking at Mayer.

"We'd like that very much, Mr. Jurgens. I'm sure my assistant has many curious questions about your broadcasting organization," he said grinning.

Stacy blushed a bit because her boss was right. She had many questions she wanted to ask. She had never been inside a Radio or TV station before and wanted to know everything.

They left the conference room and started walking down the hallway, passing the escalator and stopping at a bank of elevators where the six of them got on. Grant pushed the third floor button going up. They stepped out of the elevator onto the third floor where Stacy noticed a lot of people moving around from door to door.

Grant excused himself from the group . "I will see you all again soon. Duty calls." He then gave Stacy a sheepish grin as he turned and walked away.

Stacy watched Grant go down the hallway and thought to herself, "What a sexist jerk."

"These are our broadcasting studios where we broadcast our different language air shows around the world," Jurgens said as the four of them slowly walked down the corridor passing several closed doors with "ON-AIR" lights shining bright red on the walls beside them.

"How many people do you broadcast to around the world?" Stacy asked Jurgens.

"Over 400 million people a day listen to our broadcasts," he responded, smiling at Stacy Michaels.

Mayer then spoke up. "That's impressive. Now I understand why they wanted the telethon here."

Jurgens walked over to a studio window and pressed the button underneath it. Stacy and Mayer could see people dressed in their colorful cultural garments through the window sitting behind microphones and reading from pages in their hands.

They could see the audio engineer sitting behind his console and listened to the audio that was being broadcast coming through a speaker in the ceiling above them.

"Either of you recognize the language?" Jurgens asked Stacy and Mayer.

"It's Kurdish," Stacy replied.

"Well done, Miss Michaels. Do you speak the language?" Jurgens queried.

"Actually I *do* a little, sir" she replied.

"What other languages do you speak Miss Michaels?"

"I also speak French, Spanish, Japanese, Korean, Pashto, Russian, Persian, and Swahili," Stacy said proudly.

"WOW!" Jurgens exclaimed. "That's *impressive*, Stacy."

"Thank you, sir. Since I studied international affairs in school they recommended that I learn different languages. My father thinks I over did it," she said with a giggle.

They continued down the hallway looking into other studios and hearing different languages through the overhead speakers.

They walked down the hallway a bit before Jurgens stopped at a large metal door with a keypad next to it. He took out his ID badge and touched the keypad with it, buzzing the door open.

Stacy was curious. "Are *all* the studio doors opened that way?"

"All studios have to be opened with a key card ID badge," Jurgens replied. "Only engineers and Broadcast Operations personnel have these ID cards for security purposes. This is what we call Master Control. Here we control all the audio and video from GBN going out to the world's televisions and radios."

Stacy was amazed at the equipment used to do all this. "How much does all this cost, Mr. Jurgens?" Stacy asked.

"Well, this year's Congressional budget for us was over $400 million for full operation."

"If all goes well with this telethon I'm sure we can get an increase on that for next year," Congressman Young said, grinning at Jurgens.

"That would be great, Congressman. That's what we're hoping for," Jurgens said with a smile.

Mayer asked, "Can we see the internet servers you use Mr. Jurgens?"

"Absolutely," Jurgens replied. "They are up on the fourth floor. All our computer programs are there."

The group again all got on the elevator together and went up one story to the fourth floor. As they exited the elevator they walked down a long hallway of offices to one with two glass doors. They walked in and stood in a large lobby, seeing a sign on the wall behind a desk indicating "Computer Services."

The woman behind the desk spoke up. "May I help you, Mr. Jurgens?"

"We're here to see Director Richards. Please tell him that Congressman Young and Jonathan Mayer are with me to look at his facility for this evening's telethon."

"He knows you're coming. He'll be right out, Mr. Jurgens," she said.

Director James Richards was in charge of all computer access in the building. From internet, to broadcast programming, he oversaw what went out on the "digital air waves."

"Hello everyone," Richards said as he came into the lobby.

James Richards was a large man weighing about 300 pounds. But he was tall, at about six-foot-six, with light brown hair and glasses. He dressed like the majority of his staff, wearing khaki pants, a polo shirt and sneakers.

Jurgens introduced the group. "James, this is Congressman Young, Jonathon Mayer from Mayer Financial Corporation, and his assistant Stacy Michaels."

Richards shook everyone's hand then turned to Jurgens and asked "What would you all like to see?"

Mayer spoke up immediately. "I would love to see your trans world servers."

"Absolutely," Richards responded. "Follow me."

They all followed him down a long corridor where Richards stopped at a large metal door. Stacy noticed there were two security key pads side by side for this door. He touched his ID badge to the keypad, then quickly put in a five-number security code into the first one. He then placed his thumb print on the second keypad and the door buzzed open. Stacy noticed that Mayer was watching this security process rather attentively as was Jurgens.

"That's pretty serious security," Mayer said to Richards continuing to look at the keypads.

"We have to make sure that every server is safe from any sort of hacking," Richards explained. "That's why the money that is donated all around the world will be secured in these servers before the World Bank downloads everything to the charity's account tomorrow morning when it opens."

"That's very impressive," Mayer said with a smile looking inside the secured room to see the banks of servers stretching down the length of the room.

"We still have a few minutes before the reception starts," Jurgens said. "Why don't we go look at the TV broadcast studio for this evening's telethon?"

They all started back down the corridor heading to the elevators they came up on. Stacy looked around, curious about everything, and noticed her boss was looking around attentively as well.

They all got off back on the third floor and followed Jurgens to a very large studio known as the "auditorium" where they met Marcus Grant again. "Everything is good to go here Brian," Grant said with an arrogant, smirky grin on his face looking at Stacy.

"Very nice, Marcus," Jurgens told him. "Any issues we need to go over before we go live?"

"Not at the moment. We're all good," Grant replied.

Stacy looked around and saw a very large stage floor with eight sophisticated TV cameras at different spots around the room. On the stage were long tables with microphones at each chair. There were exactly 15 chairs Stacy counted at these tables.

She also noticed that the auditorium seated about 100 people. It was decorated beautifully with different colored flags from all the countries that had representatives there that evening.

"This auditorium has been transformed into the world's stage this evening," Jurgens said proudly. Mayer and Stacy both nodded and smiled in agreement.

"We have all the special children of our world leaders joining us this evening to speak out on the hunger issues happening to their fellow children in their own countries," Jurgens said continuing to smile.

Stacy could tell how proud he was of all the preparations he and Grant had done for this event.

Stacy stepped forward and asked, "Who is joining the telethon this evening, Mr. Jurgens?"

"We have the daughter of the President of the United States , the son of a former President, granddaughter of the Secretary of Defense, the son of the Prime Minister of England, and the son of the President of France, just to name a few, Ms. Michaels," he said to her smiling proudly.

Stacy thought to herself these were pretty "special kids" to come and speak on behalf of their countries to get rid of child hunger. She couldn't wait to meet and talk to some of them at the reception that evening, especially the President's daughter.

"Let's head on up to the reception. Our guests should be arriving about now," Jurgens said. They left the auditorium and headed back to the elevators.

When the doors opened to the fifth floor, everyone but Security Chief Charles Lee got off the elevator. He informed Jurgens he was heading down to the lobby to meet the Secret Service and President Bradshaw's daughter. Jurgens smiled and nodded as the doors started to close.

Jurgens opened the double glass doors into the ballroom. "*Wow*," Stacy whispered under her breath, seeing how beautifully decorated the room was with its crystal chandeliers and marble floors. "How old is this ballroom, Mr. Jurgens?" she asked as she scanned the paintings of past Presidents on the walls.

"The building has been around since World War II, Ms. Michaels. So almost 75 years. They used to throw big cotillion like balls here."

"It's so beautiful," Stacy replied, continuing to look around the large room.

Stacy looked over at all the buffet tables and carving stations and watched the handsomely dressed wait staff walking around with trays of fruit punch for dignitaries, security, and their charges that had already arrived at the ballroom. She understood that since this was a telethon involving children and teenagers that no alcohol was being served. But she did notice a very long dessert table that most of the young children and teens were in line for.

Jonathan Mayer grabbed a couple of glasses from the waiter's tray and offered Stacy a glass of punch, which she took with a smile. "Thank you."

"This is a pretty nice affair, don't you think, Stacy?" Mayer asked.

"It's incredible, sir. Thank you for bringing me along."

"It's my pleasure," Mayer replied with a smile.

The Presidential limousine pulled up in front of the GBN building with two Secret Service agents getting out of their front seats looking around the area. They established that there were no threats, and one of the agents spoke into his wrist transmitter. "All clear, ma'am."

The two agents that were posted at the entry door approached the limousine with clipboard in hand.

The rear door opened and a sharply dressed woman stepped out of the limousine. It was Secret Service Agent Karen Tyler. Tyler was now the lead agent responsible for the protection detail surrounding Stephanie Bradshaw, the teenage daughter of President Keith Bradshaw.

This was Tyler's fourth year of protection duty for the President's daughter who was re-elected to his second term just eight months before. Tyler's commitment to detail and keeping her charge safe, informed of her responsibilities and rules, gave her the respect of the agency and the President.

Tyler looked inside the limousine and saw Stephanie Bradshaw primping in her handheld mirror and rolled her eyes. "You look fine, Steph."

Stephanie Bradshaw was 16 years old, an only child and raised by her now single father for the past eight years after her mother passed away from brain cancer. She was the typical daddy's girl -- blonde hair, blue eyes and beautiful.

"Karen, you know I'm going to be on television. I have to look my best," Stephanie said with a smile.

"This has nothing to do with television and you know it young lady."

"I still need to look good."

Tyler looked around the front of the GBN building as the other two agents stood by the limousine. The agent with the clipboard approached Tyler. "Everyone that has arrived checks out, ma'am."

"Very good," Tyler responded. She determined it was safe and looked at Stephanie Bradshaw. "It's okay, Steph. Let's go." She looked around one more time before gesturing to her charge it was safe to get out of the car.

Stephanie Bradshaw got out of the limousine and followed Agent Tyler to the entrance of the GBN building. She stopped before she went in, turned her head back and forth as if she were looking for something - or someone - then continued in the front door with Tyler.

Lee was waiting at the security desk. He walked up and introduced himself to Tyler and Stephanie. "Good evening ladies. I'm Chief of Security Charles Lee. Thank you for coming, Miss Bradshaw."

"Thank you for having me," Stephanie responded. "This is a wonderful event for children around the world." They both shook hands with Lee and received their visitor passes.

Tyler was a bit concerned with security measures in the building noticing they didn't have to go through the metal detectors. "How many guards are on duty for this telethon?" she asked Lee.

"There are six armed guards at each entrance, four entrances, so 24 highly-trained and armed guards total for this event."

Tyler felt a little better, but still did not feel completely confident.

"May we proceed to the reception ladies?" Lee asked.

"Please, let's do," Stephanie replied, giving Tyler a smirky smile.

Tyler looked at her charge and rolled her eyes and whispered to her, "*Really.*"

Stephanie whispered back with a big grin on her face. "Don't you want me to be polite, Karen?"

"You and I both know you're here because of a boy," Tyler continued to whisper as they followed Lee to the elevator.

"Why would you even think that, Karen?" Stephanie said with a devious smile. Tyler looked at her, gave her a stern look and rolled her eyes.

"Have either of you eaten yet?" Lee asked as the three got on the elevator. "The agency has sponsored an incredible buffet for the reception?"

"Maybe something light," Stephanie replied.

Tyler looked at her with big eyes as if to indicate, "Be good."

The three of them rode the elevator to the fifth floor where the reception was taking place. The doors opened to the sound of music and people talking. Tyler and Stephanie followed Lee through the opened glass doors to find a brightly decorated ballroom, with a small three-piece band playing music in the corner. They could see long tables of food, desserts and meat-carving stations. People were waiting in line with plates in hand behind those already going along both sides of the buffet tables, enjoying everything available.

When Stephanie walked through the door and she was recognized, the room stopped to applaud her arrival. She nodded a "thank you" with a smile. Tyler smiled because she had seen a humble side of Stephanie many times and this was another example.

"Are you hungry, Steph?" she asked her.

"Not really. I'm wondering what's keeping him," she said to her protector.

"He doesn't have the transportation he used to have, remember?" said Tyler. "He's just running late. He confirmed with Marshall just this morning that he was coming."

"I know. I just haven't seen him in a while and I miss him. And I'm a bit nervous about seeing him again."

"Who are you kidding?" Tyler asked with a smirk. Stephanie smiled back.

Stephanie Bradshaw looked around the room and saw a familiar face and walked over to her. "Hi, Kristina," she said grabbing and holding her hand.

Kristina Cartwright was the 15-year-old granddaughter of Admiral James Cartwright who had recently been named Secretary of Defense by Stephanie's father, the President Bradshaw. Kristina was a bit shy, but very cute, with short blonde hair and glasses. Stephanie

53

and Kristina had hung out at the White House many times and had a lot in common since they were practically the same age.

"Hi, Stephanie," Kristina said with a smile. "You look awesome."

"Thank you. That's so sweet. Are you ready for all this?" Stephanie asked laughing. Stephanie noticed Kristina looked a bit uncomfortable with all this celebrity status put on her.

"Not really, but it's for my grandpa, so it's cool."

Tyler came over with punch for them both. "How are you, Miss Cartwright?"

"I'm good, Agent Tyler. Thank you," Kristina replied politely.

Tyler looked at Bradshaw. "Congressman Young would like to say hello and introduce you to some people, Steph."

"Can Kristina come with us, Karen?" Stephanie asked.

"Sure, I don't see why not" Tyler replied.

The three of them walked over to a small group surrounding Rep. Young. Tyler introduced the President's daughter. "Congressman Young, this is Stephanie Bradshaw."

"Miss Bradshaw, it's such an honor to have you with us this evening."

"Thank you, Congressman. It's a great cause and I'm proud to be a part of it," Stephanie said smiling. "This is my friend Kristina Cartwright. She's the granddaughter of Admiral Cartwright."

"The *new* Secretary of Defense Cartwright?" the silver haired Congressman asked with surprise.

Kristina spoke up. "Yes, sir. He's my grandpa."

"That's wonderful. Welcome, young lady. We are so happy to have you here."

"Thank you, sir," Kristina said smiling at the congressman.

The Congressman stepped aside to introduce Jonathon Mayer to the President's daughter. "Miss Bradshaw, this is Jonathan Mayer of Mayer Financial Corporation who is monitoring the donations this evening for the telethon."

"Nice to meet you, Miss Bradshaw, Miss Cartwright. Let me introduce my assistant, Stacy Michaels," Mayer said.

Stacy smiled and didn't want to look foolish in front of the President's daughter, but she was curious. "May I ask where you got your shoes? They're so cute."

"Thank you." I like her, Stephanie thought to herself. "I got them at Mackie's on sale," she said smiling.

Tyler thought the question made Stephanie less nervous about talking with the Congressman and whispered, "Thank you," to Stacy.

"No problem, Stacy replied.

A black luxury Lincoln Town Car pulled up to the entrance to the GBN building, the driver got out and opened the passenger door. A tall, handsome young man dressed in a black suit and tie got out and proceeded to walk up to the two Secret Service agents. They promptly checked his ID and allowed him to proceed through the front door alone straight up to the security desk.

"I'm Scott Matthews. I have an invitation to participate in the telethon this evening."

Just as he finished his statement to the security guard at the desk, Lee approached him. "Mr. Matthews, we thought you might not join us this evening," he said.

"The traffic in DC is terrible. Got here as quick as I could."

"How is your father? I worked for him when he was President," Lee said. "My condolences about your mother. She was a wonderful First Lady," he said solemnly.

"Thank you. Yes, she was. And my father is well" he replied.

"The reception is still going on upstairs, and the telethon starts in about 15 minutes, so you're right on time," Lee said.

"Is there someplace I can wash up before I go in?" Scott asked.

"Yes, sir. There's a men's room on the fifth floor near the reception ballroom."

The two men walked down the hall to the elevator, got on and pushed the button to the fifth floor. They exited and walked toward the site of the gala. Scott could see through the opened glass ballroom doors that everyone was having a good time. "Where is that bathroom again?" he asked Lee.

Lee pointed down the hallway to the end where Scott Matthews saw the men's room sign and walked towards it.

"I'll be right back," he said smiling back at Lee.

CHAPTER 4

THE SUN WAS STARTING TO GO DOWN OVER THE
city as another large black SUV pulled up to the front of the GBN
building, and five men wearing dark sunglasses got out of the vehicle
and immediately surrounded it.

They were all tall, fit and wearing long black overcoats. They all
converged on the passenger door and one of them opened it. A tall,
attractive Asian man got out wearing nothing but white -- a white
suit, white overcoat, and even white boots that tied.

The five men surrounded the man in white as they started heading
for the front entrance of the building. The two Secret Service agents
approached them halfway to the entrance doors. "May we see some
ID, gentlemen?" one agent asked glancing down at his clipboard.

The tall Asian man smiled. "These two gentlemen behind me
have *my* ID," he replied. The two men behind him pulled out large
handguns from their overcoats and fired two shots, each hitting both
Secret Service agents before they had a chance to pull their service
weapons. The shots were muffled by silencers and both agents fell to
the concrete sidewalk bleeding from their mouths and the wounds
in their chests, but still alive.

The Asian man walked up to them both and smiled down at
them. "You both go to a better place," he said as he stepped over

them. The two men who shot them stood over them both and fired another round into each of their foreheads and walked behind the Asian man to the front door.

The Asian man pulled out a handheld radio transmitter from his coat pocket and spoke into it. "All entry teams enter now."

"Team one, roger that." "Team two, roger that." "Team three, roger that," came the responses right after each other on his radio receiver.

He then looked around and addressed the men behind him. "Let's make this quick, gentlemen. We have a party to attend."

They walked through the front door and up to the security desk. "I'm Tanaka Amikura. I'm here for the reception and telethon," the Asian man said to the security guard sitting behind the desk.

The guard looked on the guest list that was given to him. "Sir, I don't have your name on the guest list."

Tanaka smiled at the guard. "That's okay. I brought my own invitation." The man behind him stepped up and pulled out his handgun with a silencer on it and fired a single shot into the guard's head, killing him instantly and causing him to fall backwards onto the floor.

In quick order, the remaining men behind Tanaka Amikura pulled out handguns and machine guns and proceeded to shoot the remaining five security guards near the desk, killing them all.

Over his radio Tanaka could hear similar gunfire from the other three entry locations and then he received confirmation of his team's success. "Entry one, clear. "Entry two, clear." Entry three, clear," came over Tanaka's radio one at a time.

Tanaka spoke into his radio. "Entry four, clear. Secure the doors. It has begun."

"It's time to go say hello to our important guests, gentlemen. I'm sure they wouldn't mind a few more important people joining them," he said sarcastically with a grin to his men with him.

Tanaka watched as his men dragged the bodies of the dead security guards and placed them in the large closet next to the security desk.

He then informed his entry teams over the radio, "All teams proceed to Phase Two."

Amikura and his men, with MP-5 machine guns drawn, started moving down the hallway towards the elevators, getting no resistance because they knew everyone was either on the third floor in studios or on the fifth floor for the reception.

Tanaka got on the elevator with as many as ten heavily-armed men and pushed the button to the fifth floor ballroom. One of the men handed him a long, white-handled samurai sword with a white scabbard. The handle was unique because it had a long dragon's head carving at the end. Tanaka removed his overcoat and slung the sword around his back.

Handing his jacket to one of his men, he adjusted the twin gun holsters he wore around his waist, pulling the twin 1911 silver handguns with pearl white hand grips out of the holsters and placing them back securely. The holsters were what they called "tactical," securely strapped to both legs.

Arriving on the fifth floor, they slowly exited the elevator. Tanaka's men had their weapons pointed in front and back of their surrounded Asian boss, protecting him as they started to move towards the ballroom. As they got closer, he pointed to the two hallways on each side of them, and several armed mercenaries instinctively went down each corridor to move silently into the back entrances of the ballroom. They arrived at their positions quickly and responded to their boss on the radio.

Tanaka heard "Check" twice on the radio. Then as he walked through the opened double glass doors to see everyone enjoying the reception, he remarked to those still around him, "Time to join the party gentlemen."

At the same time, his other armed men came from both side entrances at the back of the ballroom, and in seconds they had surrounded everyone.

Several security personnel guarding the children of their respective countries drew their weapons, only to be gunned down by Tanaka's armed men immediately, killing at least six people while hearing screaming and crying from scared guests not knowing what was going on.

"Good evening ladies, gentlemen, and young ones," Tanaka yelled over the hysterics.

Agent Karen Tyler knew better than to draw her gun at that moment, realizing she would be gunned down like the others if she did. Instead, she got in front of Stephanie and Kristina to shield them from the heavily-armed men.

"I know everyone is confused and scared, but I assure you no one will get hurt as long as you do what my men and I say," Tanaka reassured everyone at the fundraiser.

Looking at the dead security agents on the ballroom floor and smiling , Tanaka instructed the gathering. "Have a seat, please. The telethon will begin very shortly."

His men started moving the guests and children to the tables, some forcibly pushing them to the floor. Tanaka looked at two of his mercenaries. "Get rid of the bodies."

They both nodded to their boss and slowly dragged a couple of dead security people toward the side exits.

Stephanie Bradshaw whispered to Tyler, "What are we going to do, Karen?"

"Keep our heads down and hope they don't look for us," Tyler replied.

Stephanie could tell her friend Kristina was scared. "It will be okay Kristina. Tyler will get us out of this. She always gets me out of trouble," she said with a big grin.

Tyler looked at Stephanie and Kristina and smiled at what she said.

Stacy Michaels looked at her boss, Jonathan Mayer. "What's going to happen to us, Mr. Mayer?" she asked nervously.

Mayer looked at his assistant and reassured her, "We'll be okay, Stacy, I promise."

Stacy looked at Tyler, who she observed was trying to hide both Stephanie and Kristina, and then around the room at all the armed men. "They look dangerous, sir," she said to Mayer.

"It will be okay. I won't let anything happen to you." Mayer replied.

"WHAT IS THE MEANING OF THIS?" Congressman Young said in a loud, boisterous tone. "I DEMAND TO SPEAK TO WHOMEVER IS IN CHARGE, IMMEDIATELY!" he said.

The Congressman looked scared, but since he was in charge of the telethon he knew he needed to speak up. All the guests were there because had he invited them, and he knew it was his responsibility for the situation they found themselves in.

"Good evening, Congressman. "I am Tanaka Amikura. I am in charge, sir," he answered with a smile.

"You are a very brave man Congressman to speak up like this. We are dedicated members of the Dragon's Breath clan. We are here to have our own telethon," Tanaka said with a cackle.

Tyler recognized the Dragon's Breath moniker from a cold case she had worked without closing more than five years before.

She remembered it was a suicide bombing that killed the 11-year-old son of then President Matthews.

Stephanie interrupted her thought by asking anxiously, "Karen, where's Scott?"

"I don't know, sweetie. Hopefully, he's hiding somewhere safe if he's here."

Tanaka went and stood in the middle of the ballroom. "When I call out your name please come to the front. If you don't do it in 20 seconds or less, I will kill an insignificant person that you could have saved," Tanaka said with a sinister grin. "I *really* hope someone tests this demand. Where is my clipboard with all the names?"

Tyler, Stacy and the Congressman were stunned to see Brian Jurgens walk up to Tanaka and hear him say, with a smile, "Here it is, sir," as he handed him the security clipboard that Lee had given to Jurgens earlier upon his request.

"You're an asshole, Jurgens," Lee said with anger as he realized Brian Jurgens was working for Tanaka Amikura.

"Yes, but I'm going to be very rich, Mr. Lee," Jurgens said laughing along with Tanaka.

"Let's see. Who do we have first, Mr. Jurgens?" Tanaka asked handing the clipboard back.

"Pierre Charton, son of the French President," Jurgens read, flipping the pages on the clipboard.

The 12-year-old boy stepped forward and said, defiantly, "Your country will pay for this."

"I hope *yours* does for *your* sake," replied Tanaka with a smile. "Next?" he asked.

"Jade Chu, daughter of the Prime Minister of Japan," Jurgens continued. She stepped forward and walked over and stood next to the French President's son without fear. Jurgens continued reading from the list.

"Prince Mohammed Assan, son of the king of Saudi Arabia." Jurgens bowed as the teenaged boy walked toward Tanaka and Jurgens.

"Your Highness," Tanaka addressed him with a smile.

"Miss Kristina Cartwright, granddaughter of the U.S. Secretary of Defense," Jurgens continued from the list.

Kristina was so frightened she couldn't move and continued to hide behind Stephanie and Agent Tyler. "Miss Cartwright?" Tanaka asked. "Well, looks like we will have our first killing of the evening, ladies and gentlemen," Tanaka said with enthusiasm to everyone.

Tanaka walked over to one of the waiters, pulled one of his pearl handled handguns out of the holster and pointed it at his head and cocked the hammer.

"WAIT!" Stephanie yelled from the back of the room.

Tyler whispered, "What the hell are you doing, Steph?"

Stephanie whispered back. "Saving someone's life, hopefully." "Do what you have to do to get us out of here," she whispered to Tyler.

Stephanie then whispered to Kristina, "We'll do this together, okay sweetie." Kristina looked and nodded to Stephanie, feeling better her friend was going with her. Stephanie and Kristina both stood up and walked over to Tanaka, holding each other's hand.

"She's scared. Try a little compassion sometime," Stephanie said boldly.

"And *you* are Miss Stephanie Bradshaw, daughter of the President of the United States," Tanaka stated as he smiled at her.

"Yes. I am. And my daddy's going to kick your ass," Stephanie said with determination. Kristina grinned hearing her friend talk back to Tanaka. Both Tanaka and Jurgens snickered at her statement.

"Please stand with the rest," Tanaka told the President's daughter with a grin.

"Isn't there more, Mr. Jurgens?" Tanaka asked, knowing there were.

"Yes, sir. Scott Matthews, son of former President Daryl Matthews."

Stephanie turned white as a ghost hearing Scott's name. She squeezed Kristina's hand a little tighter knowing Scott wasn't there in the room with them. She shot Tyler a scared look.

After a very long pause, Tanaka said, "It seems our Mr. Matthews doesn't have a problem with someone dying in his name." Tanaka drew his .45 caliber handgun again from his holster and slowly walked back over to the waiter he had pointed it at previously.

"He's not here," Tyler said as she stood and starred at Tanaka Amikura.

"And who might you be?" Tanaka asked.

"I'm Secret Service Agent Karen Tyler assigned to the First Daughter's protection detail," Tyler explained.

"That hasn't worked out very well for you so far now, has it Agent Tyler?" Tanaka laughed. He nodded to one of his men closest to Tyler who slowly walked up to her and put his gun to her head, searched her and found her gun and ID. The armed henchman handed the gun and ID to another mercenary as he kept his gun at Tyler's head. The second one took them to Tanaka and handed them both to him.

"Special Agent Karen Tyler of the Secret Service," he said as he read her ID. Tanaka approached her slowly. "The President is going to be *very* disappointed in you for not protecting his daughter," Tanaka told Tyler.

"The night is still young," Tyler said to the amused Asian boss.

"Maybe you're hiding Mr. Matthews, Agent Tyler," he theorized, pointing his gun at her now.

"I haven't seen him. He obviously got here late and hasn't gotten to the fifth floor yet," Tyler replied fearlessly.

Tanaka thought about what she had just said and smiled, looking at his henchman. "Take two men and go find Mr. Matthews. Bring him back to me *alive*," he said. The three henchmen left the room, guns pointing.

"Are there anymore names on the list, Mr. Jurgens?" Tanaka asked.

"Yes, sir. Three more -- Vladimir Rykov, son of the Russian President; Xing Chao, the Chinese Prime Minister's son; and Chadwick Easton, the Prime Minister of England's son."

"Step forward, gentlemen" Tanaka demanded.

The three of them were teenage boys. All walked to the center of the room, each giving Tanaka and Jurgens hostile looks. Tanaka just smirked back at them.

"It now seems we can move on to "Phase Three" of our fun evening," Tanaka proclaimed to all. "Everyone on the list will be joining me and my men downstairs in the auditorium where the TV/radio telethon is going to take place."

Everyone looked surprised.

"Oh, we're still having a telethon," he continued. "We're just having a *different kind* of charity telethon," he said laughing.

"Those of you whose names were not called out, you will be staying here until *my* telethon is over, so get comfortable," Tanaka announced.

"If everything goes as planned, none of you will be harmed. However, my man Samson and his men have orders to kill anyone who attempts to interrupt my plans."

Tanaka looked around the room one more time and recognized Jonathon Mayer trying to hide behind Congressman Young and walked over to him. "Mr. Mayer, I'm a big fan," he said.

"I'm afraid I can't say the same," Mayer replied.

"I can respect that," Tanaka said with a chuckle. "I'd like for you to join us downstairs. Your financial insight may help our cause get more money during this telethon."

"I think I'll pass on that" Mayer said.

"But I insist, Mr. Mayer." Tanaka smiled, pointing his gun at Mayer. "Congressman, you join us as well," Tanaka added.

The guard Tanaka addressed as Samson - a big, long-blonde-haired, muscle-bound surfer type was pushing Mayer to get him to move when Stacy spoke up. "Leave him alone," she said shyly.

"Well, Mr. Mayer, looks like I'm not the *only* fan you have," Tanaka said with a grin.

"Leave her alone, Tanaka. She's my assistant. Nothing more," Mayer insisted.

"Okay," Tanaka said, eyeing his guard to stand down with the young girl.

"Let's start moving our guests down to the third floor," Tanaka ordered his men. He informed five of his armed men, including Samson, to stay in the ballroom and watch the rest of the hostages.

Tanaka looked at the clock on the wall saw it was 7:05 pm, then whispered to Samson, "At 8pm kill them all, starting with the security people first," he said with a smile.

"Yes, sir," the blonde-haired mercenary replied with a sinister grin to his boss.

Tanaka and Jurgens started walking out of the ballroom with the young dignitaries, the Congressman and Mayer, surrounded by Asian's armed group of men moving down the hallway to the elevator.

Stacy and Tyler watched as they left the ballroom and the remaining mercenaries shut the doors behind them. Samson walked over to Tyler and told her to move over to the table where they had put the remaining security staff, continuing to point his machine gun at her. Tyler got up, gave the smirking guard a dirty look and walked over and sat down next to Lee.

Stacy pulled her cell phone out of her skirt pocket and held it under the table. When the guards went around collecting their cell phones from everyone, Stacy hid hers in her skirt. She was texting frantically and just as she hit "send" Samson grabbed her hand with the phone in it.

"Who are you calling, bitch?" he screamed.

"No one, sir," she said.

"You're *lying*, bitch!" he said slapping her across the face.

Tyler stood up only to have another guard point his gun at her to make her sit back down. Stacy started crying, putting her hand to her cheek.

"I'm not lying, I swear. I didn't call anyone," Stacy said sobbing.

Samson looked at her phone and saw the text message she sent. She had written "135/157 bag, 160x127" and sent it to someone named "Tracy."

"WHAT IS THIS SHIT?" he yelled, making Stacy look at her cell phone screen as he held it in front of her face.

"It's a text to my girlfriend Tracy," Stacy told him tears coming down her face.

"THIS IS SOME KIND OF CODE, WHO DID YOU SEND IT TO, BITCH? THE POLICE?" Samson continued to yell.

"No, sir. But you are right that it *is* code, but it's shopping code," she said.

"What the FUCK is shopping code?" he demanded to know.

"135/157 is the cost of the designer bags at Mackie's Department Store" she said. "160x127 is the size of the bag, sir," she explained.

Again, Samson screamed at Stacy as he pointed his machine gun in her face. "YOU BETTER NOT BE *LYING* TO ME BITCH OR YOU'RE DEAD.

"No, sir. I'm not. I swear! Call her and ask if you want."

Samson dialed the text number and put it on speaker. "If anyone other than this woman you claim is your friend answers the phone, I will kill you where you sit," he said to Stacy.

The phone rang three times, then a woman's voice came over the speaker in a bubbly manner. "Hi, this is Tracy. Please leave a message."

"See," Stacy said. The guard seemed satisfied and hung up the phone.

Tyler shook her head thinking. "What a stupid girl, getting slapped for a handbag."

Samson threw the phone on the floor and stepped on it, breaking it in pieces. Stacy rubbed her cheek again and glanced at Tyler with a little smile.

Scott Matthews had seen the gunmen go into the reception just as he was coming out of the bathroom without being seen. He thought if he stayed hidden in the bathroom he could figure out a way to find help for all the hostages.

He continued watching Tanaka and his guards from the bathroom doorway. When he heard Tanaka tell three of his guards to go find him, he knew he couldn't stay on the fifth floor and ran down the emergency stairs to the fourth floor GBN language service offices.

Scott decided to hide in one of the office copying rooms, periodically looking out the door to see if anyone was coming. He frantically went from desk phone to desk phone trying to get a dial tone so he could call out but, all the phones somehow were dead.

Scott Matthews was the only son of former President Daryl Matthews, now 16 years old, and he still carried with him the tragic memory of losing his twin brother Steven to a similar terrorist attack five years before.

Tanaka and half of the dignitary children arrived on the third floor with six of his heavily-armed mercenaries, walked off the elevator and headed to the auditorium that had been set up for the telethon. Tanaka spoke into his radio.

"Bring the other half down now." Tanaka said as he and Jurgens stood in the doorway of the auditorium unseen and evaluated the situation.

There were eight cameramen adjusting their on-floor cameras, three people wiring the microphones on the tables, two stage managers, three TV/radio engineers, and a control booth producer, all working frantically.

Jurgens noticed Marcus Grant talking to a lovely 30-something-year-old African American woman holding a clipboard. He recognized her as Sherry Moore who was the Executive Producer for all the language TV programs, as well as in charge of the TV control room engineers. Jurgens was familiar with her through her work with TV and at the GBN gym teaching women self-defense classes. He remembered Moore was an expert in martial arts. She had only been employed with GBN for about a year.

Tanaka nodded to his men, who had stealthily gotten into position around the auditorium, and spoke into his radio. "Gentlemen, you may proceed with Phase Three."

All of the mercenaries that Tanaka brought into the auditorium ran onto the stage and down the stairs at the same time, screaming and yelling, "Put your hands on your heads NOW," and pointing their machine guns with dangerous authority. With all the GBN security guards dead there was no resistance from anyone.

The TV/radio employees were scared and put their hands in the air or on their heads almost immediately. Tanaka smiled arrogantly as he walked down the stairs of the auditorium with Jurgens.

The two of them walked over to Marcus Grant and Sherry Moore who were standing on the stage stunned at what was happening. Jurgens whispered to Tanaka as they approached them with Tanaka smiling at them both.

"Brian, what is the meaning of this? What the hell is going on here?" Grant demanded looking around the room at all the armed men.

Jurgens looked at Grant, then Sherry Moore, and said "Nothing for you to worry about Marcus, just do as he says and no one gets hurt. Understand?"

Two of Tanaka's men came down and stood behind him. "Ms. Moore, if you would be so kind as to accompany these two gentlemen to the control room, we can proceed with our telethon," Tanaka said to her.

"And what if I don't want to do that," Moore asked Tanaka defiantly.

"Well, then I'm afraid one of my men here will have to put a bullet in that very pretty head of yours, and I really don't want to do that unless it's absolutely necessary. I feel that would be a total waste.

"I'm not a complete monster," Tanaka declared with a grin.

Moore breathed deeply and then started moving up the stairs to the control room with Tanaka's men closely behind her.

The three of them then entered the control room and the two guards moved to each side of the room, pointing their machine guns at everyone there.

"Do your jobs and no one will get hurt," Moore informed the engineering staff in the control room. "We go live in two minutes," she ordered.

Jurgens looked at Grant and instructed him, "Go back to your office and wait. This will be all over soon, Marcus."

"What the hell have you gotten me into Brian?" Grant asked.

Jurgens smiled watching Tanaka walk around the stage and replied to his friend, "I made him promise nothing would happen to you. You've been a good soldier and friend to me. I haven't forgotten that."

Grant looked at his mentor, gave him a disapproving look and turned to head up the stairs to his office followed by one of Tanaka's men.

Tanaka motioned to the rest of his men at the top of the stairs, where they had been holding the children, Mayer and the Congressman at gunpoint, to bring them all down to the stage. Slowly, they all walked down the stairs where Tanaka addressed them. "Please young people, have a seat where your names are."

The tables on stage were long, with red, white, and blue table-cloths on each of them. Table-style microphones, with the GBN logo prominently displayed, were sitting in front of each chair positioned with a name card placed in front of them.

"Congressman, Mr. Mayer, please have a seat with these two gentlemen," Tanaka said pointing to two chairs on the side of the stage being guarded by two of his armed men. Tanaka escorted them both to the chairs and they sat down. "The show is about to begin," he said with a smirk.

CHAPTER 5

TANAKA AMIKURA STOOD IN THE MIDDLE OF THE stage holding a microphone when he heard "30 seconds" come over the loud speaker to inform everyone the show would be on the air. It was 7:15pm and the floor producer counted down "3, 2, 1" and pointed to Tanaka hesitantly. The camera monitors' ON-AIR red lights lit up and Tanaka Amikura was officially on worldwide television.

"Good evening, ladies and gentlemen all over the world," he said into the camera with a sinister smile.

"We want to welcome you all to the Children's Global Hunger telethon, being broadcast live at the Global Broadcasting Network here in our nation's capital, Washington, DC," Tanaka continued.

"We have a lot of surprises and some unexpected guests for you this evening, all to help generate funds for charity. I will be your host for all of this evening's festivities. My name is Tanaka Amikura," he said as he waved to the cameras.

"Our phone lines are open at 555-645-1006, and our operators are taking your calls, even international ones. "However," Tanaka said with a giggle in his voice. "We are doing this telethon a bit differently tonight."

"Do you see all of these wonderful children of important dignitaries behind me? We are so happy and proud to have them with us for this wonderful occasion," he said continuing to smile into the eight cameras positioned around the stage.

The cameraman closest to the stage panned the length of the beautifully decorated long table with microphones to show each and every one of the children/teens representing their native countries.

"We are auctioning them off to their families and countries one at a time" he smiled. "That's right. The Children's Global Hunger charity is helping the Dragon's Breath charity this evening," Tanaka explained.

"Each child will cost his or her country $100 to $150 million dollars, or I will personally execute them on world-wide television." he said with a sly grin.

"I know, I know. I can't be serious about killing children on television, you're all saying to yourselves. I'm hoping it doesn't come to that, I really am," Tanaka said as he continued smiling for the cameraman standing in front of him.

"Let's bring out our first special guest of the night. He's a U.S. Congressman from the scenic state of Virginia, Congressman David Young, the man who set up this evening's telethon," Tanaka said with a grin.

One of Tanaka's armed guards grabbed the Congressman out of his chair and pushed him over to Tanaka in the middle of the stage.

"Welcome, Congressman Young," Tanaka said as he placed his hand on Young's shoulder. The Congressman looked scared and was visibly shaking.

"Don't worry Congressman. Everything is going to work out fine. I promise." Tanaka smiled as he took out his gun, pointed it to the Congressman's forehead and pulled the trigger.

The bullet ripped through the Congressman's head, killing him instantly and dropping him to the floor beside Tanaka. Jonathon Mayer jumped out of his seat to attack Tanaka but was subdued by his two guards.

"ARE YOU FUCKING CRAZY?" Mayer screamed at Tanaka as he was being restrained by the two guards.

"Now, now, Mr. Mayer. Watch your language. After all, there are children here and we are on live TV," Tanaka replied to him laughing.

Screams and crying could be heard throughout the studio after the brutal assassination of Congressman Young. Tanaka nodded to one of his men who came over and dragged the Congressman's lifeless body off the stage, staining the floor with blood.

"I hope my message is clear to everyone," Tanaka said, looking intensely into the TV camera. "$100 million from each country. You have one hour. Sixty minutes before someone else dies. This time a child."

"Let's see who's first on the clock this evening," Tanaka continued, and smiled while looking at the scared children sitting at the long tables on the stage. "How about China?"

One of his men brought a chair to the center of the stage where Tanaka was standing. "Xing Chao, the son of President Jing Chao of China, please join me on stage," Tanaka asked enthusiastically.

One of the guards watching the table of children walked over and stood behind Xing Chao, placed his machine gun barrel into his back and motioned for him to get up and move to the stage where Tanaka was waiting for him.

The young boy defiantly got up and walked to Tanaka where he let out a tirade in Chinese that translated in English to, "My father will kill you all."

Tanaka understood every word the young Chinese boy said and responded in Chinese, telling the young boy in his native language, "That may be, but you'll already be dead," he said to him with a smile.

Returning to speaking English, Tanaka told the boy, "Please sit down, Mr. Chao. The Chinese government is now on the clock for $100 million. Call the number on your screen and our operator will inform you how to get the money to us. You have 60 minutes".

"Oh yeah, I almost forgot. It's time to end this brother OUR father waits for you," Tanaka said with a grin and a wink into the camera to everyone's confusion.

Secret Service Director Dwayne Marshall and FBI Director Michael James walked into the Oval Office where President Keith Bradshaw was pacing back and forth behind his desk. "What the hell is going on?" the President asked the two directors.

"My daughter is sitting at that table!" he yelled, looking at the television screen near his desk. "Where is her protection detail, Dwayne?" he asked nervously.

Marshall could only speculate that her detail had been compromised, that Agent Karen Tyler was somehow captured or killed during this siege. "I don't have any answers for that, sir."

Director James spoke up. "We have surrounded the building and blocked off the streets for two city blocks, Mr. President, but our spotters have informed us that the entrances are booby trapped with explosives," he said.

"We can also see they have heavily-armed men on the roof, and a frontal or aerial assault would be dangerously risky for any of our men, sir, as well as the hostages inside," James said to the worried President.

The President looked at both men and yelled, "Someone get me some answers on this son of a bitch who has *my* daughter! NOW!"

The TV news was running the Congressman's execution graphically on every channel around the world which got the President's phone lighting up like a Christmas tree from the Chinese President to the Russian President. They all wanted to know what was being done to save their children from this mad man on American soil.

"Mr. President, Secretary of Defense Cartwright is here to see you, sir," Amy Reynolds announced.

Defense Secretary James Cartwright walked into the Oval Office and addressed the President. "Mr. President, we need to talk. I'm sorry your daughter has been put into this dangerous situation. And as you may already know, my granddaughter Kristina is with her as well, sir."

"No, Admiral. I didn't know. I'm sorry," The President said.

Cartwright was a retired admiral who had worked with the President when he was a Captain in the Naval Strategic Command stationed in the Philippines 15 years ago. "I have an idea, sir, that I would like to pass by you. But *only you*, Mr. President," Cartwright emphasized.

Directors Marshall and James gave the Admiral a dirty look, who shot a smile back at them and asked, "What do you want to say gentlemen? I don't believe either of you have loved ones personally involved in this crisis."

The President looked at both directors and ordered them, "Please step outside for a moment, gentlemen. I want to hear what the Admiral has to say."

Admiral Cartwright was in charge of SEAL Team 2 in the Philippines while President Bradshaw was stationed there, commissioned to run point for the base with the Philippine government.

SEAL Team 2 was often used as a recon/surveillance team with the South Korean military, gathering information on North Korean military movements. The Admiral would send the information gathered back to the Pentagon for evaluation.

"Mr. President, I know who this Tanaka Amikura is, sir," Admiral Cartwright stated.

"One of my SEALs back in the Philippines was trained by this man's father, who was eventually murdered by his son out of hatred and jealousy, sir," the Admiral said.

"He still blames my SEAL for the demise of his family and vowed revenge over 20 years ago, sir" the Admiral explained.

President Bradshaw looked at Cartwright with his voice rising as he spoke. "So this is nothing more than a revenge match disguised as an extortion plan, with our children as pawns?"

"It looks that way, Mr. President."

"Who is this SEAL he wants so badly, Admiral?" Bradshaw asked.

"Captain Max Mason," the Admiral replied, not sure the President would know who he was.

"Max Mason? Isn't he retired from all this?" President Bradshaw asked looking confused at Admiral Cartwright knowing a bit about Max's reputation with the Secret Service in the past.

"What does *he* have to do with any of this, Admiral?" Bradshaw asked as he continued looking directly at Cartwright. "And what is this plan of yours?"

"Let me send Captain Mason and SEAL Team 2 in to defuse this situation. Their training is second to none. They have handled over 200 missions without incident, Mr. President," Cartwright replied. "The three of them have been on inactive reserves for the past 10 years, but still train four times a year together. If anyone can save our children, it's Max and his team. And I happen to know that the three of them are together for a reunion, as we speak, in Northern Virginia, sir."

"So why do you want to keep Marshall and James out of the loop on this, Admiral?" the President inquired curiously.

"Max and Marshall go way back to the Matthews administration. Max took early retirement over guilt of losing the President's son in that suicide bomber attack. It wasn't even his responsibility, sir," Cartwright explained. "Marshall took all the heat for that situation. You could say he's still a bit bitter about it.

"I know Max well, and he would only do this if he and his team have total control of the operation from the inside, sir, and don't have to worry about the Secret Service or the FBI trying to get in from the outside to interfere, Mr. President" Cartwright continued.

"So let me get this straight. You want me to put *total* control, and the life of my 16-year-old daughter in the hands of a retired, disgraced agent and his retired SEAL team, and trust them to get everyone out safely? Is that what you're asking me to do, Admiral?"

"Yes, Mr. President. That's exactly what I'm asking you to do. Bear in mind, I am also trusting Max and his team to get my granddaughter out of there safely as well. I'm asking you to let him do the same for your daughter, Mr. President," the Admiral said with a stern face.

"Okay, Admiral. But Marshall and James are *not* going to like this when they find out. I can tell you that." the President said.

"No, sir, they're not. But you're the President and what you say goes," Cartwright replied. "And one more thing, Mr. President. I don't think we should mention Max's name to either of them. He's not exactly on their Christmas card list, if you know what I mean, sir," the Admiral said with a grin.

"I can respect that Admiral, but I want hourly updates from him. Is that *clear*?" President Bradshaw mandated with authority.

"Yes, Mr. President" Cartwright replied.

"Send Directors Marshall and James back in, Amy, please," he asked over his intercom.

"Yes, Mr. President," came her reply.

Marshall and James walked back into the Oval Office to find the President sitting behind his desk and Admiral Cartwright sitting on the couch. Marshall and James looked at each other confused as to what had transpired between the President and the Admiral.

"Mr. President, we've just been informed that former President Daryl Matthews' son Scott is also in the GBN building," Marshall said.

James then added, "President Matthews is on his way here to speak with you concerning this matter, sir."

The President pushed the button on his intercom. "Amy, when President Matthews arrives, please show him into my office immediately."

"Yes, Mr. President," Amy replied through the phone speaker.

"Gentlemen, the Admiral has led me to believe that this Tanaka Amikura is extremely dangerous and has a good many armed men in the building with him," the President said. "His sources also believe that the building may be wired with explosives to keep us out."

"Mr. President, the FBI has the most highly-trained explosives experts who can defuse any bomb made," Director James explained.

"I don't want us taking any unnecessary risks that may endanger the children or others at this moment," the President said. "Secure the perimeter and stand down until I give you the okay to go inside. Do we understand, gentlemen?" the President said.

"I see the look in your eyes that you both don't agree with me on this, and I understand, but I'll not put any of these children or GBN employees held hostage in jeopardy because your pride is hurt. Do I make myself clear, Director James, Director Marshall?" the President said sternly.

Both Marshall and James responded together. "Yes, Mr. President."

"You're dismissed, gentlemen. Keep me updated every hour," the President demanded. They both nodded to the President's command and walked out the door, closing it behind them.

"One question, Admiral. If they're all retired, why would they continue to risk their lives?" the President asked.

"They do it for President, country and loyalty to each other, sir. And an occasional paycheck if I can get it for them, they do have bills to pay" the Admiral said with a chuckle.

President Bradshaw thought for a moment, then spoke. "If they can get everyone out safely, I will see to it that the three of them are compensated well for their services."

"Yes, sir, Mr. President" the Admiral replied.

"Go make your phone call, Admiral."

Cartwright nodded to the President, turned and walked out of the Oval Office, taking his cell phone out of his jacket pocket. He then ran into former President Daryl Matthews who had just arrived.

"Admiral Cartwright, congratulations on your new appointment," Matthews said, extending his hand to the Admiral.

James Cartwright took the former President's hand and shook it firmly. "Mr. President, I wished we could have met under more favorable conditions."

"As do I, Admiral," Matthews replied, continuing to shake his hand.

"We will bring our children home safely, sir. I promise," Cartwright said.

"I understand your granddaughter is also in there with my son, Admiral?" Matthews asked.

"Yes, she is, Mr. President," the Admiral responded sadly.

"How old is she?"

"She just turned 15, sir."

"Scott just turned 16, and I suspect he's keeping a girlfriend hidden from me," the former President said with a laugh.

"We can be overprotective with those we cherish most, can't we, sir," the Admiral said with a smile.

"Yes, we can," Matthews returned with a big grin.

"We're doing everything we can to get them out safely, Mr. President," the Admiral said trying to reassure him.

"I know. I'd best not keep the President waiting, Admiral," Matthews said, walking into the Oval Office with Amy Reynolds. The Admiral continued down the hallway, dialing his cell phone.

Once in the office, former President Matthews found President Bradshaw standing and looking out the window, watching the sun slowly going down behind the Washington Monument.

Matthews stood there for a moment before speaking. "I use to love watching the sun go down out that window."

"It *is* somewhat calming, isn't it," Bradshaw replied, turning to look at Matthews.

"I guess we both have children to worry about this evening, don't we, Mr. President?" Matthews said as he shook President Bradshaw's hand.

"We're both Presidents. Please call me Keith, Daryl," Bradshaw replied releasing the handshake they both enjoyed.

"Thank you, sir. What are we doing about our children, Keith?"

"We have a covert plan being finalized as we speak."

"I understand Secretary Cartwright's granddaughter is caught up in this as well," said Matthews.

"Yes, she is, Bradshaw confirmed. "She's a good friend of my daughter Stephanie. I'm glad they have each other right now. They have to be scared."

"My Scott has been a handful since his mother passed away, but I noticed a new calm in him lately. I think it's a girl," Daryl Matthews said with a big grin.

Tanaka paced the stage behind the Chinese President's son's chair, put his hands on his shoulders and looked into the camera.

"President Chao, your son is anxiously waiting for you to buy his freedom back -- $100 million in the next 15 minutes or your family will have one less rich mouth to feed. I don't want to break up a happy family. The money isn't really yours, technically, Mr. President," Tanaka continued, all the while smiling into the TV camera.

Presidents Bradshaw and Matthews intensely watched the broadcast and saw Stephanie and Kristina Cartwright behind Tanaka.

Daryl Matthews asked, "Where's Scott? He's not one of the hostages we see at the tables."

"Good question. He must be missing or hiding," Bradshaw replied quickly.

"If they had killed him, they probably would have paraded him in front of the camera by now to show everyone they mean business," Matthews speculated with a smile and hopefulness in his voice.

A voice came over the loudspeakers on the stage. It was Brian Jurgens. He had joined Sherry Moore up in the control booth to supervise.

"The Chinese government just deposited $100 million in the Children's Charity Fund account," he said his voice booming.

"That's awesome. Thank you, Mr. Chao," Tanaka spoke into the camera. "You can go back to your seat now, young Xing. Mr. Chao, I'm a man of my word. He will be returned to you safely after all is said and done.

"So, now it's time to bring another young guest to the stage and see if their country is as generous as the Chinese government has been," Tanaka stated.

"Chadwick Easton, Prime Minister Sir Charles Easton's son from Great Britain, it's your turn in the chair young man," Tanaka requested with a grin.

The 12-year-old boy stood tall as he approached Tanaka, looking at him with contempt. "My father knows the Queen," he said in his proper British accent sitting down in the chair.

"I hope he's *real* good friends with her," Tanaka said smiling at the young boy. He then looked into the main TV camera with a smirk.

"Prime Minister, you and your Queen have one hour to deposit $150 million into the account or I will kill your son on worldwide television. Your time starts now."

Tanaka walked over to Jonathan Mayer, still sitting on the side of the stage being watched by two armed guards. "How's that for entertainment?" Tanaka asked him, then walked away laughing.

Mayer shouted at him. "They won't let you get out of here alive, you know that, right?"

Tanaka smiled at Mayer's remarks. "Maybe," he said with a sly grin.

Jurgens voice came over the speaker again. "Wow, the Queen must owe the Prime Minister big time," he said laughing. "England just deposited $150 million in the account in less than 15 minutes." Tanaka looked up towards the control room and smiled.

"It seems our British friends understand the seriousness of our intentions and commitment," Tanaka said into the camera. "I believe it's time to introduce our host country's lovely First Daughter, Miss Stephanie Bradshaw," Tanaka announced.

"Miss Bradshaw is the daughter of the newly re-elected President Keith Bradshaw of the United States," Tanaka said smiling into the camera knowing that Bradshaw was watching from his Oval Office in the White House just down the street.

"Because the United States is the host country of this wonderful event, we're going to show our appreciation and give them a bit more time to present their contribution of $150 million," Tanaka announced. "You have three hours, Mr. President, starting now."

One of the armed guards stood behind Stephanie's chair and told her to get up and grabbed her by the arm. Defiantly, Stephanie shook off his grip and got up, looking him directly in the eye. "I can get up on my own, asshole," she said to the big machine gun-toting mercenary.

She walked over to Tanaka and said, with anger, in no uncertain terms, "Kill me now. The United States does not negotiate with terrorists. Or don't you know that, dumb ass?"

"Aren't we the firecracker," Tanaka said with a grin. "Have a seat, Miss Bradshaw," Tanaka ordered.

Stephanie sat down in the chair in the center of the stage and crossed her legs and arms. "My father is President. He understands what sacrifice is, and so do I," she said to Tanaka.

"We watched my mother die in front of us and had to say goodbye to her. That's true sacrifice. Something you will *never* understand, you piece of shit!" she said with tears coming down her face.

"Wow, that was heartwarming, Miss Bradshaw, but if your father doesn't send $150 million in the next three hours I'm going to splatter your emotional brains all over this stage," Tanaka said with a grin into the camera.

"You're an asshole," Stephanie Bradshaw said to Tanaka, looking up to him from the chair and getting another churlish grin from him.

Keith Bradshaw wiped the tears from his eyes, looking at Daryl Matthews. "She has a lot of fortitude Keith. You should be proud of her for that," Matthews said.

"Oh, I am. She gets that from her mother" Bradshaw said with a chuckle. "But she obviously needs to learn when it's okay to take on a psychopathic killer," he added with pride and a snicker.

Bradshaw pushed his intercom. "Amy, please get me Congressman Ryan Mitchell on the phone."

"Yes, Mr. President."

Two minutes later the phone on the President's desk rang and he picked it up. "Hello, Ryan, have you been watching the news?" Bradshaw asked.

"Yes, Mr. President. It's awful what's happening."

"I need you to crunch the numbers, Ryan. Talk to the Ways and Means Committee and find out if it's feasible for this $150 million ransom."

"Mr. President, your own daughter said on worldwide television that the U.S. does not negotiate with terrorists, and you know she's right, sir," the Congressman explained.

"Ryan, this is my *only* child. If I can't get her out in the next three hours, this crazy bastard will kill her with the entire world watching, including myself" Bradshaw explained.

"I will talk to the committee right now, Mr. President, but you need to understand this conversation may not go the way you want it to, sir," Congressman Mitchell said, hanging up the phone.

President Bradshaw thought to himself, "Let's hope Max Mason can pull this off tonight."

The GBN building was surrounded on all four sides with Secret Service, FBI, Federal Protection Police and local DC uniformed police officers moving around to get firing positions behind agency cars and SUV's. Armed with body armor, AR-15 machine guns, and the latest tactical gear they all waited impatiently for the "go ahead" to breach the building and rescue the hostages.

Directors Marshall and James had just arrived at the large black tent that had been set up across the street from the GBN building as a command center.

Large bright spotlights were beaming on each side of the building, illuminating the entire area. Generators hummed, and everyone's radio was crackling with static and chatter from all around the five-story brick building taken by armed mercenaries.

Marshall and James walked into the tent being used as the command center, looked around and saw radio transmitters, weapons on an adjoining table, and people barking orders to others through the radio.

"Who's in charge here?" Marshall asked.

"*I* am. Who are you?" the heavily-armed officer asked.

"I'm Secret Service Director Dwayne Marshall. This is FBI Director Michael James," Marshall said and they both presented their IDs to the officer.

"Sorry, sir. I'm Lieutenant Charles Adams from the Federal Protection Agency."

"Where are we, Lieutenant, with these bombs on the doors?" Marshall asked.

"The bomb squad guys have informed me they are *very* sophisticated and cannot be defused from outside the building. They have to be looked at from the other side of the door, which presents a serious problem, sir."

"So you're basically saying that we need to get someone in the building to defuse these things?" Marshall inquired.

"Yes, sir. And there are no access points to get into the building other than the roof. And our spotters have said it's heavily-fortified with mercenaries," Adams explained.

Marshall and James stepped back from the Lieutenant to speak to one another. "We can't send anyone in until the President gives the okay," James said reluctantly to Marshall.

"So what the hell are we suppose to do, sit out here in the heat with our thumbs stuck up our asses?" Marshall asked defiantly.

Marshall looked at James and said, "According to the countdown clock, the President's daughter has about 50 more minutes before Amikura plans on killing her, right? If the President's plan hasn't secured the hostages in 45 minutes, we breach one of the entrances and detonate the bomb, hopefully without casualties," Marshall said.

"The President will *not* like this if it goes sideways, Dwayne," FBI Director James proclaimed.

"His own daughter told the entire world that the United States does not negotiate with terrorists. He has to understand that as well," Marshall declared. James nodded to Marshall in agreement.

The bright spotlights lit up the outside of the GBN building like it was daylight, sending beams into the ballroom windows.

The five armed mercenaries rushed to the windows to make sure there wasn't a possibility of a breach from a SWAT team coming through the windows.

Samson looked out the window himself and angrily yelled to them, "Get back to your posts. They're not coming in."

They all returned to their positions around the ballroom, continuing to point their loaded weapons at the seated hostages.

Karen Tyler spoke up, seeing that some of the hostages were getting overheated and more scared as the situation dragged on. "We need some water over here," she demanded. "People are getting dehydrated and sick from the heat."

Tyler was apprising the situation and noticed Stacy Michaels smiling at her with a slight black and blue bruise on the right side of her face where Samson had hit her. She didn't seem scared, which Tyler thought odd for such a young, naive woman.

Samson approached Tyler, smiled and pointed his MP-5 machine gun at her face and whispered, "I'm going to enjoy killing a Secret Service agent," he said.

"That's nice for you. How about some water for these people?" Tyler requested of him with a mean look. "I'll enjoy seeing your body riddled with bullets when SWAT gets up here."

Samson laughed at Tyler, and she gave him a defiant look.

"You're a brave bitch, aren't you? In a few minutes, you're going to be a dead bitch," he informed her.

The big, blonde-haired mercenary looked at the two armed men watching the security table where the five foreign security specialists sat along with Tyler. "Take these six outside in the hallway and sit them down on the floor. Cuff them first," Samson commanded.

"Why are we being separated?" Tyler asked him.

"Because I want you to be," he said to Tyler with a grin.

The two mercenaries went to each of the security specialists and started cuffing them behind their backs with plastic security ties.

The French security agent put up a fight and was subdued by the mercenary with a hard blow to his face from the butt of his machine gun.

Tyler screamed, "THAT'S ENOUGH! You don't have to beat him senseless." The mercenary picked him up off the floor and cuffed him without resistance this time.

"I'm going to cuff you personally, bitch," Samson informed Tyler, walking towards her. "Turn around or die right here in front of everyone!" he yelled at her.

Tyler thought about resisting but realized she didn't have any recourse at this moment, so she turned around and put her arms behind her back. The blonde-haired guard put the plastic cuffs around her wrists and tightened them.

"I'm kind of disappointed you didn't resist," he said with a smile.

"Maybe later," Tyler said with a grin. Tyler looked around the room and smiled at Stacy Michaels who nodded to her.

The two guards finished cuffing the now standing security specialists and stepped back with their weapons pointing at them again.

"Take them out into the hallway and sit them down" Samson said. "And take this bitch with you as well," he said smiling again at Tyler.

Tyler looked Samson in the eyes and obnoxiously replied with a grin, "I'll see you real soon."

He smiled back at Tyler. "Not where you're going."

"I'm not there yet asshole," Tyler replied, giving Samson a big condescending smile as she was led towards the ballroom door.

Tyler and the five other security specialists were escorted out the doors of the ballroom and walked a little ways down the hallway where the armed men told them to stop and sit against the wall on the floor. Everyone stood against the wall then slid down until they were seated on the waxed floor tiles.

One of the scared waitresses from the reception asked Samson, "Where are they taking them?"

"You should worry more about yourselves," he said with a grin. "Just want you all to know that NO ONE is coming for you, so shut the hell up," he said.

Stacy Michaels looked around the room and saw that people were very frightened, uncertain about what was going to happen to them. She looked at the remaining three armed guards in the room, smiled, and rubbed her cheek thinking to herself, "You have *no idea* what's coming."

CHAPTER 6

MAX MASON WAS AS EXCITED AS A CHILD ON
Christmas morning knowing he was hosting this year's annual SEAL
team reunion for his best friends. He had set up all kinds of activities
for the guys to do for the week – baseball games, rock concerts, bar-
becues, movies, golf and, of course, the firing range competition they
had every year was also on his agenda.

Max cleaned his house from top to bottom, washing the linen,
cleaning the hardwood floors, stocking the bar in the family room
and even cleaning all the windows in the house. He hadn't seen his
two friends for almost a year but did keep in contact through email
and phone calls.

Max had been Captain and leader of SEAL Team 2 stationed in
the Philippines for six years, along with Lieutenant Jordan "Jordy"
Alexander, Commander Michael "Mikey" Stevens and Admiral
James Cartwright, the new Secretary of Defense, who was their mission control commanding officer in Manila.

They had conducted over 200-plus missions in the Pacific theater
successfully, and were still to this day considered the strongest SEAL
team in the U.S. Navy. They were a "recon and rescue" team that
Admiral James Cartwright was given clearance to put together in the
Pacific region in the late 1980s. Training started out with 28 eager

recruits until there were just the three of them. The Admiral saw something special in Max Mason, making him the team leader and never regretted the decision to put him in charge. They were all retired inactive reserves now but enjoyed training together four weekends a year with the other younger SEAL teams across the country.

It was just about 7pm when a knock came on Max's front door. He was sitting on the sofa channel surfing the cable TV when he heard the loud knock, got up, straightened his clothes and walked to the front door. After looking through the tiny peep hole, he smiled and opened the door. Two smiling faces greeted him.

"Hey boss," Jordy Alexander said to Max with a grin. "Look what I found at the airport selling flowers," he said laughing.

"I was actually stealing the flowers if you want to be technical," Mikey Stevens said to them both, chuckling and giving Jordy a smug look.

"You guys are almost an hour late," a smiling Max replied, giving each one a big hug.

"Yeah, we had some issues getting our toys through airport security," Jordy said. "Seems my gun wasn't the issue. My new laptops *were*," he said smiling.

Jordy was the communications and computer specialist for the team. He was a genius programmer, hacker, as well as the medical specialist for the team and had saved their lives many times with his keystrokes and his medical bag.

"Afraid it's my fault boss," Mikey explained. "I kinda brought more than I should have this trip," he said laughing, pointing to his huge black duffle bag at his feet. "Plus they kept asking for autographs. You know how me and Faye are about our fans, boss," Mikey said.

"What the hell did you bring son?" Max asked with a grin looking at the big black bag sitting on his doorstep.

Mikey Stevens was a hometown television star, along with his wife Faye, his son Curtis, and his brother Jeff. Mikey and his family owned a large firearms and hunting retail store in Oklahoma City where they custom made specialty firearms for celebrities. That garnered them a reality TV series called "Family Firearms" that aired on the Outdoor Network on nationwide cable outlets. They had just signed for their second season to be broadcast in the fall.

He was a damn good gunsmith, could make a working gun out of anything and could knock the wings off a fly with a sniper rifle from 100 yards away. He was also the team's explosives expert, detonating and defusing explosives.

So now, everywhere Mikey went, gun enthusiasts would come up to him and ask for autographs. He was famous and loved it.

"I brought a couple of new toys I made for you boss," Mikey said to Max. He opened his big black duffle bag on Max's porch and showed him the various firearms he had brought for him.

Max smiled and hugged Mikey. "Awesome."

"Come on in boys," Max said to them both as the three of them walked into the house. "It's great to see you both again. I've missed you," Max said grinning. "Your rooms are ready, there's booze in the bar and I bought these incredible two-inch-thick porterhouse steaks from the butcher this morning for the grill this evening."

"Will the Admiral be joining us?" Jordy asked.

Max went to the bar and picked up a bottle of 15-year-old scotch with a note on it. "The Admiral said he couldn't make it tonight but said he's in for golf on Tuesday. He wrote us a note that came with the bottle," Max said with a smile, then read it.

"Gentlemen, sorry I can't be there tonight for this joyous occasion, but I wanted the three of you to know how proud I have always been to be your commanding officer. Please drink this bottle in good health on me. 'Signed' "Admiral James Cartwright . PS. When am I going to guest star on your show, Commander?" Max laughed as he read the last part.

"Oh, hell no!" Mikey exclaimed. "He'll try to take over the show, and you know how that will sit with Faye," he laughed.

Both Max and Jordy laughed with Mikey knowing that Faye was an intense wife when it came to someone else running *her* cable show.

Max grabbed three glasses from the bar, handed one to each of them and cracked open the top on the scotch bottle. He poured a bit in each of their glasses and put the bottle down on the table.

"A toast boys," Max said raising his glass. "To our families, our comrades, our successes and our failures. May we live to fight another day for all of them," Max said with a grin.

"Here, here," both Mikey and Jordy replied. Sipping the scotch from their glasses, all three smiled with approval at the taste.

Max's phone buzzed in his back pocket. He took it out, stared at it for a moment with a stern look, then it rang in his hand.

"Hello Admiral, or should I call you Mr. Secretary now?" Max asked.

"Admiral is fine, Max," Cartwright replied with a laugh. "Sorry I can't be there, Max. Did you and the boys get the scotch I sent over?"

"Hey boss, you might want to take a look at this," Jordy said looking at the TV that was on in Max's living room.

"We did, sir. Just cracked it open and it tastes real smooth," Max told Cartwright with a laugh, not paying any attention to what Jordy said to him. Max casually glanced over at the TV screen for a moment to see what Jordy and Mikey were getting all worked up over.

"Boss! You need to see this NOW!!" Jordy shouted to get Max's attention. He and Mikey were watching and listening to the TV news while Max had been talking to the Admiral and recognized the importance of the story that was being broadcast.

Max hated being called "boss" by either Jordy or Mikey, but it was better than being addressed as "Captain Sir" which was what they both use to do in the beginning until he finally accepted being called boss.

"Can you hold for a moment Admiral?" Max asked, giving Jordy an annoyed look. Max stopped talking to the Admiral and looked at the TV screen again to see a news report coming in live from the Global Broadcasting Network where he now worked as a security clearance specialist under his friend Charles Lee.

Lee was the Assistant Chief of Staff while he and Max worked together under the President Matthews administration. Max considered him a friend and colleague while they were both in the White House.

After Max retired from the Secret Service and President Bradshaw was elected, Lee became Security Director of GBN and offered Max a job working with employee security clearances almost a year ago. Max was an "empty-nester" now and thought it was a good time to return to work again, so he accepted the position and enjoyed the job so far.

"For the second time in five years the Children's Hunger Charity has become the target of another terrorist attack in the Nation's Capital," the female news anchor said. "We warn you now, the video we are about to show is *very* graphic in nature. It depicts the murder of Congressman David Young of Virginia by the terrorist in charge."

Max understood now why Jordy needed to get his attention the second time. On the broadcast he saw an Asian man, dressed in all white, shooting a man said to be Congressman Young in the head at point blank range, then looking with an evil smile into the camera saying, "Oh yeah, I almost forgot. It's time to end this, brother. OUR father waits for you."

Max's face went flush, then turned beet red with anger at what he saw and heard. "TANAKA!" Max shouted loudly. Then he spoke into the phone.

"Did you know about what's happening at GBN, Admiral?"

"This is why I called, Captain."

Max stood a little straighter when the Admiral addressed him as Captain. He knew the conversation had switched from friendly to professional.

"Okay, Admiral," Max acknowledged.

"Seems that the Philippines are coming back to bite us *all* in the ass after all these years, Captain," Cartwright said. "This is something the entire team needs to hear, so put me on speaker please, Max."

Max thought it was interesting that the Admiral had said "please." He never used that word when asking them to do something. He just ordered them to do it.

"Yes, sir," Max replied. He then looked at both Jordy and Mikey with confusion on his face.

"The Admiral needs to talk to *all* of us," Max said, clicking on the speaker of his cell phone.

"Go ahead, Admiral," Max said putting the phone down on the table for all to hear.

"Lieutenant Alexander, Commander Stevens, sorry to ruin the reunion but I need your help this evening, gentlemen," the Admiral asked solemnly. He went on to tell the three of them about his granddaughter and President Bradshaw's daughter being guest speakers at the telethon.

"Boys, this is a personal request from me and President Bradshaw. I'm afraid this one is off the books. I am not ordering any of you to take this mission, but I'm asking as a friend and a grandfather to please help me and the President by bringing our children home safely. I know Captain Mason has an invested interest to take this mission on, but *we* and *he* could use your help as well, gentlemen," the Admiral explained.

In all the years Jordy and Mikey had known the Admiral, they had never heard him ask them for anything when it came to a mission. They both looked at each other, then at Max, smiled, and nodded in agreement.

"Aye, aye, Admiral," they said in unison.

"Thank you, gentlemen. We won't forget this."

"We all know about Tanaka Amikura from our Philippine days, and what he did to his father and Max," Cartwright stated. "Seems like he finally got up enough courage to take Max on after all these years, but with an interesting, but devastating, twist."

"Amikura is holding children and teenagers from other countries and ransoming them back to their dignitary parents and their countries. My 15-year-old granddaughter Kristina and President Bradshaw's 16-year-old daughter Stephanie are both being held by this murdering psychopath, with possibly 30 mercenaries inside the GBN building where you work, Max."

"We have less then three hours before Stephanie Bradshaw is the next victim of this asshole," the Admiral explained. "On top of all this we just got confirmation that all the entrance/exit doors are wired with explosives and armed with mercenaries, so no one can get through any of the four entrances without serious consequences."

"Not just any explosives, Admiral -- X-127," Max declared.

"How did you get that intel, Captain?" Cartwright asked surprised.

Max hesitated for a moment, then answered. "I know the man, Admiral. He was the one responsible for the Charity Gala bombing at the Majestic Hotel five years ago. I just didn't put it together until now. He used X-127 then. It makes sense he would use the rest of his stockpile in this situation. He could bring the entire building down to the ground with that much X-127, Admiral," Max explained.

"I'm going to have to talk to the President on this development right away," Cartwright responded. "Anything you boys need from me on my end?" the Admiral asked.

Max thought for a minute, grinned and looked at Jordy and Mikey.

"We're going to need access to the IRS building, Admiral," Max said with a chuckle.

"Why the IRS building, Captain?" the Admiral asked.

"Let's just say for access, Admiral" Max replied, winking at Mikey with a sly grin while Jordy continued to watch the news program.

You could hear the Admiral snicker through the speaker because he understood what Max was telling him.

"One more thing, Captain. The President wants hourly updates from you."

"Copy that, Admiral," Max replied.

"Good luck, gentlemen. Please bring our children home safely," the Admiral pleaded as he hung up the phone.

"So much for reunion weekend," Jordy said with a sigh.

"The hell, you say. We have tickets for the Washington Sentinels versus the New York Muddogs tomorrow afternoon. I'm *not* missing baseball," Max said with a big smile to them both.

"Works for me, boss," Mikey said with a laugh.

"Me too," Jordy agreed smiling.

"What about equipment and weapons, boss?" Mikey asked.

"What did you both bring with you?" inquired Max.

"I'm actually good with the laptops and communications gear," Jordy expressed, "but I only have my Sig Sauer 9mm handgun and two extra mags, boss. And I don't have my medical bag with me."

"What about you, Mikey?" Max asked.

"Well, you saw what I brought in the bag, boss. That's all I have with me. I don't think that's enough to take on 30 or more heavily-armed bad guys," Mikey stated with a grin.

Max smiled at them both. "Come with me boys. Have I got something to show you," he said grinning from ear to ear.

The three of them walked down the stairs to Max's "Theater Room" and went through the curtained entry way inside. Max was a big movie fan and loved watching DVDs and sports on his practically wall-size 82-inch big screen high definition TV.

The room was huge - at least 20 feet wide and 20 feet long - with the back walls near the entry way shelved with thousands of DVDs on both sides. The TV was secured and extended out from the wall in the middle of the room. It had four black leather recliner chairs in front of it, sophisticated audio/video, and a gaming system stored in a classy black rack on the side.

Jordy and Mikey both thought out loud, "This is way cool, boss."

"You haven't seen anything yet," Max said with a grin. He walked over to the large TV screen and pressed a sequence of numbers on a keypad on the console under it. "You're both gonna love this, especially you Mikey.

"I had this built last year," he said proudly, as both Jordy and Mikey watched as the big screen TV started moving back against the wall. Once the TV screen stopped against the back wall, two wall sections started moving towards each other from each side of the TV, exposing Max's armory of various weapons and tactical equipment.

When the two sections met in the middle it stopped, completely hiding the TV. Jordy and Mikey looked at each other smiling.

"Merry fucking Christmas," Jordy said with a big grin while looking over all the guns. Max stood there watching his SEAL teammates' surprised expressions and smiled.

On the left side was a vertical rack of five AR-223 caliber rifles and five MP-5 9mm caliber machine guns fully equipped with silencers, laser sights and sniper scopes. On the right side there were four different horizontal rows of handguns, including five SA-XD 9mm, five Sig Sauer 226 9mm, five R-95 9mm and five M&P 9mm handguns.

Both Jordy and Mikey went to the racks and looked at everything Max had, smiling like a couple of kids in a candy store. Mikey pulled one of the AR-223 rifles out of the rack, looked it over and pulled the slide to see how clean it was. "This is really clean, boss," Mikey said to Max.

"I cleaned them all two days ago anticipating our shooting competition this week," Max told his good friend.

"What kind of ammo do you have for all this, boss?" Mikey asked.

Max walked over to where Mikey was in front of the rifles and machine guns and pulled out a sliding drawer under them to show every AR rifle and MP-5 machine gun had a row of eleven loaded 30-round magazines for the 9mm caliber, and another loaded eleven 60-round magazines for the .223 caliber.

"Oh my God, boss, you have the new 60-round mags. I can't even get these for my show yet," Mikey said with a laugh, looking at everything in the drawer.

"You could say I have some pull with the Navy," Max said with a smile.

"Oh *really*," Mikey said laughing, picking up one of the new mags in Max's drawer and examining it closely.

Jordy opened the drawer under the handguns to see the different magazines for each gun lined up, eleven for each gun as well. "Why eleven magazines exactly, boss?" Jordy asked.

Max moved over a few feet to open a storage cabinet on each side of the rifles and handguns to expose holsters, tactical vests, Kevlar body armor, rifle slings, radio communication equipment, equipment bags and medical supplies. The other cabinet displayed rock climbing equipment with nylon rope, a crossbow with steel arrows, a grappling hook and gun belts that handled ten magazines for handguns, rifles and machine guns.

"Oh, now I understand. One in the gun, ten on the belt," Mikey said with a big grin.

"Okay, where are the toys that go boom, boss?" Mikey asked with a smile.

Max pulled out a long drawer that was directly under the rifle and handgun magazine drawers to show four rows of different color-coded canisters and pointed to each row one at a time.

"Concussion grenades, flash bang grenades, tear gas and smoke grenades," Max replied. Then he picked up mini C-4 packs, detonators and digital timers and showed them all to Mikey.

"*Nice*, boss!" Mikey said impressed.

"Take what you need gentlemen. We leave in 10 minutes," Max told them as he grabbed one of the large nylon duffle bags and started filling it with gear. He grabbed the crossbow and arrows, checked the scope and put it in one of the bags.

Jordy saw him put the crossbow in the bag and asked, "What the hell you need that for, boss?"

Max just smiled at him and continued loading the large black bag with weapons, rock climbing gear and two nylon ropes. Jordy looked puzzled at what Max was bringing on this mission.

When Max was finished filling the second of the two bags he had, he started getting dressed with a Kevlar vest, black tactical shirt, his magazine-loaded gun belt and a fully loaded tactical vest. He grabbed his SA-XD 9mm handgun, checked it, loaded a magazine in it and placed it in his holster and secured it. He put his black leather jacket on and looked at both Jordy and Mikey arming themselves accordingly.

Max, like Jordy and Mikey, preferred the AR-223 rifle more than the smaller MP-5 9mm rifle and they each grabbed one out of the rack, checked the scope, put in a 60-round magazine, attached them to slings, loaded the rest of the magazines in the gun belts, looked at one another and smiled. Max added two MP-5 machine guns plus extra magazines to his other open bag.

Mikey had given Max twin 9mm mini handguns with three-inch silencers that he had constructed in Oklahoma, as well as a .22 magnum mini machine pistol with three 50-round magazines. "These are sweet. Thank you," Max said expressing his appreciation for the gifts from his friend as he placed them in the bag.

"You're welcome, boss. Wait till I show you how special the 9mm minis are," Mikey responded with a sinister grin.

The three of them stood and evaluated the gear they had, made sure everything was secure, grabbed the bags on the floor and headed up to Max's garage.

Jordy grabbed his communications bag with his special laptops and audio/video communication devices in it, and the medical bag from Max's cabinet. Mikey grabbed the "boom bag," as he liked to call it, and his AR-223, and they both headed up the stairs.

Max was waiting in the garage for them with the back door of his SUV open to accommodate the bags they brought up with them.

"Does anyone have to use the restroom before we take on the bad guys?" Max asked them both with a big grin on his face.

Mikey and Jordy loaded their gear in the back of the SUV and turned to one another. "I'm good, you?" Jordy asked Mikey.

"Yeah. I'm cool. But can we stop for ice cream, or maybe chicken and waffles before we get there, boss" Mikey asked Max sarcastically with a smile.

"Smart-ass redneck country boy," he responded with a laugh.

"Aye, aye, sir," Mikey returned with a proud grin.

The three of them got into Max's SUV and backed out of his driveway heading to DC -- the GBN building – and to take on Tanaka Amikura.

CHAPTER 7

PRESIDENT KEITH BRADSHAW WAS PACING BACK
and forth behind his desk, continuously looking out the window
of the Oval Office, worrying more and more about his daughter
Stephanie and the terrorist situation that was happening again to the
Children's Global Hunger Charity.

The phone on the President's desk buzzed. Bradshaw pushed the
speaker button and heard Amy Reynolds' voice. "Mr. President, I
have Congressman Mitchell on the line for you, sir."

"Thank you, Amy. Put him through please."

"Yes, sir."

Bradshaw put the Congressman on speaker, anxiously waiting to
hear the decision on his request. "What did they have to say?"

"Mr. President, I'm afraid I have bad news," the Congressman
stated. "The Ways and Means Committee voted down your request
to give the ransom money for your daughter, sir."

There was dead silence for a moment. Then President Bradshaw
lashed out at the Congressman.

"MY daughter is not going to die because a bunch of *old fools*
thinking they run the country don't agree with MY politics!" he
screamed at Mitchell.

"I won't forget this, Ryan. There will come a time when your committee will need *my* vote for something in the next four years. That vote may or may not be there because of this exact moment," Bradshaw exclaimed. Before Congressman Mitchell could respond President Bradshaw hung up on him.

The phone buzzed again and Keith Bradshaw abruptly yelled, "WHAT?"

"Sorry, Mr. President, but Defense Secretary Cartwright is here to see you," Amy said.

"I'm SO sorry Amy. Please send the Admiral in.

"Yes, Mr. President. Not a problem, sir."

The Admiral walked into the Oval Office and the President asked immediately, "Any progress Admiral?"

Admiral Cartwright shook the President's hand and stepped back.

"Captain Mason and his team are in route to the GBN building as we speak, Mr. President."

"Do you think they have a chance Admiral?"

"If I know Captain Mason and his team, they have a *very* good chance of being successful, Mr. President," Cartwright replied. "But we have a serious problem. Captain Mason believes that the building is rigged with X-127 explosives."

"I read about that explosive in a CIA memo about three years ago," said the President.

"Yes, sir. Just one of those charges can bring that entire building down around everyone, and they have *all four* entrances wired with this stuff," the Admiral said hesitantly.

"What does Mason say about getting into the building?" Bradshaw asked nervously.

The Admiral gave him a slight grin. "Let's just say, Mr. President, that Max Mason has creative ways of getting in and out of places we would never consider."

"Does he need anything from us on our end, Admiral?"

"Funny you should ask that, sir," Cartwright said with another grin.

Max, Mikey, and Jordy arrived at the GBN building but drove right past it when Max saw Secret Service Director Dwayne Marshall standing in front of the mobile command center with FBI Director Michael James.

"What's up, boss?" Jordy asked, noticing they were not stopping at the GBN building.

"My old boss with Secret Service seems to be in charge here with the FBI Director," Max replied.

"That doesn't sound like a good thing, boss," Mikey responded.

"It's all good, boys. Wasn't going in that way anyway," Max said to them with a smile.

Max parked his black SUV in front of the IRS building, which was next to the GBN building but separated by Interstate 95 north and south, an eight-lane highway.

"Looks like they stopped traffic for us at least," Jordy said with a chuckle to Max and Mikey.

It was a security protocol to block the streets and highways involved in any criminal activity for a two-block radius. The three of them got out of the SUV and opened the back. "Let's grab the gear and get inside before anyone sees us," Max ordered.

"Where are we going, boss?" Jordy asked.

"THERE, into the IRS building. Their security should be expecting us," Max said looking at Mikey who was now grinning at Max. Jordy looked confused but figured Max knew where he was going.

The three of them grabbed all the bags and slowly, cautiously - so not to be seen by any of the law enforcement personal patrolling the perimeter of the GBN building - walked into the lobby of the IRS building where several uniformed security guards approached them.

Max looked around the lobby of the building to see metal detectors, glass offices, several banks of elevators, and the huge information/security desk sitting in the middle of the floor with six uniformed armed guards awaiting their arrival, hands on their guns.

"Are you Captain Mason?" one of the guards asked.

"Yes I am," Max replied, and produced his Virginia driver's license to the guard.

"I'm Sergeant William Fowler with the Federal Protection Police," he said. "I understand from my supervisor that both the President and the Secretary of Defense ordered that I'm to escort you and your men to the roof," he explained.

Jordy looked at Mikey and Max in horror. "The ROOF?" he said.

Mikey started laughing knowing this would be Jordy's reaction when he found out he had to go up to the roof. Max kind of smirked but had to be commanding and serious knowing his friend was a little scared of heights.

"Let's get the bags into the elevator, Lieutenant," Max said looking at Jordy with a stern look.

"We're going down into the basement, aren't we boss?" Jordy asked with a smile as he placed the last bag in the elevator.

"Tanaka would expect us to come through the basement tunnels," Max replied to his colleague.

There were delivery tunnels that ran under the highway and connected the IRS building with the GBN building. Access was in the basement of the GBN building through a steel security door.

Max expected that door to be heavily fortified with either mercenaries or wired with X-127 because it would be something Tanaka would almost certainly do.

"He's not a stupid psychopath," Max informed Jordy. "He knows I'm coming. He just doesn't know *how* I'm coming," Max said with a grin.

"Good luck, gentlemen," Sergeant Fowler said to Max and his team as the elevator doors started to close.

Max pushed the seventh floor button and saw Jordy grab hold of the railing to steady himself and sheepishly smiled to Mikey. Mikey just kept his head down grinning, knowing how this was affecting his friend.

"Can we talk about this plan, boss?" Jordy asked nervously.

Max looked at Jordy. "You'll be fine, Lieutenant."

The elevator door opened on the seventh floor and Max stepped out to find the floor completely abandoned. The IRS had a strict 9am-5pm work schedule for their employees, so he knew no one would be there at that time of night. "Let's get the bags up to the roof," Max said as he headed down the hallway.

Jordy hesitantly grabbed two of the bags and followed Max towards the sign "Roof Access", mumbling to himself the entire time. Mikey followed close behind them with the other two bags. Once inside the doorway they headed up the stairs.

Max slowly opened the door to the roof and stuck his head out and looked around to make sure it was safe. He walked out onto the gravel roof top with his SA-XD handgun pointed in every direction he looked. He determined it was safe and opened the door and motioned Jordy and Mikey to come out.

The wind was blowing a bit more than usual up on the roof and Max could tell Jordy was getting a bit nervous about being there. "Are you okay, Lieutenant?"

"Permission to speak freely, sir," Jordy asked.

"Go ahead, Lieutenant," Max replied with a smile, knowing Jordy never asked to speak unless he was pissed about something.

"When did this plan become a goddamn parachute jump, sir?" Jordy asked sarcastically to his commanding officer.

"Who said anything about a parachute, Lieutenant?"

"OH, SHIT, here it comes!" Mikey said out loud with a grin.

Max opened one of the equipment bags they brought, pulled out the crossbow, arrows, the black nylon rope and a pair of high powered binoculars.

"Remember that mission in Burma?" Max asked them both with a smile.

"Are you fucking kidding me, Captain?" Jordy replied. "I almost died on that mission. Sir, I know you have all this fucking bizarre training, but some of us aren't *special* like *you, sir,*" Jordy said respectfully to Max.

"If it's any consolation Lieutenant, I'm going first this time," Max said with a grin.

"Does that mean if you die, the rest of us can do it differently?" Jordy asked with a smile.

Mikey looked at Max and smiled. "He does have a point, boss."

Max just smiled at them both and picked up the binoculars. "Gear up boys," he said to them playfully.

Max looked through the binoculars in the direction of the GBN building's roof which was two floors down from the IRS roof. He stared through them for a few moments, then put them back in the bag.

"Looks like Tanaka has a few boys on the roof as well," Max said to his team.

"Let's work on the tunnel plan now boss," Jordy said to Max, understanding his recon about mercenaries being on the GBN roof.

"At ease, Lieutenant," Max said with a grin.

Mikey looked through his sniper scope on his AR-223 rifle towards the GBN rooftop. "I see three hostiles, boss," he said to Max.

"That's what I saw too," Max replied. "How far do you think the shot is Mikey?"

"About 300 feet, boss. I can get one from that distance, but the other two will have to be at close range," Mikey explained. "Or they'll know we're coming."

Max stood there for a moment and thought about what Mikey had said. He looked at the equipment he pulled out of the bag and smiled to himself knowing what he was about to do. He walked over to the edge of the roof and looked down the side of the IRS building thinking to himself, "That's going to hurt if I don't make this."

Max shifted his stare over to the GBN rooftop to see the three mercenaries *only* being together when they had to check in on the radio, which Max calculated as every 15 minutes. He looked at his watch and started the stopwatch on it. "We have exactly 15 minutes to get ready," he told Jordy and Mikey.

Jordy and Mikey were already "geared up" and watched Max work on the steel arrow he was going to use with the crossbow.

"I appreciate you making this for me, Mikey. Shame we didn't have this in Burma," Max said grinning.

The arrow had a specially made arrowhead that would go through solid concrete because of a .357 caliber bullet insert that upon impact would give the arrow more power going into the concrete, enabling it to hold up to 400 pounds of weight.

"Yeah, I made it for you for rock climbing; if we had this back then Jordy might not be afraid of heights," Mikey said laughing.

"Fuck you very much, Commander," Jordy said sarcastically.

Jordy handed Max and Mikey ear bud communicators and tested them. "Can you two assholes hear me," Jordy said laughing.

"Copy that" both Max and Mikey replied laughing.

"Time to get serious, guys," Max commanded looking at them both.

"Yes boss," they both answered.

Max loaded the arrow on the crossbow and attached the black nylon rope to the arrow's steel tether. He looked through the scope to adjust its elevation and sights.

Jordy looked at Max. "I still don't like this, boss."

Max grinned back at Jordy. "Look at it this way -- you can be the first to say I told you so."

"Aye, aye that, Captain," Jordy said laughing.

"Good luck, boss," they both said to Max.

Max's alarm on his watch buzzed, he looked through the crossbow's scope to see the three mercenaries walk over to the far end of the roof to check in on the radio.

Max aimed at the top of the concrete entryway he knew led to the stairs into the building and pulled the trigger on the crossbow. The arrow flew straight and fast, hitting the concrete wall of the stairwell entry, exploding the .357 round farther into the concrete with a loud bang.

"I'll be damned. It worked," Mikey said laughing.

Mikey and Jordy grabbed the nylon rope and pulled it tight to secure it to the steel water pipe on top of the IRS building, tied it off and gave Max the thumbs up sign that he was good to go.

Max had brought three nylon straps that were about three inches wide, grabbed one, and left the other two for Mikey and Jordy to use. He grabbed the rope and wrapped the nylon strap over it and stood on the ledge of the roof. "Take your shot, Mikey," Max commanded.

"Aye, aye, sir," Mikey replied, looking through the scope of his AR-223 sniper rifle.

Max took out his SA-XD handgun, twisted the silencer to the barrel, grabbed both ends of the strap with one hand and jumped, sliding down the rope to the GBN building roof.

Mikey had one of the mercenaries in his scope sight, pulled the trigger and the bullet hit him in the forehead, killing him instantly and causing him to fall to the ground next to his two friends. "Nice shot, Mikey," Jordy acknowledged to his friend, putting his hand on his shoulder.

Max slid down the rope holding both ends of the strap with one hand and shot the other two mercenaries with his other, killing them both before landing beside all three of them. Max checked all three bodies to make sure they were dead before looking back up at Mikey and Jordy on the IRS rooftop, giving them a thumbs up.

"Send over the bags first," Max ordered.

Mikey and Jordy hooked up the bags to the rope extending over to the GBN roof and slid them down. Max received them and placed them beside the dead mercenaries.

"Who's gonna be first? Over." Max asked with a grin on his face.

Mikey looked at Jordy and said, "I'll go first so you know it's cool, okay?

"I still want to go on record that this is a bad idea for me," Jordy replied.

"I hear you, buddy," Mikey replied smiling.

Mikey grabbed his strap, tossed it over the rope and wrapped both hands around them, climbed up on the ledge and jumped. Jordy looked over the ledge and saw how easy and fast Mikey had gotten down to the GBN roof with Max. "This may not be so bad after all," Jordy thought to himself. He grabbed the last strap left for him, slung it over the rope with confidence, climbed up on the ledge and said out loud, "Please, God, let me die from a good fuck," closed his eyes and jumped.

Jordy was sliding down the rope and almost to the GBN roof when the rope from the arrow snapped. Max instinctively dove to the ground grabbing the runaway rope as Jordy's weight started pulling the rope down.

Jordy noticed he wasn't getting to the roof and braced himself against the building's outside wall about ten feet from the top, grabbing the rope with both hands, realizing that he wasn't sliding anymore, he was falling. Max and Mikey pulled the rope up slowly, then grabbed their friend and slung him over the edge of the roof to the gravel surface.

"REALLY?" he said looking at Mikey. "Next mission I get to make the goddamn plan. And *nice arrow* by the way," Jordy said viciously but relieved his two best friends were there to save him...*again*, just like Burma.

"I brought an extra pair of shorts in my bag. Do you need them?" Mikey asked Jordy laughing.

"Not yet, but keep them close by," Jordy replied with a smile still lying on his back on the roof looking up into the night sky.

The three of them sat on the rooftop together for a moment, had a good laugh, then Max got up first. "Time to go to work, gentlemen."

"I'm hoping the rope wasn't our only way out, boss," Jordy said with a smile.

Max smiled back. "That depends on Mikey being able to get us out the front door."

"Not a problem, boss. I've never met a bomb I couldn't defuse," Mikey stated with a laugh.

"These aren't just regular C-4 bombs, Commander," Max informed him. "This is that X-127 shit that levels buildings."

"I'm still good, boss," Mikey said, smiling confidently.

Jordy opened his bag and pulled out the mini laptop that attached to his left forearm, booted it up and started hacking into the GBN surveillance cameras to see what was happening in the building with the mercenaries and hostages.

"It seems there are hostages in the fifth floor hallway, the third floor TV studio, and the ballroom, each with armed hostiles," Jordy said looking at his screen intently. He then looked a little closer." You better take a look at this, boss," he said to Max.

Max eyed Jordy's screen. "I know," he said with a stern look on his face.

Mikey came over and looked at the screen. "Interesting," he said with a grin.

"Show me the hostages in the hallway again," Max requested.

Max looked at the screen and recognized several security people he knew, but one person in particular caught his eye. "TYLER!" he said out loud.

"Who's Tyler, boss?" Jordy asked looking at his screen.

"We worked together for a few years at the Secret Service. She's a good agent."

"SHE?" Mikey asked with a big grin.

Max looked at Mikey and flashed him an annoying look.

"It's all good, boss. Let's go rescue the nice lady," Mikey said with a snicker. You think she has a sister for Jordy?"

Max just rolled his eyes. Mikey looked at Jordy and they both grinned together.

Max got all his gear situated, including the new "toys" Mikey had given him, and started heading towards the door to the stairwell. "Everyone good?" Max asked them both.

"Good to go, boss," they both acknowledged to their Captain.

Max looked at Jordy. "It's clear to the fifth floor exit boss," Jordy said.

CHAPTER 8

THE THREE OF THEM MOVED SLOWLY WITH THEIR AR-223 rifles pointed, covering each other looking down the stairwell and back the way they came. They were all in SEAL team mode and the joking had to be put aside for now.

Scott Matthews was still in the fourth floor office when he heard voices coming towards him. He carefully raised his head above one of the cubicle walls to see two mercenaries coming down the hallway. He knew they would find him if he stayed there, so he slowly crawled across the floor to another open office where he sat for a moment thinking what his next move would be.

He stood up cautiously and looked around to see the two armed men were moving away from him, saw the stairwell exit door and decided to go back up to the fifth floor. He crawled over to the door, raised up and saw that the mercenaries had their backs to him. He stood up and went through the door. Just as he managed to get through it, one of the men turned and saw the door closing behind him.

"He went up the stairs." The two mercenaries conferred and moved quickly through the door and up the stairwell.

Scott had just gotten to the fifth floor when he heard the two mercenaries clamoring up the stairs behind him. He looked around and the only place to hide was the men's bathroom he had hidden in previously, so he ran inside. He stood in the middle of the restroom and couldn't think what to do other than hide in the last stall and hope they wouldn't come in after him.

He locked the door behind him and climbed on top of the toilet seat so they couldn't see his feet from underneath the stall, then pulled out of his pocket a letter opener he had found while he was hiding in the office below. He thought if he was going to die, he was going to try to take someone with him. A gallant plan, he thought to himself.

The two mercenaries opened the door to the fifth floor, looked down the hallway and realized the only place Scott Matthews could have gone was into the men's restroom, and both walked in.

"We know you're in here, kid," one of the men said. "If we have to look for you, we're going to hurt you," he continued. "The boss said he wanted you alive, but he didn't say we couldn't put a few bruises on you," he said laughing with his partner. They slowly moved toward the stalls, kicking the first stall door open with a loud bang.

Max opened the door to the fifth floor, scanned the hallway and slowly walked out, his AR-223 aiming where he looked. He heard a loud noise down the hallway and headed toward it. He looked back at Jordy and Mikey. "Check on the hostages in the other hallway, but don't do anything until I get there," Max commanded.

"Copy that, boss," Jordy replied. Mikey and Jordy watched as Max headed towards the men's bathroom and Jordy couldn't resist commenting, "Thought we told you to go before we left, boss," he said with a grin.

Max turned and smiled at Jordy then put his finger to his lips giving him a soft "Shsssh!"

Max slowly and quietly opened the hallway restroom door then slightly cracked opened the interior door directly into the bathroom. He could smell the stale air of a boy's locker room then stepped in to see two big, heavily-armed men.

He quickly concluded they were part of the terrorists working for Tanaka Amikura. They were equipped with tactical gear and machine guns. Max observed them kicking in a bathroom stall door, obviously looking for someone, so quietly took out his handgun and slowly walked up behind the terrorist closest to him.

The second terrorist kicked in the third stall door just as Max said to the one he was behind, "Excuse me." The armed man turned to see a smiling Max Mason who promptly hit him across the jaw with his handgun, knocking him unconscious and dropping him to the floor. The second terrorist turned and saw Max right in front of him.

"Who the *fuck* are you?" he yelled.

Max smiled and replied sarcastically, "Just here for the party."

The terrorist turned his machine gun in Max's direction. Max grabbed it and pushed it up away from him just as it discharged several rounds into the ceiling. Max punched the mercenary in the stomach and ribs twice, then hit him hard in the face. The muscular man took the punch but returned one of his own to Max's jaw, spinning him around and knocking his handgun to the floor. Max came back with another punch to the mercenary's now swollen face and blocked his next punch with his other arm. The mercenary's knees buckled and Max struck him with another hard punch to his head, knocking him to the floor.

Max leaned over him and said with a grin, "That had to hurt," then punched him hard in the face one last time, knocking him unconscious, watching him fall face down on the floor of the bathroom.

He then walked over and picked his gun up off the floor and put it back in his holster.

Max felt there was someone still in one of the bathroom stalls and slowly moved to the fourth and last stall. Just as he grabbed the handle, the door burst open and Max saw a blade weapon coming towards his face.

Max stepped back but was grabbed and wrestled to the floor by a tall young man in a suit. Max had to keep the shiny blade from reaching his face, grabbing the man's wrist and punching him in the ribs. He then twisted the blade out of his hand and tossed it across the floor. Max thought to himself, "This kid knows how to fight a little."

Scott Mathews proceeded to land a forearm blow to Max's jaw. Max tossed the young man aside, got to his feet and rubbed his jaw thinking that was a good close quarters punch.

"I'm not going to let you kill her," he said to Max as they both got up off the bathroom floor.

"Kill who, kid?" Max asked confused, looking at the young man in front of him in a fighting stance.

Max looked at the young man and recognized the Rocky squirrel pin on his lapel. "SQUIRREL!" Max said loudly, smiling.

"Max, is that *you*?" Scott asked, relieved.

"Yeah, kid. What the hell are you doing here?"

"I'm here for the telethon. Got an invitation to speak from the President's daughter Stephanie," Scott explained.

Max looked at Scott Matthews, who was standing there brushing off his suit. "What did you mean you weren't going to let them kill her?"

Scott shyly looked the other way which Max remembered was his way of not wanting to tell him something.

"*Really?* You're involved with the President's daughter, Squirrel?" Max asked with a big smile. Scott turned red with embarrassment knowing Max figured out what he was doing there.

"It's all good kid. I was your age once many years ago," Max said laughing.

"I missed you Max, so did Tyler. Why did you disappear on us?" Scott asked sadly.

Max didn't have a really good reason other than he thought it was best after what Scott's family had been through the past five years.

"Nothing personal, kid. Just needed Mason family time, that's all."

Max smiled and walked towards the former President's son and gave him a hug.

"Nice to see you again kid. You grew up well."

Scott Matthews extended the hug and replied, "Good to see you too, Max."

"We need to get out of here before others come," Max said. "Help me tie these two idiots up and gag them."

After tying their wrists behind their backs tightly with plastic zip ties, then gagging them, Scott asked, "Where are we putting them, Max?"

Max smiled at Scott and opened the last stall door.

"Shall we?"

That got a big grin from Scott. The two dragged both of the terrorists into the stall and tied them both to the toilet, embarrassing them just a bit more.

Looking back to the stall as Max and he were leaving, Scott smiled toward it and said, "Assholes."

"What's going on boss? We heard gunfire?" Jordy asked Max through his earpiece.

"We're on our way, Lieutenant," Max replied, moving down the hallway with Scott Matthews in tow. Max had managed to take one of the bathroom terrorist's radios and could hear chatter from the others checking in from their assigned posts in the building.

"*We're,*' on our way, boss?" Mikey inquired confused. Just as Mikey finished his question, Max and Scott came around the corner and knelt down beside them both.

"Who's this, boss?" Jordy asked.

Max was just about to answer when Mikey said, "This is Scott Matthews, President Matthews's boy."

"Yep. How did you know?" Max asked Mikey.

"He was all over the news this week about coming to this shindig after what happened five years ago."

Scott looked at Mikey. "Are you Mikey Stevens on Family Firearms?"

Mikey smiled and looked at Max. "Another fan. What can I say, boss?" he said grinning.

"Wait a minute. You watch *his* show too, Squirrel?" Max asked surprised. "I thought your mom & dad didn't allow you to watch violent shows after what happened."

"I'm a teenager. Of course I watch shows I'm not supposed too," Scott said with a condescending smile.

"You got good taste, kid," Mikey said shaking Scott's hand.

"Can we get on with why we're here," Jordy interrupted, rolling his eyes at Mikey. "Remember the bad guys?" he asked with a grin. "And by the way, I'm Jordy, kid," he said to Scott shaking his hand.

"Oh, I haven't forgotten," Max replied to Jordy. "Squirrel and I left two tied up and unconscious in the bathroom," Max said with a grin looking at Scott.

"I see you haven't given up that "No Killing" code yet, boss" Jordy stated.

"It's not really a code, Lieutenant. It's more of a guideline. Let's deal with these security hostages, shall we gentlemen?" Max said, changing the subject.

The four of them moved slowly down the hallway to the other side of the building near the ballroom. Max kept Scott Matthews behind them because he was a civilian and didn't want him getting hurt if there was a confrontation or firefight with any terrorists along the way.

"What does it look like, Lieutenant?" Max asked.

Jordy looked over his computer screen attached to his arm. "I see three bad guys watching six hostages, including your girlfriend, boss."

"She's *not* my girlfriend," Max said insistently, giving Jordy a look.

"Who are they talking about, Max?" Scott asked, anxious to know.

"Agent Karen Tyler is one of the hostages in the hallway," Max replied to the concerned teenage boy.

"OH, SHIT!" Scott shouted. "That means Stephanie is in danger, Max. Tyler is her Secret Service protection. She's known about us from the beginning," he said nervously.

"Tyler knew about you two seeing each other?" Max asked surprised.

"Yeah. She didn't approve at first, but she eventually saw how we felt about each other and decided it was okay. She even started helping us see each other two or three times a month."

"Interesting" Max said with a smile.

"What's the plan, boss?" Jordy asked Max.

"We rescue the hostages and try not to get killed," Max replied with a grin.

"I like that plan, boss" Mikey said. Jordy smiled and nodded in agreement.

"Let's try to take them alive, guys," Max requested. Mikey and Jordy looked at one another and shrugged their shoulders and rolled their eyes.

"Show me what you got on screen, Lieutenant" Max commanded, ignoring the looks they both gave him.

Jordy typed on his small computer for a moment, then moved the screen towards Max so he could see it better as the hallway video camera came on to show them the hostage situation.

There were three armed terrorists with machine guns standing in front of six hostages, including Karen Tyler, sitting on the floor with their backs against the wall.

Max noticed that all the hostages had their hands secured in back of them, so he knew getting help from any of them was out of the question at this time.

"Looks like this is on us, guys," Max relayed to Jordy and Mikey in a low voice.

"They'll see us coming, boss," Jordy said looking at his video screen.

"Not necessarily, Lieutenant," Max replied grinning. "See the door behind them?"

Jordy, Mikey, and Scott looked at the video screen seeing the door behind the three terrorists that Max pointed out.

"That door goes into the GBN Agency Director's office. He has a side entrance down the other hallway where we can get in without being seen," Max explained.

Jordy smiled at Max. "I'm beginning to see where this is going, boss."

"We sneak out the door and take the three of them by surprise. No one has to die, gentlemen," Max said sternly.

Jordy and Mikey acknowledged Max's plan with an "Aye aye, sir," but weren't overly enthusiastic about it, Max noticed.

The four of them moved slowly back down the hallway away from the armed terrorists guarding the hostages, and came to a door with a plaque on the wall indicating Agency Director John Raymond's office.

Raymond was the overall Director of the Global Broadcasting Network, appointed by President Bradshaw two years ago.

Director Raymond was overseas visiting broadcasting affiliates and had appointed his Director of Broadcasting Operations Brian Jurgens to look after the charity telethon, so Max knew his office would be empty.

Just as they were about to go through the door Max heard a noise in the office across the hall from the Director's. Max looked at Jordy and Mikey and gave them the sign to cover the door.

Max noticed that this was Broadcast Operations Chief Marcus Grant's office and slowly moved towards the door with Mikey and Jordy on each side of it, guns poised.

Max pulled his handgun out of its holster and slowly turned the doorknob to the office. Max slung the door open to find Marcus Grant shredding papers on his desk nervously.

"I swear I didn't know what he was doing," Grant said out loud, seeing the gun pointed at him, raising his hands in the air.

"Didn't know what *who* was doing?" Max asked a confused Grant, standing there with his hands in the air.

Max, Jordy, Mikey and Scott Matthews hurried into Grant's office and shut the door behind them.

Realizing it was Max Mason pointing the gun at him, Grant got defensive and yelled. "Who the fuck do you think you are, Mason, pointing guns at me? Don't you know who I am?"

"Yeah, a dumb ass that's going to prison it seems,"Max answered as he smiled at his friends. "I never liked you, Grant. You're an arrogant kiss-ass that deserves what he gets." Max said to him harshly.

"I didn't know what Brian was doing. I'm innocent of all this," Grant stuttered.

"Interesting that Brian Jurgens is behind this scam with Tanaka," Max thought out loud. "Jurgens isn't that computer savvy, and Tanaka just wants to kill me," Max said to his three friends, ignoring Grant still standing behind his desk with his hands in the air.

"There's someone else we don't know about here, pulling Jurgens' strings," Max deduced. "We need to keep moving," he told them.

Max looked at his watch and understood they still had just under two hours before Tanaka's deadline but knew he needed to get back to the ballroom and all the hostages NOW.

"What about him, boss?" Jordy asked, looking at a now pissed off Marcus Grant.

"Leave him. Let him sweet talk his way out of his own mess," Max said looking Grant in the eyes and smiling.

"You know if Tanaka catches up to him, he's DEAD, boss," Mikey said, knowing Grant could hear him.

"Like I told you before, Commander, it's a guideline, not a code," Max said smiling at Grant as he walked out the door.

Mikey glanced over at Jordy and Scott and grinned, looked at Grant and shook his head. The three of them headed out the door behind Max, their guns pointed again.

"I won't forget this, Mason," Grant yelled angrily.

"Prison will *not* be kind to you," Mikey said to Grant, laughing as they all left his office and walked across the hall to the Director's door.

The four of them walked slowly and cautiously into the Agency Director's office looking around to make sure the terrorists guarding the hostages in the adjoining hallway didn't hear Grant's angry rant to Max. Max slowly opened the door, his gun pointed, and walked in.

"Clear," Max said in a low voice to his comrades, who followed him in and closed the door.

"Check the video again, Lieutenant." Max commanded.

"Nothing's changed, boss. They're right outside the door here," Jordy whispered.

"Scott, you stay here. Mikey, take the one on the left. Jordy, the one in the middle," Max commanded. "I'll take the one closest to Tyler on the right."

"Copy that boss," Mikey and Jordy replied."

Just as Max and his team were about to open the office door to the hallway to free the hostages, Jordy glanced at his video screen on his forearm one last time.

"*Wait*," he said with urgency, grabbing Max's arm before he opened the door.

The three terrorists had moved together to talk to one another and the situation was compromised.

"The three of them are talking about something, boss," Jordy said.

Max looked at the screen and saw Jordy made the right call to stop him because there wasn't a chance at surprise now.

The three terrorists looked at one another, and one said to the other two, "It's 8 o'clock. Samson said Tanaka wants us to kill these assholes now. Put blindfolds on them, then we'll shoot them."

They started putting black clothe blindfolds on each of the six security hostages. When they got to Tyler, she looked at the terrorist with contempt.

"What's the matter, asshole? Don't have the stomach to look us in the eye when you shoot us?" she said defiantly.

The terrorist ignored her and roughly put the blindfold over Tyler's eyes. Tyler tried shaking it off as he put it on but to no avail. Max watched this from Jordy's video screen and could wait no longer.

"We go in *now*" he ordered.

The three terrorists went back to their original spots in front of the hostages. They took out their magazines from their machine guns, checked the ammo and put them back in the guns.

This was Max's chance to go in before they had a chance to chamber a round into their weapons. Max, Jordy and Mikey walked out of the office and slowly got behind each terrorist undetected.

Nodding to one another, all three of them at the exact same time put a double-armed choke hold on all three terrorists making them gasp for air, their arms flailing to try to get away, eventually losing consciousness. Slowly the three terrorists were lowered to the ground unconscious, and Max and his team released them, standing over them.

Scott Matthews watched the whole thing unfold from the office doorway and was impressed as hell at how well Max and his friends worked together. "Cool," he thought to himself.

Max walked over to Tyler, still blindfolded and sitting on the floor, smiled and said to her, "After all we meant to one another, you don't call, you don't email, and you don't text."

"I know that voice," Tyler responded. "Max Mason! Untie me, you asshole," she said again defiantly.

"WOW, now is that anyway to talk in front of the children?" Max asked laughing.

Max slowly took the blindfold off of her and helped her to her feet, cutting the plastic cuffs from behind her back. Tyler rubbed her wrists to get the circulation going again, then smacked Max across the face.

"What the hell was that for?" Max asked surprised.

"That's for not calling me back five years ago," Tyler said with a grin. Jordy and Mikey looked at each other and smirked.

"What was that, you two?" Max asked them annoyed while rubbing his cheek.

"Nothing, boss," they both said grinning.

They then turned their attention back to the unconscious mercenaries, rolling them over and securing their wrists with their plastic cuffs. Scott walked out of the office and went over to Tyler.

"Where's Steph?" he asked.

"SCOTT!" Tyler said excited to see him safe. "Tanaka has her on the third floor," Tyler told him. "Are you okay, Scott?"

"Yeah. I mistakenly beat up Max in the bathroom," Scott said with a grin to Max.

"That's not too hard to do," Tyler said facetiously.

Jordy couldn't help himself and started laughing, then stopped when Max gave him an evil look.

"Sorry, boss," Jordy said with a smile. Max gave him a grin to let Jordy know it was okay.

Jordy walked by Max to observe the other side of the hallway and whispered, "I like this one boss. Can we keep her?"

Tyler walked past Max giving him a smile then went over to help untie the other security specialists she had been with. Max walked over to Charles Lee, took his blindfold off and helped him to his feet.

"Max, what the hell are you doing here? You're supposed to be on vacation?" Lee asked relieved.

"Long story. Are you okay, boss?" Max asked his friend.

Jordy heard what Max said and looked over at Mikey and said with a grin, "Looks like *our* boss has his *own* boss."

"Stay focused, Lieutenant," Max said to Jordy hearing what he said.

"Let's secure these assholes someplace where the Fed's can find them when they get in here," Max said to Mikey and Jordy.

"Aye aye, sir" they replied.

Tyler heard their response "Who the hell are you? Captain Hook?" she asked laughing.

"No, ma'am, He's *our* Captain," Mikey said to Tyler seriously.

"What's that supposed to mean?" she asked with a confused look at Max.

Jordy looked at her. "We're SEAL Team 2, ma'am. Captain Mason is our C.O." he said respectfully.

"It's okay Jordy, Mikey," Max said to them. "Allow me to introduce my team," he said proudly to Tyler. "This is Lieutenant Jordan Alexander, our communications, computer and medical specialist."

Jordy nodded his head in Tyler's direction and said, "Ma'am."

"And this rugged, handsome devil is Commander Michael Stevens, our demolition and weapons specialist," Max said with a smile.

"Ma'am. And thanks, boss," Mikey said with a smile.

"Wait. I know you," Tyler said to Mikey. "You're the Outdoor Network guy," she said with a smile, a little star-struck.

"*Really*? Does everyone watch your show, Commander?" Max asked laughing.

"They *do* love me, boss, And, yes ma'am, I am," Mikey said beaming with pride.

"We've been activated and sent in by Defense Secretary Cartwright and President Bradshaw to recover the hostage children and GBN employees," Max informed her.

"I have to get Stephanie Bradshaw and Kristina Cartwright out of here Max. It's my job," Tyler said sternly.

"It's *our* job now, Agent Tyler," Max said pulling rank on her.

"I got news for you. I don't work for you, CAPTAIN MASON," she said angrily.

Tyler walked over, grabbed one of the unconscious terrorist's handguns out of his holster, as well as three magazines, and looked at Max.

"I'm going after MY charges. You're welcome to come along CAPTAIN. Just stay out of MY way," Tyler said, com-promisingly but sternly. Max looked at Jordy and Mikey, who both nodded to their Captain.

"Okay, but we have to go to the ballroom and free the hostages there first before we head down to the third floor," Max said to Tyler.

"Yeah, I can do that. I kind of have a score to settle there," she said with a grin.

Jordy looked at Mikey. "Can we marry this girl?" he said with a smile.

"I don't think the boss is gonna like you chasing his girlfriend," Mikey said loud enough for Max to hear.

"She's *not* my girlfriend," Max said to his men, starting to turn red.

"No, but I could've been if you'd bought me dinner that night five years ago," Tyler said with a smile as she walked by the three of them heading to the ballroom ahead of them. Max smiled then gave Jordy and Mikey a dirty look. Jordy and Mikey smiled at each other and followed behind, Scott Matthews and the rescued security specialists bringing up the rear.

They slowly made their way to the ballroom. The double doors were still open and you could see everyone sitting at tables, some laying their heads on them.

Max looked at Tyler and informed her that his team would go in first and eliminate the threat before everyone else went in. That didn't sit too well with her. She wanted Samson alive to make him pay for how he treated the hostages while she was one of them.

"I'm going in with you, Max," she said sternly. Max didn't want to fight with her anymore, so he conceded letting her go with them because he knew she could take care of herself in a firefight if it came down to that.

"What do you have, Lieutenant?" Max asked Jordy as he stared at his wrist computer screen.

"I got three armed hostiles in the room, boss," Jordy replied. "One on the left, one on the right, and one standing beside a lone female hostage. Jordy looked at Max and showed him the situation on his video screen.

"REALLY," Max said out loud. Tyler looked at him with a confused look on her face.

"He's fine. Just go with it," Jordy said to her with a grin.

"Jordy, take the one on the left. Mikey, the one on the right," Max commanded. "I'll take the one in the middle," he said sighing heavily. "Tyler, stay behind me, please."

"On my mark, gentlemen," Max said looking at his two men.

Waiting a moment he commanded, "GO," and the four of them moved quickly into the ballroom. Jordy shot first, hitting his target right between the eyes, killing him instantly and watching him hit the floor. Mikey's shot was almost identical to Jordy's, dropping the terrorist on the right side of the ballroom floor instantly.

Just as Max was about to take his shot, the terrorist Tyler knew as Samson grabbed the nearest hostage, put his gun to her head and screamed, "DROP YOUR WEAPONS OR I'LL KILL THIS BITCH!"

Mikey and Jordy moved up next to Karen Tyler, their guns still pointed at the last terrorist in the room, watching what Max was going to do next.

"I SWEAR I'LL KILL THIS BITCH IF YOU DON'T DROP YOUR GUNS... RIGHT NOW!" Samson shouted at Max.

Tyler recognized the hostage as Stacy Michaels, Jonathan Mayer's assistant.

"Shouldn't have called her a bitch," both Mikey and Jordy said together. Tyler heard them and looked at them both strangely.

Max looked at the young woman being held with a gun pointed to her head, seeing her smile and wink at him. Max rolled his eyes knowing how this was going to end.

The young woman grabbed Samson's arm around her neck, then took his gun, grabbing the slide so he couldn't fire it. She twisted it from his hand and smacked him hard in the face with it, then tossed it across the floor.

Samson was bleeding from his nose profusely and screamed, "YOU BROKE MY NOSE, BITCH!"

Again she smiled at Max, who stood there watching curiously, shaking his head, continuing to point his AR rifle at the two. The mercenary tried punching her, but she grabbed his arm and twisted it to bend him over where she sent her knee into his face.

She then came down with her elbow on his twisted arm, producing a loud crack followed by his screams of pain, breaking his arm.

Max continued to watch the young woman manhandle the large muscular terrorist with ease, glancing back at Jordy and Mikey who were both watching the scene, intently smiling.

Stacy again brought another knee to his jaw as he whimpered in pain, knocking him unconscious, his body dropping on the floor by her feet.

She looked at Samson slumped on the floor, shifted her skirt down some, flipped her long brown hair out of her face before she started walking towards Max and his colleagues.

Max stood there looking at the young woman, watching her compose herself, closed his eyes and shook his head again several times.

"Who the HELL *is* this woman?" Tyler asked out loud, confused by what she just witnessed.

The young woman looked down at Samson, smiled and said, "That's for smacking me across the face, asshole." Then she walked over to Max and said, "Hi, Daddy," and kissed him on the cheek.

Tyler looked at both Jordy and Mikey.

"Daddy?" she asked.

"Yes. *Daddy*," Jordy replied with a confirming nod and smile from Mikey.

Stacy Michaels was, in fact, Stacy Marie Mason, Max's 21-year-old daughter.

"Did you have to hurt him so bad sweetheart?" Max asked with a scowl on his face.

Stacy smiled at her father. "He shouldn't have smacked me so *hard*," she replied with a sly grin.

Max hugged his baby girl tight. Stacy loved hugging her father. He was always so comforting and protective when he did. He looked at her and said, "Hello Princess, are you okay?"

"Yeah, I'm okay, Daddy," she said with a smile. Then she pushed away from him and hit him hard in the chest.

"What was that for?" Max asked surprised, putting his hand on his chest.

"You're late. I sent that text to you over an hour and a half ago. Where have you been?" she asked annoyed. "Did you bring *my* bag?" she asked with a smile.

"Yes. Mikey has it with him," Max replied, still a bit annoyed she hit him.

"Very cool. Thank you, Daddy," she said smiling enthusiastically.

"What are you doing here in the first place, Stacy?" Max asked as she was walking over to Mikey and Jordy.

122

"Hi, Uncle Jordy," she said, totally ignoring her father's question.

"Hi, sweetie," Jordy replied, giving Stacy a hug.

"Hi, Uncle Mikey. How's Aunt Faye?" she asked, also hugging him.

"Hi, sweetheart. She's doing great. Wants to know when you want to be on the show again."

"Am I the *only one* who *doesn't* watch your show?" Max asked Mikey frustrated.

"I guess so, boss," Mikey said with a frown on his face.

"Really, Commander, the boo boo lip? I thought she only gave *me* that." Max said, laughing as he looked at Stacy smiling at him.

"Daddy, you need to watch Uncle Mikey's show. It's awesome. I got to pet a big bear on his show," Stacy told him beaming from ear to ear. Mikey handed Stacy one of the black duffle bags they brought and she said, "Thank you," with a smile.

Max looked at Mikey with a disapproving stare. "A BEAR COMMANDER? REALLY?"

"He was a little bitty fellow, boss. I swear," Mikey replied, giggling but knowing Max wasn't happy.

Tyler was standing beside Jordy and looked at him confused.

"You're her Uncles?" she asked.

"We're actually her and Jacob's godfathers," Jordy explained to her. "They've been calling us 'Uncles' since she was 6 and Jacob was 8 years old."

"Can we get back to my question, young lady? Why are you here in this situation?" Max asked concerned.

"I came with my boss, Jonathan Mayer. I've been working as his assistant and secretary for almost two years down at the beach," Stacy explained to Max. "Remember that accounting job I told you I got down at the beach? This is the job," Stacy said to her dad.

Stacy placed the black duffle bag on a table and opened it. She pulled out a sealed plastic bag with clothes in it, opened it and pulled the black pants out.

She kicked off her high heels and slowly slid the pants up her legs, buttoning them under the skirt she was wearing, then dropping her skirt to the floor. She put her black tank top on, then her tactical boots, and continued to pull things out of the duffle bag, placing them on the table.

"This whole family reunion thing is real touching, not to mention entertaining, but it's not getting the President's daughter away from that psycho Tanaka," Tyler said getting annoyed. "We have *no* clue what we're up against right now. We need a plan Mason," she demanded looking at him, then the others.

"Stacy?" Max queried his daughter while smiling at Tyler.

"There are at least 27 mercenaries, Tanaka. . . oh yeah, and Brian Jurgens," Stacy said. "There are only two hostiles now at each entrance on the first floor guarding the X-127 explosives wired to the doors."

"How do you know its X-127?" Tyler asked, knowing how devastating that explosive could be.

"I over heard Samson telling one of his men on the radio to be careful or the whole building would go up with them in it," she replied with a grin. "The *only explosive* I know that will do that is X-127." Stacy explained.

"Continue please," Max requested.

"Mostly 9mm side arms, AR's and MP-5's, but most of them are wearing body armor, so shooting them means in the head if you want them to stay down," Stacy said. "Tanaka Amikura is carrying two long Japanese samurai swords, one black and the other white with a dragon carving on the end."

Tyler was getting pissed off at the time they were wasting not going after the President's daughter Stephanie and spoke up.

"Why the HELL are we listening to someone who ONLY fetches coffee and sets up meetings?" she asked angrily.

"EXCUSE ME!" Stacy responded with a stern look at Tyler.

Max looked at Tyler and laughed. "You don't understand, Karen.

"I know. I'm not relying on intel from a secretary like the rest of you are," Tyler replied.

Jordy and Mikey looked at Tyler and smiled. Then Jordy piped in saying "She's NOT a secretary."

"She's Naval Intelligence," Max said proudly, looking at Tyler and flashing Stacy a proud smile.

"I like her, Daddy. She's spunky," said Stacy with a smile as she finished getting dressed, putting on her Kevlar armored vest and buckling up her twin SA-XD holstered gun belt. "So, who's the hottie?" she asked her dad with a grin.

"This is Agent Karen Tyler of the Secret Service," Max said to her.

"NOT HER," she said with a big smile looking at Tyler. "HIM!" Stacy pointed out with a devilish grin, turning her head and nodding over her father's shoulder. Max had not realized that Scott Matthews had come into the room by now and was standing behind him.

Tyler looked at Max. "So you think *I'm* a hottie?" she asked him smiling, glancing over at Stacy who returned the grin with a wink.

"Smooth, boss," Jordy whispered, passing him to look down the hallway. Max knew he was turning a bit red but knew he had to stay on task.

"It's about time, Daddy. It's *only* taken *five years*," Stacy said to her father, approving the potential relationship. "Let's get back to the hottie. Who is he?" Stacy asked with a smile, loading her MP-5 machine gun and adjusting the laser sight on it.

"This is Scott Matthews," Max replied, watching Scott shake his daughter's hand.

"No fucking way! THEE Scott Matthews? The son of President Matthews?" she asked curiously.

Stacy looked at Scott. "You grew up well," she said with a grin. "You like older women?" she asked jokingly to Scott with a smile.

"You didn't finish telling me why you're here with Mayer,"Max asked his daughter again.

"It's strictly business, Dad," she said in a condescending tone.

"What is your mission, Ensign Mason?" Max ordered sternly.

"Really, Dad? You're going to pull rank?" she asked getting mad.

"You're not just here to hold Mayer's books and get him coffee are you Ensign" he asked.

Max didn't like the fact that his only daughter was in the same building with a man who had been trying to kill him for over 20 years. He knew it wasn't a coincidence.

"My mission is on a need-to-know basis, sir," she replied standing at attention.

"In the hallway, Ensign…NOW," Max commanded.

"Aye aye, Captain Mason," Stacy said, pissed at her dad.

Stacy followed Max into the hallway away from everyone and continued to stand at attention in front of him. They both looked down the hallway on both sides of them to see exit doors to the stairwells.

"Tanaka is here to kill me, nothing else," Max stated to her. "He's not here for any ransom money, whatever that shit is about. He killed that Congressman on TV to get MY attention, nothing more. Whatever your mission is, you have to stand down so you don't get hurt," Max said concerned.

"Permission to speak freely, sir," Stacy Mason asked still standing at attention.

"Granted" he repkied.

"The Admiral placed this mission in my hands, sir. I'm afraid I *only* answer to him, Captain," she said defiantly.

"Okay. We can fix that," Max said with a grin. Max pulled out his SAT cell phone and dialed the Admiral's private number.

The phone was answered on the other end.

"Captain, have you gotten my granddaughter out of there safely?" Admiral Cartwright asked Max, concerned.

"Not yet, Admiral. Calling to give you and the President an update and to help with a possible problem," Max explained.

"Continue Captain," Cartwright said.

"We have safely secured 46 hostages from the fifth floor ballroom, eliminating 11 terrorists, five of them dead, sir," Max said over the phone. "We have reasonable intel to believe that GBN Director of Broadcasting Brian Jurgens and his assistant Marcus Grant are responsible for the ransom idea, sir," Max continued.

"Good work, Captain," the Admiral said.

Just as Max was about to ask the Admiral about Stacy's mission, two terrorists came through BOTH stairwell exit doors at the same time.

Without hesitation both Max and Stacy drew their handguns and fired two rounds, each at opposite ends of the hallway, dropping both of the terrorists to the floor with gunshots to the head.

"Mine hit the floor first," Stacy said with a smile.

"*Really*, Ensign?" Max said to Stacy with an intense look on his face.

"Well, he did," she said turning her eyes away from his.

Max returned to the Admiral on the phone. "We need to go Admiral, but there seems to be an unexpected wrinkle here in the form of my daughter Stacy saying she's under orders to you, sir," Max declared.

"That's correct, Captain. I recruited Ensign Mason over a year ago to recon the Mayer Financial Corporation down in Virginia Beach, and to specifically keep an eye on Jonathan Mayer, the company's CEO," Admiral Cartwright said. "We had our suspicions that Mayer was laundering money for terrorist organizations in the Pacific area. Ensign Mason got us some valuable intel on Mayer over the past three months concerning this charity telethon, Captain. You should be very proud of her."

"I'm always proud of my children Admiral, but what I'm seriously concerned about is that YOU, Admiral, put her up against a sociopath corporate thief with serious ties to possibly the most dangerous assassin in the world who wants ME dead without even a word to me, SIR," Max said with respect, but angry.

"We can continue this awkward conversation at a later date, Captain," the Admiral said, understanding how Max was feeling.

"Yes, sir. We *will*," Max said annoyed.

"I need you to transfer her to my team, Admiral," Max requested.

"Wait a minute, sir," Stacy complained out loud, hoping the Admiral could hear her.

"Hand her the phone, Captain," Cartwright asked.

Stacy took the phone and spoke. "Ensign Mason here, sir."

"Ensign Mason, this is Admiral Cartwright. You are hereby reassigned to Captain Mason's SEAL team for the duration of this operation. You will now take your orders from him," he informed her, because he knew he now owed Max. "Please put Captain Mason back on the phone and good luck, Ensign," he said.

"Aye aye, sir," Stacy replied, handing the phone back to her father, now her commanding officer.

Max took the phone from her. "Admiral," he said.

"*Her* mission is now *your* mission, Captain. Find out why Mayer is there and what he's planning with the charity money Tanaka has already collected."

"Yes, sir," Max replied.

Max and Stacy returned to the ballroom and Max looked at Charles Lee. "I need you and the rest of these security representatives to get these hostages down to the first floor. My two guys will go down with you." Max gave Lee a loaded 9mm handgun he'd taken from one of the captured terrorists and two full magazines. "Remember what we did at the range," he said to Lee.

"What do we do when we get to the first floor?" Lee asked Max.

"Wait until my guys can get one of the bombs defused, then get everyone out of the building."

"What about Tanaka and the hostages on the third floor, boss?" Jordy asked.

"I'll take care of Tanaka. This has gone on long enough," Max replied angrily.

"Once Mikey defuses the explosives on one of the doors, you two get back up to the third floor immediately and help with the young hostages," he said to Jordy.

"Aye aye, sir," Jordy replied with a nod from Mikey.

"I'm going with you, Max," Tyler said sternly.

"No, you're not," Max replied, staring at Tyler.

"Once again, I don't work for you, Captain Mason," Tyler said. "MY job is to get President Bradshaw's daughter and her friend out of here safely. YOUR job is to get ALL the hostages out of here safely, not mine."

"Technically, my job IS to get the President's daughter and the Admiral's granddaughter out of here safely," Max said to her, remembering Admiral Cartwright's personal plea to him and his men.

Max thought about what she said and knew she wasn't going to listen to him, as he pulled out a MP-5 machine gun and several loaded magazines from the black duffle bag and handed them to Tyler. "Please don't make me regret this," Max told her with a smile.

"I'm going too, Max," Scott Matthews said boldly.

"That's not happening, Squirrel."

"I promised Stephanie I would be there for her. I'm not letting her down," the tall teenager said. "I swear, Max, if you send me away I'll sneak away my first opportunity and come back for her," Scott said getting angry.

"I'll keep an eye on him, Daddy," Stacy said, thinking how noble Scott was being for his girlfriend.

Max looked at how defiant Scott was being, taking up for himself like he did all those years ago and wanting to protect someone he loved, and smiled. "You do everything Ensign Mason tells you to do. Do you understand?" he said to Scott.

"Yes sir," a relieved Scott Matthews replied.

"Stacy, don't be going all Rambo on these terrorists, do you understand? I need you BOTH out of here in one piece. Copy that, Ensign?" Max said, smiling to his daughter.

"Yes, sir. Copy that," Stacy replied with a smile.

"Mikey, give Scott a gun and a couple of mags out of the bag," Max commanded.

Mikey handed Scott Matthews a SA-XD handgun and two 20-round magazines. "Try not to shoot yourself in the foot kid," Mikey said with a grin.

"Do you know how to use that?" Stacy asked, watching Scott look at the gun in his hand.

Scott ejected the magazine from the gun, checked the ammo, reinserted the mag, pulled the slide back to load a round, then looked at Stacy. "You're not the ONLY kid your father taught how to use a gun all those years ago," he said with a smile.

Stacy smiled back at him. "I knew I was going to like you."

"Everyone set to do this?" Max asked.

"Copy that, boss," both Jordy and Mikey said.

Max looked at Scott, Stacy and Tyler. "All three of you leave Tanaka alone. He's mine. Get the children and your charges down to the first floor as fast as possible," Max said to them. "And Mikey, you have to get that fucking bomb off the door."

"Aye aye, boss" Mikey replied giving him a playful salute.

"Everyone be safe," Max said, taking Tyler's hand, squeezing it and smiling at her.

"You too," Tyler said as she smiled and squeezed his hand back. "And remember you still owe me dinner."

Max turned and looked at Stacy with a smile and said, "Love you Princess. Please be careful."

"Love you too, Daddy," she said hugging him, kissing him again on the cheek. Stacy looked at Jordy and Mikey and smiled. They both smiled back at their goddaughter and nodded.

Jordy looked at everyone and said with a big grin, "Time to make the donuts," remembering an old TV commercial he loved, trying to lighten the mood.

Max looked at Jordy and Mikey and smiled. "Guess it's time to poke the bear in the cage," he told them.

Mikey laughed. "This should be fun, boss."

"You *do* understand, boss, that's a public channel you're about to broadcast on, that even the Feds outside will hear your conversation," Jordy said.

Max gave him a sheepish smile. "I know." Max took the radio out that he had taken from one of the unconscious, captured terrorists, pushed the transmitter button, and spoke.

"Hey, Tanaka. I understand you've been asking about me. What can I do for you, asshole?" he said with a grin, looking around at everyone.

CHAPTER 9

TANAKA AMIKURA WAS PACING BACK AND FORTH behind an angry and nervous Stephanie Bradshaw who was still sitting in the chair in the center of the TV studio stage when he heard a familiar voice come over one of his guard's radios a few feet away. He motioned to the guard standing behind Jonathan Mayer to hand him his radio, pushed the transmitter button and spoke.

"*Finally*, my brother. I was beginning to believe you were taking the coward's way by not facing me," he said with a smile, releasing the button to hear his response.

Max Mason's voice could be heard through the entire room from Tanaka's radio.

"First of all, you psychotic asshole, I'm NOT your brother," he said harshly.

"My father thought of you as a son, so that makes us brothers," Tanaka replied, grinning holding the button down and releasing it again to hear Max's comment.

"I NEVER was, NEVER will be" Max continued. "You killed several good friends of mine tonight. I want you to understand I'm going to bury you in the deepest hole I can find," Max said angrily to Tanaka.

"I understand over the years you preferred not to take a life when you *could* have, my brother," Tanaka stated, smiling as he put his lips closer to the radio.

"I'm thinking real hard about changing that philosophy with *you*," Max said into the radio, looking at both Stacy and Tyler still sitting there.

"My father's sword was yours for the taking. Why didn't you take it? *And* the clan?" Tanaka asked, knowing everyone around him could see this conversation was starting to anger him.

"Because it wasn't mine to take. It belonged to YOU or your sister. You couldn't see past your petty jealousy to understand that," Max answered, releasing the transmitter button and lowering the radio from his mouth.

Max thought for a moment, then brought the radio back to his lips. "You killed your father for no other reason than jealousy and rage, Tanaka. YOU will face justice for your actions," Max said.

"My father was a fool. His death sent my sister to live with YOU, and he taught me to KILL...then decided what he taught me was wrong," Tanaka said angrily. "My father went against the old ways -- the way of the ninja," Tanaka yelled into his radio angrily.

"You're such an arrogant prick. Your father was smart to send Yuki to my family so *you* couldn't corrupt the ideas he taught her," Max said into his radio to a now fuming Tanaka Amikura.

Max remembered Yuki Amikura as a beautiful young girl who was practically a sister to both Stacy and Jacob when they lived in Manila. Sensei Amikura put a request in his will that upon his death, Max and his wife would take care of Yuki until his brother - Yuki's uncle - could retrieve her and take her back to Japan, because he felt her brother's influence on her could have serious consequences later in her life.

"Why don't we discuss this face to face, my brother, so I can give you my father's sword personally like he always wanted?" Tanaka asked.

"I'll be right down, you piece of shit" Max replied into the radio.

Max checked his AR rifle and handgun, looked at everyone and gave Tyler a wink. "I believe I got his attention."

Max gave everyone the okay to move the ballroom hostages down through the stairwell with Jordy on point, and Mikey bringing up the rear, AR-223s pointing front and back. Max, Stacy, Tyler and Scott Matthews waited until everyone had gone through the door before they went through behind them. "Tyler take the rear" Max commanded. Tyler dropped back behind Scott and Stacy, her MP-5 machine gun pointing behind them.

Outside in the command center across the street from the GBN building, Secret Service Director Dwayne Marshall and FBI Director Michael James were informed by the communications officer that he had recorded some significant conversation with the terrorist in charge and an unknown person, who seemed to have a grudge with him, inside the building.

"Play it back for us," Marshall commanded. Marshall put the headphones on as the officer rewound the recording. The audio came through Marshall's headphones and he had a confused look, recognizing the voice. "MAX MASON!" he said out loud taking off the headphones and tossing them on the table in front of the officer.

"Who the *hell* is Max Mason?" Director James asked.

"Max Mason worked for me almost five years ago. He was a *really* good agent until that fiasco with former President Matthews's son," Marshall explained.

"The death of the President's son by the suicide bomber. Now I remember him," James said to Marshall.

"He took the fall for that, even though it wasn't his fault, and took an early retirement. My career took a serious hit because of him," Marshall said out loud with some animosity. "I heard he took a security job with one of the Federal agencies about a year ago. Now it's all starting to make sense."

Marshall looked at the communications officer with a scowl.

"Get me Max Mason's Federal employment file immediately, Lieutenant," he demanded.

"Yes, sir" he said as he started typing furiously for Marshall.

"Do you think he's working for the terrorists?" James asked.

"Not a chance. He's too much of a fucking Boy Scout," Marshall replied with a grin. "But I bet Admiral Cartwright had something to do with this. HE was Mason's commanding officer with the SEAL's many years ago before he worked for me. We need to head back to the White House and discuss this development with the President."

Marshall looked at the officer. "Have someone bring our car around, Lieutenant."

"Right away, Director," the young officer replied.

Max, Stacy, Tyler and Scott Matthews stood outside the third floor stairwell door leading to the main TV studio down the long hallway. Max knew that's where the child hostages, terrorists and Tanaka would be . . . waiting for him.

Mikey, Jordy and the rest of the ballroom hostages slowly continued down the stairs to the first floor. Max looked at Mikey who was behind everyone.

"Good luck, Commander" giving him a nod.

Mikey nodded in acknowledgement to his captain.

Stacy and Tyler continued keeping their eyes and guns focused up the stairwell they had just come from, watching for anyone that may surprise them from behind.

Max got on his knees and slowly opened the door, peeking out into the long third floor hallway. "It seems clear," he said to the three of them over his shoulder. He then turned and looked at the three of them.

"I need all three of you to listen carefully," Max asked. "I need you to wait ten minutes before you come down the hallway. I have a score to settle with Tanaka concerning his father."

"You said to *never* make a mission personal," Stacy said to her father.

"I still believe that sweetheart, but this is something I owe Sensei Amikura." he said.

"I remember him. He was always sweet to me. Used to give me flowers and taught Jake martial arts before you did," Stacy remembered.

"Then you understand why I owe him to right HIS wrong with Tanaka," Max replied.

"I do. Just be careful," Stacy said to her father.

Max looked at Tyler who grinned and seemed to understand. "You still owe me dinner," she said with a smile.

"It's a date," he said to her with a grin.

"Who said anything about a date? Be careful, Max. He wants to kill you . . . badly" she replied with a concerned look on her face.

Max looked at Scott Matthews. "Your mom, dad and Steven would be *very* proud of you right now, Squirrel," Max said to the tall teenager with a smile. "Rescue your girlfriend and get the Hell out. Deal?" Max asked putting his hand on his shoulder.

"Deal," Scott replied.

Max looked back at Tyler smiling. "By the way, we need to have a discussion about you playing cupid with those two," Max said to her laughing. Tyler blushed and smiled.

"I love you, Daddy. Don't be silly with him," Stacy said to Max, concerned as she grabbed his hand. Max laughed at his daughter's comment because she knew him too well.

"Sweetheart, have you met me?" Max said laughing, squeezing her hand back to reassure her.

Max checked his weapons and smiled at Stacy. "I love you too, Princess," he said before slowly opening the stairwell door and walking out into the hallway where he immediately put himself against the wall, a tactic every military and law enforcement officer knew to do in a criminal conflict.

Stacy checked her watch and looked at Tyler and Scott. "Ten minutes starting now," she said.

Max continued to slowly move down the long hallway looking repeatedly in both directions with his AR 223 rifle. He glanced back at the stairwell door as it slowly closed, hoping that everyone would be safe.

As Max slowly walked down the hallway towards the auditorium he could hear a faint whispering as he approached the audio engineer's lounge on the right side of the building. Knowing that Tanaka's men had gone through every room on this floor and had rounded up the remaining hostages, placing them up in the ballroom with everyone else, Max thought these voices could be a couple of Tanaka's men waiting for him.

Max stood at the side of the lounge door and looked down the hallway where he could see the big security mirror up on the wall showing three armed terrorist's at the end of the long hallway on the other side. Max noticed they were guarding the auditorium entrance doors and knew he would have to deal with the three of them in order to get to Tanaka Amikura.

Max quickly went inside the engineer's lounge, his AR rifle pointing in all directions, when he was surprised by two people hiding behind the personal staff lockers.

"Don't shoot! Don't shoot!" they shouted with their hands in the air.

Max lowered his rifle seeing a man and a woman walking towards him, their hands high in the air.

"You can put your hands down. I'm one of the good guys," Max said, suddenly recognizing the two people coming towards him.

"Max? Is that you?" the man asked seeing Mason standing there in full tactical gear with a machine gun pointing at them just a second before.

"Yeah, it's me, Jimmy," Max replied smiling. Max knew that Jimmy Collins was a broadcasting engineer who ran the audio boards for the various language services radio programs. He and Max had a love for the same baseball and football teams and talked daily about them when they saw each other in the hallways.

"What are you doing here, Max? Why are you dressed like that?" the young woman standing behind Jimmy asked hesitantly, still scared that the terrorists might find them.

"Let's just say I'm in the wrong place at the right time," Max said to her smiling. Max knew that the young woman was Natalie Korsa, another audio engineer that worked with Jimmy. She was a married mother of two kids who Max had known for a couple of years while at GBN.

"We need to move you two downstairs and get you both out of here," Max said walking back to the doorway and glancing at the hallway mirror to see one of the terrorists heading their way.

"I'm afraid we may have a little problem," Max said to them both with a sheepish grin, knowing the terrorist was going to find the three of them in the room.

"I need you both to trust me and sit at the table in front of me," Max asked as he started taking his tactical gear off and placing it on the floor in the corner of the room. The only thing he kept was the large tactical knife that he slid in his belt in the front of his pants.

Max started talking to them both about their families to distract them for what was about to happen as the terrorist walked in hearing the conversation as Max stood with his back towards him.

"Very slowly put your hands where I can see them," the armed man said to the three of them as he came into the room.

Max smiled at Jimmy and Natalie then nodded for them to do as the man said, watching as they both raised their arms above their heads. The terrorist watched the two of them raise their hands just as Max quickly spun around, pulled the knife from his belt and slid it straight into the terrorist's throat as he grabbed the trigger guard of his machine gun so the terrorist couldn't get a shot off to warn the other two at the auditorium door.

Max watched as the terrorist slowly died, his eyes starring into his as he made quiet gurgling sounds as blood oozed down Max's knife hand. The dead terrorist fell to the floor at Max's feet as Jimmy and Natalie watched in shock and horror at what Max had just done to another human being.

Jimmy stood up from the table and looked at Max stunned, as his GBN colleague bent over, pulled his knife out of the dead man's throat and wiped the blood on the man's military style jacket.

"Who the *fuck* are you, Max?"

Max walked over to his tactical gear and started putting his Kevlar vest and tactical gun belt back on, and looked Jimmy in the eye saying with a smile "Just someone trying to do the right thing," he answered as he picked up his AR rifle from the floor.

Max looked out the doorway one more time and saw that the other two terrorists hadn't moved from the auditorium door, then looked back at his two friends.

"Let's go, you two."

Max touched the com link in his ear, turning it back on.

"Mikey, do you copy?" he asked smiling at the two scared engineers.

"Right here, boss," Mikey Stevens said into Max's ear.

"I have two friendlies here on the third floor I need you to extract for me. Copy?" Max asked as Jimmy Collins and Natalie Korsa listened beside him.

"I'll meet them at the second floor stairway door, boss," Mikey replied.

"Copy that, Commander," Max responded with another grin to his two friends standing there.

"My colleague will meet you both and get you safely out of here," Max said to both of them smiling and holding open the third floor stairwell door.

They shook Max's hand and told him to be careful, then headed down the stairs towards Mikey as Max turned and walked back towards the hallway.

Max came to the other hallway and slowly looked around the corner to see another terrorist had joined the other two standing guard with automatic weapons at the auditorium door leading into the main TV broadcasting studio.

Max could see that the three of them were wearing Kevlar armored vests. He turned back against the wall and thought for a moment.

Max closed his eyes took a deep breath, let it out and walked around the corner firing three rounds from his rifle, hitting all three of them in the chest. Because of the silencer on his rifle, no one in the TV studio heard his shots, and the three mercenaries didn't have a chance to get a shot off. Max knew his shots didn't kill them because of their vests, but he knew they seriously knocked the wind out of each of them and he had to subdue them quickly before they got back up. He practically ran to the three of them laying in front of the studio door, saw the first one stirring on the floor and promptly apologized.

"Sorry about this," Max said right before he hit him square in the jaw with the butt of his rifle, knocking him completely unconscious again.

Max moved to the next one who was starting to get up on his knees and also hit him in the face with his rifle, knocking him back down to the floor unconscious.

The third mercenary managed to get to his feet but was still disoriented facing the door. Max put his AR rifle against the wall and drew his handgun from its holster. Max quietly walked up behind him now holding the SA-XD handgun in his hand said quietly, "Excuse me," and promptly hit him across the jaw with the butt of the handgun as he turned, knocking him out and to the floor with his comrades.

Max quickly flipped the three unconscious men over onto their stomachs and cuffed their wrists behind them with plastic cuffs.

He figured they wouldn't wake up for a while in their condition, three less terrorists he had to worry about.

Stacy, still in the third floor stairwell, anxiously glanced at her watch and saw that only five minutes had expired. She then looked at Tyler and said, "I'm going in now."

Tyler grabbed her arm, smiled and told her, "Trust your father's instincts. He knows what he's doing."

"I hate waiting, and he *knows* it," Stacy said smiling, but still worried.

"I know. Me too. And I've been waiting for Max Mason a lot longer than you have," Tyler replied with a big grin.

Max slowly and cautiously opened the door to the main TV studio, walked in and knelt down, looking at the stage from a small walkway that wrapped around the stage above the control room. There were stairs on both sides of the walkway leading down to the stage.

Max noticed at least 15 rows of audience seating with no cover standing between him and the stage. He discreetly looked into the open-windowed control room seeing at least two armed mercenaries inside with the engineers and other hostages.

Max looked back down on the stage to see the long table with children and teenagers sitting behind it, with microphones in front of them, and three mercenaries standing in back of them. He could see from his perch that on the right side of the stage a lone man sat in a chair with two mercenaries watching over him. He wasn't sure who the man was but suspected it was Jonathan Mayer.

Max could see that a few feet away from him sitting in the center of the stage was Stephanie Bradshaw, the President's daughter. He also recognized one of the teenagers sitting at the table to be Kristina Cartwright, the Admiral's granddaughter. He remembered them both from pictures the Admiral sent to his SAT phone earlier. He saw that there were at least seven armed mercenaries and nine hostages, not counting those in the control room or the camera operators on stage.

Max turned his focus to the tall, stylish Asian man dressed in all white pacing impatiently behind Stephanie Bradshaw.

"*Tanaka Amikura,*" Max said to himself.

Tanaka stopped pacing abruptly and stood directly behind Stephanie Bradshaw's chair for a moment. He looked up the stairs towards the control room, then motioned to one of the mercenaries keeping Jonathan Mayer sitting in his chair to come over to him.

"He's here somewhere in the studio," Tanaka said quietly to the guard. "I can feel his presence. Take another man and search the room," Tanaka ordered.

As the mercenary was walking away Tanaka grabbed his arm and whispered, "I want him alive. Do you understand?" The mercenary nodded to Tanaka, then motioned to one of the guards watching the children, and the two of them talked for a moment before disappearing backstage.

"Welcome, my brother, I'm so pleased you could join us," Tanaka said loudly looking up into the studio air.

Max realized he lost the element of surprise and wondered how long Tanaka knew he was there. Max's question was answered rather quickly as the two mercenaries sent to apprehend him came from both directions on the walkway. Max figured Tanaka wanted him alive so he could kill him himself, so dealing with his men without fear of being killed was Max's advantage.

"I'll be right down after I take care of the piece of shit scumbags you sent up for me," Max yelled down from the top of the stairs to Tanaka.

Max stood up to address the two mercenaries charging at him. He spun and kicked the one coming up behind him, knocking him backwards, then turned to punch the other in the face.

The mercenary behind him tried to grab Max's arm, but Max punched him in the throat, making him gasp for air, grab his throat with both hands and stagger backwards.

Evidently the mercenary Max punched in the face decided killing him was better than capturing him and pulled a large tactical knife out of its scabbard and swung at Max twice before stepping back. He lunged at Max with the knife. Max quickly took it away from him in a twisting motion and shoved it up into his head under his chin, killing him while holding him up by his vest and staring into his dying eyes.

Max realized the other mercenary had somewhat recovered from his throat jab and started reaching for his handgun after watching Max kill his comrade. Still holding the dead mercenary up, Max yanked the knife out of his chin, turned quickly and threw it into the second mercenary's head. It hit right between his eyes just as his gun cleared his holster. Already dead, he dropped to his knees then toppled over face down.

Max let go of the vest of the first mercenary, who dropped to the floor at his feet, his blood starting to flow down the stairs in front of them.

Max straightened his own vest and slowly started down the stairs pointing his rifle at Tanaka, his laser sight sparkling on Tanaka's white-clothed chest. "I guess it's hard to find good help these days," Max said to Tanaka with a smile, looking back at the two dead men laying on the stairway.

"It's good to see you after so many years, my brother. Your sense of humor has not changed," Tanaka replied.

"When are you going to get it through that bad wiring in your head that I am NOT your brother," Max said keeping the bright red dot on Tanaka's chest as he navigated down the stairs.

Max noticed the TV cameramen were keeping their cameras on both him and Tanaka. Seeing the bright red light on top of each camera told Max they were broadcasting everything live worldwide.

"You will always be a member of the Dragon's Breath clan. It's what my father wanted since the day you came to him," Tanaka said.

Max shook his head and rolled his eyes at Tanaka. "If I'm not mistaken, *you* took *me* to *him*, dumbass," Max replied, keeping his rifle pointed at Tanaka's chest.

Max remembered when he was an 18-year-old Navy Ensign SEAL trainee in Manila. He got a three-day furlough and decided to take in the sights alone that weekend. The first day, he met a few Philippine guys his age at the Buddhist Shrine and hit it off.

They decided to go to a couple of bars and talked him into going with them. They had a few drinks then decided to go to another bar to see some girls. Max was cool with that.

They all left by a side door leading to an alley, and when they got outside the Filipino group started beating up on Max, calling out anti-American slurs, while kicking and punching him harshly. Max

143

got a couple of good punches in, remembering his SEAL training, but unfortunately was overwhelmed because it was five against one.

Just as he was about to lose consciousness from the beating he was taking, he watched a young man with a staff take on the five men, beat the hell out of them and scare them off. It was a young Tanaka Amikura.

Max remembered that he threw him over his shoulder fireman style and took the injured SEAL to his father's home where he woke up the next day staring at Yoshi Amikura, his son Tanaka and his very young daughter, Yuki, all kneeling beside him.

Sensei Yoshi Amikura taught martial arts with his son near the Naval base in the fighting art of "ninjitsu"- or "ninja." His family did this for generations, training hundreds of men and women. They were known as the "Dragon's Breath" clan, feared and respected by all the martial arts schools in Manila and Japan.

Max stayed with them that weekend, recovering and learning Yoshi Amikura's philosophy of "the way of the ninja." When he returned to base he reported the weekend situation to Admiral Cartwright who immediately investigated Amikura and his son.

Cartwright told a young Max Mason that Yoshi Amikura was a well respected, honorable, good man, but found his son Tanaka less disciplined, and less likely to share his father's honorable ideas. In other words, he didn't trust Tanaka Amikura.

Max asked the Admiral for permission to train with Yoshi Amikura, arguing that it could only enhance his SEAL training. The Admiral agreed as long as Max did it on weekends, away from his SEAL training. For almost six years Max Mason was tutored by Sensei Amikura and became one of his best and brightest students.

One cloudy Saturday morning, Max came to the school to find Sensei Amikura dead in the training room, his son Tanaka standing over him with his father's bloody dragon head sword in his hands.

Max approached Tanaka to confront him after what he had done, but Tanaka smiled at Max and threw a small explosive at him. Max dove to the side of the room to avoid being harmed, but Tanaka disappeared in the smoke, his father dead on the floor of the dojo. Max covered Sensei Amikura's body with a sheet and called Admiral Cartwright.

Max still remembered that horrific day and angrily continued down the stairs one by one, keeping his rifle and red laser sight on Tanaka as two of his mercenaries came up behind their boss with their MP-5 machine guns pointed at Max.

"I see you have more idiot scumbags working for you," Max told him.

"My father considered you ninja and wanted you to take over the clan when he was gone," Tanaka said, starting to get angry.

"First of all, your father was my friend who understood I didn't believe in your so-called "way of the ninja," Max said. "I was *only* there for training to make myself a better Navy SEAL," Max explained.

"You learned to kill like the rest of my father's students," Tanaka said, turning red with frustration.

"I *only kill* when it's necessary to save lives. You and your students kill because you *like* it. That just makes you a homicidal psychopath," Max replied.

"I plan on killing you today, my brother, and giving you your rightful place next to my father," Tanaka informed Max.

"You're gonna *try,*" Max said with a smile. "I'm not so easy to kill," Max informed Tanaka.

"Drop your guns. We'll do this the *old* way, the way of the ninja," Tanaka commanded Max.

"I don't think so. I plan on taking you to jail, asshole," Max replied keeping his AR rifle pointed at the Asian ninja.

Tanaka walked over to a VERY scared Stephanie Bradshaw still sitting in the center of the stage, pulled out one of his pearl-handled 1911 handguns and placed it against her head. "Drop your guns, my brother," Tanaka demanded," or you'll have to explain *again* to a President why *another* child had to die in your care."

Max continued down the stairs and finally got to the stage, his rifle still pointed at Tanaka, the bright red dot still shining on his nice, clean white suit. He walked up the couple of stairs to the stage floor, and walked onto the stage. Max could see in Tanaka's eyes he meant to kill Stephanie if he didn't do as he was told.

CHAPTER 10

JORDY AND MIKEY HAD FINALLY REACHED THE first floor stairwell door with all the hostages in tow.

"We are proceeding to get the hostages out, boss," Jordy said to Max who was still listening through his ear bud receiver.

"Copy that, Lieutenant," Max replied, staring at Tanaka still holding Stephanie Bradshaw at gunpoint.

"So we have friends about, do we?" Tanaka asked. "Let the others downstairs know there are mice in the building," he told one of his guards, laughing in front of Max as he spoke.

"These mice have sharp teeth," Max responded smiling after Tanaka's attempt at humor.

Jordy peeked through the door and could see one of the four entrances being guarded by two armed mercenaries. Studying the glass doors, he could see the explosives attached to them.

"Looks like you're gonna have your hands full up here, Mikey," he said to his friend still behind the hostages.

Jordy studied the mercenaries to see neither of them was wearing a protective vest like the others they encountered. Charles Lee came up to Jordy still peeking through the door.

"What does the situation look like?" he asked.

"Two guards and explosives wired to the door. A real party," Jordy replied jokingly, trying to get Lee to relax.

Jordy looked across the hallway and saw a room with a sign that said "Conference Room" and knew Lee worked there so he would probably have the information on it Jordy needed.

"How big is that conference room?" he asked Lee.

"Pretty big. We hold international seminars there regularly."

"Can all these people stay there safely while we try to get the door opened?" Jordy asked.

"The door locks from the inside and it's got tinted windows all around, so if everyone is quiet it could be used to hide everyone," said Lee.

"Cool. Good to know," Jordy replied with a smile. "Pass it along to everyone that we're headed into the conference room," Jordy said to Lee, who nodded to confirm.

"But what if the guards see us crossing over?" Lee asked.

"Let me take care of the two guards," Jordy replied.

Jordy slowly walked out into the first floor hallway, his rifle pointed at the two mercenaries at the entrance. He walked slowly towards them both when suddenly one turned to see him and pointed his machine gun at him. Jordy fired a short silenced burst from his machine gun, watching the bullets rip through both mercenaries, dropping them both to the floor. Jordy slowly walked towards the shot-up terrorists and found both of them dead.

Jordy turned to go back to the stairwell door to direct the people over to the conference room, seeing the two dead mercenaries on the floor in front of him, when another mercenary slowly and without warning came up behind him.

He cocked his gun pointed at Jordy's head. Jordy knew he was a dead man and closed his eyes as he heard two shots ring out. He opened his eyes when he realized after a moment he wasn't dead and saw the mercenary drop to his knees then fall face down on the floor beside him.

Lee was standing behind the fallen terrorist holding a smoking gun, visibly shaking and staring at what he had done. Jordy walked slowly up to Lee who still hadn't moved, still looking at the dead terrorist at his feet and gently lowered Lee's gun with his right hand. Jordy looked Lee in the eye.

"Thank you. I won't forget that" Jordy said with a grateful smile.

Lee broke his trance after hearing Jordy's words and smiled. The two of them headed back to the stairwell door and quietly opened it, looking at the other hostages hovering around it.

Jordy and Lee started moving the ballroom hostages over to the conference room five at a time. It took them a few minutes but they finally got everyone inside.

Mikey caught up to Jordy and asked, "Any issues?"

Jordy was a bit hesitant.

"Nope, nothing, Everything is under control," he responded as he smiled at Charles Lee who returned the gesture.

Max could see Tanaka was serious about killing the President's daughter if he didn't drop his weapons, so he laid his rifle on the floor and took out his handgun and placed it beside his rifle.

"Now, get on your knees, my brother," Tanaka said forcefully.

"I don't think so, asshole," Max replied arrogantly.

Tanaka cocked the hammer of his handgun pointed at Stephanie Bradshaw's head and repeated himself.

"I *SAID*, GET ON YOUR KNEES!" Tanaka said with fire in his eyes.

Max slowly got on his knees and put his hands behind his head, looking up at Tanaka defiantly.

"What now, asshole?" Max asked with a condescending grin.

"Now we finish this the ninja way," Tanaka said, smiling at Max. One of the two mercenaries still on the stage handed Tanaka a black samurai sword. Tanaka promptly released the hammer on his pistol and returned it to its holster, then unbuckled the double holster and laid it on the floor. He then looked at Stephanie Bradshaw and smiled.

"It's *not* your day to die, little one," he said. Tanaka walked over and placed the black sword on the floor in front of Max.

"What the hell is this for?" Max asked confused.

"The ninja way," Tanaka told Max with a grin.

Stacy looked at her tactical watch, then looked at Tyler.

"Ten minutes are up," she said.

Tyler nodded in agreement with Stacy who was already checking her weapons.

"Are you comin', kid?" Stacy Mason asked Scott Matthews with a smile, seeing he was a bit nervous sitting there.

"Yeah, sure," Scott said with a bit of concern in his voice, looking at the gun in his hand.

"Everyone is in the main TV studio," Stacy said addressing Tyler. "There are two ways to get in. I'll take one, you and the hottie go get his girlfriend through the other," Stacy said giving Scott a wink.

Tyler smiled and said, "Okay, but be careful."

As Stacy was about to go out the door, she turned to Tyler.

"By the way, he's always had a thing for you. Never stopped thinking about you or what might have been," Stacy said to Tyler with a big grin.

"I love my Dad, but he's just a bit slow when it comes to women *not* my Mom," Stacy said with a giggle. "He used to buy her red roses once a week for years thinking she loved roses. She really *only* liked orchids, so he can be a bit dense," Stacy said laughing. Tyler blushed and laughed with her.

Stacy, Tyler and Scott slowly walked out of the stairwell with their guns pointing. Stacy motioned to Tyler to go one way down the hallway with Scott and she was going the other way. The three of them looked at each other, smiled acknowledging to one another to be careful and started slowly going their own way down the hallways.

Stacy slowly walked to the second hallway and looked around the corner to see the three secured, unconscious mercenaries her father had left on the floor by the TV studio door. She stepped over them and smiled as she looked down at them before slowly opening the door. Stacy thought to herself "Nicely done, Daddy."

Tyler and Scott had managed to get to the other door without detection but found the door locked and couldn't get in without making some serious noise.

Tyler quickly grabbed him by the arm and turned him around to find a secondary entrance through an unlocked office door next to the TV studio.

Max looked up at Tanaka from his knees.

"So what am I supposed to do with that?" he asked as he looked at the black samurai sword on the floor in front of him.

"Either use it, or die without it," Tanaka said, grabbing the white sword with the dragon's head on the handle from the guard standing next to him.

Max looked around and saw the cameramen still pointing the cameras at him and Tanaka and asked, "Are you guys okay?"

The four cameramen nodded to Max that they were okay, but he could tell they were scared.

Tanaka was getting impatient with Max and yelled at him, "PICK IT UP!" referring to the sword in front of him.

Max paused for a moment to think.

"I understand now. This isn't the ninja way. It's the Japanese way," Max said to Tanaka with a stern look on his face.

"You want me to kill you for killing your father…so you can atone for your sin. That's why you want to do it in such a public forum, so when I kill you on worldwide television the world will feel sorry for your sorry ass," Max explained with a smile, watching Tanaka turn red with anger.

"It's about honor and family, something you can NEVER understand," Tanaka said to Max angrily.

"HONOR? You killed your OWN father! Where's the honor in that, dumb ass?" Max asked stubbornly. "I know more about family and honor than you'll ever figure out."

"Did you know it was me who orchestrated the car accident that killed your wife 15 years ago?" Tanaka said to Max bragging. "That left you without a mother for your children?" He said continuing to smile.

Max looked at Tanaka with hate in his eyes, hearing this for the first time.

"DAD!" Stacy screamed coming down the stairs to the stage, seeing her father on his knees and hearing what Tanaka said about her mother. Stacy turned on the laser sight on her MP-5 machine gun and placed the bright red dot on Tanaka's chest.

"Well, look at this. The Mason family is here to watch you die," Tanaka said to Max laughing.

"STACY, GET OUT OF HERE" Max yelled up to his daughter.

"You are no longer the little girl that played with my sister, I see," Tanaka said to Stacy grinning.

"You haven't changed either. You're still a smug asshole," Stacy yelled down at Tanaka, then glancing back at Max.

"Is the daughter as good as the father?" Tanaka asked slyly, spinning around and throwing two steel blades at Stacy.

Stacy used her machine gun like a baseball bat to block the blades from hitting her, impaling one of the blades into the wall across from her and the other to the seats below.

Tanaka smiled. "Very impressive," he said to Stacy.

"I was trained by the best and you're about to get your ass kicked by him, asshole," Stacy said, giving her dad a grin.

"She's a feisty one," Tanaka replied laughing.

Max looked up at Stacy and gave her a smile.

"You have NO idea," he responded to Tanaka's comment.

Tanaka glanced up with a smile at the control room and the glass window slowly slid open with one of the mercenaries hanging out of it pointing his machine gun down at Stacy.

"STACY, ABOVE YOU!" Max yelled as he saw the glass window slide open and the machine gun appear.

Stacy stepped back, and up a step, as the guard's bullets ripped up the wall beside her just barely missing her, the empty cartridges flying down to the seats below.

Stacy glanced up to the control room and opened fire at where the mercenary was shooting from, hitting him several times, his dead weight crashing him through the glass opening to the empty seats below.

Tanaka grabbed his dragon sword, raised it above his head and swung down in Max's direction thinking he would get a surprise blow to end Max's life. But he hesitated for a moment, glancing back at Stacy on the steps killing his man in the control room and watching him fall to the seats below.

Tanaka was so busy watching Stacy and his dead guard that he didn't see Max put his hands behind his back and pull out two black steel telescoping baton's Mikey had made him a couple of years ago that he wore under his tactical vest. Max brought both batons up, crossing them to catch Tanaka's blade as it came down towards him, almost slicing into his forehead.

Tanaka pushed down hard on his sword with both hands, but Max pushed back harder, slowly raising himself to his feet.

"You can't fight with a sword, can you?" Tanaka asked, his sword still locked with Max's steel batons.

"I don't like swords, and I surely don't need one to kick your ass," Max said with a grunt pushing up harder.

Max remembered what Tanaka said about his wife Sylvia and kicked him hard in the chest, pushing him backwards and surprising Tanaka, knocking him back against the wall. Max stood there in a defensive pose remembering how he met his wife Sylvia Michaels when they both were stationed in Manila.

Sylvia was one of the base nurses that took care of the SEAL team when they got injured during their training or missions. Max asked her out one day after she patched him up and surprised him when she said yes. They were married on the base a year later by Admiral Cartwright.

Sylvia died in a car accident in Manila after they celebrated their ten-year anniversary leaving Max to raise their two children on his own. The three of them moved to Virginia the next year when Max got the job with the Secret Service...with Admiral Cartwright's recommendation to then President Matthews.

Tanaka came at Max swinging his sword left and right. Each time Max blocked the strikes with his steel batons. Tanaka stepped back, then thrust his sword at Max who spun around and elbowed Tanaka in the head as he went by. The blow to Tanaka's head dazed him for a moment as Max stood waiting for his next move, smiling at him.

"That had to hurt," Max stated grinning.

Stacy had slowly made her way back up the stairs to the control room and she cautiously looked down to see her father waiting for Tanaka to strike again.

She took a quick peek through the window into the control room to see Brian Jurgens holding a gun on the control room staff now sitting on the floor, along with the other armed mercenary standing next to the open window.

Stacy bent down almost sitting on the floor at the side of the wooden door of the control room, her machine gun reloaded and pointing at the door.

She knocked with a smile on her face, something she knew her dad would do to piss off those inside.

"Knock, knock," she said outside the door giggling to herself as bullets ripped up the middle of the door just like she thought they would, making a large hole where the mercenary thought she would be standing in front of the door.

Stacy laid down and looked inside pointing her MP-5 through the hole in the door to see the mercenary reloading and fired a short burst through the hole hitting him several times in the chest knocking him backwards out the already broken window of the control room into the seats below like his partner before him.

Max and Tanaka looked up as the second guard's body fell, crashing down into the seats near them, right next to the other one Stacy had shot and killed.

"Looks like you're running out of scumbags to play with," Max said to him with a grin. "That's MY girl," Max said proudly trying to piss off Tanaka a little more.

Tanaka turned red with anger, rushing at Max again swinging the dragon sword in his clinched hands but getting blocked each time by Max's quick baton responses. Max had had enough of this toying with him and countered Tanaka's next swing with a block, then a backhand swing hitting Tanaka square in the jaw with his steel baton. Tanaka fell backwards, then steadied himself, wiping the blood that appeared from his mouth on his nice white suit.

"That's a stain you're not going to get out anytime soon," Max said laughing.

Tanaka loved his white suit, and getting his *own* blood on it enraged him. Max's condescending comments continued to infuriate Tanaka and he started swinging his sword wildly, hoping to catch Max by surprise. The *only* surprise Tanaka got was Max's spinning roundhouse kick to the back of his head knocking him to the floor.

"*That* was for my *wife!*" Max said looking angrily down at him. "Get up, asshole," he said, taunting him now.

Tanaka got up off the floor and screamed, "I'LL KILL YOU!" as he ran towards Max, thrusting with his sword again.

"Yeah, yeah, I know. Shut up and do it already. You're boring me," Max said to him sarcastically waiting for his strike.

Max blocked the sword once again and smacked Tanaka across the face with his baton, knocking out some teeth on the floor. "That was for your FATHER, you piece of shit," Max said harshly.

Tanaka was bent over holding his jaw and spitting out blood all over the floor when he glanced up at the control booth.

Brian Jurgens watched the beating Tanaka was getting from Max Mason from the control room window and decided it was time to run. He screamed out to Stacy through the door. "I'LL KILL THIS WOMAN! I SWEAR I WILL," his gun pointed at the head of producer Sherry Moore.

"I don't care. I don't know her," Stacy said sarcastically through the large hole in the shot-up door.

Jurgens grabbed Sherry Moore's hair making her scream out, "Please don't let him hurt me," she said crying.

"Damn," Stacy thought to herself. She yelled back. "Let her go Jurgens."

"You know that's not happening. Let me out of here and I SWEAR I'll let her go when I'm clear of this place."

There was something about this situation that just didn't seem right, and she thought for a moment. "What would my Dad do?" then she realized Jurgens wasn't going anywhere because the entrances were still wired and she needed to get to the stage to help her boss Jonathan Mayer and the kids from the other two mercenaries.

"I'll let you go if you promise not to hurt her," Stacy said rolling her eyes.

Jurgens shouted out "I promise I'll let her go when I'm clear of this place." The door slowly opened and Stacy stood with her machine gun pointed at Jurgens as he hid behind Sherry Moore, his gun still pointed against her head. With her laser sight Stacy placed the bright red dot in the center of Jurgens' forehead in case he decided to shoot his way out. Jurgens and Moore walked past Stacy and out into the hallway, the door closing behind them.

Stacy looked back down at the stage to see her father and Tanaka staring at each other. The children and Mayer were still being guarded by three mercenaries hiding behind them, continuing to use them as human shields. She slowly walked down the stairs again looking at her father as if to say to him, "Finish this." She pointed her machine gun at the three mercenaries.

Max saw Stacy coming down the stairs and smiled. Tanaka glanced up to see Stacy smile at her dad.

"Isn't that sweet? After I kill you, I'm going to kill her *very* slowly," Tanaka said to Max, blood still coming out of his mouth.

"My money's on *her*, asshole," Max said with a grin.

Tanaka had had enough of Max's glib remarks and decided to end this fight. He swung his sword back and forth but was blocked furiously by Max's batons. He spun around to try to cut Max but wasn't fast enough. Max knocked Tanaka's sword out of his hands with both batons, sending it above their heads. Max dropped his batons on the floor, hearing them bounce on the wooden stage with a hard thud, and grabbed Tanaka's sword out of mid-air and thrust it into his white-clothed chest, looking him in the eyes.

"And THAT'S for my *children*, taking their mother from them," Max said with a scowl on his face.

Tanaka, blood gushing from his mouth now gave Max one last sarcastic grin and said, "I will see you soon, my brother."

"Don't count on it asshole" as he twisted the blade with both hands in Tanaka's chest, killing him and dropping him to the floor.

He looked down at Tanaka's lifeless body at his feet."I told you I'm NOT your brother, asshole. I'm just a pissed off *father*," Max said exhausted.

Looking up at Stacy coming down the stairs he smiled and exhaled knowing she was okay.

The three mercenaries guarding the hostages saw Tanaka lying dead on the stage floor with his own sword in his chest and grabbed Stephanie Bradshaw, Kristina Cartwright and Jonathan Mayer.

They started shooting their machine guns at Max and Stacy, who immediately dove between the rows of seats, bullets ripping the foam out of the seats around them. As bullets flew over their heads they looked at each other.

"You always said you wanted more father/daughter time together," Max said to her with a smile lying on the floor beside her as she handed him one of her loaded SA-XD handguns

"*Most* fathers take their daughters to dinner or the movies, *not* a damn gun fight, Dad" Stacy said with annoyance, yet smiling at her father.

Max could see that the other children were lying on the stage floor under the long table to try to avoid the mercenaries shooting in the room.

"We need to get those kids out of here," Max said to Stacy.

"I *got* this," she replied, raising her head up to see where the mercenaries were.

One of the mercenaries stayed back standing on the stairs, continuing to fire his machine gun at Max and Stacy still hiding behind the seats, looking up as his two comrades hurried up the stairs ahead of him with the three hostages.

Max could hear the familiar click of an empty magazine, aimed the handgun he got from Stacy, stood up and fired three rounds into the mercenary standing on the stairs as he was changing magazines in his machine gun.

Stacy stood up too and aimed at the mercenaries running up the last few stairs with the hostages.

Max yelled at Stacy, "Don't fire in the kids' direction."

"*Really*, Dad?" she yelled at him sarcastically, raising her machine gun. She fired two short bursts above their heads, chasing the mercenaries, the two teenagers and Mayer up the remaining stairs, making sure not to hit anyone as her father had ordered.

Stacy looked back at her father who gave her a sheepish grin. She smiled back. "We need to get the hell out of here," she said to him.

"*See*, we are bonding," Max said to her laughing in agreement as they both ducked back down between the seats as the other two mercenaries continued firing at them.

The two mercenaries and their three hostages managed to get up the stairs firing bursts behind them toward Max and Stacy. Bullets flew by as they watched the mercenaries run out into the hallway.

"Where's Jurgens?" Max asked Stacy.

"He got away with a black female hostage. He can't get far. Uncle Mikey hasn't confirmed the doors out of the building being opened yet."

"I'm going after him, you help get the kids down to Mikey and Jordy on the first floor," Max commanded handing her gun back to her.

"What about Mayer?" Stacy asked.

"Get the kids downstairs *first* Ensign, then you can go after your boss. That's an *order.*" Max said prioritizing the situation. He still didn't trust Mayer but knew Stacy could handle herself with him if it came down to it. He had a bigger scumbag to chase…Brian Jurgens.

Stacy got the rest of the kids hiding under the table on stage gathered together to explain the situation to them. She informed them they were going downstairs to the first floor conference room to wait for the doors to open so everyone could go home to their parents. She told the older ones to look after the younger ones so they wouldn't be scared. She took one of the little one's hands and led them up the stairs of the studio and through a door until all six were out in the hallway.

Max smiled watching his daughter hold the scared little girl's hand, thinking to himself, "She's not a little girl anymore."

Max grabbed his batons off the stage floor and returned them to their holsters behind his back, then put his handgun back in its holster, picked up his rifle and replaced the spent magazine with a new fully-loaded one. Once he was situated to his liking he headed towards the stairwell door to try to find Brian Jurgens.

He knew Jurgens ruled his Broadcasting Department with an "iron fist" along with Marcus Grant, and a female H/R sympathizer named Patricia Johnson. The three of them had become the most despised people in the building.

They had continued to terrorize the audio/video engineers union for years, denying leave, handing out suspensions, putting people on administrative leave with pay just for spite, and making up rules as they went along under Jurgens' definition of "best practices."

They even covered up sexual harassment and discrimination cases against each other, this was all part of Jurgens' plan to become Director one day.

Max had several of Jurgens/Johnson cases against his own people come across his security desk and always did his best to help them.

159

Jurgens was a scumbag, and now he was a criminal scumbag with a gun needing to be apprehended. Max smiled at how the mighty had fallen and it was his job to bring him to justice.

The two mercenaries slowly went down the hallway with their three hostages heading to the stairwell door just as Tyler and Scott Matthews came around the corner from the locked studio door.

Stephanie Bradshaw saw her friend and yelled, "KAREN!"

Scott Matthews saw his girlfriend and yelled, "STEPHANIE!"

"SCOTT!" Stephanie responded, relieved to see him.

Scott saw the mercenary holding Stephanie's arm and rushed him, throwing himself on top of the armed man knocking them both down onto the floor. Scott's gun and the guard's machine gun slid across the floor away from them as they continued to roll around on the floor together.

The other mercenary engaged Tyler, trying to shoot her with his machine gun. Jonathan Mayer saw that both mercenaries had their hands full with the others and weren't paying attention to him anymore and saw his chance to flee, leaving through the stairwell door and heading down the stairs.

Tyler saw Mayer run out the door and thought to herself, "What an asshole," as she pinned the mercenary's machine gun against him with both hands then pulled it towards her only to shove it back really hard into his face,knocking him backwards and dropping the weapon. The dazed mercenary grabbed Tyler in a bear hug that was beginning to squeeze the air out of her.

Scott started punching the guard in the face, who returned his own punch to the left side of Scott's ribs causing him to groan in pain. Stephanie stood beside Kristina with fear on both their faces as they watched Scott and Tyler fight the two big mercenaries.

Scott got to his feet holding his side looking at Stephanie when she said, "Scott look out." He turned to receive a hard punch to his jaw that knocked him backwards into Stephanie and Kristina. The force of the punch pushed Scott into Kristina who fell down to the side as Scott fell on top of Stephanie, falling to the floor. The guard stood over Scott and Stephanie smiling, then slowly pulled his pistol from its holster pointing it at both of them. Cocking the hammer and saying with a grin, "I voted for the other guy."

"*Fuck* you. My Daddy didn't *need* your pathetic vote anyway," Stephanie said flashing her own grin.

Tyler head butted the big mercenary in the face, causing him to grab the side of his head and buckling his knees a bit as he let go of his hold on her. She looked over at the mercenary pointing the gun at Scott and Stephanie and screamed. "NOOOO!"

Two shots rang out and Tyler's face went cold looking at the two young lovers lying on the floor. The mercenary holding the gun on Scott and Stephanie slowly dropped to his knees and fell face down revealing a shocked Kristina Cartwright behind him holding Scott's gun the barrel still smoking.

"Oh my GOD! I KILLED him!" Kristina Cartwright screamed.

Scott and Stephanie stared at each other, then looked at Kristina with a sense of shock, relief and appreciation on their faces. Scott helped Stephanie to her feet, both still looking at Kristina in shock at what she did.

Tyler hit the other guard hard in the jaw with her right fist then put a hard knee into his groin dropping him to the floor. As he laid there rolling back and forth holding his groin Tyler sent a swift kick to his left jaw with her right foot, knocking him out.

Tyler ran to Kristina and slowly took the large handgun out of her clasped hands, consoling her as she continued to cry for what she had just done.

Tyler looked at the mercenary lying on the floor in front of them and realized he was wearing an armored vest and quickly rolled him over and cuffed his wrists from behind with the plastic cuffs Max had given her before they separated. The three teenagers watched with confusion as she did this.

"He's not dead, sweetie," Tyler said to Kristina trying to calm her down. "He's wearing a bullet-proof vest," she explained to her.

The guard started to stir, trying to roll over, and Kristina saw she hadn't killed him. "I *didn't* kill him," she said looking at Tyler with a smile.

"No you didn't, sweetie" Tyler replied with her own smile, still kneeling beside the mercenary making sure he was secured.

She didn't like the fact that he was conscious, so she bent down, looked him in the eye and said, "You should have stayed asleep, dumb ass," then punched him hard in the face with her right fist knocking him out again. She looked back at Kristina grinning. Kristina smiled back.

"You saved our lives, Kristina," Scott said to her taking her hand to say thank you.

Stephanie ran to her and hugged her friend hard and kissed her on the cheek. "Thank you, thank you."

Kristina smiled, closed her eyes and appreciated the big hug she got from her best friend.

"You three need to get downstairs and out of this building," Tyler said to them.

Stephanie Bradshaw looked at Tyler asking "Aren't you going down to protect us, Karen?"

"You three don't need protecting from what I just saw. The three of you know how to protect each other," Tyler said with pride and a grin.

"You were so brave," Stephanie said to Scott Matthews, hugging him and kissing him hard on the lips. "Thank you for coming after me," she said kissing him again.

"You're welcome," Scott said blushing and holding her tight.

Watching this exchange, Tyler smiled and thought to herself, "Maybe I *will* have dinner with Max."

Tyler touched the transmitter in her ear and spoke. "Jordy, I have Stephanie, Kristina and Scott headed your way in a couple of minutes. Copy?"

"Copy that, ma'am" came through her ear.

"Okay, enough of this," Tyler said with a smile. She picked up two handguns and handed them to Scott and Stephanie.

"You both know how to use these. Do what Max and I taught you" Tyler said looking at Stephanie, then Scott.

"Yes, ma'am," Stephanie replied.

"Shoot them in the ass if you're not sure where to shoot them," Tyler said to them smiling. The three of them laughed at that remark.

Stacy Mason, with the other kids, came around the corner to find the four of them standing there. Tyler looked at Stacy and nodded in appreciation of her helping the kids get back to their families.

"What kept you?" Tyler asked Stacy smiling.

Stacy Mason rolled her eyes at Karen Tyler. "Needed to fix my makeup," she said with a sarcastic smile.

Tyler looked at Scott, Stephanie and Kristina and commanded them.

"Head down the stairwell to the first floor and get these children down to Jordy. Remember to watch your front and back going down. Jordy is waiting for all of you now."

The three teenagers smiled and each gave Tyler a hug and headed towards the stairwell door with Scott leading the way. Stephanie looked back at Tyler.

"Where are you going, Karen?"

"You could say I'm going to collect on a date," Tyler responded, looking at both her and Stacy with a grin.

The three of them walked through the door with the rest of the children and it closed behind them.

Stacy sat next to Tyler in the stairwell reloading her guns. "Is everything okay with them?" she asked Tyler.

"They're incredible," Tyler said with a proud grin. "Where is your dad?" Tyler asked.

"He went after Brian Jurgens. Seems my dad has a bit of a hard-on for him right now," Stacy said laughing. Tyler laughed back.

"You are a sailor, and YOUR father's daughter," she replied. Tyler then touched Stacy's bruised cheek that Samson had smacked hard earlier that night. "Does it still hurt?" she asked.

"A little, but it was worth it," Stacy said with a giggle.

"You got smacked for handbags," Tyler said condescendingly.

"NO, that's what I told him the *code* was for," Stacy laughed.

Tyler had a confused look on her face at Stacy's statement.

"Then what the hell did you send in that text to Tracy?" Tyler asked.

Stacy laughed again at Tyler's question.

"There *is* no Tracy. I sent that text to my Dad," she explained.

"But we all heard her voicemail," Tyler said confused.

"My Dad, my brother and I have been playing with codes and secret texts since I was about ten years old. I sent 135/157 bag 160x127 to my dad's SAT cell phone," Stacy explained, smiling at Tyler. "135 means hostage situation, 157 no more communication, 160 means building wired with explosives, and x127 was the type of explosive used on the doors."

"What does "bag" mean," Tyler asked. ?

"It means bring my mission bag with my guns in it," she said laughing. "The voicemail was set up in case my bluff was called," Stacy said with a giggle. "That was my friend Brenda's voice. It was the first time I used it. Surprised it actually worked."

Once they got their weapons loaded and were ready to go again, Stacy asked Tyler, "Are you going to help my Dad?"

Tyler smiled and blushed. "If that's okay with you, sweetie."

"Are you kidding? You two exhaust me," Stacy said laughing. "Get a room already."

"Now wait a minute, young lady," Tyler expressed with a grin.

"Yeah, whatever," Stacy said laughing. "I'm going after Mayer. He has to show his hand by now."

"You need to be careful. Something about him," Tyler replied.

"I will," Stacy confirmed.

Max started down the stairwell looking for Jurgens and the hostage he took from the control room, touched his earpiece and spoke.

"How's it coming with that door, Commander?"

Mikey had just started looking at the X-127 explosives wired to the door and could see the armed police outside waiting to storm the building.

"We have some *very* impatient Fed's outside the front door, boss," Mikey relayed to Max. It's going to take a bit of time to get these off the door."

Looking intensely at the wiring, Mikey came to a dangerous conclusion.

"They seem to be able to be set off by a remote detonator. Captain, someone has their finger on the trigger of all four of these bombs," Mikey said nervously.

Max stopped where he was in the stairwell.

"Mikey, are you telling me there's a detonator in someone's pocket that can bring this building down around us?"

"It looks that way, boss. Each one has multiple relays and LED binary codes attached to each bomb," Mikey explained.

"Can they be defused, Commander?" Max asked his expert.

"Sure, boss. But all four bombs need to be defused at the same time. If one is defused without the others at the same time, they *all* blow," Mikey explained.

"Shit! This sucks" Max said pissed. "So we need to clear out the bad guys that are guarding the doors first before we can get to the bombs?"

"Seems that way, boss." Mikey answered.

"Jordy, do you copy?" Max asked.

"Right here, boss."

"So you heard *all* that, right, Lieutenant?" Max asked his friend.

"Affirmative, boss. Sounds like we're all fucked," Jordy said with a laugh.

"What is your evaluation of the security people you have there, do you think they could handle a firefight?" Max asked.

"Not sure, boss. I believe Lee can. Not really sure about the others," Jordy said, knowing Charles Lee had saved his life earlier.

Lee had asked Max if he would train him in firearms in case he ever needed to use one and became quite proficient with both a handgun and AR-223 rifle after many times at the range with Max, so Max knew he could handle a gun. Max now regretted allowing Stacy to go after Mayer when Mikey could have used her in this bomb situation, but he knew Tyler was taking the child hostages to the first floor and they could use her expertise down there.

"Jordy, has Agent Tyler brought down the kids yet?" he asked.

"The kids got here a few minutes ago, boss. Tyler wasn't with them."

Max thought to himself that she probably went with Stacy after Mayer if she wasn't with the kids. "Jordy, I need you to recon intel on the other three doors and the hostiles guarding them. Do it quickly and quietly," Max told him.

"Copy that, boss," Jordy replied, knowing they had one door secured.

Jordy reloaded his AR rifle with a fresh magazine and slowly made his way down the side of the wall to the next hallway. From there he could see all three doors which were about 300 feet away in three directions. He lay on the floor, took out a small pair of binoculars and looked at each door to see how many mercenaries were manning them. He was confused about why there weren't more of them guarding the doors right now.

"Hey, boss. Did something happen upstairs you haven't told us about?" he asked quietly, almost whispering.

"Tanaka Amikura is dead," Max replied.

"That explains a few things," Jordy said giggling, still looking through his binoculars.

"What do you mean, Lieutenant?" Max asked.

"There are *only seven* hostiles guarding the three doors, boss. They all look like they're getting ready to bug out themselves," Jordy said, watching the mercenaries packing up explosive and weapons bags.

Max thought for a moment. "They have another way out of the building."

"The basement," Max and Jordy said together.

"I *knew* it wasn't wired! Jordy said with a scowl on his face and hearing Mikey laugh in his ear piece.

"Dully noted, Lieutenant," Max said snickering himself. Max understood where his friend was coming from but had to be serious now. Jurgens *always* had a backup plan to get out of the building, Max thought to himself.

"We still need to take care of those seven hostiles and get people on the bombs so Mikey can help them defuse these damn things… before someone drops this whole damn building on top of all of us," Max declared.

"Copy that, boss," Jordy replied.

Jordy quickly talked with Charles Lee and Scott Matthews about the bomb's being defused, handed them each a radio and a loaded handgun.

Jordy, Mikey and Scott Matthews slowly headed down the hallway. Before they left, Mikey handed Lee and Scott a knife to cut the wiring when they were all synched together by radio.

Max decided that his two best friends had this under control and continued through the second floor stairwell door into the hallway looking for Brian Jurgens and the female hostage he had taken. Max thought to himself that it either had to be Jurgens or Mayer that had the detonator on them.

He believed one of them or *both* of them were going to escape through the basement and blow the building to avoid capture during the hysteria and confusion of the building collapsing.

Max's SAT phone started buzzing in his pocket and he realized he hadn't checked in with the Admiral in a while. "Hello, Admiral," Max said into the phone.

"Where the HELL have you been, Mason?" Cartwright yelled through the phone.

"Sorry, Admiral. Been a little busy."

"What's the status on my granddaughter and the President's daughter, Max?"

"They're safe, or as safe as they can be, Admiral."

"What is that suppose to mean, Captain?" Cartwright asked angrily because he hasn't heard from Max in a while.

"I'm afraid there are some serious complications here, Admiral, that we didn't take into account," Max replied to his commanding officer.

Max went on to explain about the X-127 on all four doors, the remote detonator someone in the building possessed, the synchronized defusing of all four bombs to get everyone out, the possibility of a secondary escape for the terrorists, and how Kristina saved the President's daughter and her boyfriend Scott Matthews.

"What about Tanaka Amikura?" the Admiral asked, a bit relieved hearing about his granddaughter. "The feed was cut off just as you and he faced off against one another," Cartwright said.

Max thought for a moment, then realized when Stacy shot up into the control room and killed the mercenary it knocked the live TV broadcast off the air, so no one saw the fight between the two of them.

"Tanaka is dead, Admiral."

"Good riddance. He's been a thorn in our side for over 20 years."

"Did you know he killed Sylvia, Admiral?" Max asked.

"I had no proof, Max, but I suspected he had something to do with it."

"Why didn't you *tell* me you suspected he killed *my wife*, SIR?" Max asked angrily.

"We had no proof of his involvement, Max. You needed to take care of your two children. They just lost their mother. I continued to investigate the accident but found nothing over the years. If I had something concrete, I would have told you. You have to believe that."

Max was exhausted and needed to concentrate on getting everyone out.

"We can discuss this at another time, Admiral."

"Do you need anything, Max?" the Admiral asked.

"I need everyone outside to calm down. It looks like the FBI is planning an assault on the building and that's the last thing we need right now, sir. You need the President to tell them to stand down."

"I can do that, Max, I'm headed there now. What about Mayer, Max?" Admiral Cartwright asked concerned.

"My *daughter* has gone after him, sir," Max said, not happy. "She feels responsible for him at the moment, yet he still hasn't shown his true colors."

"I still don't trust him, Max. Too many things with the man don't add up."

"Copy that, Admiral."

"You and your men be careful, Captain, and keep the President's daughter and my granddaughter safe," the Admiral commanded.

"Aye aye, sir." Max hung up the phone and returned it to his pocket continuing to look for Jurgens on the second floor.

Jordy, Mikey and Scott Matthews slowly crept up behind the two mercenaries near the north side entrance. Mikey aimed his AR rifle and shot both mercenaries in the head, killing them both instantly, dropping them to the floor. Mikey's thought was, "The only good terrorist is a dead terrorist." He didn't have a problem with killing if it meant protecting those around him, especially Jordy and Max. Jordy looked at Mikey with a confused look on his face.

"WHAT?" Mikey asked.

"We might have been able to take them alive," Jordy replied.

"You know damn well the boss wouldn't want the kid to be put in unnecessary danger, especially *this* kid," Mikey explained.

Jordy stood there and thought for a moment, then shrugged his shoulders and realized Mikey was right. Jordy and Mikey dragged the two bodies over to the wall and laid them on top of each other. Mikey made sure Scott's radio was on the same frequency that Charles Lee had on *his* radio and handed it back to him.

"Here kid," Mikey said with a grin. "Stay put. We'll let you know when we're ready to go, okay?"

Scott Matthews nodded in agreement. Mikey started to leave when he turned smiling at Scott Matthews and said. "Oh yeah, and shoot *anything* that's not *us*."

It was just Mikey and Jordy now moving a little quicker to the last two entrances. They knew they had at least four more mercenaries to deal with, and that the hostiles were trying to get out of the building now before the hostages did.

Just as they got to the corner wall of the west entrance they turned to see what the situation was like and ran smack into both mercenaries heading to the stairwell door.

"OH SHIT!" Jordy said surprised, grabbing the closest one to him and taking him to the floor, knocking the bags out of his hands. The two men rolled on the floor trying to get away from one another, both throwing punches.

Mikey looked at the other mercenary standing in front of him surprised, smiled and said, "What's up, asshole," then punched him in the jaw, quickly staggering the muscular mercenary backwards. The dazed man looked at Mikey and could hardly believe what he was seeing.

"You're Mikey Stevens of Family Firearms."

"Well, yes I am," Mikey said enthusiastically. Here, let me autograph that large bruise on your forehead," Mikey said with a grin.

"What bruise?" the mercenary asked.

"*This* one," Mikey replied, hitting him hard with the butt of his Sig 9mm handgun he had pulled out of his holster, knocking the star-struck mercenary to the floor unconscious. "Always willing to give back to my *fans*," Mikey said laughing.

The mercenary sitting on top of Jordy, who was still lying on the floor, had pulled out a large knife and was trying to stab Jordy in the head with both hands wrapped around the knife hilt.

Jordy, who was holding the large mercenary's wrists with both hands, looked up at Mikey and asked, "Why is it I always get the big ones and you get the ones who want to shake your hand," Jordy said grunting.

Mikey had rolled his assailant over and cuffed him with the plastic cuffs, then looked back at Jordy smiling, holstering his gun. "Are you through yet?" Mikey asked, rolling his eyes at his friend.

"I guess so. Mine's uglier than a mud snake," Jordy replied with a smile.

He then hit the mercenary in his left ribs several times with his gloved right fist while still holding the knife away from his head causing the large mercenary to roll off of him and jump to his feet.

Jordy was still lying on the floor when the mercenary reached for his holstered handgun forcing both Mikey and Jordy to pull and fire their handguns.

Both of their bullets struck the mercenary's head at the same time and they watched him fall to the floor next to his unconscious partner.

"Can we get back to work now?" Mikey asked smiling at Jordy.

Jordy got back on his feet and shook his head at his friend, looking a bit tired and rumpled after his scuffle with the now dead mercenary.

"YOU go take care of the last one. I'm staying here," he told Mikey, breathing heavily and leaning against the wall.

"Do you need a nap, Lieutenant?" Mikey asked laughing.

"I could really use a steak and a beer along with that nap, Commander," Jordy replied sarcastically.

Mikey grabbed his AR rifle, checked the magazine and smiled at Jordy and headed down the hallway to the last entrance still controlled by the mercenaries. Looking back several times, Jordy was waving him off with a grin indicating he was fine.

Mikey slowly moved down the wall to the last entrance hallway, peeked around the corner and saw not one, but three mercenaries standing by the entrance door. Mikey touched his earpiece. "This might take a moment," he said to Jordy.

"Do you need to make *friends* first?" Jordy asked patronizing.

"No, but I could use a third arm," Mikey said with a laugh.

Jordy realized what he said now, knowing there were three mercenaries at the south entrance instead of the one they both expected.

"What's the plan?" Jordy asked.

"Don't get killed, or Faye gets everything," Mikey said laughing out loud.

Mikey looked around the corner again and saw that the three mercenaries had separated from each other. One mercenary was standing by the door, one by the metal detector and the other leaning up against the wall on the left side of the door. Mikey thought to himself he would need three accurate shots in rapid succession to take down all three before they could get a shot off at him, something he'd never done before. Mikey took a deep breath, let it out then went around the corner. He had gotten about ten feet down the hallway when the first mercenary by the metal detector saw him and aimed his MP-5 machine gun at him.

Mikey fired first, hitting him in the face and knocking him to the ground screaming in pain but not killing him.

The second mercenary shot several rounds at Mikey who dove to the floor and rolled over, shooting the hostile several times in the chest, dropping him to the floor. Mikey went to shoot the last mercenary but as he took aim he watched the mercenary slowly drop to the floor with a hole in his forehead.

"You and the Captain aren't the *only* ones who can hit a beer bottle from 100 feet" Jordy said behind him, standing down the hallway a bit.

"Look at you being all *you* can be," Mikey said with a grin to his friend. "I taught you well."

"That's the Army, dumb ass. And *you* didn't teach me, Stacy did," Jordy said with a laugh.

"Remind me to kiss my niece when I see her," Mikey replied. "Nice shot, by the way," he added sincerely.

"Do you think we can get these damn doors opened so I can get something to eat? I'm fucking starving." Jordy told Mikey smiling.

They both walked over to the mercenary screaming in pain and Jordy knelt down to look at him.

"He'll live, it's a through and through, Jordy said. "Looks like the bullet went through the other side of his jaw. He'll be eating with a straw for awhile, but he'll be okay," Jordy evaluated.

"Good," Mikey replied as he hit him hard on the other jaw with the butt of his rifle, knocking him unconscious so he would stop screaming.

Jordy headed back to the entrance he was assigned to by Mikey and picked up the radio. "Are we *all* ready to do this?" he asked.

Mikey hit the transmitter button on his radio. "Everyone look around for hostiles first, then check in," he said. Mikey needed all three of them to be on the same page with him to do this with *no* distractions or hesitations.

"This is Charles Lee. Everything is fine here, Mr. Stevens."

Scott Matthews spoke into his radio. "Everything is cool here, sir."

"Okay, gentlemen, this is Bomb 101 class," Mikey said with a chuckle. "I need each of you to do EXACTLY as I say *when* I say it," Mikey said seriously.

CHAPTER 11

IT WAS GETTING CLOSE TO MIDNIGHT WHEN THE intercom on the President's desk beeped. Keith Bradshaw pushed the button.

"What is it Amy?" he asked politely, remembering he was abrupt to her a while back.

"Mr. President, Secret Service Director Marshall and FBI Director James are here to see you," she said through the speaker.

Bradshaw was still worried about his daughter Stephanie being held captive at the GBN building and was continuing to pace back and forth in front of the Oval Office window, while former President Daryl Matthews sat on the couch waiting to hear any information about his son Scott who was there as well.

"Send them in, Amy," Bradshaw replied.

"Yes, Mr. President."

Directors Dwayne Marshall and Michael James walked into the Oval Office and were surprised to see Daryl Matthews there with the President. Marshall walked up to him and extended his hand. "Mr. President, it's been a long time," he said.

"Hello, Dwayne. How are you doing?" Matthews asked, pleasantly smiling.

"Doing well, sir. Thank you. I was sorry to hear about Mrs. Matthews passing," Marshall said sadly.

"Thank you, Dwayne," Matthews said continuing to shake his hand.

FBI Director James walked over and shook Matthews' hand and said, "It's good to see you again, Mr. President."

"You as well, Michael," Matthews replied.

"Do you have any new information concerning my *daughter* or Scott Matthews?" President Bradshaw asked the Directors.

Dwayne Marshall turned to look at Daryl Matthews with surprise and asked, "Is *Scott* in the GBN building *as well*, Mr. President?"

"We believe so Dwayne, he was invited and scheduled to speak at the telethon," Matthews said. "We haven't been able to confirm if he's in the building or not."

"I spoke to Scott this morning, sir. He told me he wasn't sure if he was going or not," Marshall said surprised. "I know that Miss Bradshaw put his name on the guest list, but he sounded apprehensive about participating. I only mentioned his name in passing to Agent Tyler just in case he showed up.

"I'm afraid we don't have *any* information on any of them right now, sirs," Marshall said to the current and former Presidents.

"Then *what* are you here for, Director?" President Bradshaw asked harshly, still pacing back and forth behind his desk.

Dwayne Marshall looked at his former boss Daryl Matthews with a bit of concern, then back to President Bradshaw.

"We have reliable information that a former Secret Service agent under President Matthews and my employ, Maxwell Mason, is in the GBN building taking on the terrorists, Mr. President," Marshall replied.

"MAX?" Daryl Matthews asked surprisingly.

Marshall turned to look at Daryl Matthews.

"Yes, sir. We got chatter from several hostile radios in the building and one of the voices antagonizing the person in charge was Max Mason, sir," Marshall explained.

"Are you sure it was Max?" Matthews asked, now standing up glancing at President Bradshaw.

"Yes, sir. His voice print analysis confirmed it was him," Marshall replied.

President Bradshaw was staring out the office window looking up at the moon and listening to Dwayne Marshall, then asked, "So you have NO information on my daughter or President Matthews' son at this moment?"

"No, sir. Nothing yet," Marshall said thinking about the President's coy attitude without questions when he brought up Max Mason's name.

"You knew, Mr. President, didn't you, sir?" Marshall asked forcibly. "You knew Max Mason was in the GBN building. This was Admiral Cartwright's plan all along, wasn't it, sir?" Marshall asked annoyed.

"That will be enough, Director," Bradshaw said looking at Marshall with authority. "Yes, I knew Mason and his team were going in the building. I'm the one who sanctioned it."

"Admiral Cartwright had information vital to possibly getting my daughter and the rest of the hostages out safely and I approved of his plan," Bradshaw continued, looking at Daryl Matthews.

"Max Mason has knowledge of this situation no one else does. That's why I'm trusting Admiral Cartwright's plan on this," President Bradshaw said with conviction.

Again the intercom on President Bradshaw's desk beeped and he answered, "Not really a good time, Amy," Bradshaw said nicely.

"Mr. President, Admiral Cartwright is here to see you, sir," she said.

"Send him in please, Amy," Bradshaw said anxiously.

"Yes, sir, Mr. President."

Admiral Cartwright walked into the Oval Office to see everyone staring at him.

"Gentlemen, Mr. Presidents," Cartwright acknowledged, wondering why he was the center of attention right now. Keith Bradshaw gave him a concerned looked and the Admiral put it together that everyone in the room knew about Max Mason being in the GBN building.

"Who wants to go first?" the Admiral asked with a smile on his face. He then turned to Daryl Matthews.

"You deserve the first question, Mr. President. After all, Max worked for you the longest," Cartwright said, not shy about his knowledge of Max being involved.

"Is *my son* alive in that building?" Matthews asked the Admiral.

"Yes, sir, and doing quite well for himself, I understand," Cartwright said with a smile. "Your son Scott has shown incredible bravery in protecting his girlfriend," Cartwright said with a grin, looking at President Bradshaw.

"It seems, Mr. President, that your son has been seeing Stephanie Bradshaw for the past year now," Cartwright continued, smiling at Daryl Matthews.

"What the HELL are you talking about, Admiral?" Keith Bradshaw asked angrily.

"It seems the fathers are always the *last* to know when it comes to their teenage children falling in love with someone," Cartwright said grinning.

"That makes a lot of sense now," Daryl Matthews replied with a smile of pride. "Are you sure he's okay, Admiral?" he asked wanting to be reassured.

"He's safe, Mr. President. And I understand he's pretty good in a fight," the Admiral said putting his hand on Matthews shoulder.

"What about my *daughter*, Admiral?" President Bradshaw asked somewhat annoyed.

"She's safe as well, Mr. President, and it seems you raised a spitfire of your own, sir," Cartwright replied. "She took on Tanaka to save my granddaughter's life. I thank YOU for that," he said smiling. "She's a *very* brave young woman. You should be very proud, sir."

Keith Bradshaw smiled at the Admiral and nodded in appreciation.

Dwayne Marshall had had enough of this praising the teenagers enveloped in this crisis and interrupted the Admiral.

"Where the fuck is Max Mason, Admiral?" he asked annoyed.

"Why did you send him in there when WE have capable people that could go in there and get the job done?" Marshall continued harshly, staring at Cartwright.

"FIRST off, Director, Special Agent Karen Tyler is fine. And I'm sure she would be overwhelmed by your relief that she's okay," the Admiral said to him sarcastically.

"SECOND, you had NO clue who you were up against in this situation and Max Mason did. You just can't handle that a former agent went in to fix the problem outside of YOUR control, Director," Admiral Cartwright added with a smile.

"And THIRD, you need to stand your men down from breaching the perimeter entrances or they'll blow the X-127 charges that are attached to each door," he said harshly to Dwayne Marshall.

"Mr. President, I don't have to stand for this bullshit," Marshall said angrily. Marshall looked at James and said, "Our men have orders to defuse the bomb at the east entrance ONLY and get the hostages out the same way."

"Are you insane? Someone has a remote detonator," the Admiral explained. "The moment they see your men trying to defuse their bomb they'll blow it, killing everyone inside. When are they supposed to go in, Director?" the Admiral asked sternly.

Marshall looked at his watch, then at the Admiral. "In five minutes they breach," he said.

"Mr. President, are we going to trust a civilian to save the world leaders' children, or are you going to allow the use of government professionals to go in and show that the American President will not cower in fear to terrorists, sir?" Marshall demanded.

"Just so you know, Dwayne, Max Mason and his team have KILLED or CAPTURED nearly all the terrorists in the building, including killing Tanaka Amikura himself," Cartwright told Marshall. "And he hasn't lost a hostage in his care yet."

"Stand down, Director," the Admiral ordered. "The entrance doors have to be defused simultaneously or they send a signal to each other to detonate."

"You don't get to give me orders. I don't work for you, Admiral," Marshall replied.

"No, but you work for *me*," President Bradshaw said. "Stand down, Director Marshall. Call off your men NOW," he said with authority hearing the Admiral's explanation.

Marshall reached into his pocket and pulled out his cell phone and quickly called to the command communications center outside the GBN building. The phone was picked up immediately and Marshall spoke.

"Lieutenant, abort the breach on the east entrance doors."

"Sir, the demolition team has already proceeded to the doors under radio silence. They are moving in as we speak," the young officer replied to Director Marshall.

Marshall looked at President Bradshaw with despair on his face.

"Mr. President, it's too late. The demolition team has already proceeded to the doors. They have orders to go to radio silence on their approach, sir. I can't stop them," Marshall explained to Bradshaw with his head down.

"You incompetent fool! YOU killed them all," Admiral Cartwright yelled at Marshall, knowing his granddaughter was still in the building with Max.

The FBI's demolition team slowly came up to the east entrance doors to find a tired and nervous Charles Lee locked in on the other side of the doors waiting to hear from Mikey Stevens on how to defuse this bomb sitting in front of him. Lee tried to wave the men off on the other side of the protective glass but they misunderstood him thinking he was glad to see them.

Lee rolled his eyes and shook his head knowing they didn't understand anything he was trying to say because the doors were soundproof as well as bulletproof. He took out a piece of paper and a pen from his pants pocket and wrote quickly, "EVERYONE WILL DIE IF YOU DON'T GET BACK".

The FBI demolition team took Charles Lee's threat seriously because they backed away from the doors immediately. Lee smiled and thought to himself, "I'm SOOOO in trouble for that."

"Everyone ready to do this?" Mikey asked over the radio.

"Check," Scott Matthews confirmed.

"Check, but I have a lot of anxious FBI agents looking at me right now," Lee said into his radio, staring at the armed men outside his glass door.

"Check. Ignore them; we always do," Jordy replied laughing.

"Okay, listen carefully and do exactly as I say," Mikey said seriously. "Each bomb has a metal access housing on the front of it. I need all of you to slowly pry it off with your knife," he instructed.

"Don't let your knife touch any of the exposed relays behind the access panel. Check in after you have all done that."

"Check," Scott Matthews replied.

"Check," Lee said nervously.

"Check, Commander," Jordy said to his friend.

"Well, we're all still here. So far, so good," Mikey said to everyone laughing. "Now comes the fun part. You each have four different colored wires and four different colored relays. Each wire has to be cut precisely at the same time by all four of us, so we cut on three," he explained.

"WAIT...do we cut on the number three, or is it 1, 2, 3 CUT?" Jordy asked cautiously.

"1, 2, 3 CUT is fine guys. Here we go," Mikey told everyone. "Orange wire first, 1, 2, 3 CUT.

"Nice, we're all still here," Mikey said laughing again.

"Ready...blue wire 1, 2, 3 CUT," the demolition expert said into the radio. "Next the green wire, 1, 2, 3 CUT. Okay, now the red is the last wire. 1, 2, 3 CUT."

Mikey smiled knowing they all did great.

"Now comes the hard part," Mikey said snickering.

"The HARD part?" Jordy complained rolling his eyes.

"The bomb relays are VERY sensitive. Any awkward movement will set them ALL off," Mikey explained. "Let's do this slowly and carefully," he said, encouraging the three of them.

Max slowly moved down the second floor hallway heading towards Brian Jurgens office. He had taken his communications ear-bud out to prevent any noise issues with Mikey, Jordy, or their two recruits defusing the bombs at the entrance doors.

He knew the FBI was monitoring and recording everything from the terrorists' radio frequency, so he pulled out the radio he had, turned down the volume on it and tied the microphone transmitter button back with one of the plastic cuffs he had and stuck it in his back pants pocket.

Max knew if Jurgens was captured he would try to use any means possible to get out of the charges against him and that getting a confession out of him would be the *only* evidence he could use against him in court. Max knew Jurgens was a "talker." He loved to hear the sound of his own voice. Max also knew that Jurgens considered himself a "lady's man" and thought he was charming with the opposite sex. Max decided to use his vanity against him.

Max slowly moved to the corner intersection, his AR rifle pointed down the hallway. He knew Jurgens' office was on this hallway and peeked around to see two mercenaries standing outside his office door, proving to Max that Jurgens was inside.

Max moved back around the corner and stood against the wall thinking about his next move. He peeked around the corner a couple of times at the two mercenaries thinking about what to do to get into Jurgens office with less violence.

Max didn't like his options -- either kill both mercenaries, kill one and be captured by the other, or surrender and hope Mikey and Jordy were on their way up to help, which would have meant they got the entrance doors open. Max had a lot of faith in his team but knew this could be a bit much for everyone involved. He decided to just "wing it" - as Jordy would say - and walked around the corner with his hands in the air. The two mercenaries saw him come around the corner and ran to him, their machine guns pointed at his head.

"DOWN ON YOUR KNEES!" they screamed at Max as they took his rifle and handgun away from him.

Max slowly went down to his knees smiling. "I bet you're wondering why I'm here?" he asked sarcastically.

One of the mercenaries smacked Max across the face with his open hand. "Shut the fuck up," he said.

Max turned his head to look at him with a pissed scowl on his face.

"You both understand that Tanaka Amikura is dead, right?" Max asked, puzzled at their response.

"Shut up, asshole. We don't work for him," the mercenary who smacked him said.

"Oh, *really*. Who do you work for then?" Max asked politely.

"THEY work for ME," a voice behind Max said. Max turned his head in the direction of who was speaking to see Brian Jurgens standing there holding the door to his office open with a big grin on his face.

"Bring him in here," Jurgens ordered.

The two mercenaries grabbed Max by his arms and dragged him through the glass doors and tossed him on the floor in front of Jurgens and his large shiny metallic desk. Max looked around the office to see two additional mercenaries standing together in the left corner of the office.

"Max Mason, boy have you been a thorn in my ass the past year," Jurgens said laughing.

Max knew this was his opportunity to get Jurgens talking.

"Nothing personal, just trying to give your people a fair shake," said Max.

"A lot of MY people don't deserve a fair anything," Jurgens replied.

"You understand everyone's meal ticket, Tanaka, is dead, right?" Max asked.

Jurgens laughed. "Tanaka was just window dressing and muscle, nothing more."

"So YOU are the brains behind Tanaka's little takeover? Is that what you're saying?" Max asked smiling.

"I planned everything, including letting him know you worked here," Jurgens said, continuing to laugh. "The ONLY problem with that was you took vacation time the same week as the telethon," Jurgens said.

"Don't you hate it when that happens?" Max replied, now laughing himself. "You didn't get that much, did you?" Max asked, continuing to get Jurgens to talk.

"Tanaka was good enough to get us $250 million. That's a lot of little umbrella drinks on an island with NO extradition," Jurgens said with a smile.

"Splitting it with Jonathan Mayer has to suck. He hardly did anything for the cause," Max expressed.

"Mayer?" Jurgens said with a grin. "Mayer had nothing to do with the money. He has his own agenda here" Jurgens snickered.

"That's hard to believe. I know you don't have the kind of computer skills he does," Max said trying to get him to tell him more.

Jurgens smiled at Max.

"I see what you're doing, trying to get me to tell you everything. But what the hell, I know you're going to die in a few minutes," he said continuing to laugh at Max.

Max smiled back, not at all fearing for his life.

"Mayer's company is going bankrupt. He has a personal corporate insurance policy on the business that if anything tragic were to happen to him, the company would pay out $500 million to an offshore account disguised as his favorite charity," Jurgens explained.

Max could see on Jurgens face that he was telling the truth.

"So what did Tanaka have to do with it?" Max asked.

"Tanaka set it up with Mayer for $50 million to help fake his death here in the building," Jurgens said grinning.

"Mayer has the detonator," Max said.

"You're pretty smart for a dead man, Mason," Jurgens replied.

Max noticed that while Jurgens was talking to him, the four mercenaries were now standing side by side in back of Jurgens' long metallic desk keeping their machine guns on him.

Max rose up to stand, and while putting his hands up noticed the reflection on the lower part of the desk standing right in front of the four mercenaries, while Jurgens continued to stand at the right side of his desk. Max showed four fingers on each hand, then he lowered his two middle fingers.

"Too bad Tanaka didn't get to kill you, Max," Jurgens said.

"He's been waiting to die a long time by me. Thought I'd finally help him out," Max replied.

Max now had three fingers on his hand raised and slowly started dropping each finger one at a time.

"It's a shame you had to come here alone, Max. Now you're gonna die alone," Jurgens said, slowly moving away from the desk while the four mercenaries' guns were still pointed at Max.

"Who said anything about coming ALONE?" Max asked, dropping his last finger on his hand making a fist.

Shots went through the glass office doors, shattering them both and hit the two outside mercenaries splattering their blood against the wall.

Max lowered his arms quickly and the two mini handguns Mikey had made him slid out of his sleeves on metal rails. He raised them quickly, shooting the two mercenaries standing in front of him in the forehead, watching them slowly drop to the floor with the other two. Max turned quickly to Jurgens, who was stunned at how fast everything happened, and pointed his two guns at him.

"I guess it sucks to be you right now," Max said to him with a grin.

Jurgens looked at Max with rage in his eyes,

"That was so cool," Jurgens said to Max with a grin.

"Glad you enjoyed it," Max replied reaching over the desk and hitting Jurgens square in the jaw knocking him backwards.

Mikey and Jordy came through the office doors, glass everywhere on the floor, their guns still pointed at the four dead mercenaries lying on the floor.

"How did you know we were here, boss?" Jordy asked.

"You had your rifles pointed at the floor until you shot, which is procedure. Your lasers hit the bottom of Jurgens desk and I caught a glimpse of them," Max explained.

"Aren't you glad we figured out your hand signals boss?" Jordy asked laughing.

"Aren't you the clever ones," Jurgens said sarcastically.

Max looked at both Jordy and Mikey. "I take it you got the bombs off the doors?"

"Yeah, boss. Then all the Feds ran in securing the hostages. You should have seen poor Mr. Lee with all those guns pointed at him," Mikey said grinning.

"We thought we would get up here as fast as we could, boss, and avoid all kinds of drama and explaining," Jordy said with a chuckle.

"Well, now I need you both to get down to the basement," Max commanded. "I have a feeling Mayer is down there with Stacy and Tyler."

Jordy looked at Jurgens with contempt.

"What about this asshole, boss?" Jordy asked with a grin to Jurgens.

Jurgens looked at Jordy saying "Maybe I'm an asshole, but you're just a poor, uneducated redneck hired gun."

"I'm not the one going to get ass fucked in prison. AND I'm HIS uneducated redneck gun for hire, asshole." Jordy said back to Jurgens, looking over at Max and smiling.

"That's enough, Lieutenant," Max said, smiling at his friend.

"Sure, boss," Jordy replied, smiling at Jurgens.

"Are you going to be okay, boss, if we leave?" Mikey asked.

"I'll be fine. Jurgens isn't smart enough to do his own killing," Max said to his two friends.

Mikey and Jordy loaded up their guns and slowly walked out of the shattered glass doors of Jurgens office into the hallway and disappeared towards the stairwell door to find their goddaughter Stacy and Agent Tyler.

Max took out plastic cuffs from his pocket and smiled at Jurgens.

"I've waited a long time to do this…since the first day I met your smug ass," Max said, forcibly turning Jurgens around to cuff him.

"Well, it looks like you may have to wait a little longer," Jurgens replied to Max smiling. Max looked at him with a confused look on his face, then felt the cold barrel of a handgun pushed against the back of his head.

"Did this bad man hurt you, baby?" a female voice asked Jurgens.

"No, sweetheart. Mason and I were having a little chat about old times," Jurgens said, smiling at Max and rubbing his jaw.

"Drop your toys, Mason," Jurgens ordered then surprising him with a hard fist to his jaw.

Max moved his jaw around giving Jurgens a smile saying "You hit like a girl".

Max slid his sleeves up one at a time and undid the mini rail guns attached to his forearms and placed them on the floor in front of him.

"Kick them over to the side," Jurgens ordered.

Max lightly kicked the pair of guns over towards the door.

"That's a good boy, Max," the female voice said to him from behind.

The gun barrel left the back of his head and the woman walked around to face him. It was Sherry Moore, the hostage Jurgens was supposed to have taken from the control room.

"You look surprised," she said walking up to Jurgens and kissing him on the lips with a smile, but not taking her eyes or her gun off of Max.

"Not surprised, disappointed someone so young is going to spend the rest of her life in prison," Max replied to the attractive black woman.

"We have all the money we will ever need. We just have to enjoy spending it," she said, ignoring Max's comment.

"What happens when he gets tired of you?" Max asked her.

"He loves me," she said to Max smiling.

Jurgens looked over at Max from where he was standing and gave him a sinister smile. He then walked over to his desk, pulled open a drawer and took out a small key ring with a flash drive on it. He looked at Sherry Moore still holding the gun on Max and smiled.

"I'm going up to the servers to download the transfer code. You take care of him and meet me up there, baby," Jurgens told her.

Sherry Moore smiled at him and said, "Love you, baby. See you in a minute."

Jurgens clutched the key ring in his hand and gave his attractive accomplice a passionate kiss to reassure her of his commitment. He then smiled over at Max.

"See you in Hell, Mason," he said, walking out the door and heading to the stairwell.

Max looked at Moore with contempt.

"What now?" he asked as he saw that Karen Tyler was slowly walking up behind Moore with gun in hand. Tyler smiled at Max and he smiled and looked directly in Moore's eyes.

"I should have asked you out for dinner five years ago" he said with a grin.

Moore looked at him confused.

"I didn't even know you five years ago, asshole," she said pulling the hammer back on her gun.

"Not YOU! HER!" Max replied with a smile.

Tyler smacked Sherry Moore in the back of the head with the butt of her handgun and she fell to the floor unconscious, dropping her gun. Tyler looked at Max and smiled.

"Just for the record, I like red roses" she said.

Max understood what she meant, knowing she and Stacy had a talk.

"Yes, ma'am," he said smiling at her.

Tyler walked up to Max and kissed him passionately on the lips, and the two stood there enjoying it for a long moment.

"Hey, boss, we seem to have a problem down here," Jordy told Max over the communicator he had put back in his ear.

Max and Tyler broke their embrace.

"What's the problem, Lieutenant?" Max asked, annoyed.

"We seem to be surrounded by Feds, boss." Jordy replied.

"Feds? *Not* hostiles?" Max asked.

"Affirmative, boss," Mikey chimed in.

"Is there any alternative route to the basement, Commander?" Max asked.

"Negative, Captain. We would have to shoot our way out of this corridor against friendlies," Mikey replied.

Max thought for a moment then told them, "Drop your weapons, and surrender to them."

"WHAT, boss? *Really*?" Jordy asked.

"Give me five minutes to talk to the Admiral," Max said.

"Aye aye, sir, but I don't like it one bit," Jordy said looking at Mikey, who shrugged at his partner.

Admiral Cartwright was still in the Oval Office with Presidents Bradshaw and Matthews as well as Directors Marshall and James when the phone buzzed in his pocket and he quickly answered it.

"What's going on with the hostages, Captain?"

"Admiral, I need you to call whomever is in charge over here and release MY men," Max requested with a sense of urgency. "They are in custody and I still *need them* in here, sir."

"Does that mean *all* the hostages have been rescued, Max?" the Admiral asked excitedly.

"Yes, sir. We got them all out about ten minutes ago. EVERYONE is safe. Your granddaughter is safe, sir," Max said with a smile.

"Well done, Captain, to you and your team," Cartwright expressed.

"Sorry to be abrupt but I need my guys *now*, sir. Jurgens and Mayer are *both* still running loose in the building. We can talk about everything over the scotch when we get Jurgens and Mayer, sir," Max said.

"Copy that, Captain," Cartwright replied as he looked over at President Bradshaw and smiled.

The Admiral hung up the phone and put it back in his pocket.

"Mr. President, Max Mason's team is in Federal custody inside the GBN building and are *still needed* by Captain Mason," he explained.

"Does this mean MY daughter is safe, Admiral?" Bradshaw asked nervously.

"Yes, sir. *Everyone* is okay," Cartwright said looking at Daryl Matthews. "But it's imperative we release Captain Mason's men, Mr. President. NOW, *sir!*"

"I can't believe we are doing this," Jordy said to Mikey with a grin. "I *hate* being in handcuffs."

Mikey looked at Jordy and smiled, then slowly removed his SIG 9mm handgun from its holster and placed it on the floor beside his AR-223 rifle in front of him. Jordy did the same beside him. They both slowly went to their knees and put their hands on top of their heads just as the FBI Special Operations agents came around the corner with guns pointed at both of them.

"DON'T MOVE, ASSHOLES," the lead agent screamed, not knowing who the two men were sitting on their knees.

Jordy looked at Mikey, smiled and whispered, "Assholes?"

"It's what they do," Mikey said sarcastically as he smiled back at Jordy.

"We are SEAL Team 2 under Admiral James Cartwright's command," Jordy explained to the agent.

"I don't give a shit. Put your hands behind your back, asshole," the agent ordered Jordy.

Jordy, being who he was, quickly responded. "Don't have to be rude about it, dude."

That angered the agent and he pushed Jordy to the floor face down, where he put his knee in his back and grabbed both of his arms.

Jordy grimaced in pain as the agent put steel handcuffs on him. After securing the cuffs, he rolled Jordy back over and screamed, "You're under arrest, motherfucker!"

Defiantly, Jordy looked at him and smiled. Mikey, still with his hands behind his head, looked at the agent who had been overly rough with his friend and said, "You really shouldn't have done that, son. You seriously need to talk to Admiral Cartwright or FBI Director James about us," Mikey explained.

"Shut the hell up," the agent said.

"Okay. It's your job on the line, not mine," Mikey said with a smile as he was being handcuffed aggressively. "Whoa, cowboy, don't have to be so rough. We're all on the same side here."

Another agent searched them both to find only their driver's licenses and handed them to his commander.

"Jordan Alexander and Michael Stevens," he read out loud from their licenses.

The other agent leaned over to his commander and whispered something which made the commander respond.

"You have to be shittin' me!"

The commander of the Special Operations unit looked at Mikey and asked, "Are you the TV gun guy?"

Mikey looked at Jordy and grinned while Jordy just rolled his eyes at him exasperated.

"Yes, sir, I am. Do you watch the show?" Mikey asked nicely in case he was a fan.

"My agent here watches your show," the commander replied. "Still doesn't tell us why you two are here."

Jordy spoke up thinking they could reason with the commander now, "Call your boss, and ask FBI Director James or Defense Secretary Cartwright if they know who we are, please," Jordy asked.

Max and Tyler stood over Sherry Moore's unconscious body, then Tyler bent down and rolled her over to cuff her hands behind her back. Tyler saw her eyes were closed, so she relaxed to get the plastic cuffs out of her back pocket.

Moore's eyes opened and she swung her legs around to knock Tyler off of her while Max just stood there in silence and surprise.

Both women stood up and looked at one another with contempt. Max looked at Tyler who he could tell was pissed at being knocked to the ground and asked, "Need any help?"

Tyler smiled at him, then looked back at Sherry Moore with anger in her eyes. "I got this bitch," she said.

"Yes, ma'am," Max responded, raising his hands up and leaning against the wall to stay out of her way.

Tyler looked at Moore and went into a fighting stance, getting a smile from Moore.

"Oh, I'm going to enjoy kicking your ass, bitch," she said to Tyler.

Watching Sherry Moore get into her own fighting stance, Max could only smile and think he was about to watch a real "chick fight."

Tyler looked at him with a frown on her face knowing what he was thinking.

"*Really*, Mason?" she said to him.

Moore threw a punch at Tyler with her right fist. Tyler blocked it with her left arm and swung to connect to Moore's left jaw with her own right-handed punch. Moore stepped back, rubbed her jaw and smiled at Tyler.

"You hit like a girl," she told Tyler.

Tyler spun around to try to kick Moore but was blocked and kicked by Moore in the stomach, bending her over in pain.

"That had to hurt," Moore said laughing.

Tyler knew she couldn't get angry and go after her half cocked. Max taught her back when they trained together to be patient and make her opportunities count.

Tyler straightened up and waited for Moore to attack her, which she did, throwing another right-handed punch at Tyler's face. Tyler ducked down to avoid it and landed her own right hand into Moore's ribs, staggering her backwards.

"I guess that had to hurt a little too," Tyler said to Moore with a smile.

"You bitch! I'm going to *kill* you!" Moore said to her, as Tyler watched her hold her ribs in pain.

Tyler looked over and asked Max with a grin, "Why is it they always say that right before they get the shit knocked out of them?"

Max looked at Tyler with a smile and shrugged his shoulders.

This pissed off Sherry Moore even more and she went towards Tyler and gave her a roundhouse kick that nearly landed upside Tyler's head. But instead, Tyler kicked her standing leg out from under her and she fell to the floor hard, hitting her back and head. Dazed from the knock to her head, Moore got up again and swung at Tyler wildly without thinking. Tyler hit her twice in the jaw in rapid succession causing her to bleed from her mouth. Moore could barely stand, now battered and bruised, but she was still defiant. She looked at Tyler with blood dripping down her chin and taunted her.

"I bet you haven't been laid in years, bitch."

Tyler looked at Moore and grinned, then looked over at Max, then looked back at Moore, continuing to grin.

"Things are looking up, bitch" she said looking over at Max and giving him a wink.

Tyler punched her hard in the face, knocking Moore to the ground unconscious for the second time. She bent down and as she rolled Moore over and said, "Let's try this again," and placed the plastic cuffs on her wrists and tightened them securely.

She got up and walked over to Max who was smiling, looked him in the eye and asked, "What the Hell are *you* smiling about Mason?"

"Nothing, champ," Max replied with a big grin.

"Good thing." she said with a grin.

CHAPTER 12

MAX MASON KNEW HE HAD TO GO AFTER BRIAN Jurgens who was on his way up to Computer Services, but he was worried about his daughter Stacy going after Jonathan Mayer, now that they knew what Mayer was about to do. Tyler could tell Max was worried about Stacy.

"Go take care of Jurgens. I'll go make sure Stacy is okay" she said to him.

Max knew not to argue with Tyler once she made up her mind about something. He grabbed her and kissed her hard on the lips.

"We still have a dinner date," he said to her with a smile.

"You better not stand me up again," Tyler said to him as he headed to the stairwell door.

"Not a chance. I've seen how hard you hit," Max yelled back, laughing as he entered the door to the stairs.

FBI Director Michael James was sitting on the President's couch in the Oval Office when the phone buzzed in his suit coat pocket. He took it out and saw from the caller ID that it was from the command center in front of the GBN building.

"Excuse me, gentlemen, I have to take this," James said to the Presidents, Director Marshall and Admiral Cartwright.

"What is it, Lieutenant?" James asked in a whisper.

"Director, we have two men here in full tactical gear who claim they are friendlies, sir," the young Lieutenant said into the phone.

"Do they have IDs, Lieutenant?" James asked.

"Yes, sir. One is Jordan Alexander from Florida, and the other one, sir, is kind of weird," he said to James.

"What the Hell do you mean weird, Lieutenant?" James asked raising his voice so everyone could hear.

"His driver's license says he is Michael Stevens from Oklahoma, sir."

"So, who the Hell is he, Lieutenant?" James yelled now at his young agent.

"He's the TV star of a cable gun show that a lot of my men watch, sir," he replied to James cautiously.

"A *TV* STAR?" James yelled back into the phone.

Admiral Cartwright heard what James said into the phone and walked over to him.

"Give me the phone, Michael," he ordered with a stern look on his face.

"Excuse me, Admiral," James said defiantly looking over at Dwayne Marshall with confusion on his face as to what to do next.

Cartwright looked over at Keith Bradshaw.

"One of Max Mason's men is Mikey Stevens, a TV star on the Outdoor cable network, Mr. President."

Bradshaw looked at Director James who was avoiding eye contact with him and asked, "Is that call about Mason's men, Director?"

James looked at Marshall again, shrugged his shoulders as if to say, "He's the President," to his friend, then handed Admiral Cartwright the phone and said, "Yes, Mr. President."

Cartwright looked at James with contempt but still said "Thank you" for handing him the phone and spoke into it.

"This is Admiral James Cartwright, the Secretary of Defense. Who am I speaking with?"

"This is Lieutenant Charles Adams of the Federal Protection Agency, Mr. Secretary, here in the command center outside the GBN building siege, sir."

Cartwright watched as Director James whispered something to Marshall and asked, "Lieutenant, do you have Jordan Alexander and Michael Stevens in custody?"

"Yes, sir. The FBI's Special Operations Commander has them both in custody inside the building," Adams replied.

Admiral Cartwright nodded to President Bradshaw acknowledging that they had his men in custody.

"Connect me to the commander immediately, Lieutenant," Cartwright ordered.

"Yes, sir, Mr. Secretary," Adams replied.

Lieutenant Adams went on the radio and told the commander the Secretary of Defense wanted to speak to him and switched the Admiral's phone call to the commander's radio.

"I have the commander on the line, Mr. Secretary." Lieutenant Adams told Cartwright.

"Commander, you have two men in custody -- Jordan Alexander and Michael Stevens. I need you to release them both immediately," Cartwright ordered.

"I can't do that, sir; not without *my* director's authorization," the commander replied.

Cartwright looked at Director James and smiled, put the phone on speaker so everyone could hear and said, "It's for you," handing James the phone.

"Commander, this is FBI Director Michael James, identification code 1006 omega," he said hesitantly looking at President Bradshaw. "Release both men you have in custody. Give them back their weapons and gear. They are *not* hostiles. I repeat, they are *not* hostiles. Let them go and leave them be. Do you understand, commander?"

"Yes, sir. Copy that."

Director James looked at Admiral Cartwright with an angry expression, placed his cell phone back in his pocket and asked, "Happy now?"

Admiral Cartwright smiled and replied, "You have NO idea how many lives YOU just saved,"

The commander understood what he had to do but still didn't like it because the two men were nothing more than Presidential hired guns and he was in command of a federal Special Forces unit.

He walked over to Mikey and clipped the plastic cuffs from his wrists and tossed them on the floor at his feet.

"Appreciate it," Mikey said politely with a grin.

He moved to Jordy and roughly grabbed his arms from behind.

"Easy dude, we're on the same side," Jordy said feeling the pain in his arm. The commander clipped the cuffs and tossed them on the floor in front of Jordy in contempt. Jordy brought his arms around to the front and rubbed his wrists one after the other getting the circulation back into them. The commander looked at the agent standing beside Jordy and Mikey and said, "Give these two assholes their weapons and gear and get them *out* of *my* sight."

"Yes, sir," the agent replied.

The commander turned to walk away when Jordy said, "Hey, dude, you forgot something."

As the commander turned to see what Jordy meant, he received a hard right hand punch to his jaw from Jordy, knocking him backwards. The stunned commander collected himself then took a step towards Jordy to retaliate, but Mikey put his hand on his chest to abruptly stop him in his tracks.

"You *had* to know that was coming," Mikey said to the commander laughing, watching Jordy collect his gear and start walking away from them both.

"Do your job and we'll do ours," Mikey declared picking up his AR rifle and gear. He nodded to the commander who replied with his own nod, still rubbing his painful jaw.

Mikey caught up with Jordy heading to the stairwell door. "Nice punch," Mikey said with a grin.

"He had it coming," Jordy replied, still pissed off at the way they were treated.

"Yes, he did," Mikey said, smiling at his friend.

"Thanks for backing me up back there," Jordy replied.

"If you didn't hit him, *I* would have. Then Faye would have been pissed at me for the negative publicity," Mikey said making his friend laugh. Mikey Stevens touched his ear com and said, "We're back in the game boss. What's your plan for us?"

Max Mason stopped in the stairwell on his way to the fourth floor upon hearing his comrade and replied, "Welcome back boys. Sorry about the inconvenience with the Feds, but it couldn't be helped."

"It's all good, boss, but you owe Jordy big time," Mikey said laughing.

"Yes, you do, boss," Jordy added.

"Got in a bit of trouble, did you?" Max asked Jordy.

"He deserved it, boss," Jordy replied with a giggle.

"Have to go with the Lieutenant on this one, boss," Mikey said backing up his friend.

"So what did we miss, boss?" Jordy asked.

"I'm afraid you missed Tyler kicking the bad-ass black chick's ass who worked for Jurgens," Max said laughing.

"A *chick* fight and we *missed* it, boss? Bummer!" Jordy replied laughing. "Was it hot?" he asked sheepishly looking at Mikey. "I bet it was *hot*," Jordy said to them both out loud.

"We really need to get you a girlfriend, Lieutenant," Max said laughing.

"Nah, way too much maintenance, boss," Jordy replied smiling and slowly moving through the stairwell door, his AR rifle pointed down the stairs.

"For you or for them?" Max asked laughing and continuing to look down the hallway for Jurgens.

"Maybe both," Jordy responded laughing.

"On a serious note, I'm a bit concerned about Stacy. She hasn't checked in since she went looking for Mayer," Max said over the com link.

"She's a big girl, boss. She was trained by the best," Mikey said trying to calm her father down.

"I'm not sure what Mayer has in mind right now. Remember he still has a detonator," Max said peering down the hallway through the fourth floor stairwell door.

"Agent Tyler went off to see if she needed any help. Now I'm worried about both of them," Max said.

"Hey, boss, we both like Tyler. She's a good agent. You can do worse," Jordy said smiling.

"Yeah, boss. I'm thinking about asking her to be on the show next month," Mikey said laughing awaiting their orders inside the stairwell.

"Really, you two," Max said condescendingly but with a grin on his face.

"What's our assignment, boss?" Jordy asked Max.

"I have a bad feeling there are more explosives in the basement than there were on the doors, Mikey," Max said addressing his explosives expert. "I need you both to go down there and see what is what, and to look out for Stacy and Tyler," Max requested. "Mayer may still have the basement rigged to collapse the building."

Both Mikey and Jordy responded, "Aye aye, Captain," and slowly descended the stairs towards the basement.

Stacy Mason cautiously opened the stairwell door, standing in the entry way to the basement level of the building. She pointed her MP-5 machine gun back and forth down the hallway, looking both ways to make sure it was clear of mercenaries.

Slowly she moved out into the hallway with her back against the wall, constantly looking up and down the hallway, pointing her machine gun in both directions. When she got to the corner of the first hallway junction, she quickly looked down to the end of the hallway.

While Stacy did not see anyone, something caught her eye -- a metal box on the wall with bright red and green lights on top of it.

She noticed the metal box was placed on one of the large concrete pillars that ran along the interior of the basement.

She thought out loud saying, "I wish Uncle Mikey was here right now," because she had a feeling this metal box was a bomb and her Uncle Mikey would know how to defuse it. She grabbed the radio Tyler had given her, hit the transmitter button and realized that the battery was dead. So she had no way of communicating with anyone about this situation. "Damn it," she said at her predicament as she stared at the metal box on the wall.

She laid the radio quietly on the floor, not wanting to make any unnecessary noise. She walked back down the corridor from where she'd come, into the main hallway again. Standing at the corner, she glanced both ways down the hall and saw four armed mercenaries, two coming from each direction. Two of the mercenaries were carrying several of these metal boxes she had just found in the other hall. She watched as they stopped at both ends of the hallway, ripped off two adhesive strips from the back and placed two boxes on the concrete pillars at each end, pushing hard on the casings to secure the bombs to the pillars.

They opened the boxes with a battery-powered screwdriver, revealing a large quantity of C-4 explosives connected to wiring.

Stacy continued watching as one of the mercenaries continued to use the screwdriver inside one of the boxes, connecting two loose wires to the C-4, then closed the metal door acknowledging the red and green lights on top lit up. Stacy figured that meant the explosive box was now armed.

She stood against the wall, closed her eyes and thought about what she could do. She didn't have any bomb defusing training like her godfather, she didn't have any communications capabilities at the moment, and she had four mercenaries walking towards her with no cover.

"Note to self: if I get out of this alive, remind me to ask Uncle Mikey for Bomb Squad 101 training," Stacy said to herself with a grin, continuing to look at the mercenaries down both hallways.

She looked in her bag and took out the two flash-bang grenades her dad had given her, stared at them and - with a grin realizing she so inherited her father's warped sense of humor - said, "This could be interesting. I love it when Daddy gives me party favors."

She took out both of her SA-XD 9mm handguns, checked the magazines, reloaded and placed them both on the floor at the edge of the hallway junction. She placed ear plugs in both her ears, because she knew it was about to get loud.

Stacy sat down on the floor beside both her guns, quickly glancing down the mercenary-filled corridor with the grenades in both hands. She looked down both ends of the hallway one last time, seeing the four mercenaries were getting closer, about 20 feet away now and still not seeing her,concentrating on attaching the bombs.

Stacy pulled out both pins on the grenades and released the metal handles, which flew in the air in front of her. She lay down and rolled them both towards the mercenaries in each direction down the hallway.

A tremendous roar erupted and smoke filled both ends of the hallway as the grenades exploded, stunning all four mercenaries, who dropped the boxes and placed their hands over their ears to shield them from the horrific sound and blinding light.

Stacy laid straight down on her back looking at all four mercenaries staggering from the explosion, aimed both her guns out to her sides and fired at least 15 rounds, moving her head back and forth. She hit all four in the chest multiple times, killing all of them. She stayed lying on the floor for a moment to see if anyone moved or if anyone else came down the hallways. She then raised up to a sitting position, keeping her guns aimed down both ends of the hallway and said with a big smile on her face, "I can't believe that just worked."

Stacy heard a noise coming down the right side hallway and glanced down, her gun pointed as she quickly recognized Karen Tyler making her way down towards her position through the smoke from the other end of the hallway.

Tyler saw Stacy sitting on the floor and asked with a laugh, "Do you need a moment sweetie?" as she stepped over two of the dead mercenaries Stacy had just put down.

"Huh?" Stacy asked with a confused look on her face as she took the earplugs out, not being able to hear what Tyler said.

"Was this you?" Tyler asked looking back and forth seeing the four dead terrorists on the floor at both ends of the hallway.

"Yeah," Stacy said not happy about what she had done. "They shouldn't have tried to blow up the building with ME still *in* it," she explained angrily.

Tyler helped Stacy back on her feet as she holstered her two guns and dusted herself off after lying on the floor. "Is my dad okay?" Stacy asked Tyler concerned.

Tyler smiled and blushed a bit.

"He's great sweetie. He went after Jurgens."

Stacy smiled back seeing Tyler blush and asked, "Did my Dad finally kiss you?"

"Let's not talk about that right now," Tyler replied shyly.

"He *did*!" Stacy said to her smiling. "About damn time," she said looking at Tyler who was starting to turn red. "Can I talk to my Dad? My radio died on me a while ago," she told Tyler pointing at the dead radio lying on the floor at her feet.

"Sure, sweetie," Tyler replied grabbing the radio out of her back pocket and then speaking into it.

"Hey, Max. Someone here wants to talk to you."

"Are you okay, Tyler?" Max asked.

Tyler smiled and handed the radio to Stacy.

"Hi, Daddy. I like how you asked if *she* was okay first. One *kiss* and you forget all about *me*, huh?" she said with a giggle, smiling at Tyler.

Max smiled thinking about his kiss with Tyler earlier, then realized he was talking to Stacy.

"Are you okay, Princess?" he asked, ignoring her comment about Tyler.

Stacy pushed the transmitter button looking at Tyler.

"Nothing a good hot bubble bath and *your* chocolate chip pancakes wouldn't cure," she said to her father laughing.

"I think that can be arranged when we get out of here, sweetheart. Have either of you located Mayer yet?" Max asked with concern in his voice.

Before either Tyler or Stacy could answer, Jonathan Mayer stood at the end of the hallway behind them with three mercenaries standing beside him, their guns aimed at both of them.

"I guess you're looking for me," Mayer said laughing.

"Drop your guns and slowly turn around," Mayer said to them both.

Tyler placed her MP-5 machine gun on the floor in front of her, then slowly took her Sig 9mm handgun out of its holster, bent over and placed it on the floor next to the MP-5.

Stacy hesitated dropping her guns and slowly turned to face Mayer.

"A couple of my men said you were good with those," Mayer said to her, referring to her two holstered handguns. "But I don't think you're that fast," he said smiling at his former assistant, then smiling at the three armed men beside him.

"Why don't we pace off twenty feet and you and I can find out," Stacy said with a grin, her hands touching both of her guns.

"I like my chances this way," Mayer replied looking at his three bodyguards with their weapons pointed at the two women. "Now drop the guns or die bitch," Mayer said forcibly.

Tyler looked at Stacy and the two of them smiled at one another. Stacy slowly unbuckled her gun belt and lowered her guns to the floor, then put her hands on top of her head.

Mayer walked over and picked up the radio Stacy had also placed on the floor and spoke into it.

"Who do I have the pleasure of speaking to?" he asked arrogantly.

Max hesitated for a moment then spoke.

"Max Mason here, Mayer," he said.

"The man who killed Tanaka Amikura," Mayer said impressed, staring at both Tyler and Stacy in front of him.

"That's right. And what are you going to do with the detonator you're holding?" Max asked with authority.

"I'm going to disappear with it," Mayer replied laughing into the radio. "You might want to worry about these two lovely ladies I have down here," Mayer said to Max.

Max knew that Tyler and his daughter could take care of themselves and replied to Mayer, "I don't EVER have to worry about *my* girls. But YOU do," Max said laughing.

Just as Max replied to Mayer, Stacy pulled two throwing knives out of sheaths attached to both of her wrists that had been hidden under her long sleeves while her hands were behind her neck and threw them both at the two nearest mercenaries, impaling both blades into their necks, dropping them both to their knees as they bled profusely and tried to pull the knives out. Blacking out, they both fell to the floor face down, blood spreading around them in a puddle on the floor.

The third mercenary looked at what Stacy had done to his two colleagues as blood continued to pour out of their necks in spurts. He turned to fire at her when Tyler grabbed his machine gun and pointed it upwards as bullets ripped through the barrel into the ceiling tiles above. He grabbed Tyler by the throat with one hand.

She started gasping for air as he raised her up off the floor when Stacy leveled a hard kick to his side, hurting his ribs and causing him to drop the machine gun and release his grip on Tyler's throat, dropping her back on her feet.

Mayer saw that his last body guard was getting his ass kicked as the other two lay dead in their own blood, blades sticking out of their necks, and decided he needed to escape. He ran down the hallway away from all of them.

Tyler coughed several times then composed herself to help Stacy with the big mercenary left standing. She landed a hard right-handed punch to his face knocking him to his knees.

"YOU GOT THIS?" Stacy yelled at Tyler referring to the mercenary on his knees watching Mayer run down the corridor away from them.

"Yeah. Go after him!" Tyler responded smiling at Stacy who was already running after Mayer. Tyler picked up her MP-5 from the floor and swung it at the mercenary's face, connecting to his jaw and knocking out several teeth that went flying out of his mouth. He rolled his eyes, then shut them and fell face first onto the floor.

Tyler quickly pulled out plastic cuffs and strapped them around his wrists behind his back. "Asshole," Tyler said to him as she got up off the floor moving her sore neck back and forth.

Stacy started running towards Mayer who turned and saw her coming after him. He pulled out a small cell phone-like device from his suit coat pocket and pressed one of several buttons on it. Stacy didn't see the metal explosive box filled with C-4 on the pillar as she ran past it chasing Mayer.

The explosion crumbled the concrete pillar, closing the hallway entrance with rubble. The force threw Stacy to the ground, knocking the wind out of her. She slowly caught her breath, coughing several times, and rose to her hands and knees to find Mayer standing there with one of her handguns pointed at her head and the detonator in his other hand with the concrete rubble now separating him and her from Tyler.

Stacy felt a sharp pain coming from her right arm and saw a big cut with blood slowly oozing out, but she knew she couldn't worry about that at the moment. She needed to concentrate on Mayer.

"You just blew up your *only* way out. What the HELL are you going to do now?" she managed to ask Mayer who also was exhausted and in pain from the blast.

Mayer smiled at the young woman, her clothes covered in concrete dust, now sitting up on her knees.

"This IS the way out," Mayer said pointing his finger to the "emergency door" sign to the IRS building her Uncle Jordy wanted to use earlier that day.

"But before I go, I still have to level the building so no one realizes I'm not dead. It will take them months to figure out I'm not in here with all of you," he bragged to Stacy laughing. "Meanwhile, I'll be on a beach somewhere getting a tan."

Mayer pushed the last button on his device and looked over to a larger metal box on the concrete pillar and smiled as the red & green lights came on, then he looked at Stacy.

"Wish I could have fucked you before all this, because in five minutes you're not going to look so good to me anymore," he said laughing.

Stacy looked at Mayer defiantly.

"I like my men a little on the *sane* side. My Dad's gonna fuck you up when he finds you, asshole."

"DUMB BITCH. Your dad's going to die in this building too, but not before you," Mayer said with anger standing over Stacy, still pointing the gun at her head and pulling back the hammer.

"HEY, ASSHOLE," Tyler yelled from where the rubble had closed off the entrance...except for a small opening where Tyler had her MP-5 rifle barrel and red laser sight pointing at his forehead. Just as Mayer looked up to see Tyler, the bullet ripped through his forehead killing him instantly and dropping him to the floor beside Stacy, blood slowly oozing out of the bullet hole and down his forehead, his dead eyes staring up at the ceiling.

"You *shouldn't* have called her a *bitch*," Tyler said loudly through the partial opening, bringing a smile to Stacy's face. Stacy could barely see Tyler through the hole but smiled and winked at her anyway to show her appreciation for saving her life.

Stacy collected herself and yelled to Tyler through the rubble.

"I need Uncle Mikey down here NOW! There's a big ass bomb here that's going to blow up the building in less than five minutes."

Tyler got on the radio and inquired, "Where *are* you, Commander Stevens?" Just as she finished asking her question she quickly turned her rifle on Jordy and Mikey, who raised their hands just as they arrived next to her.

"Stacy's in there with a large explosive device that's going to go off in less than four minutes that will surely level the building," Tyler explained to the two of them.

Jordy frantically started moving the large concrete slabs between the three of them and Stacy, but some were just too heavy.

"She's going to have to disarm the bomb herself," Mikey said to Tyler and Jordy, both looking at him worried. Jordy managed to make the partial opening a bit bigger so everyone could see Stacy standing at the large metal box attached to the pillar in front of them.

"Hey, sweetheart, you look like a mess," Mikey said with a smile.

"Gee thanks, Uncle Mikey," Stacy replied with a grin, knowing how she must have appeared covered in dust.

"I need you to disarm this bomb with me, okay?" he said calmly.

"Okay, but if we all die Dad's gonna be *pissed*," she said laughing. Mikey laughed with her.

Jordy pushed Mikey's bomb tool kit through the opening and Stacy picked it up off the floor and opened it.

"I need you to take the metal cover off the front slowly, but not too slowly," Mikey yelled to his scared goddaughter.

Stacy took out the battery-powered Phillips-head screwdriver and removed the four screws from the front and took the panel off to expose the bomb mechanism.

"There's a *shitload* of C-4 in this case," Stacy relayed.

"Tell me what colors the wires attached to the timer are," Mikey asked loudly.

"Red, green, white, black, and blue wires, and there's 2:45 left on the timer," she yelled back.

"Okay. I need you to cut the wires in this order, sweetheart," Mikey instructed. "Start with the blue one."

Jordy looked at Mikey and asked, "Why the blue one first?"

Mikey looked at Jordy and smiled.

"Because the blue one doesn't do anything. It's a common trick among bomb makers. I'm more concerned with the white one. There weren't any white wires in *any* of the bombs we disarmed coming down here. That's new. Now shut up and let me do this with her," Mikey said concerned but still managing a grin at Jordy.

Stacy slowly cut the blue wire with no detonation and smiled. "Not sure if I like doing this," she said to herself. Stacy yelled, "Done!" after cutting the wire.

"Now cut the green wire," Mikey told her.

Stacy slowly put the wire cutters on the green wire, closed her eyes and cut the wire. She opened her eyes smiling again.

"Done!" she yelled through the opening.

"Now cut the black wire," Mikey yelled through the opening.

After having already defused several of these bombs on his way down to Tyler and Stacy, Mikey now knew the cutting sequence of the wires by heart. But he still had no clue about the extra white one in this particular device.

Meantime, Jordy and Tyler together had been pulling the concrete rubble away from the entrance as best and as fast as they could, making the opening a little bigger each time while Mikey was instructing Stacy on how to disarm the bomb.

Stacy wiped the sweat from her forehead and placed the cutters on the black wire this time. She pressed them together, severing it without incident again.

"Done, Uncle Mikey!"

"You're doing great, sweetheart," Mikey said for reassurance while smiling at her through the now larger opening.

"Only two more, sweetie. Then we can all go home. How much time is left?" Mikey asked.

"1:15," Stacy yelled looking at the remaining wires nervously.

"Okay. Plenty of time," he told her hoping to calm her down. "I need you to cut one more wire, then it will be all over," Mikey said confidently. "Cut the red wire."

Stacy put the cutters on the red wire, closed her eyes then opened them.

"WAIT!" Mikey yelled putting his hand on Jordy's shoulder beside him.

Stacy pulled the cutters away from the red wire at the last moment and yelled, "WHAT THE *FUCK*, UNCLE MIKEY?"

"Cut the WHITE wire, Stacy," Mikey said firmly looking her in the eyes.

"Are you sure?" Stacy asked.

"Yes, I'm sure," Mikey confirmed.

"You didn't sound all that sure a moment ago," Stacy said sarcastically.

"CUT THE GODDAMN WHITE WIRE! THAT'S AN ORDER, ENSIGN," Mikey yelled knowing there were only seconds left.

"Okay, okay," Stacy replied, pissed off that he pulled rank on her. Stacy put the cutters to the white wire, closed her eyes and cut through it with NO reaction, the timer stopping at 28 seconds remaining. Stacy opened her eyes and smiled, then yelled enthusiastically, "It *worked*, Uncle Mikey! It *WORKED!*"

"How did you know it was the *white* wire?" Jordy asked Mikey with confusion on his face.

Mikey turned and sat on the rubble below the opening, wiped the sweat from his forehead and smiled.

"Tanaka was an arrogant creature of habit. He designed these bombs. He loved anything *white*," Mikey laughed, remembering everything Tanaka Amikura wore was white and even had pearl white handles on his guns.

"What the *hell* is going on down there guys?" Max yelled into Mikey and Jordy's earbuds as he moved down the fourth floor corridor towards the Computer Services office.

"Oh, hey boss. Sorry. Stacy was defusing a big ass bomb here in the basement and we had to temporarily turn our coms off," Jordy said grinning to Mikey.

"Are you fucking *kidding* me, Lieutenant?" Max yelled annoyed. "Are Stacy and Tyler okay?" Max asked hesitantly.

"They're both fine, boss. But it's gonna be a bitch to get out of here," Jordy replied rolling his eyes.

Stacy put the wire cutters back in Mikey's tool bag, put the strap over her head and looked up towards the opening that Jordy, Mikey and Tyler were making bigger. She could see their full faces looking down at her and started climbing up the concrete rubble to see if she could get out. When she got to the top, Tyler stuck her arm through the opening and grabbed her hand.

"Are you okay, sweetie?" she asked.

"Yeah, thanks. Nice shot, by the way. Did my dad teach you that?" Stacy asked smiling.

"He might have had something to do with it," Tyler said grinning.

Stacy pulled her arm back and started throwing some of the concrete rubble that she was able to pick up down to the floor on *her* side, making the opening a little bigger each time. Finally, it was big enough for Stacy to squeeze through. She took Mikey's tool bag from around her neck and handed it to Jordy on the other side and started crawling through the opening head first.

Jordy and Mikey grabbed their goddaughter and helped her through until she was able to stand on the floor below them. Jordy saw she was bleeding from a deep cut on her arm.

"Have a seat and let me look at that cut."

"We need to go help my Dad. I'm fine," Stacy replied anxiously to Jordy.

Jordy could see that the cut was deep and needed stitches immediately or she was going to lose a lot of blood. He looked at his goddaughter sternly.

"I SAID, have a *seat* Ensign and let me look at that wound. That's an *order.*"

Stacy looked at Mikey, and he smiled and nodded indicating Jordy was right about the wound.

"Yes, sir," Stacy acknowledged as she took a seat on the concrete rubble.

Jordy grabbed his medical kit from the back of his tactical vest and started going through it to get what he needed for her bleeding wound.

"I'm going to have to stitch this up for you," Jordy told her grabbing the needle and thread from his bag.

"Can't you just give me a Scooby-doo band-aid and a lollipop, and send me on my way?" Stacy asked snickering.

Jordy gave her a condescending smile.

"NO, you need stitches! Now hold still" he ordered.

Threading the needle with the medical thread, Jordy slowly punctured the skin on both sides of her wound and pulled the thread through.

"Goddamn that hurts, Uncle Jordy!" Stacy yelled at him as he slowly punctured the skin again for another stitch through the cut.

"Stop whining like a little girl," Jordy replied smiling at her.

Tyler looked at Jordy, then Stacy as if to say, "Oh *no*, you *didn't* just say that to her," watching Mikey laugh at them both.

"I love you, Uncle Jordy," Stacy said knowing he was only helping her and she shouldn't be cross with him.

"I love you too, sweetheart. We're almost done," Jordy replied with a smile as Stacy winced with each stitch he had to make. Jordy finished the final stitch and tied the thread off, then he took out the small alcohol bottle and showed it to Stacy. "This is the bad part sweetie," he informed her.

Stacy looked at him and actually gave him a boo boo lip.

"It's gonna hurt like *hell* for a moment, but it has to be done, sweetheart," Jordy explained.

"I know. Just do it," she said bravely.

Jordy took a big piece of medical gauze from his bag and soaked it in alcohol.

"Take a deep breath," he told Stacy, already tensing up. Stacy inhaled deeply and Jordy rubbed the alcohol-soaked cloth on the stitched up cut.

"OH, MY GOD!" Stacy screamed, tears coming down her cheeks having never felt that kind of pain before.

"Breathe, sweetheart, breathe," Jordy said trying to comfort her.

The initial shock of extreme pain was subsiding and Stacy was only feeling a sharp sting of pain as Jordy slowly cleaned the stitched-up wound. Stacy wiped away her tears and watched as Jordy covered the wound with a large medical patch on her arm above her elbow.

"Is this gonna leave a scar?" Stacy asked looking at the now bandaged wound on her arm.

"Yeah, I'm afraid it will," Jordy replied.

"Cool. My *first* Navy SEAL battle scar," Stacy said, her smile now beaming to everyone around her.

"You know you're SOOOO getting a SEAL tattoo when we get out of here," Jordy said with a grin.

Stacy looked over at Mikey, who smiled and nodded in agreement of that idea.

"Can't hurt as bad as this did," she said laughing as she wiped another tear from her face. Jordy and Mikey looked at each other and snickered.

Stacy tried to get up and stand on her feet but she was a bit woozy, and Jordy had to catch her from falling back to the floor.

"I need to help my Dad," she said, falling into Jordy's arms.

"You're not going anywhere for a bit, Ensign," Mikey said to her.

"Your dad will be fine. I promise," Mikey said to her as she was lowered back to a sitting position on the floor.

"What's your status, boss?" Mikey asked Max, touching the com link in his ear.

"I'm on the fourth floor heading to the Computer Services office. That's where Jurgens was headed, copy," Max replied.

"I'm afraid we're not going to be much use to you, boss," Mikey said. "Mayer is dead, and the main bomb has been defused down here, but he managed to detonate a smaller one and there's rubble everywhere. Gonna be a while for us to catch up to you."

"Remind me to have a talk with you three about letting the "newbie" defuse the bomb in the basement," Max said with a chuckle.

"She didn't have much of a choice boss, and besides she wanted to do it," Mikey said laughing.

"Of course she did. What 21-year-old recruit with *no* experience wouldn't want to defuse a live bomb that could kill hundreds of people," Max said sarcastically to his friend.

"Tell Stacy I love her and that I'm *very* proud of her," Max said to his longtime friend. "I think I'm losing battery power in my com link. It keeps going in and out, so this may be our last conversation, Commander," Max said solemnly.

"Aye aye, Captain," Mikey replied, respectfully looking over at his three companions sitting on the mound of rubble.

"You and Jordy get everyone out of the building in case Jurgens has any surprises like Mayer had," Max replied.

"Oh yeah, and tell Tyler we *still* have a dinner date when this is all over," Max said laughing.

"Yes, sir," Mikey replied with a grin. He then looked at everyone and smiled. "Seems the Captain wants us to get everyone out of here while he goes and takes on Jurgens by himself."

He looked at Tyler, raising his eyebrows and cocking his head as he relayed Max's message to her.

"By the way, dinner is still *on*."

Tyler smiled back as Stacy tried to get up again without Jordy's help.

"I have to go help my father," Stacy said to everyone, staggering as she stood up.

"We have our orders, Ensign. Your father will be fine," Mikey said to her in a stern voice.

Jordy looked at Mikey with concern because they had *never* been separated before until now.

Mikey looked back at Jordy understanding the look on his face.

"He'll be fine. He's been in worse situations than this before, you know that," Mikey replied.

Jordy still couldn't help wonder whether they would see Max again after this night.

"We still have work to do," Mikey said to the three of them. "I can see at least three bombs that need defusing before we can head upstairs," he said looking at the two bombs lying on the floor and the one down the corridor attached to a concrete pillar.

"Thank God Mayer didn't activate them before we took him out," Tyler said with a smile to Stacy.

Stacy was finally feeling better as she watched Mikey and Jordy work together to defuse the two bombs on the floor beside the dead mercenaries.

"Do you think my Dad will be okay against Jurgens?" she asked Mikey.

"I do. The three of us have been through much harder missions than this, sweetie," Mikey said trying to comfort her.

"We met Jurgens. He's a pussy. Your dad can kick his ass easily," Jordy said to Stacy with a grin, then looked back at Mikey, changing his facial expression to worried.

CHAPTER 13

MAX CAUTIOUSLY MOVED DOWN THE THIRD floor corridor and reached another hallway to his right, his AR rifle pointed in front of him. He slowly looked around the corner to see a lone masked mercenary standing guard outside the Computer Services office.

Max knew there was only one way in or out of the office because of the highly sensitive security data servers located there. He also knew about all the security protocols in the building, especially the special safeguards put in place for the data servers because of his security job at GBN.

Max figured that Jurgens or the mercenary standing there had killed the armed security guard GBN had stationed at the door because of the large pool of blood he could see on the floor under the mercenary's boots. This angered Max a lot more, because he had a friendly relationship with most of the armed uniform security staff in the building. He knew that most of the guards had families and loved ones that Jurgens, Mayer, and Tanaka Amikura destroyed by killing the guards just for money and revenge.

Max needed to get into the Computer Services office the masked mercenary was guarding quietly to surprise Jurgens and believed he had just two options -- kill the mercenary from the corner where he stood with his AR rifle, which would alert Jurgens that he was there by dropping the mercenary in front of the door, or draw the mercenary away from the door quietly and take him out one-on-one.

Max still didn't want to kill unnecessarily so he looked around the hallway to see what he could do with the mercenary. He knew Jurgens wasn't getting into the server room very easily but figured he had a plan already in motion.

He looked up and realized that as his back was against the wall there was a steel ladder bolted to the concrete wall above him that went up to the ceiling about fifteen feet where a large metal electrical box was located.

He climbed up the ladder to evaluate the height from the ceiling to the floor and figured he could ambush the mercenary quietly if he made a distraction below to catch him by surprise.

Max quietly maneuvered down from the steel ladder, stood against the wall and thought for a moment. He glanced quickly around the corner again, looking down the hallway while the mercenary continued to stand guard at the office door. He noticed there were two other offices with glass doors halfway down the hallway on both sides of the corridor and saw the reflection they made with the lighting fixtures above them. He smiled and thought this was his way to get the mercenary away from the door without Jurgens getting suspicious.

Max took out his universal multi-tool from its sheath and promptly pulled out the screwdriver. He carefully unscrewed and detached the red laser sight from the accessory rail of his AR rifle and switched it on down the hallway behind him to make sure the battery was working. The red beam shone brightly, so Max turned it off, satisfied the battery was good. He got down on his knees near the hallway entrance and positioned the small laser mechanism on top of a cardboard box he found in a hallway closet, concentrating the red beam towards the closest set of glass doors. He switched it on for a split second to see where the beam would reflect off the glass door and realized it bounced to the other glass door across the hallway, a few feet down closer to the mercenary's position.

Max quickly turned the beam off before the mercenary spotted it. He needed to get ready now that he thought this would work.

He grabbed one of the steel batons he used against Tanaka out of its holster in the back of his tactical vest and extended it to its full length. He slid it between his vest and his gun belt in front of him to hold it in place before he climbed the ladder. He positioned the laser to reflect the bright red beam off both glass doors near the mercenary and the Computer Services office door, hoping it was just enough to make him curious to see what it was at the end of the hallway.

He switched on the laser sight sitting on the strategically-placed cardboard box and immediately climbed the ladder at the corner of the two hallways getting as high as he could.

Holding on to a rung with his left hand and taking out his baton with his right, Max waited to see if Jurgens' hooded mercenary would leave his assigned post to investigate the mysterious light.

Max watched from his perch, seeing the bright red beam go down the hallway...but knew he had to wait for the mercenary to be in position to subdue him. Max thought about how much he hated to wait for anything. He twisted himself around so he could hold on and see the mercenary coming from around the corner above his head. Max wondered if his friends in the basement were doing okay as he waited on the steel ladder.

The masked mercenary caught a glimpse of something red in the glass door of the office opposite his position. He hesitated at first but decided to walk across to it anyway to see what was shining through the glass. He looked into the office through the doors and didn't see anything red or shiny from where he was standing. He shrugged it off and was returning to stand guard at the Computer Services door when he glanced over at the other office door across the way and saw the same shiny red reflection in that glass.

The masked mercenary became suspicious, having now seen two shiny red reflections on separate glass doors. He aimed his loaded MP-5 machine gun down the hallway as he headed towards the bright red beam he could see reflecting into the second office door.

He slowly and cautiously looked into the office but again couldn't find any shiny red reflection coming from inside.

Now a bit confused, the mercenary looked down to the end of the corridor and saw that the shiny red beam was coming from a corner at the end of the hallway where it split. The armed mercenary slowly headed towards the bright red light. Max had positioned the red laser beam to reflect off both office glass doors to disorient the terrorist and it seemed to work.

The mercenary slowly turned the corner of the hallway, his machine gun pointed, and saw nothing down the corridor except the cardboard box the red laser sight was sitting on and he went towards it. Just as he completely rounded the corner, he casually glanced up to see Max Mason jumping down on top of him, boots first, from the ladder on the wall.

Max hit the masked mercenary hard to the floor, knocking his machine gun several feet away from him. Max stood over him smiling.

"Not really your day today now, is it," Max said as the dazed gun-man looked up at him.

The masked man shook off Max's initial attack and thrust-kicked him to the midsection, sending him backwards, surprising Max but not knocking him down. It was just enough time to allow the merce-nary to get to his feet.

"We've been expecting you, asshole," the large masked assailant said to Max.

"Well, I do hate being late to a party," Max said laughing.

The mercenary swung at Max with his right fist but Max blocked it with his steel baton, causing the masked man to shake his hand in pain.

"Damn, that's gonna hurt a little," Max said to him grinning.

"I'm going to kill you myself. I don't care what special plans Jurgens has in mind for you."

"Oh, now you went and spoiled the surprise. Your asshole boss isn't gonna like that," Max replied sarcastically.

"Fuck Jurgens," the mercenary replied to Max as he slowly took his large combat knife out of its sheath. "I'm going to slowly skin you alive," he said as he ripped his black wool mask off, revealing a completely burnt, scarred face smiling at Max.

"Wow! You're just an *ugly* mother fucker. I bet you don't get a lot of dates," Max said continuing to laugh at and taunt the scarred mercenary.

Max figured the element of surprise was gone, knowing that Jurgens was waiting for him, so keeping quiet wasn't necessary any more. The now unmasked mercenary screamed at Max as he moved towards him swinging his big knife.

"I'LL *KILL* YOU, ASSHOLE!"

"Now is that anyway to talk with all the children in the building?" Max asked stepping back and reaching behind his head. He pulled out Mikey's last gift to him, a mini .22 magnum machine pistol with a 30-round magazine holstered to the back of his tactical vest close to his neck.

Max promptly fired a long burst of ten to fifteen rounds into the attacking mercenary, watching as the bullets ripped through his upper torso, putting a look of shock on his face as he died staring at Max.

"Don't you just hate it when that happens?" Max said to him as his body fell to the floor, blood starting to flow from the many bullet holes in his chest. Max stood over the dead mercenary, his gun barrel still smoking.

"Sorry dude, just the way it had to be. Wrong job at the wrong time."

Max looked at his new gun and realized .22 magnum rounds can cause some serious body damage. He then looked around the corner of the hallway with Mikey's new gun in hand to make sure no one else came running out of the office to help the dead mercenary. After a few minutes and no one appearing, Max figured they were all waiting for him inside the office. He said to himself, "I would kill for a pizza right now," laughing about how hungry he was.

Max stood there for a moment wondering what Jurgens had in store for him in the computer office…reloaded his mini .22 magnum with a full magazine, checked his handgun magazine and slid it back in its holster. He decided to leave his AR rifle behind, leaning it up against the wall in the hallway, using the smaller machine pistol as his primary weapon going into the office. It was easier and more compact in a close-quarters situation. Mikey Stevens, the gunsmith, knew how to make a good reliable gun, Max thought with a smile.

Max shook his arms and head to get into the right frame of mind and decided it was time to go arrest Jurgens and stop him from taking the $250 million dollars from all those poor hungry kids. Max was a father and that pissed him off.

He slowly moved down the hallway, continuing to hug the wall, looking back and forth until he came to the double glass doors of Computer Services office.

Max stood to the side of the doors, glancing down at his feet to see the blood-stained carpet and closed his eyes for a moment in sadness.

He then opened the door and moved quickly inside seeing only the receptionist's desk and the back of her chair under the big "COMPUTER SERVICES" sign on the wall behind it. In the lobby area, he saw a couple of chairs, a coffee table and several plants.

Max had been in this office many times and thought it was a pleasant place for their employees to work. He remembered it was the *only* office in the GBN building with closed circuit TV cameras directly fed to the FBI's cyber-division across town because of the high security information servers it housed.

Max cautiously moved from the glass door towards the lobby desk, holding his machine-pistol with two hands pointing at both the right and left open hallways on each side of it. He knew he had to stop Jurgens from downloading the bank codes to the secure servers or the telethon money would be lost forever, with *only* Jurgens able to access the money whether he was in prison or not. Max remembered Jurgens bragging about the bank being in a country with no extradition treaty and knew he needed to stop the download to keep the money for the kids in the U.S.

"You can't even be on time for your own death," a voice came from behind the receptionist desk.

Max stopped in the middle of the lobby and watched as the receptionist's chair slowly turned to reveal Jurgens sitting there with his arms folded, his hands hidden by the desk.

Max smiled then lowered his head and shook it back and forth laughing loudly at Jurgens, his gun still pointed at him.

Max looked at Jurgens with a big grin.

"Frankly, I'm *extremely* disappointed you're not holding a white cat," he said making a sarcastic reference to a couple of his favorite secret agent movies.

Immediately after his comment, Max felt severe pain in his right hand and dropped his new gun on the floor. Looking at the back of his hand he saw a steel-bladed throwing star deeply embedded in his skin causing blood to ooze out of the wound around it. Max pulled the steel blade out of his hand angrily and painfully and threw it to the floor.

Max quickly removed the glove covering his blood-soaked hand. He put pressure on it to stop the bleeding with his left hand, immediately grimacing with pain. He looked at Jurgens, now pointing a gun at him, and saw to his right a black-clad figure standing in the adjacent hallway, his face covered with a mask.

"Well, this is a fine mess you got yourself into, Mason" Jurgens said laughing as he continued sitting in the chair with a gun in his hand pointed at Max.

Max looked over at the masked assailant and then to Jurgens.

"Another ugly friend of yours?" Max asked, still holding his injured right hand. "Seems you *only* have ugly friends who have to wear masks. Now I understand why they can't get laid," Max said, smiling while looking at Jurgens' new friend.

"Now is that any way to talk to the person who's gonna determine if you die quickly, or slowly?" Jurgens proclaimed grinning.

Max looked at Jurgens with contempt in his eyes.

"I think you have the wrong guy, dude. I determine how I die, not some ninja wannabe," he said angrily watching the black ninja take a step towards him. "Come on, asshole, let's dance," he said smiling at the black ninja who was obviously infuriated at his challenge.

"Now now, boys. Mayer and I paid a lot of good money for this fight. Let's not cheat us out of it," Jurgens said as he got up out of the chair, his gun still aimed at Max.

"Before we get started, drop your weapons on the floor and kick them to the side," Jurgens ordered.

Max slowly unbuckled his gun belt with his left hand, trying not to use his painfully-injured right one, and dropped it to the floor in front of him.

"Now take off the vest. Wouldn't want you using any of those special toys you have hidden in it," Jurgens said to Max grinning.

Max unzipped and removed his tactical vest and laid it on top of his gun belt already lying on the floor.

"Who's your pet monkey?" Max asked Jurgens, referring to the silent black ninja standing next to him.

"You didn't think we wouldn't have a backup plan, if by chance you managed to kill Tanaka now, did you?" Jurgens replied.

"Tanaka found him in a psychiatric hospital five years ago. Trained him to kill anyone he needed dead."

Max listened to Jurgens but continued to stare into the ninja's eyes and found something peculiar about them, like they were dead already.

"After Tanaka helped him escape the hospital, he took him to Japan where he's been ever since," Jurgens explained. "He's killed over 100 men, women and - yes - children. They have a special name for him there," Jurgens said with a smile.

"The Demon," Max said before Jurgens had a chance to.

"YES, so you've heard of him. Good, because you're going to die by him," Jurgens said with a serious look at Max.

Max remembered hearing rumors years ago about a man in the Japanese mountains who was obsessed with killing but only killed when his Master told him to. He only used his sword to kill in the dead of night, making him a ghost, some calling him a "demon."

Because of that, he became known as "The Demon". Max thought it a bit silly but he knew others who were truly scared of his reputation.

Two more black-clad ninjas came and stood in the left hallway just as Jurgens moved around from behind the receptionist's desk.

"Oh look, he brought friends," Jurgens said sarcastically to Max.

"Goodbye, Mason, and good riddance," he said, walking behind the two ninjas close to him.

"I'll see you in a few minutes, asshole," Max said loudly to Jurgens as he started to leave. Jurgens turned and gave Max a smile and flipped him off as he walked away.

Max looked at the three ninjas and smiled. "Which one of you wants to go to *hell* first?" Max asked confidently.

The ninja called Demon, who seemed to be in charge of the other two, looked at them both and motioned for them to attack the injured and unarmed Max Mason. Max went into a defensive fight stance as he watched the two black-clothed men pull long steel bladed swords from scabbards above their heads. Max looked at Demon standing in the hallway watching.

"Two against one. Kinda seems unfair to *them*, don't you think?" Max said, continuing to smile at all three of them.

The Demon motioned with his hand and one of the ninjas stepped back allowing the other to go one-on-one with Max.

The ninja ran towards Max, his sword above his head slicing down at Max's head. Max stepped aside and smacked the ninja hard in the face with his open left hand then jumped back into his fighting stance.

"I thought Tanaka taught you all how to fight. I guess you must have missed that class," Max said toying with him to make a mistake. "Maybe he taught you how to die."

The ninja stopped and rubbed his cheek through his mask thinking Max got a lucky shot and advanced again, swinging his sword towards Max's throat. Max ducked under it and came up under the ninja's arm, landing his injured right fist into his midsection, staggering the ninja backwards and causing him to grab his ribs.

Max shook his right hand and grimaced in pain as well, noticing blood coming from the wound again. He looked over at the ninja everyone called Demon and still noticed something strange about his eyes, something very familiar, but he couldn't place them.

The ninja thrust his sharp sword at Max, but he was able to move to his right, out of the way, and landed another hard right-handed punch to the ninja's jaw, again hurting Max's hand in the process. Max shook his hand and rubbed it with the other as he watched the ninja rub his jaw with rage in his eyes.

Max knew this was going to have to come to a quick end because his hand was hurting much more than he wanted it to and he had two more bad guys to take on before he could go after Jurgens again.

Max stood in a defensive posture, waiting for the ninja to attack again. He noticed the leader nodding to the other ninja waiting to engage Max as well. Max gave a quick glance over at his tactical vest on the floor where his batons were as both ninjas attacked from different directions at the same time. Max remembered what Sensei Amikura taught him about using multiple opponents' own energy against each other. He ducked under one blade while maneuvering the other ninja to strike his partner's blade, stopping it before it cut Max.

Max quickly landed a hard left kick to one of the ninja's midsection, knocking him backwards into his leader. The ninja leader looked pissed at Max and pushed the ninja away from him forcefully.

"Don't worry, you'll get your turn, asshole," Max said flashing a quick smile at The Demon and turning his attention back to the other ninja coming towards him.

Max watched as both ninjas were about to attack together, looking at each other to decide who was going first.

One ninja swung his sword at Max who stepped into the swing and grabbed the ninja's hands on the hilt and reacted to the other ninja's blade coming towards his head. He forced the blade up to block the ninja's strike, elbowing the ninja he had hold of in the face several times, relieving him of his sword as he fell to the floor behind Max.

Max quickly went on the offensive now that he had a sword of his own to use and he clashed blades over and over with the ninja still armed. Max knew how to use a sword, he just didn't like to.

The now unarmed ninja tried to sneak up behind Max who spun around to land a hard roundhouse kick to his head, knocking him to the floor yet again. The ninja's sword came down as Max spun back around to face him, and it managed to cut Max on his left arm, forcing him to grab it and hold the sword with the injured right hand.

Max evaluated the cut on his arm as not too deep or long. In fact, he brushed it off as a simple flesh wound, a minor painful inconvenience. He glanced back to see the ninja getting back up on his feet as the other stood in front of him smiling through his mask.

"I hate this ninja crap," Max said to them all.

He looked at the smiling ninja, wiped the blood off his arm with his fingers and said, "Come get some, asshole," raising the sword above his head in classic Japanese samurai form.

Max timed his move perfectly, watching the ninja's sword lunge towards him as the other ninja tried to take him from behind. Max moved sideways, spinning out of the way as the ninja's sword slid into the heart of the ninja behind him, surprising them both.

Max moved behind them both, slicing his sword down on the other ninja's back, almost cutting him in half. Both ninjas fell to the floor dead, and Max stood over them, his sword dripping with their blood. He turned and smiled at the ninja leader Jurgens & Mayer had hired to kill him.

"I guess it's your turn now," Max said as he looked down at the two dead ninjas, then back at The Demon. "We *could* call it a day and you could get out of my way so I can go get Jurgens."

The ninja finally spoke to Max.

"I've waited five long years for this moment." he said through his mask.

"Do I know you? Have we crossed paths before?" Max asked, looking puzzled and thinking that the ninja's eyes looked familiar.

The ninja slowly slid his sword out of the scabbard from behind his back and brought it to his side.

"Tanaka Amikura rescued me from a life of imprisonment and trained me the past five years for revenge," he said to Max.

"I have no idea what you are talking about. Tanaka was a homicidal lunatic who killed his own father and now he's dead," Max replied.

"You killed MY mentor, MY Master, and MY friend," the ninja said as he began swinging his sword aggressively in front of Max to intimidate him.

"He was an asshole," Max said to him defiantly with a grin.

What Max said did not sit well with the ninja, which gave Max exactly what he wanted - the agitated ninja making the first move against him.

Demon swung his sword at Max, who countered, and the clang of their swords hitting each other emitting sparks echoed down the hallways.

The ninja pushed his crossed sword against Max's with intense strength until they were face to face. Max smiled at him, still pushing his sword into the ninja's but felt a rush of pain to his forehead as the ninja head butted him, staggering Max backwards.

"Very nice, asshole," Max said smiling, as he collected himself and looked directly in the ninja's eyes, still wondering where he might have seen them.

The Demon attacked again, swinging his sword back and forth. Max countered each swing with steel hitting steel. He let his right hand slide off his sword and connected with a full force jab to the ninja's face, knocking him backwards a few feet.

"Doesn't feel good, does it, asshole?" Max said with a serious look on his face this time.

This angered the ninja even more and he came at Max swinging his sword swiftly, catching Max a bit off guard. The Demon ninja managed to cut him on the chest, ripping Max's shirt and revealing the Kevlar protective vest he was wearing.

"So I guess I have to cut your head off," the ninja said through his mask.

"Take your best shot, asshole," Max replied smiling.

Max's condescending attitude made the ninja angrier and he moved quickly towards Max who countered with a sidekick to the ninja's ribs, causing him to fall to the floor holding them. He quickly got back on his feet and swung his blade anxiously, enabling Max to counter and come down with his blade cutting his left arm. The ninja stepped back to evaluate his wound as it bled down his arm through his long sleeve, dripping onto his hand and then to the floor.

"Damn, that has to hurt. I know mine does," Max said to him as the ninja continued to watch his blood drip onto the floor.

"YOU should have made BOTH of those Presidential brats use the restroom that night," the now injured ninja screamed at Max.

"WHAT?!? . . . . "WHAT did you say?" Max asked the bleeding ninja. The ninja stood in front of Max and slowly removed his mask with his free hand, finally revealing his face to Max.

"JASON CARPENTER!" Max yelled, shocked. "You're supposed to be dead," Max said confused.

"But I *am* dead, Max Mason," the ninja said to Max smiling.

Max studied his face for a long moment and noticed this Jason Carpenter's face didn't have the small scar under his left ear he got from a hot bullet casing that flew back at him at the firing range and burned and scarred him.

"You're NOT Jason Carpenter. You look like him, but you're NOT him. Who are you?" Max demanded.

The ninja started laughing "He worked with you for almost a year and you didn't know he had an identical twin brother locked up in a mental hospital did you, Max?" Carpenter's brother asked.

"Jason kept to himself, never talked about his family," Max said to him cautiously, knowing now that he was unstable.

"My brother left me in that Hell hole to rot after our parents died, but I forgave him because we were connected by birth. We were family, but then *you* had him killed," Carpenter's twin said to Max.

"So what does this vendetta have to do with me and Tanaka?" Max asked moving slowly away from him.

"Sensei Amikura rescued me from MY padded HELL, and told me how you helped in killing MY brother that night five years ago," the blood dripping ninja said slowly gripping his sword with both hands.

Carpenter moved quickly towards Max swinging his sword while Max countered each swing with his own. They both broke off and started circling each other while Max looked his opponent in the eyes.

"Tanaka was the one who planted the bomb that killed your brother and a precious little boy Jason swore to protect that night, NOT me you crazy fuck," Max yelled at the demented ninja.

"That homicidal maniac trained you to kill me because he didn't have the stones to do it himself until tonight, and look where that got him," Max continued, pissing his opponent off even more.

Carpenter turned red with anger hearing what Max said about his Master and rushed at Max again. He thrust his blade forward as Max blocked each lunge, then Max hit him hard in the jaw with his injured right fist, staggering Carpenter backwards again.

Max shook his right hand several times feeling the pain from the contact. Carpenter stood there for a moment and rubbed his jaw sneering at Max Mason with hatred and contempt in his eyes.

"Jason was a good agent, and a good person. He didn't deserve what he got" Max said trying to calm Jason's twin brother down.

"Tanaka used people. He used *you* just like he used that woman to carry the bomb that killed him five years ago," Max tried explaining.

Max could still see the hate and anger in Carpenter's brother's eyes and realized this wasn't going to end well. "I don't want to kill you, and you don't want to be dead" Max said to the ninja who was ready to attack again.

"You killed my Master and my brother. Now I'm going to kill you, Max Mason" Carpenter yelled running towards Max with his sword over his head.

Max stood waiting for him and ducked under his swinging sword and swung his blade under his midsection, slicing the flesh open in a spray of blood, knocking the ninja down to the floor.

Carpenter got to his knees holding his bleeding wound next to the tactical gear and weapons Jurgens had made Max remove. Carpenter looked shocked that he was severely wounded. He looked over and saw Max's gun belt with his SA-XD 9mm handgun still in the holster.

Max knew exactly what the wounded ninja was thinking as he looked at his gun belt, so he dropped his sword and dove over the top of the receptionist's desk just as Carpenter came up with Max's gun, firing at the desk Max was now hiding behind.

Carpenter stopped firing briefly, holding onto his wounded side. It gave Max enough time to pull out the .380 automatic pistol he kept in his right ankle holster and crawl to the other side of the desk. Carpenter slowly walked around the end of the desk, blood dripping heavily from his wound now, to find Max lying on his back with his gun pointed at him.

Max looked at him with sad eyes and spoke "Don't do it. Don't make me kill you."

The ninja smiled at Max and slowly started to raise the gun in his hand, forcing Max to fire three rounds into him at point blank range.

Carpenter lowered his gun and slowly fell to his knees as blood starting flowing from his mouth. He looked at Max still on his knees in front of him, smiled and said, "My name is Joshua Carpenter," then closed his eyes and fell over sideways, his blood starting to cover the floor under him.

Max laid there for a long moment staring at the now dead ninja… closed his eyes and shook his head. He slowly and painfully got up off the floor, took his gun out of Jason Carpenter's brother's lifeless hand, walked over to his gear lying on the floor and put his gun belt and vest back on.

He slid his handgun back into its holster. Max stood there for a moment looking at Joshua Carpenter lying dead on the floor in his own blood thinking how Tanaka and Jurgens used and destroyed *his* life for petty revenge.

Max was so angry that he flipped the desk over and threw the chair against the wall, scattering broken pieces. He stood and looked at what he just did, shook his head and screamed one word: "JURGENS!"

CHAPTER 14

BRIAN JURGENS WALKED INTO JAMES RICHARDS'
office with two mercenaries, one on each side of him, and stood in
front of Richards who was sitting behind his desk.

"What the *hell* is the meaning of this Brian?" Richards asked,
looking up from his desk.

"I need to get into the server room James," Jurgens replied smiling.

Richards stood up behind his desk and asked defiantly, "Do you
have clearance from security, Brian?"

Jurgens looked at the two mercenaries who stood beside him,
then back to Richards.

"These are the *only* security clearances I need at the moment," he
replied, continuing to smile at Director Richards. "Now if you don't
mind, I'm kinda in a hurry."

"What are you trying to do, Brian?" Richards asked angrily.

"I'm not *trying* to do anything, James. I'm ROBBING the Federal
Government of $250 million dollars," Jurgens replied laughing.

James Richards walked around his desk and stood in front of
Brian Jurgens watching the two mercenaries point their machine
guns at him.

Jurgens grabbed Richards ID and yanked it off from around his
neck. "I'm gonna need this soon," Jurgens said to the startled Director.

"You're going to take the children's telethon money out of the server?" Richards asked, realizing what Jurgens was about to do.

"I'm afraid so," Jurgens replied continuing to giggle.

"What makes you think I have *any* intention of helping you, Brian?" Richards asked with contempt.

"Because, James, you're no hero, and it's not YOUR money I'm taking *anyway.*"

"You'll have to KILL me before I allow you in the server room. That money belongs to the children," Richards said to Jurgens angrily.

Jurgens looked at the two mercenaries and said, "Step outside."

The two armed men looked at Richards, then nodded to Jurgens and walked out of the office.

"Give me the entry code and I will give you some of the money to *your* bank of choice," Jurgens said hoping he could be bribed. "You can give it to whatever charity you want," Jurgens assured him.

"I'd rather be dead," Richards replied angrily.

"You're such a sentimental putz," Jurgens said. "Suit yourself."

Jurgens pulled his handgun out from behind his back and waved it towards the door to get Richards to head to the server room ahead of him.

Richards started walking towards the doorway when he suddenly turned and tried to grab Jurgens gun from his hand. The loud bang could be heard down the hallway as the bullet from Jurgens gun hit Richards in the lower part of his midsection and went out through his lower back.

Blood started pouring out of both wounds and Richards fell to the ground looking up at Jurgens in shock at what he did.

"Goddamn it, James, look what you made me do," Jurgens said holding the discharged firearm in his hand.

"Fuck you, Brian," Richards said defiantly as he slipped into unconsciousness, his body lying at Jurgens' feet.

Jurgens stood there with his head bowed and eyes closed thinking that this was never his intention, but he was way past feeling guilty and yelled, "Get in here you two."

The two mercenaries came back into the office and saw Richards lying on the floor and Jurgens standing over him with a smoking gun in his hand.

"Give me a knife," Jurgens ordered with no remorse whatsoever for what he had just done.

Max Mason heard the gunshot from the other side of the hallway and headed in that direction, still feeling the pain in his hand and arm from the fight with Carpenter's twin brother and his two ninja friends.

Max stopped for a moment halfway down the hallway, pulled his handgun from its holster, ejected the empty magazine, and replaced it with a full 20-round one before he started walking towards the server room and James Richards' office.

Max cautiously rounded the corner of the hallway, his gun pointing everywhere his eyes went and came to Richards' opened office door. Max slowly walked in to find his body lying on the floor in a large pool of blood in front of his desk.

Max sadly stood beside the body as he looked over Richards' desk, shuffling papers from one side to the other hoping to find a code book or clue that might help him get into the server room to stop Jurgens.

Frustrated that he couldn't find anything to help, Max turned to leave when a soft breathing James Richards grabbed his ankle, looked up at him and said something Max could not make out.

"Hang in there, James. I'll get you some help," Max said to his seriously injured GBN colleague.

Again, Richards said something to Max he couldn't understand.

"What are you trying to say, James?"

"SHOOT THE SERVER," Richards yelled before collapsing and dying in front of Max.

Max walked over to the couch a few feet from Richards and grabbed the blanket to cover his dead fellow employee. Max stood there for a moment staring at the lifeless body getting angrier at how he found him.

Max Mason was extremely pissed now and remembered that James Richards and he had had lunch many times together over the past year and thought of him as a friend and a good person who *always* did the right thing. They had been to several Sentinels games over the past season and his love of baseball was unsurpassed. He didn't deserve this, Max thought, and he understood that Jurgens was responsible for all this happening and Max needed to end it.

Max left Richards' office and headed towards the server room down the hallway.

As Max was about to turn the corner, one of Jurgens two mercenaries opened fire on him with his machine gun ripping bullets into the wall next to him. He quickly ducked back around the corner avoiding the deadly rounds.

Max smiled and thought to himself that Jurgens' hired guns couldn't shoot worth shit. "Jurgens must have found these guys at some carnival shooting game" he said out loud thinking of how he was going to get down that hallway.

Max stood against the wall where the two corridors intersected and simply put his gun around the corner and fired five or six rounds, not seeing where he was aiming. He just wanted to start some confusion for whoever was firing at him.

Max reached behind his back and grabbed the two smoke grenades from the small bag attached to his tactical vest. He knew he wasn't going to make it down that hallway without some cover or distraction. He thought that enough smoke would hide his advancement, but he also realized that the downside was he wouldn't be able to see the angry mercenary shooting at him until he was practically right next to him.

He rolled his eyes, took a deep breath and pulled the safety pins on the grenades and quickly tossed them both down the corridor towards the lone mercenary standing in the doorway to the server room.

The white phosphorus smoke from the grenades started filling the hallway, not allowing either Max or the mercenary to see either end of the hallway or each other. Max knew he had about fifteen bullets left in his handgun, so he knew he would have to finish this quickly. He turned the corner and ran hard close to the opposite wall. He was half way down the corridor when he saw the mercenary still standing in the doorway taking aim at him with his machine gun. Max dove head first with his gun out in front of him. As he was sliding down the last half of the slick-tiled hall, he fired bullets in the direction of the doorway while bullets from the mercenary's machine gun flew just above his head.

Max's shots hit the mercenary several times in different parts of his body causing him to jerk uncontrollably and fall to the floor, his face looking at Max's just inches away.

"Fuck you, asshole," the mercenary said with one last defiant breath to Max, blood pouring out of his mouth from the bullet wounds Max had inflicted on him.

"Damn, that's harsh. Are you sure those are the last words you want to leave this world with?" Max asked sarcastically, smiling at the now dead mercenary.

Max stood up over the body and grabbed the 9mm MP-5 machine gun out of the dead man's hands, pulled out the ammo magazine and saw there were about 20 rounds left in it. He looked at the man's holstered handgun and realized it was a .40 caliber pistol not compatible with his SA-XD.

Max knew he had emptied his handgun into the mercenary, so he slowly took the 9mm bullets out of the machine gun magazine and reloaded his empty handgun magazine until it was completely full. Max knew he could have used the machine gun but preferred his handgun, a less complicated weapon in close combat. He left the now empty rifle on the floor next to the dead mercenary.

Max rolled the lifeless body over in the doorway to see what else he had, thinking, "What the Hell, he's not gonna need it anymore." He found a working radio on the man's tactical vest and snatched it off quickly so it wouldn't get soaked in the blood pouring out of his chest. Max figured he was *very* lucky that none of the bullets he put in the guy hit the radio, inspecting it thoroughly. He pushed the transmitter button, brought the radio to his lips and spoke.

"Jordy, do you copy?" he asked. Waiting a moment, Max spoke again. "Jordy, come in."

"Hey boss, nice to hear you're still with us," Jordy replied, coming over the radio's speaker.

"Yeah, a little banged up but still alive so far," Max responded laughing. "Is everyone okay?"

"Yes, sir. Stacy's a bit excited about her first SEAL scar, but other than that everyone is fine, boss," Jordy said smiling at Stacy, knowing he was poking the bear in the cage once again.

Max blew off what Jordy said about Stacy and spoke into the radio.

"I'm going to need a *big* favor Lieutenant," Max said cryptically.

"Whatever you need, boss," came Jordy's reply over the speaker.

"Well, I need you to hack into the Federal Government's high security entry codes for GBN's computer server room," Max said releasing the transmitter button with a grin.

"Oh, is *that* all? Not ANYTHING I can get forty years in prison for, huh boss?" Jordy said looking at Mikey standing beside him with concern on his face. "I was hoping you wanted me to make your credit score higher," Jordy said laughing over the radio.

"YOU can *do* that?" Max asked jokingly.

Jordy looked at Mikey again, rolled his eyes, and the two of them laughed. Jordy took a big breath, looked at Mikey, then asked, "When do you *need* this boss?"

Max looked at his watch, saw that it was exactly 2:45 am and needed the door opened by 3am.

"I need the server door opened in fifteen minutes, at exactly 0300, Lieutenant."

"Aye aye, Sir," Jordy replied, believing he could get it done by then. "Good luck, boss," he said to Max.

"Get everyone out of the building," Max ordered one last time before his radio finally went silent.

Max played with the radio for a minute and realized the battery was dead. He dropped it on the hallway floor beside the mercenary's lifeless body and checked his gun one last time before heading to the server room.

Max was still a little sore from the wounds he had sustained even though they had both stopped bleeding. He took his glove off and flexed his hand several times to get the circulation going and to see if it would start bleeding again, which it didn't. He put the glove back on and headed down the hallway.

Brian Jurgens was standing in the hallway, almost to the server room, when he had heard the multiple gunshots, thinking to himself that Max might have killed another one of his men and was on his way to him now. Jurgens didn't have a lot of faith in his men at the moment since most of them were dead by Max's hand.

Jurgens looked at the lone mercenary standing beside him and yelled, "DAMN IT, that son of a bitch Mason is STILL alive. Why can't any of you kill ONE man?" Jurgens asked, very annoyed that Max was still pursuing him.

"Looks like I'm going to have to kill him *myself* then. No one else seems *capable* of doing the job," Jurgens said to the confused mercenary looking at the gun in Jurgens' hand pointing at him.

Jurgens looked at his armed companion and asked, "Do you think you could kill this asshole for me, or do I have to kill you first, then *him* MYSELF?"

"Yes, sir," the mercenary replied waiting for his boss's approval.

Jurgens looked at the mercenary with big eyes suggesting that he get moving, then yelled, "Go already!"

The mercenary started back down the hallway in the direction of where they'd heard the gunshots a few minutes before. Jurgens watched as the mercenary left to stop Max Mason once and for all, or at least he hoped so. Jurgens turned and slowly walked down the hallway, alone now with gun in hand, trying to reach the server room without anymore distractions or interruptions.

Max came around the corner of the hallway and literally ran into the mercenary. The collision knocked both against the wall causing Max to drop his handgun to the floor where the mercenary kicked it down the hallway. Max grabbed him by the vest with both hands and head butted him hard, staggering them both.

"That's my *favorite* gun, asshole!" Max yelled at him.

The mercenary came back at Max with a hard right hand jab to his midsection causing Max to gasp for air.

He recovered quickly, stepped back and front-kicked the mercenary in the chest, knocking him hard into the wall behind him, then to the floor where he stared up at Max, who could see the rage in his eyes.

"That had to hurt...a lot," Max stated to the big mercenary with a smile on his face. "Shouldn't have kicked my gun" Max told him as he started getting up in front of him. The mercenary then pulled a big knife from behind his back and showed it to Max.

"Are you trying to say *big* knife, *little* DICK?" Max asked grinning, hoping it would piss off the large man even more.

"I'm going to carve my name on your chest, asshole. My boss told me I could kill you" he said angrily.

Thinking to himself, Max smiled and thought, "I guess I did piss him off."

"I'm hoping your name is AL," Max replied laughing as he glanced at the floor behind him where his gun was lying about fifteen feet away.

The mercenary didn't find Max's comment funny at all and lunged at him with the large knife. Max jumped backwards watching the blade swing across in front his body, missing him by just inches. The mercenary walked towards Max swinging the blade up and down as Max backed up a step at each swing. Max continued to look behind him as the tall, violent man continued to swing the large blade at him. Finally, Max had had enough of this dancing around and front-kicked the knife-wielding mercenary in the chest, staggering him backwards a few feet.

This gave Max the time he needed, and he dropped to the floor and grabbed his gun, now within hands' reach, and fired four rounds into the mercenary's chest, surprising him as he stepped towards Max one more time still swinging the large knife.

"Didn't your daddy ever teach you to *never* bring a knife to a *gunfight*, asshole," Max expressed with a grin, laying on the floor with his gun still pointed at him in case he came at him again. The mercenary fell to his knees, then face down on the floor, a puddle of blood starting to form around him.

Max got up and walked over to him and rolled him over to make sure he was dead, watching the blood pour out of the four bullet holes in his chest. Max searched him for anything he could use against Jurgens, finding only some more 9mm ammo he could use.

He took another moment to reload an empty SA-XD magazine with the ammo he took off the dead mercenary and put it in the magazine holder on his gun belt. He looked at his watch and saw he still had over ten minutes before Jordy opened the server room door. Max grabbed the dead mercenary's knife, slid it behind his back into his gun belt and headed for Jurgens, who he knew was waiting for him now.

Jordy, Mikey, Stacy and Tyler were all a bit confused by Max's request over the radio to hack into the server room. Then Stacy remembered from her tour of GBN that the director of Computer Services had to enter a five-digit security code to open the server door, and he was the *only* one with the code.

"Dad needs your help with the code because Mr. Richards must be dead," she said to Jordy, figuring out what Max needed and informing the rest.

"I need to get somewhere where there's a better Wi-Fi signal for me to do what the boss needs," Jordy said to them.

The four then started down the hallway to get to the stairwell to take them back up to the first floor so they could help Max.

"Will you be able to hack into *all three* security protocols, Uncle Jordy?" Stacy asked.

"I believe so, sweetie," Jordy replied, thinking he had to because his Captain was counting on him.

Stacy and Tyler volunteered to take point, their MP-5 machine guns aiming down the hallway, so Jordy could focus on watching his wrist computer for better Wi-Fi signal strength, with Mikey coming up from the rear to protect his SEAL teammate's back. Jordy concentrated intently for a better signal as they moved down the hallway.

Stacy and Tyler came around the corner first, starting to head down the hallway to the stairwell when they saw two mercenaries standing at a concrete pillar near the stairwell door, looking into the opened panel of a familiar looking bomb they had already attached to the wall.

Stacy grabbed Tyler and pulled her back quickly before the two men saw them, then peeked around the corner. The two mercenaries continued wiring the bomb so they obviously hadn't seen the two women. Tyler looked at her three colleagues.

"Do we take a shot?" she asked.

Mikey looked around the corner quickly and said, "No, we might hit the bomb."

"I have an idea, but you may not like it, Tyler" Stacy said smiling.

"Oh, this can't be good" Tyler replied with a grin, looking at both Mikey and Jordy.

Stacy leaned over and whispered in Tyler's ear what her plan was.

"Are you *serious* girl? *You* have a VERY devious mind!" Tyler said laughing.

Stacy smiled at her response and nodded to her.

"You and I are going to have a serious talk after all this," Tyler said to her, shaking her head laughing.

Jordy and Mikey were puzzled by what the two women had up their sleeves.

"*Trust* us," Stacy said to her two uncles with a *big* grin, putting her machine gun on the floor at her feet and watching Tyler do the same.

Both Stacy and Tyler then took their vests and gun belts off, placing them gently and quietly on the floor next to their MP-5 machine guns.

Jordy and Mikey looked at one another and scratched their heads, *still* wondering what they were both up to. The two women giggled and smiled at both Jordy and Mikey and continued with their plan.

Stacy took off her black tactical T-shirt. She was wearing nothing under it but a black, low-cut lace bra. Tyler unbuttoned her white long sleeve shirt and then took her white bra off, exposing her breasts to a stunned Mikey and Jordy.

"Forget what you saw, gentlemen, or I'll have to kill you both in your sleep," Tyler said smiling at the two shocked men staring at both her and Stacy.

Tyler grinned and giggled at Stacy as she started re-buttoning her shirt, but only half way up so her breasts could be partially seen, her hard nipples protruding through her white shirt.

"I know this might be a REALLY stupid question -- but what the HELL are you two up to?" Jordy asked with confusion on his face.

"You men are SO predictable," Stacy started explaining.

"Most men believe women are nothing more than fragile, defenseless sex toys they can play with," Tyler added.

"Men think with their dicks when they see a sexy woman, and their fantasies run wild when they see *two* together," Stacy said smiling at Tyler.

"Watch and learn boys," Tyler continued as she and Stacy walked around the corner hand in hand towards the two mercenaries.

"That's *so* sexist," Jordy said looking at Mikey.

"Don't look at *me* dude. I've been married for fifteen years," Mikey said back to him smiling.

The two women in their state of undress started giggling and laughing, playfully looking at each other as they moved toward the two mercenaries. They wanted them to hear this and make them believe the women didn't know they were standing there.

The two men stopped what they were doing when they saw the two half-naked women walking towards them.

"Don't MOVE, either of you," the closest one said pointing his machine gun at them.

Stacy grabbed Tyler and embraced her as if she were scared, but in a very affectionate way.

"*Please* don't shoot us," Tyler begged holding onto Stacy and rubbing her hands over Stacy's hips.

"How did you TWO get down here?" the mercenary asked staring at the two beautiful women and licking his lips.

Stacy gave him a sweet smile and said, "We both came downstairs for some alone playtime," as she placed her hands on Tyler's face, turned it towards hers and kissed her softly on the lips, surprising Tyler.

"No one's supposed to be down here," the second mercenary said to both women, walking up next to his partner.

"There's a private office no one uses on the other side that we like to use when my girlfriend here gets a little horny during work," Tyler explained rubbing Stacy's right breast through her bra, watching both mercenaries coming closer to them, as Stacy squirmed under her touch, looking at Tyler with BIG eyes, grinning and surprised.

"We NEED to search you both," the closest one said to the two women.

"That's okay with me. We both like *boys* too," Stacy said with a smile and a giggle.

"And you're both so strong, handsome. . .and dangerous," Tyler said smiling, rubbing her leg up and down on Stacy's as the two mercenaries watched them.

Jordy and Mikey continued to sneak peeks around the corner to watch the show and realized that neither mercenary even glanced in their direction. Jordy whispered to Mikey, "Do we tell the boss about this?"

"Oh, hell *no*. I'm afraid of her," Mikey softly replied smiling, continuing to watch the two women seduce the two armed terrorists.

The first mercenary walked up to Stacy smiling and patted her down from her ankles to her waist, stopping to grab her ass, hearing Stacy moan with excitement as he did it. The second mercenary searched Tyler, stopping to cup her breasts through her shirt with both hands.

Both Stacy and Tyler turned their backs on their targets and rubbed their asses up against their crotches, getting them place their machine-guns against the wall and start kissing on both of their necks. Tyler looked at Stacy, smiled and nodded. Stacy smiled back acknowledging her.

Both women turned around quickly and punched each mercenary hard in the face with their right fists causing them to stagger backwards. Stacy front-kicked her assailant in the chest before he had a chance to react to her first attack, bending him over at the waist.

Stacy looked over at Tyler who was connecting right and left hand punches to the mercenary's jaw, and even saw her knock a tooth out to the floor. Stacy walked over to her man and grabbed the back of his hair to raise his face up to hit him but he managed to back hand slap her across the face, pissing her off more.

Tyler saw the slap and smiled because she knew Stacy wouldn't stand for that, and she roundhouse kicked her mercenary upside his head, pushing him backwards towards the bomb.

The mercenary fell right below the bomb and looked at Tyler and smiled. "Oh, SHIT!" Tyler thought as she watched the mercenary reach up and hit the timer switch on the bomb detonator, causing the clock to start counting down from thirty seconds.

"WE GOTTA GO, STACY" Tyler yelled as she hit the mercenary in the jaw as he tried to get up, watching the clock count down to fifteen seconds. Stacy saw the fear in Tyler's eyes and hit her mercenary one last time knocking him to the floor near his partner.

"I was really beginning to like you," Stacy said sarcastically to Tyler as they ran down the hallway together before the bomb went off.

"Wait till you taste my cooking," Tyler said laughing.

Stacy and Tyler ran hand in hand around the corner to the other hallway just as the bomb went off, throwing them both into Jordy and Mikey. The four of them lay on the floor as the smoke and dust started coming down their hallway.

"Are you two okay?" Mikey asked as Stacy and Tyler got up off the floor slowly.

Tyler looked at Stacy and smiled as she got up off the floor and dusted herself off.

"I think you were beginning to enjoy that."

Stacy smiled back as she got to her feet and giggled to that remark.

"Maybe" she replied with a smile.

Jordy and Mikey looked down the hallway and saw the explosion had blocked the stairwell entrance with concrete rubble on top of the two now dead mercenaries and realized there was no way they were getting out that way. He opened up his wrist computer and saw that the explosion had now made the Wi-Fi signal weaker.

"We have less than ten minutes to get into the server room for the boss," Jordy explained.

"How are we gonna get out of here, guys?" Tyler asked as she and Stacy started putting their clothing and gear back on.

Stacy thought for a moment. "We *could* go back and crawl through the hole we made to get me out" she said to the three of them.

"That seems to be the *only* viable option right now," Mikey said.

"We gotta move NOW," Jordy ordered, knowing he had very little time to get the server room security code to Max.

The four of them started running down the long hallway until they came back to the rubble-blocked entrance way Stacy had had to crawl through to get to the others after Tyler killed Mayer. Stacy climbed up and looked into the small hole they had made to get her out and saw Mayer lying on the floor on the other side where Tyler had shot him.

"Guess I'm not getting a reference from him for *my* next job," she said smiling back at the other three.

"*Really*," Tyler replied laughing at her comment. "You *so* have your father's morbid sense of humor, that's for sure."

"Thank you. I like you too," Stacy said to her new friend.

The four of them worked together to try to make the hole bigger, pushing rubble down both sides of it so they could all get through. Jordy continued to monitor the Wi-Fi signal as he helped move the heavy rubble next to the hole.

"I still don't have decent signal strength yet to do the hack," Jordy said anxiously, waving the arm around that had the computer attached as he looked for better reception.

"Maybe we just need to get on the other side for better reception," Mikey told his nervous comrade.

Jordy looked at his watch and saw it was 2:58 am and realized he might not get the entry code to Max in time. The hole was finally big enough for both Stacy and Tyler to crawl through to the other side, which they did. They stood on the rubble looking back through at both Jordy and Mikey.

Jordy's watch alarm went off to tell him it was 3:00 am and he started to get upset about still having no signal on his side of the rubble. He tried to squeeze through the hole but it still wasn't big enough.

"GODDAMN IT," Jordy cursed loudly.

Mikey could see how upset Jordy was, not wanting to fail his commanding officer, and tried to calm him down.

"Hey, buddy, we will get on the other side soon enough. You need to be patient," Mikey informed him.

"THE OTHER SIDE," Jordy yelled with a smile at Mikey who was now confused by his sudden enthusiasm.

Jordy took his mini computer off his wrist, ripping the Velcro straps away and holding it in his hand.

"TYLER, I NEED YOU!" Jordy yelled through the rubble.

Tyler stuck her head through the hole.

"What do you need, Jordy?" she asked seeing how anxious he was.

"I need you to complete the hack for Max on THAT side of the rubble as close to the escape door as you can get," Jordy explained to her.

Jordy handed his computer to Tyler through the hole and she climbed down the rubble with Stacy watching diligently.

"Tell me what the signal strength is in the lower right hand corner," Jordy yelled to her.

"Thirty-eight percent and climbing," she said smiling and yelling back at Jordy.

"Awesome," Jordy said to Mikey, sitting beside him looking through the hole at Stacy and Tyler near the IRS escape door.

"When it gets to sixty percent I need you to press the ENTER button," Jordy yelled to Tyler through the opening in the concrete rubble. "That *should* be enough signal strength to set the hack in motion."

He had already prepped and calibrated his computer to enter the numerous entry codes to the server room after Max had made his request, and before he gave it to Tyler, knowing all she had to do was press one button.

"It's at sixty percent, Jordy," Tyler shouted, while Stacy stood beside her also looking at the screen.

"Press ENTER *now*," Jordy commanded.

Tyler put her finger on the ENTER button and pressed down. She watched as the codes quickly downloaded to Jordy's computer, thinking it was so cool to have a mega computer this size.

"DOWNLOAD COMPLETE," came over the small screen prompting Tyler to yell back at Jordy as she smiled at Stacy.

"I think it worked!"

Jordy looked inside the large hole and smiled at both Stacy and Tyler.

"Nice job, you two" he expressed.

Tyler frowned at Stacy and then asked her laughingly, "What did *you* do?"

"Oh, I was here for *cuteness* points," Stacy said smiling and sticking her tongue out at Tyler playfully.

"We still need to get out of here, you two," Mikey yelled at the two women, admiring what they had done.

Tyler looked at Stacy and smiled.

"We're already through. We should leave your sorry asses here," Tyler said laughing.

"Please don't," Jordy responded, looking exhausted and worn out.

Tyler put Jordy's computer on the floor next to the door so it wouldn't get damaged by the rubble, then she and Stacy headed back up to where the two men were and started moving more concrete pieces away from the opening.

Once wide enough, Mikey was the first one to crawl through, handing his AR rifle and pack to Tyler first before he finally joined the women on the other side. Jordy waited till Mikey was clear through the opening before he started crawling through, finally standing with the other three by the IRS escape door.

Jordy picked his mini laptop up off the floor and opened the small screen to his horror. The screen repeatedly flashed a red error message: "DATA CORRUPTED, DOWNLOAD INCOMPLETE". Jordy saw that the download was only 98 percent finished when it crashed.

"OH, MY GOD." Jordy said looking at his screen. His three colleagues could visibly see he was very upset.

"What's the problem, Uncle Jordy?" Stacy asked worried.

"I don't know if the entry codes got through for your dad. The server codes have been corrupted," Jordy explained panicking.

"I did everything you said," Tyler said to Jordy.

"I know you did," Jordy said not letting her take any blame.

"Sometimes the corruption can be in the processor sending the signal," Jordy told the three of them. "We have to hope Max got the door opened before the signal got corrupted."

"What if we send the codes again outside where there are no Wi-Fi issues?" Mikey asked.

Jordy smiled at Mikey and replied, "That could work, Commander."

The four of them opened the escape door to the IRS building and quickly ran down the hallway to the other building, then to the elevator bank. They pushed the up button on the elevator and then looked over and saw the stairwell exit door.

The overhead indicator showed the elevator was coming from the seventh floor. And as if they'd read one another's minds, they all headed through the stairwell door, believing the elevator was too slow, and they ran up the stairs to the first floor lobby.

They then ran out of the first floor stairwell door right into the teeth of the FBI Special Weapons Unit positioned there with their guns pointing at them. The FBI was set up to capture any of the terrorists who tried to escape using the IRS tunnel from the GBN building.

"WHOA! DON'T SHOOT! WE'RE THE GOOD GUYS!" Jordy yelled as they all put their hands up.

"Get on the ground NOW," the commander of the unit shouted at them.

"Not *again*! We're Alexander and Stevens. We've been cleared by your Lieutenant Adams. CALL HIM, PLEASE!" Jordy shouted back as they all started getting on the floor.

The commander talked softly into his radio, continuing to have his men keep the four of them covered with their weapons. He put his hand to his ear piece and said, "Roger that, sir," and walked over to the four suspects now lying face down on the polished floor in front of him.

"Sorry, Lieutenant Alexander, Commander Stevens. I had to make sure you weren't part of this shit across the street," the young commander explained looking at the GBN building through the window and offering his hand to help Stacy and Tyler up off the floor.

"No problem. I need to use my computer," Jordy said anxiously opening his mini laptop and rebooting it. The computer came online and Jordy went to work to resend the entry codes to Max in case they hadn't worked the first time because of the signal interruption in the basement.

He pressed the ENTER button and watched as the download proceeded again. Jordy realized looking at his small computer that he now had one hundred percent signal strength in the IRS lobby surrounded by all the Wi-Fi repeaters they had. The entry code download went quickly and a "DATA DOWNLOAD COMPLETED" message came over Jordy's small screen.

"Now we wait," Jordy said to the three of them huddled around him, still looking at his laptop screen. Stacy and Tyler looked around the IRS lobby at all the security, then looked at each other, a bit concerned for Max still in the GBN building.

Mikey could read the worry on their faces, looked at the two of them and smiled.

"He'll be fine," he said, trying to reassure them. "But I think we all need to be over at the GBN building to meet him when he comes out."

Stacy, Tyler and Jordy all smiled, nodded to Mikey and headed out the IRS front door into the warm July night air, hoping Max was on his way out as well.

CHAPTER 15

THE FLOOR SHOOK HARD UNDER BRIAN JURGENS as he stood in front of the secured server room door. It made him think one of the bombs had gone off on one of the floors below him. He also heard the multiple gunshots from the far end of the hallway. He wondered if this was the last he'd seen of Max Mason, or if he was on his own because he ran out of mercenaries...all *because* of the lone Navy SEAL.

Jurgens looked at his cell phone as he glanced at the security measures on the wall next to the door incorporated by James Richards. He took out Richards ID card and waved it over the security scan pad and watched as the light went from red to green with an additional buzz, accepting his ID.

Now came the hard part, as Jurgens knew he needed a five-digit numerical code to be punched into the keypad and had no clue what it was. He was aware that *only* Richards knew the code, and the problem with that was he lay dead in his office from the fatal accidental gunshot.

Jurgens was a man who used information on those who worked in his division, or around him, and he'd downloaded all their personnel records to his personal cell phone. He brought up Richards' personnel file and started reading intensely, seeing if there were any five number combinations he could use to try to open the door. He read that he was once married but lost his wife Janet to cancer two years ago. They had one daughter named Samantha, born in January of 2011.

Jurgens continued to read, feeling some sadness over the outcome with Richards, and thinking he never meant to hurt him, let alone kill him by accident. He felt bad that Richards' daughter would now grow up without either parent in her life.

He understood how that felt, having lost his own daughter to divorce almost twenty years ago having no contact with her since his ex-wife and she moved to Texas.

He continued reading until he came to the end of Richards' file and stood there looking at the small print on his phone thinking, "What did I miss with him?"

Jurgens continued to scroll up and down the file looking for anything that might resemble a numerical combination, when suddenly he stopped and smiled. "Are you serious?" he said out loud to himself. "That's got to be *way* too easy," he thought.

Jurgens looked at the screen on his phone and proceeded to push the numbers one at a time on the digital keypad. When he pushed the last number on the pad he waited a moment, then watched as the red light changed to green and then buzzed just like the first security measure did.

"HOT DAMN!" Jurgens said out loud. He thought to himself how simple it was to figure out Richards' code using his daughter's birthday January 11th, 2011 or 1-1-1-1-1. Jurgens smiled as the second security measure was solved now. If he was going to get the $250 million Tanaka had extorted, he now only needed to hack the third and final security measure to get inside the server room so he could download his bank code from the flash drive he brought on his key ring.

Jurgens reached into his back pocket and pulled out a bloodied piece of cloth and slowly unwrapped it in the palm of his hand, revealing a severed thumb from James Richards' left hand. He picked the bloodied thumb up with two fingers and pressed it against the fingerprint scanner, rolling the tip of the thumb to make sure the entire fingerprint was scanned.

He stood there for a moment with no results so he decided to do it again, pressing harder on the fingerprint scanner with the tip of the dead man's thumb. The red light changed to green and the door buzzed and opened for a now relieved Brian Jurgens.

He knew now that it was too late for Max Mason to stop him from stealing the money from the server. Jurgens dropped the bloodied severed thumb to the floor. Even if Max Mason got in and used it he wouldn't be in time to stop the download to his bank in the Cayman Islands. He walked through the steel door and pushed it closed behind him, locking the server door securely.

Max felt the building shake just as he got to the server room thinking to himself that maybe he was too late to stop Jurgens, and that Mayer had used his detonator to start setting off more bombs that Jordy and Mikey couldn't find.

He stood in front of the server room door looking at the three security measures with their red lights shining brightly on top of each of them. He knew that the red lights meant everything was secured and that there was no way inside until they turned green, but that didn't stop Max from trying to kick the door in several times, only stopping after he realized it wasn't going to give.

Max looked at his watch and saw it was past 3:00 am and wondered where Jordy's computer hack of the security codes were. Max was starting to get frustrated when he noticed the bloodied severed thumb lying on the floor by the server room door.

Max remembered Richards lying on the floor of his office in a pool of his own blood and noticed the thumb on his left hand had been cut off by a knife, yet he still stayed alive long enough to give Max a message before he died. Max thought to himself, "That's a true hero." He was pissed now and said out loud in frustration, "I'm going to KILL you, Brian."

Jurgens made his way down to the main server terminal and pulled his keychain from his pants pocket. He slowly unhooked the mini flash drive from the metal key ring and opened it. He stood in front of the server terminal and inserted the flash drive into the open USB port, wiggling it back and forth to make sure it was secure.

He pulled the keyboard out from under the video screen and proceeded to enter his transfer code one number at a time. He had memorized the numerical code so no one else knew it. After entering the full sequence of numbers, Jurgens pushed the ENTER button to start the download.

What he wasn't expecting was that a timer screen came on and projected how long it would take to complete the download. Jurgens would have to wait twenty minutes before it was finished.

He looked around the small room and saw a video camera in the corner of the ceiling with a red light shining on top of it, understanding that the Feds now knew everything he was doing. Jurgens looked directly into the camera, smiled and flipped it off laughing.

Max was starting to get anxious about not getting in the locked metal security door, hoping Jordy, Mikey, Tyler and Stacy were okay and not in the area of the explosion that rocked the fourth floor where he was.

He started looking around for anything he could use to try to pry the door open but couldn't find anything sturdy enough. His frustration finally caught up to him and he started beating on the metal security door with his fists.

"YOU HAVE TO COME OUT EVENTUALLY, YOU PIECE OF SHIT!" Max yelled loudly through the door, not knowing if Jurgens could hear him or not, but he didn't care.

He picked up a chair from a nearby desk and in frustration started beating the door with it, knowing nothing was going to happen. The door was highly secured. It just made him feel better because he couldn't take it out on Jurgens...*yet*.

Max hit the security door one more time, hard enough to finally break the chair into pieces. He looked at the shattered pieces and realized Jurgens had caused him to lose control, and that pissed him off even more. He walked over to the desk from where he had taken the chair and sat on it. Staring at the server door and hoping to come up with an idea to get into it, he suddenly saw *all* the red lights change to green and a buzzing noise coming from the ID scanner. He got up with a grin and watched as the digital scanner also buzzed, the fingerprint scanner followed with the door buzzing open.

"Thank you, Jordy Alexander," Max said out loud holding the door so it didn't close before he got in.

Max took out his handgun and slowly walked through the door to see rows and rows of computer servers down long hallways. Their blinking colored lights made Max think about Christmas and the lights he and his kids put on their tree each year.

Max figured that Jurgens needed to do his download at the main computer terminal which he knew to be at the very end of the server racks. He cautiously moved down the hallway continuing to look at all the blinking lights on the servers as he passed them one at a time, rack by rack. Max also noticed the cold temperature in the secured room, thinking it probably had to do with keeping the servers cooled down from their excessive use.

Brian Jurgens was sitting in a chair watching the download clock count down at 13:00 when he heard the loud buzzer of the door opening, alerting him to the fact that someone had come into the server room.

He got up out of his chair and glanced at the video camera on the wall, then got behind the last server rack to hide. He thought to himself, "Looks like I get to *kill* Mason after all," assuming it was him who came in. He took his handgun out of his belt to check how much ammo he had left. "DAMN," he said aloud, realizing he only had two bullets remaining in his gun's magazine.

He pulled out the big knife he used to cut off James Richards' thumb from the back of his belt. Staring at the blade and admiring it with Richards' dried blood still on it, Jurgens said to himself with a smile on his face, "Guess I'll have to kill him the old fashioned way."

Max slowly made his way past the rows of servers halfway down when he caught a glimpse of Jurgens sticking his head out from the corner of the last server, which made Max believe that's where the main download server was. Max stood behind a server and yelled at Jurgens, "Why don't you come over here and let me put these cuffs on you, asshole. It's been a long night," he said with a grin. Max quickly looked around the server he was behind and saw Jurgens' gun and jumped back.

Jurgens fired a shot in Max's direction, missing him badly, then shouted, "Why won't you die, Mason?"

Max smiled and shouted, "God wants me to kick your ass first."

"You know you're too late to stop me" he decried.

"If that was true, you'd give yourself up," Max replied.

"Why give up, when I can kill you and still be rich" Jurgens yelled back to him.

Max rolled his eyes figuring he was going to have to go after Brian now quickly glancing around the server he was behind.

"You need to come and get me, Mason," Jurgens yelled as he peeked around the server rack.

"Not a problem, asshole. I'll be right there," Max replied loudly, moving away from the server he was using as cover, his gun pointed in Jurgens' direction.

Jurgens looked around at the main terminal to see the download clock reading seven minutes left, then concentrated on killing Max Mason. Looking around the server, he saw Max moving towards him and took his *last* shot, hitting the server next to Max. "Did that one get you, Mason?" Jurgens yelled laughing.

Max quickly ducked back behind the server after Jurgens' shot had ricocheted off of it. The shot had creased Max's left shoulder, tearing his shirt and causing his shoulder to bleed.

Max looked at it with a scowl on his face and said, "Damn, I loved this shirt." Really pissed now, Max put his gun in his left hand and applied pressure to the cut with his right, shaking his head in confusion. "Why am I the *only* one getting shot and stabbed," Max asked himself laughing.

Jurgens realized he was out of bullets and needed to surprise his determined pursuer in order to kill him with the large knife he had. He checked the download clock one more time, seeing it read just under five minutes remaining to completion. With his knife in hand,

Jurgens slowly and quietly walked around the servers to try to sneak up behind Max Mason.

Max removed his hand and saw that the cut on his shoulder had stopped bleeding, then looked around the corner of the server to see if he could still see Jurgens.

"What's the matter, Brian, you're awfully quiet for an obnoxious and arrogant prick," Max yelled, hoping to get a response from Jurgens.

When he didn't get a response he figured Jurgens was trying to surprise him somewhere. Max cautiously moved to the next server rack keeping his gun pointed where his eyes went. He continued to move from server rack to server rack, keeping his head swiveling in case Jurgens attacked.

Max finally made it to the to the main download terminal without spotting Jurgens. He could see the terminal counting down the banking code program and noticed he only had about three minutes left to figure out how to stop the download or the $250 million would be lost to Jurgens. Max wished Jordy or James Richards was here.

Max was studying the download terminal when Jurgens came around the corner of the server with a large knife in his hand swinging down at Max. Max reacted quickly by blocking the knife with his handgun. The knife hit Max's gun hard, knocking it out of his hand and onto the floor by Jurgens' feet. Jurgens quickly kicked the gun across the floor so Max couldn't reach it, smiling at him. Max stepped back in a defensive posture and asked, "Why do you bad guys *insist* on kicking MY gun, I paid good money for that damn gun," he said with a grin.

Brian Jurgens laughed at that remark and waved his big-bladed knife as he prepared to attack again.

"I'm going to enjoy killing you, Mason."

Max and Jurgens started to slowly circle each other. Max pulled out the knife he took off the dead mercenary from behind his back. He waved his weapon at Jurgens and grinned.

"Mine seems to be bigger than yours, Brian…and I have a bigger *knife* too."

"You're such a smug asshole, Mason."

"Maybe. I actually like to think of it as part of my charm," Max replied smirking as the two men stood in front of each other ready for combat.

"After I kill you, I'm going to kill that little girl of yours," Jurgens said to him with a smile. Max laughed out loud making Jurgens turn red with rage.

"I would enjoy watching my baby kick your slimy ass all over the floor. But she's going to have to stand in line right now, because I have waited a long time for this myself," Max said with a big grin.

Jurgens lunged at Max, who easily blocked the swinging steel blade with his own, then hit Jurgens in the face with his open left hand. Jurgens stepped back and rubbed his cheek in pain.

"Oh, don't give up yet. I'm not through bruising you," Max said smirking.

Jurgens came at Max again, swinging his knife left and right furiously, managing to make a cut on Max's chest, ripping his shirt again and exposing his Kevlar vest.

"Damn, *AGAIN*! I loved this shirt," Max said, disappointed he was going to have to throw his favorite tactical shirt away because of the damage.

Jurgens smiled as he looked at Max's ripped T-shirt, knowing he had pissed him off.

"Your tailor is not going to be very happy with you, Mason," he said, laughing again and waving his knife at Max.

"WOW, that was actually kind of funny, Brian. You can be in charge of the prison talent show when you're not getting butt-fucked by your cellmate," Max said laughing. "Now *that* was *very* funny," he said to an enraged Brian Jurgens.

"I'M GOING TO KILL YOU, MASON!" Jurgens said, poised to attack again.

"Blah, Blah, Blah. Are you going to talk me to death?" Max asked.

Jurgens came at Max swinging his knife uncontrollably with Max dodging and ducking each swing. Finally, Max hit Jurgens in the ribs with a hard right-handed fist, knocking him backward. Before

Jurgens could catch his breath Max hit him with his left fist upside his jaw, knocking his head against the server room wall. Jurgens slid down the wall bleeding from his mouth and laughed hysterically looking at his download clock counting down the last seconds before completion.

Max picked his gun up off the floor and walked back to the download terminal, watching Jurgens lie on the floor against the wall, and saw the final ten seconds counting down.

Max pointed his gun at the main terminal and fired as many rounds as he had left in his magazine into the server, remembering what James Richards had said to him before he died -- SHOOT THE SERVER!!!

The download clock went to five seconds and stopped. A bright red error message flashed across the screen. "DATA CORRUPTED, INCOMPLETE DOWNLOAD".

Jurgens screamed, "NOOOOOO!" when he saw that Max had stopped the download to his bank.

"I guess you could say you finally had your five seconds of DEAD AIR" Max said to Jurgens with a grin, knowing that was one of Brian Jurgens' pet peeves about broadcasting...*no* dead air.

"You *killed* a lot of *my friends*, tonight," Max said to Jurgens, reloading his gun with a fresh magazine and pointing it at Jurgens' head. "You should be dying tonight as well," Max continued, still aiming his gun at Jurgens.

"You can't kill me, Mason. It's not in *your code,*" Jurgens said.

"Like I told someone earlier this evening, asshole. It's not really a CODE. It's a GUIDELINE," Max responded, putting the barrel of his SA-XD handgun against Jurgens' forehead.

Jurgens looked up nervously and seeing the security video camera, said, "If you kill me, you'll be a murderer, no better than me, and everyone will see on THAT camera."

Max stared into Brian Jurgens' eyes with contempt, then swung his gun in the direction of the video camera up in the corner and without looking, pulled the trigger and blew the camera off the wall.

"You mean *that* video camera?" he asked with a grin. Max watched as Jurgens' eyes got very big. He actually saw fear on his face for the first time.

Max picked Jurgens' knife up off the floor and flung it down the hallway, then reached down and grabbed Jurgens by the coat collar, his gun still pointed at his forehead.

"You tried to kill my daughter, you son of a bitch. I should kill you for that alone," Max said angrily.

Jurgens smiled at Max knowing he wouldn't kill him. He figured Max wanted him to go to prison and slowly started to stand up, his mouth still bleeding from the beating Max gave him. Max kept his gun pointed at him, continuing to stare him in the eyes, but didn't notice a miniature remote device hidden in Jurgens' left hand until it was too late.

Max hit Jurgens in the left jaw hard enough to knock him to the floor again and reached down and grabbed the remote device from his hand. Jurgens sat on the floor rubbing his jaw and laughing out loud. "Afraid it's too late, Mason," he said continuing to laugh.

"What did you do, Brian?" Max asked looking at the blinking green light on the small remote.

"YOU and your friends were too busy with the hostages, Tanaka, Mayer, and the explosives on the first floor and basement that you had *no* clue there were secondary explosives all over the third floor auditorium," Jurgens said grinning proudly.

"Why would you do that? I'm sure my friends have gotten everyone out of the building by now," Max asked confused.

"There's *no one* left in the building to kill, dumb ass," Max said with a stern look on his face.

"There's YOU," Jurgens said laughing. "You took MY money, and I have NO intention of letting you take me to prison…not to mention I just *don't like you*, Mason," Jurgens said with a bloodied grin. "So I get to take *you* with me. Who's the dumb ass NOW?" Jurgens said to Max.

Max grabbed Jurgens again by his coat collar and yelled, "How much time do we have?"

Jurgens just smiled, but when Max reared back his right fist to hit him again Jurgens put his hands up to protect his face speaking up quickly.

"Ten minutes, ten minutes," he said not wanting to get hit in the face again, knowing it was too late anyway. Max looked at his watch and started his timer to count down ten minutes.

The cell phone of FBI Director James buzzed in his pocket as he sat on the couch in the President's Oval Office waiting patiently for more information on the GBN crisis. He had just been reprimanded by the President of the United States for withholding information on his daughter being held hostage and wasn't about to lose his political career over a vendetta Dwayne Marshall had with Max Mason. He took his phone out to answer it.

"My apologies, Mr. President," James said answering his cell phone. President Bradshaw looked at Director James and nodded in acceptance.

"Director James here," he said into the phone.

"Lieutenant Adams here, sir, at the GBN command tent. You asked to be informed of any new developments, sir."

"Proceed, Lieutenant," James replied placing his phone on speaker as he looked around the room at President Bradshaw, former President Matthews, Admiral Cartwright, and Director Marshall.

"Well, sir, the entire building has been evacuated of all GBN personnel and visitors. Everyone is safe."

"That's wonderful, Lieutenant. Well done," James replied smiling and looking around the room at everyone.

"We have taken thirteen terrorists into custody without incident. Seems we found them all cuffed and unconscious on various floors, sir." the Lieutenant informed him, uncertain as how this happened. "And a *whole lot* of dead terrorists, sir."

"Good work, Lieutenant. Tell all the team commanders they did a great job," James said.

"That's just it, sir. *We* didn't kill or capture them," Lieutenant Adams replied.

Of course James knew who did but wasn't going to share the information with the Lieutenant.

"Document what you know, Lieutenant" Director James requested.

"Yes, sir. However, sir, we are receiving several heat signatures from the third floor."

"I thought you said the building was clear, Lieutenant," James asked confused.

"It is clear of *people,* sir. These are active *explosive* heat signatures, about ten located in different areas of the third floor," Adams said apprehensively. "They didn't come on until just a few minutes ago, after everyone got out, sir. We believe they were remotely started from inside the building. We don't know how long before they detonate so we're afraid to send a bomb disposal team into the building, sir," the Lieutenant said, worried how the Director would react.

"ONLY EXPLOSIVE heat signatures, Lieutenant?"

"Yes, sir. That's all we're reading inside."

"Keep everyone back and continue to monitor the heat signatures," James ordered the young Lieutenant.

"Yes, sir," Adams replied hanging up the phone.

Director James put his cell phone back in his pocket looking at everyone a bit confused at what his young Lieutenant just told them all.

Knowing now that the building was wired to explode and collapse, President Bradshaw asked, "Are we sure EVERYONE has been evacuated, Michael?"

"You heard what I did, Mr. President, that there are NO body heat signatures in the building anymore, *only explosive* heat signatures which are on a different heat wave signature than humans," Director James explained.

"So our *children* are safe?" Bradshaw asked.

"Yes, sir. We have them safely secured," James replied seeing relief on the President's face.

"Where are Max Mason and his team?" Admiral Cartwright asked James.

"I don't have that information, Admiral. I just know there are NO hostages or GBN personnel in the building anymore."

Admiral Cartwright pulled out his SAT phone and dialed Max's number, but got no response after letting it ring several times. Cartwright looked at the President, and then James and said, "I need to talk to your commander at the crime scene."

James nodded and pulled his phone out of his pocket again and dialed the number.

Lieutenant Adams answered after seeing it was the Director's number on the caller ID. "Yes, sir?"

"Lieutenant, this is Admiral James Cartwright. I need to talk to your crime scene commander immediately."

"Yes, sir. I will connect you to his com-link." Once he did, Adams said, "Okay, go ahead Admiral."

"Commander, I need to speak to Max Mason or one of his team immediately," the Admiral ordered.

"We don't have a Max Mason here with us, Admiral," the commander said.

"Do you have Commander Stevens in custody?" the Admiral asked.

"He's not in custody, sir, but he is here," the commander replied seeing the two men and two women walking towards the command center, already knowing who they were. "I'll put him on, sir."

Mikey, Jordy, Tyler, and Stacy had walked from the IRS building over to the GBN building command center to wait for Max when they were approached by the crime scene commander and two other officers.

Tyler stepped in front of Mikey, Jordy, and Stacy and addressed the commander before he could speak.

"I'm Secret Service Agent Karen Tyler, I *need* to see the President's daughter IMMEDIATELY," Tyler demanded to the commander. Tyler knew she was still on duty to protect Stephanie Bradshaw and she wanted to get back to her and Kristina Cartwright's side.

"She's in the next command tent with the others, ma'am," the commander replied. He looked at one of his men standing watch and said, "Show Agent Tyler to the President's daughter."

Tyler nodded with a smile to Mikey, Jordy, and Stacy to say thank you and left with the officer to find Stephanie and Kristina.

"Commander Stevens, Admiral Cartwright would like to speak to you" the crime scene commander said as he handed his radio to Mikey.

"Admiral, nice to hear your voice, sir," Mikey said pleasantly.

"Commander, is Captain Mason with you?" the Admiral asked.

"No, sir. He went after Jurgens in the server room on the fourth floor. He hasn't come out of the building yet."

"Commander, there are several explosive heat signatures, but no *human* heat signatures in the building," Admiral Cartwright told Mikey.

"That can't be, sir," he responded nervously. "We defused ALL of the explosives on the doors and in the basement. There have to be at least two human heat signatures for Max and Jurgens, sir."

Mikey realized that no one had even thought about looking for bombs on floors other than the first and basement. Jurgens and Tanaka had pulled a fast one that might kill Max.

Jordy was listening beside Mikey and motioned him to give him the radio.

"Admiral, this is Lieutenant Alexander speaking. Captain Mason's and Jurgens' heat signatures could be masked by the server room, sir."

"What do you mean by that, Lieutenant?" Cartwright's voice asked over the radio speaker.

"The server room has to be sealed and kept at a certain cooler temperature to keep the computer hard drives from overloading from heavy use, sir. It's *very* possible that Captain Mason and Brian

Jurgens are still in the server room, Admiral," Jordy told him with worry in his voice. "That would explain why their heat signatures aren't being seen."

"I can't get through to him on his SAT phone, Lieutenant," the Admiral said.

"The server room doesn't allow any other carrier waves inside but its own, sir," Jordy said.

"The Captain knows *everything* that's going on around him, sir. Trust him on this as well, Admiral," Jordy said to him trying to reassure his commanding officer.

"I'm on my way to my granddaughter, Lieutenant. Hopefully Max will be there by the time I get there. Copy out," Cartwright said to Jordy.

"Aye aye, sir. Copy out," Jordy replied and handed the radio back to the FBI commander.

Jordy looked at Mikey and Stacy and shrugged his shoulders.

"I'm sure he's okay," he said with a slight grin.

"My Dad needs to get the Hell out of there NOW," Stacy said so loudly that everyone around her could hear.

"Your dad is the smartest man we *know*, sweetheart. If anyone can get out of there alive, it's *him*," Mikey said squeezing her hand for reassurance. "Besides, his new girlfriend won't allow him to die. She's a *very* stubborn woman," Mikey added with a grin.

Stacy smiled back.

"I like her too," she said.

Karen Tyler stood outside the second command center and thanked the officer for the escort, then walked in and spotted Stephanie, Kristina, and Scott Matthews sitting at a table drinking canned sodas like normal teenagers would do. Tyler smiled watching the three of them.

"This looks cozy. Got one for me?" she asked.

"KAREN!" Stephanie Bradshaw screamed, turning to see her protector. Stephanie got up and ran to Tyler, hugging her tightly as Kristina and Scott smiled.

Tyler was a little taken aback by how emotional Stephanie was but blew it off and hugged her charge for a very long moment.

"Is *my Dad* coming to get me," Stephanie asked as she stepped back from her embrace.

Tyler wasn't sure of the answer but said, "I'm sure he's on his way, sweetie."

Tyler then went over to get a hug from Kristina and to shake Scott's hand.

"Where's Max?" Scott asked as he and Tyler shook hands.

"He's on his way," Tyler replied, knowing how much Max meant to him …and now to *her* too.

CHAPTER 16

MAX LOOKED AT JURGENS ON THE FLOOR AND, still pointing his handgun at his face, gave him an order.

"Get up and put your hands out."

"You're going to cuff me before we die? How noble of you Mason," Jurgens retorted as he got up and presented both of his hands in front of him. Max put the plastic cuffs on Jurgens and tightened them securely.

"We're not dying today, asshole," Max told him smiling.

Jurgens stood in front of Max with a confused look on his face and was about to say something when Max hit him in the jaw full force with his right fist knocking Jurgens unconscious slumping over Max's left shoulder. Max rose up and carried Jurgens over his shoulder fireman style out the server door and towards the stairwell.

Jurgens was a bit heavy unconscious but Max didn't want anyone to die with a building falling on top of them, not even Brian Jurgens. Max especially wanted Jurgens to rot in prison for what he had done, so he endured his weight going through the stairwell exit.

Max looked down the stairs, and then headed up the stairs to the fifth floor. He had an idea, but even he wasn't too keen about it but thought it was the best possible way to live through this crazy night.

"I have TWO body heat signatures heading to the fifth floor," Lieutenant Adams said shouting out loud to Mikey, Jordy and Stacy huddled behind him and his equipment.

They all smiled at one another knowing one of those heat signatures was Max. Mikey looked at Jordy and gave him a big smile because he knew what Max was about to do.

"*No…he wouldn't do that again, would he*?" Jordy asked whispering to Mikey thinking the same thing his friend was thinking. Mikey laughed at Jordy.

"*Maybe*" Mikey said with a smirk.

"He nearly broke his neck the last time," Jordy said to Mikey in a low voice so Stacy couldn't hear him.

Admiral Cartwright informed President Bradshaw and former President Matthews that their children were secured and safe outside the GBN building. He then told them that it was possible the entire building could be leveled by explosives planted on the third floor that no one found because they had not been looking there.

The Admiral made sure they all knew there was no one else in the building, keeping to himself the possibility that Max Mason and Brian Jurgens were still inside. He had faith in Max and knew he would somehow get out okay and frankly didn't care about Jurgens living through this.

President Bradshaw picked up his phone.

"Amy, please have Chariots 1 and 2 brought around to the front." Then he hung up.

"Is that a good idea, Mr. President?" Director Marshall asked figuring the President was heading to the GBN building.

"I'm going to pick up *my* daughter Dwayne. Do *you* have a problem with that?" Bradshaw asked still a bit pissed at his Secret Service Director.

"I'm asking because there's a building about to fall to the ground, sir, and we don't want you to get hurt," Marshall explained. "I can have your daughter rushed back here by one of my men, sir."

"She needs to see me there, Dwayne," Bradshaw insisted. "She needs to know her father came for her," Bradshaw said looking at Daryl Matthews smiling.

"Yes, sir. I understand, sir. But you're the President of the United States, and it's *my* job to keep you safe."

"Not tonight, Dwayne. I'm just a father going to pick up his little girl," Keith Bradshaw said defiantly.

Daryl Matthews looked at the relieved and happy President and simply said, "I'll drive if he doesn't want to Mr. President," with a big grin looking over at Dwayne Marshall.

"Admiral, would you like a ride?" President Bradshaw asked.

"Yes, Mr. President, I would if you don't mind, sir. I'm sure about now my granddaughter would like to see me as well."

Marshall pulled out his phone and spoke.

"I need three protection teams at the front door NOW," he said. "Bring Chariots 1 and 2 to the front of the building."

President Bradshaw's phone buzzed and he answered it, listened, and then spoke. "We'll be right out. Thank you, Amy."

The five men walked out of the Oval Office together to the front entrance of the White House where two long, stretch limousines awaited at the bottom of the steps with Secret Service agents surrounding both of them.

"Gentlemen, if you wouldn't mind accompanying me in the first car, we can be on our way," President Bradshaw said looking down from the top steps of the White House.

They all slowly descended the stairs and an agent opened the back passenger door. Former President Matthews and Admiral Cartwright got in and moved over to make room for President Bradshaw.

FBI Director James and Dwayne Marshall were waiting behind Bradshaw to follow him inside the limo when Bradshaw turned to them both standing at the car door.

"Dwayne, why don't you and Michael meet us over there in your own cars?"

Both Marshall and James watched as the President got inside the limo and the agent closed the door behind him. They watched as the two limos headed out towards the main gate.

FBI Director James looked at Marshall with a scowl on his face and said, "This is all *your* fault...all because you have a hard on for Max Mason."

Marshall looked at James with anger.

"Shut up, Michael." Marshall thought to himself, "This was all Max Mason's fault" and he wasn't going to forget about it...EVER.

Max managed to carry Jurgens through the fifth floor stairwell door and tossed him on the floor as gently as he could so he could catch his breath. Max looked at his watch and saw he had about six minutes left before the explosives went off.

He noticed that Jurgens was starting to stir and wake up, so he hit him hard again in the jaw to put him out again. As he did it, he said laughingly, "I have to say, Brian, I never get tired of hitting you."

Max looked down the fifth floor hallway to locate the roof access stairwell, picked up Jurgens' unconscious body and put him over his shoulder again. Max moved down the corridor as quickly as he could with Jurgens' dead weight over his shoulder and entered the roof stairwell door. He looked up and sighed, then started up the stairs to the roof access door.

Mikey and Jordy didn't want Stacy to know what Max was about to do because she definitely wouldn't have approved of his idea, but they both thought they should be there in case he needed backup.

Jordy looked at Stacy with a grin on his face and said, "Sweetheart, not to be so blunt, but Mikey and I have had to take a piss for over two hours now. We'll both be right back."

Jordy watched as Stacy rolled her eyes and smiled at both of them as they turned to head out of the command center. Jordy looked at Mikey and nodded. The two of them walked over to Lieutenant Adams and Jordy asked, "Where's the head, Lieutenant?"

Adams looked up from his scanner equipment at Jordy.

"Out the tent, to the right…down the street a bit. You can't miss them."

"Thanks," Mikey replied, and they both walked outside of the tent leaving Stacy with the young Lieutenant in charge.

Standing outside the tent door, both Mikey and Jordy checked their handguns and placed them back in their holsters. They went left towards the National Health Building, because they knew that's where Max was going, and made sure they weren't being followed.

With Jurgens still unconscious and over his shoulder, Max opened the roof door and walked out into the warm summer air. It felt good on Max's face since he had been stuck inside the building for most of the night. Jurgens' weight was starting to give Max pain in his lower back, but he still managed to make it to the roof's edge.

Max dropped Jurgens on the coarse gravel roofing, stretched and looked up at the full moon. He made sure Jurgens was still unconscious, then quickly walked over to the side of the building.

Looking down, Max said chuckling to himself, "I remember this NOT working out so well for me the last time." He quickly went over to the three dead terrorists he, Mikey and Jordy had left on the roof and found his crossbow and equipment bag still beside them where he had left them. Max checked the bag for the other repelling rope he had and another crossbow arrow. He smiled when he saw Jordy had packed a small roll of duct tape and said to himself, "I love that guy."

Max took the bag and crossbow over to the edge of the building where he could see the National Health Building across the freeway approximately fifth yards away and put them down next to him. He looked at his watch again and saw he had just over three minutes before the explosives detonated on the third floor.

He took out the rope, duct tape, arrow, and the collapsible steel grappling hook and placed them all on the ground by the bag near the edge of the building.

Max looked over at Jurgens, saw he was still unconscious, and proceeded with his crazy escape plan. He unfolded the grappling hook and attached the rope to its end, tying it in several knots to make it tighter than it was when Jordy came over to the GBN building.

He smiled at the thought of Jordy yelling at him and Mikey after they pulled him up. Max took the crossbow arrow and the duct tape and taped the grappling hook to the shaft of the arrow. He unfurled the rope, cocked the crossbow string back, and placed the arrow in the crossbow.

Max looked over the side of the building and saw lights on in a second floor office of the Health Building and decided *that* was his target.

He picked the crossbow up with his makeshift arrow and grappling hook, then all of a sudden dropped it to the ground immediately when he realized Jurgens had put his cuffed hands over his head causing the plastic cuffs to choke him.

Jurgens was seriously determined to strangle the life out of Max. Max was gasping for air and trying to pull Jurgens hands back over his head to no avail. Finally Max took a big breath and started elbowing Jurgens in the ribs.

Again, and again Max's elbow blows hit Jurgens' ribs, still pulling at the cuffed hands around his neck with the other. Finally, Max threw his entire weight back to cause Jurgens and him to fall backwards on the roof, with Max landing on top of Jurgens. Max continued to elbow Jurgens ribs and finally felt his grip around his neck loosen and grabbed his cuffs and pulled them from around his neck. Max rolled off of Jurgens coughing for more air and got up just as Jurgens did.

"You understand I'm starting to enjoy beating the shit out of you, right?" Max asked a defensive postured Brian Jurgens.

"Fuck you, Mason," Jurgens yelled back.

Max smiled and spun kicked Jurgens in the face, knocking him to the ground, his mouth and nose bloodied again. Jurgens got up and raised his clinched fists and ran screaming towards Max, who promptly moved out of the way and stiffed armed him under his chin hard to his throat to knock him to the ground.

Max walked over to Jurgens lying on the roof gravel and stood over him smiling. The bloodied and bruised Jurgens looked up at Max who told him, "I still *never* get tired of hitting you." Then he punched Jurgens hard in the face one more time to knock him unconscious once again.

Max looked at his watch and saw he had less than two minutes to get off the roof before the explosives went off. He picked up the crossbow and stood on the edge of the roof and fired the arrow with the duct taped grappling hook through the second floor window of the National Health Building office, shattering the glass.

Max yanked the rope back towards him to secure the grappling hook to the window frame and pulled it tight to secure it to the large steel gas pipe above his head at the edge of the GBN building...again tying it in several knots.

"Now I understand why Jordy hates my plans so much," Max said to himself laughing.

Max thought for a split second to leave Brian Jurgens there unconscious on the roof of a soon collapsing building and said out loud, "I guess it *is* more of a *CODE* than a guideline."

Looking down at the unconscious Jurgens, Max smiled as he said, "Looks like you caught me in a good mood, asshole."

Max grabbed one of the straps they had used earlier and threw it over the rope and grabbed Jurgens by the coat collar with both hands and stood him up just as he felt the first rumble and shake of the building under his feet. Max realized the bombs in the building were starting to go off one at a time as he felt one shock, then another. The next one almost knocked him and Jurgens off their feet onto the gravel roof. The roof continued to move as Max's watch alarm was sounding off. He knew it was jump or die so he threw Brian Jurgens over his shoulder again and grabbed both ends of the strap with his free hand and screamed, "OHHH, SHIIIIT," as he jumped off the GBN roof, sliding down the rope towards the shattered office window, holding on to Jurgens tightly with his other hand.

Tyler, Stephanie, Kristina, and Scott Matthews walked into the communications command tent where Tyler had left Mikey, Jordy, and Stacy, but found only Stacy and Lieutenant Adams.

"Where are Mikey and Jordy?" Tyler asked Stacy.

"They had to go to the little boy's room," Stacy replied laughing, then smiled at Stephanie Bradshaw.

"Hello again, Miss Bradshaw," Stacy said to her. "I still love your shoes," Stacy added with a smile.

"Is your dad okay, Stacy?" Stephanie asked.

Stacy smiled so the young girl would not see how worried she was saying "He'll be fine. He always lands on his feet."

Scott Matthews smiled at Stacy and nodded, agreeing with her about Max. Stacy smiled & winked back at him.

"Hey, hottie. Glad you made it. My Dad would have *killed* us all if you didn't make it out alive," she said sarcastically.

The explosions started blowing out the windows on the third floor of the GBN building, sending fire and debris out into the night air. More powerful explosions from the building started to shake the ground causing some of the police and security staff to fall to the asphalt pavement from the seismic intensity.

Tyler and Stacy gasped seeing the building on fire and feeling the ground shaking under them. Stacy squeezed Tyler's hand hard watching the burning building start to implode into itself.

"Don't worry, sweetie. Your dad wasn't in there," Tyler told Stacy to reassure her.

"I know," Stacy replied with a sheepish grin.

Explosion after explosion went off inside the GBN building making things in and around it shake as if an earthquake had hit. It caused the 75-year-old steel girders supporting the building to start bending in the middle and the structure began to collapse.

Jordy and Mikey had been halfway to the National Health building when the GBN building started exploding, causing the ground under them to shake and rumble. They had barely been able to stay on their feet. They saw the fire shooting out of the third floor windows and looked at one another with concern.

"I'm sure he's fine," Mikey said.

"He *better* be. He still has that bottle of good scotch the Admiral gave us," Jordy said with a smile.

"What the Hell was that?" Jordy asked hearing someone scream above his head.

Both Mikey and Jordy looked up to see Max with what looked like someone over his shoulder sliding down a rope from the GBN building roof top to an open office window in the Health Building.

"I *told* you he was going to do it again," Mikey said to Jordy laughing.

Jordy looked at Mikey with another concerned look saying "Yeah, I remember. He was in the infirmary for almost a month the last time too."

"Yeah, he was. Gave him a lot of time to spend with Sylvia," Mikey responded grinning back at Jordy.

Max Mason, still holding on to the unconscious Brian Jurgens with one hand and the strap sliding down the rope with the other, realized the exploding bombs on the third floor were collapsing the GBN building to the ground a little faster than he expected, because he noticed the slack from the rope and thought, "This is gonna hurt… AGAIN." He was hoping to slide through the second floor office window, but he had a secondary plan if this were to happen. He wasn't fond of the idea but knew it might be necessary to live through this.

The National Health Building was the *only* federal building with its own "reflecting pool" incorporated on its property to encourage its employees to enjoy the outdoors during the spring, summer, and fall months. It had tables and chairs around it for eating and socializing. The reflecting pool itself had a three-foot wall all the way around it and filled with fresh, self-cleaning water with a fountain in the center. It measured approximately one hundred feet long and about forty feet wide. Max had seen it when he concocted his escape idea.

The GBN building was a mess of steel, concrete, and glass falling to the ground with fire and dust shooting into the warm summer air. Halfway across the freeway with Jurgens in tow, Max realized they weren't going to make the open window where he'd shot the rope, so he knew he had to go to "Plan B." He thought to himself that Jurgens was the lucky one, because he was unconscious and wasn't going to feel what Max was about to do to him…but Max knew he *himself* would!

As Max continued to slide down the rope, it was slipping lower and lower when finally they were over the reflecting pool. When they were about 20 feet above it, Max let go of Jurgens who dropped into the pool. He hit the water hard, sending a large splash of water into the air. Max then let go of the strap and hit the water on the other side of him about 20 feet away, causing Max to gasp for air and feel intense pain from the impact. He blacked out face down in the pool.

Jurgens raised his head out of the water gasping for air, wondering where he was and how he got in the pool with his hands still cuffed. He looked around and saw Max Mason face down in the water and smiled, thinking he was finally dead.

Jurgens slowly walked through the three foot-deep water to the edge of the pool and climbed out and looked around through the thick dust cloud that surrounded the whole area.

Max raised up quickly from the water gasping for air, coughing and spitting out water. He thought he might have cracked a couple of ribs from the hard impact with the water because of the harsh stabbing pain.

He was soaked from head to toe and hated wearing wet clothes. As he slowly stood up, Max grabbed the left side of his ribs, looking around the pool for Jurgens through the thick fog of concrete dust. But he wasn't anywhere in sight near where Max had dropped him.

Max could see through some of the dust cloud at the GBN building that only the top three floors had completely collapsed. Max thought to himself, "That building is going to need a shitload of windows and doors."

Jurgens walked away from the reflecting pool quickly after he saw Max Mason rise up out of the water on the other side. He managed to get to the other side of the building without Max seeing him. "Don't worry Mason, *you* and I have *unfinished* business," Jurgens said out loud.

He tried to bite his cuffs off without success as he walked to the other end of the National Health Building and turned the corner, thinking he was free from this fiasco. But he ran right into Mikey and Jordy coming from the other side of the freeway. "*Shit!*" Jurgens said knowing he wasn't going to get away now.

"Hey there, are you lost little boy?" Jordy asked him laughing while slowly pulling his gun out of its holster.

Jurgens turned quickly to try to run from the two men, but Mikey grabbed him by the cuffed left arm, swung him around and hit him hard in the jaw with his right gloved fist, knocking Jurgens to the ground. He looked up at the two SEALs, wiping away blood from his mouth.

"Why do you assholes always have to hit people in the face?"

"I see now why the boss likes hitting him," Mikey said to Jordy laughing.

"Yeah, he's a *dick,*" Jordy replied picking Jurgens up off the ground by his wet cuffed arms.

"You made quiet a mess, asshole" Jordy told Jurgens looking over at the partially demolished GBN building. Jurgens just smiled at them both.

Max Mason came around the corner of the building, his gun pointed at the three men standing there.

"Hey, boss, did you lose something?" Jordy asked with a grin as he saw his soaking wet Captain standing there.

"I would have found him eventually. He's too stupid not to get caught" Max replied grinning at Jurgens and still holding the left side of his ribs. "He knows he's going to prison without a dime now," he said to his two friends laughing painfully.

"*Fuck* you, Mason," Jurgens said angrily.

Jordy was still holding his cuffed arms and smacked Jurgens in the back of the head with his open hand.

"Be nice to the Captain, asshole," Jordy said to a surprised and now pissed off Brian Jurgens.

The three men started walking back to the command tent dragging Jurgens with them. Max looked at Mikey and asked, "Are the girls okay?"

"Yeah, boss. They're both great," Mikey replied looking at Jordy and flashing him a smile.

Jordy knew what that grin meant and looked away from Max. He thought to himself *he* wasn't going to be the one to tell his Captain that his new girlfriend showed both of them her tits in the line of duty. He looked at Max and smiled.

"We are *soooo* getting Stacy a SEAL tattoo now boss," Jordy said laughing.

"I'm not so sure about that, boys," Max said with a big grin.

"We'll get her drunk first. She won't feel it," Jordy said looking over at Mikey who was shaking his head with a no.

"You *do* understand we're still talking about MY little girl, right Lieutenant," Max said with a stern look and a smile.

"Sorry, boss. *My* bad," Jordy said giving Mikey an evil grin.

"And what's this about a *scar*?" Max asked them both with a fatherly look.

Jurgens was getting annoyed by all this family talk and remarked, "The three of you are *so* cute together."

Max hit Jurgens in the back of the head like Jordy had done and said, "Shut the fuck up, Brian."

The four of them were walking up to the Federal command center when five heavily-armed officers approached them with their guns pointed. Max suggested they raise their hands just to be safe so no one got trigger happy.

"Inform your commander that Captain Max Mason is here with a prisoner," Max asked politely to one of the officers as the others surrounded them.

The officer walked away and spoke into his radio. "Yes, sir," he said then turned back to face Max.

The President's limousine pulled up on the other side of the command center and several Secret Service agents got out and secured the area before they allowed the President to get out of the car. Once the area was secured to their liking, one of the agents opened the rear passenger door and President Bradshaw stepped out, followed by former President Matthews, and Admiral Cartwright.

Lieutenant Adams was contacted and informed by the checkpoint officer that the President's limo had come through his secured barrier and went outside the command tent to welcome them. Adams quickly saluted President Bradshaw and stood at attention.

"Where's my daughter?" Bradshaw asked

"She's right this way, Mr. President," the young lieutenant replied. He took him inside the next tent and Bradshaw saw his daughter standing with several others, including Agent Karen Tyler, and tears of joy ran down his face.

"DADDY!" Stephanie Bradshaw screamed running into his arms, hugging him tightly.

"Are you okay, sweetheart?" he asked squeezing her tight and whispering "Thank you" to the heavens.

"Yeah, thanks to all of *them*, I *am*, Daddy," Stephanie said smiling and looking at Tyler, Stacy, Kristina, and Scott.

President Bradshaw walked over to Karen Tyler and took her hand unexpectedly.

"Whatever I can do for you, Karen. Thank you for saving my baby," Bradshaw said with a smile.

"Mr. President, I was only doing my job."

"No, you weren't; you did more than that, you saved a lot of lives tonight; I appreciate everything you've done," Bradshaw said thinking about what she must have had to endure in the GBN building.

Stephanie grabbed her father's hand happy to be safe again.

"There's someone I want you to meet, daddy."

President Bradshaw noticed Stacy behind Tyler and put his hand out to her.

"And who are *you* young lady?" Bradshaw asked with a smile.

Stacy stood at attention a little embarrassed at how she looked, a bit bruised and bloodied from her ordeal. She saluted her commander in chief.

"Ensign First Class Stacy Mason of SEAL Team 2, Mr. President."

Hearing herself say that she was an official Navy SEAL made Stacy smile from ear to ear. She only wished her dad was here to see her with the President.

"Thank you, Ensign, for saving my daughter's life," Bradshaw said to Stacy.

"It wasn't just me, sir. I was proud to help, Mr. President," Stacy said smiling at Tyler, who returned her smile with a wink.

Admiral Cartwright and former President Matthews walked into the command tent to see Kristina and Scott standing there next to Tyler, Stacy, and President Bradshaw.

"GRANDPA!" Kristina yelled when she saw her grandfather, running to him and hugging him.

Admiral Cartwright hugged his granddaughter tightly.

"You gave me such a scare, young lady" Cartwright said as he kissed her forehead.

"I'm okay. I shot a guy, but I didn't kill him," Kristina told him smiling.

When he heard that, Admiral Cartwright's eyes got really big.

"I'll tell you later, sir," Tyler whispered to him.

Daryl Matthews walked over to his son Scott who smiled and said, "Hey, Dad."

Matthews grabbed him and hugged him tightly.

"I am *so* proud of you son. Your mother and brother would be, too" he whispered in his ear.

"Thanks" Scott replied watching tears come down his father's face.

"There's someone I would like you to meet" he said with a grin to his father.

A soaking wet Max, Jordy, Mikey, and a handcuffed soaked Brian Jurgens were escorted by the Special Weapons Unit to the command center where Secret Service agents watched over the entrance, which led Max to believe the President was inside. Before they walked in, Max looked at the two agents at the door and suggested they take Jurgens somewhere else because he was a criminal now and shouldn't be in the same room with the President.

One of the agents told him that the President had asked to see him before they took him to be processed. Max found this confusing and a bit of an unorthodox procedure.

Max walked into the command center and saw everyone standing and talking.

"DADDY!" Stacy screamed, seeing her dad first.

Stacy realized she had screamed really loud and promptly apologized.

"Sorry, Mr. President."

President Bradshaw smiled at Stacy.

"As you were, Ensign."

"Thank you sir" she replied with a smile.

Stacy ran to her father and almost literally jumped in his arms to hug him. "Easy, Princess. Dad's had a rough night," Max said to her still feeling pain in his side.

Stacy kissed him on the cheek.

"You're all *wet*, Daddy."

"Yes, I am. Long story sweetie." he replied with a painful smile.

"Where are Uncle Jordy and Mikey?" Stacy asked concerned.

"They are standing outside for a moment," Max said a bit apprehensive about why.

Tyler walked over to Max and whispered with a big grin, "Hey sailor, new in town?"

"You may want to hold up on that for a moment," Max said to her with a stern look.

"What's wrong, Max?" Tyler asked a bit confused.

"I'm not sure yet," Max replied as Jordy and Mikey escorted Brian Jurgens into the command center.

Seeing Jurgens in the same area as the President, Tyler and Stacy drew their handguns and pointed them at Jurgens.

"What? No love and kisses from anyone?" Jurgens asked with a smirk, his clothes dripping wet like Max's as Jordy and Mikey dragged him in front of the President.

Scott Matthews got in front of his father and pulled his gun out and pointed it at Jurgens and asked, "What the Hell is this, Max?"

"My apologies to everyone," President Bradshaw said. "I requested that he be brought here," he continued. "You can all lower your weapons," Bradshaw informed everyone.

They did so but kept them at their sides in case Jurgens tried something stupid. Daryl Matthews lowered Scott's gun and took it from him, smiling how proud he was of his son wanting to protect his father.

"I knew there was a reason why I voted for you," Jurgens said to President Bradshaw just as he received a hard right-handed punch to the jaw that knocked him to his knees again. Looking up and rubbing his jaw, Jurgens realized it was the President who had hit him and was now pissed at him.

"You tried to kill my daughter and hundreds of other people for money, you asshole!" President Bradshaw screamed at Jurgens in anger.

"You hired a psycho killer to kill children in front of millions of international TV viewers. And, you blew up a government building to help hide your escape."

"Everyone has a bad day," Jurgens said to the President smiling and bleeding from his mouth.

"I'm going to bury you so deep in prison, you'll *never* see the sun shine again," Bradshaw yelled at Jurgens.

"We'll see," Jurgens said with a smirk.

"Get this piece of shit out of my sight," Bradshaw said to one of the Secret Service agents standing by the entrance.

As Jurgens was being led away, the President came over to Max Mason and extended his hand.

"I want to thank you from all of us, Captain Mason. You and your team have served your country incredibly this evening."

Max took the President's hand firmly, shook it…then leaned in and whispered, "Nice *right,* Mr. President."

President Bradshaw smiled back at Max.

"Admiral Cartwright and I have an idea that may interest you and your team, *after* you get some rest. I'm gonna go hug my daughter now if you don't mind, Captain," Bradshaw said with another firm hand shake.

"Yes, sir, Mr. President," Max replied.

Daryl Matthews then came over to Max and shook his hand.

"Thanks Max, for not letting me lose everything."

"You and Heather raised a *very* smart young man, Mr. President." And, by the way, he hits like a mule," Max said laughing and rubbing his jaw.

"He's missed you a lot," Matthews said to Max.

"I've missed him too, sir," Max said looking over at Scott Matthews with Stephanie Bradshaw. "But I think you have bigger problems, sir," Max said laughing.

The former President looked at his son staring at Stephanie Bradshaw.

"Were *we* that in love at that age, Max?"

"Not me, sir. I just wanted to get laid," Max said in a quiet chuckle.

"Me too, but don't tell *him* that," Matthews said laughing with him. "Guess I need to go get this over with. Her father's *not* going to take this well."

"No, he's not, sir. Good luck with *that,*" Max said laughing.

The former President walked over to his son who promptly introduced him to his girlfriend Stephanie, who introduced President Bradshaw to her boyfriend Scott. The two Presidents looked at one another and smiled because they knew their children were safe again.

Tyler walked over to Max and grabbed his hand and squeezed it tight, looking him in the eye.

"When are we having that date, Captain?" she said with a smile.

"Do you like baseball?" Max asked with a grin on his face.

"I'm more of a football girl," Tyler replied still smiling at him.

"I can work with that," Max said laughing the two of them headed towards the door where Jordy, Mikey, and Stacy were standing.

Directors Dwayne Marshall and Michael James walked up to the entrance of the command center as the five of them stepped out into the night air.

Marshall looked at Max with anger on his face, then looked at Karen Tyler.

"Where do you think you're going, Agent Tyler?"

"Hopefully to get something to eat, and then sleep, sir," she said not caring what he wanted right now.

"I'll be *expecting* your report on my desk at 9:00am this morning, Agent Tyler," Marshall ordered.

"It's Sunday, sir, MY day off. I'll have it for you by Monday morning."

"You will have it on my desk *this morning*, agent," Marshall said with authority bellowing out his order.

Stacy stepped up in front of Tyler and looked the agitated Director in the eye.

"It's her day off. She said she'll have it for you *Monday morning*," Stacy said sternly.

"Listen up, *princess*! *You* don't get to tell *me* how to run *my* office!" Marshall screamed, getting into Stacy's face. Stacy turned and smiled at Tyler.

"Hey, *Dwayne*!" Max said from behind Marshall. Marshall turned to see what Max wanted when he felt severe pain in his face and jaw that knocked him to the ground and made him spit out blood.

Max rubbed the knuckles on his right hand and looked down at the Director.

"Shouldn't have called her a *princess*. Only her *Daddy* gets to call her a princess," Max said smiling as he looked over at Stacy standing with Tyler. Stacy returned the smile.

Marshall got back to his feet and noticed James smirking at what Max had done to him.

"What the fuck are you smiling for?" Marshall yelled at James who ignored him and walked into the command center where the President was.

"I'm going to press charges, Mason, you son of a bitch," Marshall yelled as the five of them ignored him and started heading back to the IRS building where Max had left his SUV parked.

"You might want to let it go, Dwayne," Admiral Cartwright said to him. He had just come out of the command center when he saw Max hit Marshall and thought, "Good for him."

"I don't work for you, Admiral, so fuck off," Marshall said defiantly.

"No, you don't, but as of Monday you work *with* Max Mason," the Admiral proclaimed walking away to let Marshall stew and think about what he'd said.

"That will NEVER happen," Marshall replied as he headed back into the command center.

Admiral Cartwright laughed as he watched Marshall walk angrily into the command center. And he said to himself, "You have *no idea* what's about to happen."

"Captain, a word please," the Admiral asked walking up to the five of them as they were heading towards the front of the IRS building.

Max looked at and addressed his four companions.

"I'll meet you all at the car."

"This is for their benefit as well, Captain," Cartwright said.

Jordy, Mikey, and Stacy stood at attention next to Max and saluted Admiral Cartwright who returned the salute.

"At ease, boys and girls," he said smiling at them. I'm *very* proud of *all* four of you. You saved a lot of lives tonight, including my granddaughter and the President's daughter. That means the world to *both* of us."

Max looked at everyone and spoke.

"We did it for country and family, Admiral, nothing more sir." he said.

"I understand. But I have been given authority to compensate the three of you - like you asked Max - for your heroic service."

"Just these two knuckleheads, Admiral. Not necessary for me," Max said as he smiled looking at Jordy and Mikey.

Admiral Cartwright handed Jordy, Mikey, and Max each a sealed envelope and all three looked at them confused. Max opened his and saw a check made out to him for $500,000. "A half a million dollars, sir?" Max asked smiling. Jordy and Mikey opened theirs fast to see what *they* were given, smiling at one another.

Both got checks for $500,000 as well. Jordy scratched his head and looked at Max, who smiled at him and handed his check back to the Admiral.

"Give it to the kids, Admiral." Max said smiling at Tyler and Stacy who had stunned looks on their faces.

"That's *my Dad,*" Stacy said proudly.

Jordy looked at Mikey and shrugged his shoulders.

"I'd only blow it on *really* bad choices," he said to his friend extending his hand with the check to the Admiral.

Mikey laughed hearing what Jordy said and also handed his check to the Admiral.

"Faye would kill me if I didn't give it back."

Admiral Cartwright looked a bit shocked at the three checks now back in his hands and smiled at the three men.

"The Children's Hunger Charity thanks the three of you for your generous donations," he said smiling and shaking his head at the noble gesture. "If you won't accept the money, maybe this will suffice."

He walked over to Stacy Mason who stood at attention again and handed her Lieutenant bars. "Congratulations, Lieutenant Mason," the Admiral said shaking her hand as she looked at her dad watching with pride.

"Wait a minute! Now I have *no one* to boss around," Jordy said out loud annoyed.

"I'm not so sure about that, Commander," Cartwright said to Jordy with a smile.

"COMMANDER?!" Jordy said out loud with a big grin on his face looking at Max and Mikey.

"Congratulations, Commander," Cartwright said shaking Jordy's hand.

"With all due respect, sir, my wife is going to kick your ass, Admiral, if Jordy can boss me around" Mikey said laughing at his friend.

"I think I'm safe, Captain," Admiral Cartwright addressed Mikey shaking his hand and congratulating him.

"Damn, I was *this* close," Jordy said to Mikey laughing and holding his two fingers slightly apart.

"Max, we have something else in mind for you, though you will still be promoted to the rank of Rear Admiral," Cartwright said seeing the scowl on Max's face about the rank promotion. "We want you to be the Director of the new Secret Service Domestic Terrorism Division starting Monday morning."

Max looked at Admiral Cartwright and smiled.

"You know this doesn't fix the problem you and I *still* have, sir," he said sternly remembering how he'd put Stacy in danger with the deadly Tanaka Amikura.

"I know, Max. We can discuss that at another time," the Admiral said feeling bad for his actions.

"May I hire my own staff?" Max asked.

"Yes, except for Lieutenant Mason. She still has sea obligations even *I* can't get her out of."

"Does she *still qualify* as a SEAL, Admiral?" Max asked with Jordy and Mikey listening intensely

"After tonight, I think she earned it, she'll however still have to go through the training in Key West" Cartwright reassured him.

"YESSSSS!" Jordy said out loud looking at Stacy and smiling at his brave goddaughter. He rolled up his sleeve to show her his SEAL tattoo and pointed at her smiling. Stacy smiled and nodded to Jordy in agreement. Mikey reached over and pounded her fist in congratulating her as she beamed. Tyler reached over and grabbed her hand and squeezed it and smiled at her.

"I'll make sure her file is appropriately updated to Key West Command" Admiral Cartwright affirmed to Max.

"Thank you, Admiral. I'll see you Monday morning with my ideas, sir."

"Very good. Congratulations, Director Mason." He then turned to head back to the command center to be with his granddaughter. But then he stopped short and turned back around asking, "By the way, Max, what happened to Mayer?"

Max looked at both Stacy and Tyler, then back to the Admiral and replied, "Dead, sir."

Cartwright thought for a moment, then looked over at Stacy with a smile before he left.

"Well done, Lieutenant." he said turning back towards the command tent.

The five of them were tired, hungry, bruised, and bloodied, but they smiled at one another knowing it was over and once again started walking towards Max's SUV.

Jordy, Mikey, Tyler, and Stacy were almost there when Max asked from behind them, "Who wants chocolate chip pancakes?"

"I do, I do!" Stacy replied raising her hand high in the air. Though she was an adult now with a gun and a new rank, she still loved her daddy's pancakes.

"Want to try my pancakes, Agent Tyler?" Max asked with a smile.

"So you're offering to make me breakfast, tough guy?" she asked with a grin.

"Yes ma'am, *anytime* you'd like," Max replied grabbing her and kissing her hard in front of everyone.

"Daddy, *really*," Stacy interjected.

"*Really,* boss? Can't that wait until you two get a room?" Jordy asked annoyed that he had just given away half a million dollars and no one to *comfort him* about it.

Tyler looked at him sternly, which made Jordy uncomfortable, and he slowly got behind Mikey to avoid her gaze. Mikey laughed at his friend as Tyler smiled.

They all arrived at Max's SUV, got in and sat there for a moment each taking a deep breath, then looking at one another relieved that the ordeal was over. Jordy, not one to shy away from anything, looked at Mikey and grinned, then asked Max, "Are we still going to the baseball game this afternoon, boss?"

Everyone busted out laughing except for Jordy who was confused by the laughter and simply asked, "*WHAAAT*?!"

Max started up the SUV and looked around at everyone.

"Let's go home." he said with a smile.

MAX MASON

RETURNS IN

PERFECT SCORE

The Misadventures of

Max Mason

Volume Two